Marrying the Millionaire

Charming, handsome and rich…
What more could three sisters want?

Three passionate novels!

In July 2006 Mills & Boon bring back
two of their classic collections, each
featuring three favourite romances
by our bestselling authors...

MARRYING THE MILLIONAIRE
by Lynne Graham

An Arabian Marriage
The Disobedient Mistress
The Heiress Bride

AFTER OFFICE HOURS...

The Irresistible Tycoon
by Helen Brooks
A Professional Marriage
by Jessica Steele
Marriage on the Agenda
by Lee Wilkinson

Marrying the Millionaire

AN ARABIAN MARRIAGE

THE DISOBEDIENT MISTRESS

THE HEIRESS BRIDE

by
Lynne Graham

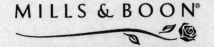

MILLS & BOON®

MILLS & BOON and MILLS & BOON with the Rose Device
are registered trademarks of the publisher.
Harlequin Mills & Boon Limited,
Eton House, 18-24 Paradise Road, Richmond, Surrey, TW9 1SR

MARRYING THE MILLIONAIRE
© by Harlequin Enterprises II B.V., 2006

An Arabian Marriage, The Disobedient Mistress and *The Heiress
Bride* were first published in Great Britain by Harlequin Mills &
Boon Limited in separate, single volumes.

An Arabian Marriage © Lynne Graham 2002
The Disobedient Mistress © Lynne Graham 2002
The Heiress Bride © Lynne Graham 2002

ISBN 13: 978 0 263 84964 6
ISBN 10: 0 263 84964 3

05-0706

Printed and bound in Spain
by Litografia Rosés S.A., Barcelona

AN ARABIAN
MARRIAGE

by

Lynne Graham

Lynne Graham was born in Northern Ireland and has been a keen Mills & Boon® reader since her teens. She is very happily married with an understanding husband, who has learned to cook since she started to write! Her five children keep her on her toes. She has a very large dog, which knocks everything over, a very small terrier which barks a lot and two cats. When time allows, Lynne is a keen gardener.

Don't miss Lynne Graham's exciting new novel
Mistress Bought and Paid For
**out in September 2006 from Mills & Boon
Modern Romance™**

CHAPTER ONE

'IT IS a matter of family honour...' King Zafir's voice was thin and weak but fierce longing burned in his gaze as he addressed his only surviving son. 'You will bring your brother Adil's son home to us and we will raise him to adulthood.'

Crown Prince Jaspar murmured tautly, 'Father, with all due respect, the child has a mother—'

'A harlot *unfit* to be called a mother!' In a sudden explosion of anger, King Zafir raised himself from the pillows and thundered, 'A shameless creature who danced until dawn while her child fought for his life in hospital! A greedy, grasping Jezebel...' At that point a choking bout of serious coughing overcame the irate older man and he struggled in vain to catch his breath.

Instantly, the King's medical team was rushed in to administer oxygen. Pale and taut, dark eyes intent, already stunned by the furious outburst that had brought on the attack, Jaspar watched the physicians go about their work and willed his parent to recover. '*Please*, Your Royal Highness,' his father's closest aide, Rashad, begged with tears in his strained eyes. 'Please agree without further discussion.'

'I had not realised that my father held Western women in such violent aversion.'

'His Majesty does not. Have you not read the report on this woman?'

As he registered in relief that his father was responding to the treatment the worst of the tension holding Jaspar's

5

lean powerful frame taut ebbed and he breathed in deep. 'I have not.'

'I will bring the report to your office. Your Royal Highness.' Rashad hurried off.

A thin hand beckoned from the great canopied bed. Jaspar strode forward and bent down to hear King Zafir's last definitive words on the subject, uttered in a thready tone of deep piety that nonetheless held a rare note of pleading. 'It is your Christian duty to rescue my grandson…'

As soon as the immediate emergency was over and his father had been made comfortable, Jaspar left the room. As he crossed the anteroom beyond, every person there dropped down on their knees and bent their heads. In receipt of that respectful acknowledgement of his recent rise in royal status, he clenched his strong jawline even harder. Reflecting on the recent death of his elder brother, Adil, who had been Crown Prince since birth, only made Jaspar feel worse than ever.

One day he would be King of Quamar but he had not been brought up to be King. In the instant that Adil had died, Jaspar's life had changed for ever. He had loved his brother but had never been very close to him. Adil had, after all, been fifteen years older and cut from a different cloth. Indeed, Adil had often cheerfully called his younger brother a killjoy. But, almost inevitably, Adil's excessive appetite for food and fat Cuban cigars had contributed to his early demise at the age of forty-five.

In the splendid office that was now his, Jaspar studied an oil painting of his jovial brother with brooding regret. Adil had also been an unrepentant womaniser.

'I adore women. *All* of them…' Adil had once told Jaspar with his great beaming smile. 'My wife, my ex-wives, my daughters included, but why should I settle for only one woman? If only we were Muslim, brother, I might have had four wives at a time and a harem of concubines. Do you never think of what life might have been like had our honoured ancestor, Kareem I, not founded us as a Christian dynasty?'

So, when Adil had not been carrying out his duties as Crown Prince, he had sailed his pleasure yacht, *Beauteous Dreamer*, round the Mediterranean with a string of beautiful fun-loving Western women aboard. Rumours of his eldest son's discreet double life had occasionally caused King Zafir great disquiet but Adil had always been a most gifted dissembler and his women had always been willing to cover his tracks for him.

It seemed painfully ironic that the much-wanted son which Adil had failed to father with any of his three successive wives should have been born out of wedlock. Had that child been born within marriage, he would have been second in line to the throne but his illegitimacy barred him from what should have been his rightful place in life. Jaspar suppressed a heavy sigh. In his generation, the al-Husayn royal family had had little luck when it came to producing male heirs, although, having fathered several daughters, Adil had remained excusably optimistic that a son would eventually be born.

And just two years ago, a baby boy *had* been born to an English woman in London. During the hours that Adil had survived before the second heart attack had struck and proved fatal, he had confessed that shocking fact to their distraught father. Unsurprisingly, the news of that unknown grandson had become an obsession with the grieving older man but extensive confidential enquiries had been required even to track the woman down. In fear of a scandal that would reverberate all the way back to Quamar, Adil had gone to considerable lengths not only to disassociate himself from that birth, but also to conceal all evidence of the child's existence.

It was a mess, an unholy mess, that he was being asked to sort out, Jaspar reflected bleakly as Rashad scurried in with much keen bowing and scraping to deliver a sealed file to his desk. His parent was too ill to be made to consider practicalities, but to bring Adil's child back to Quamar, shorn of the supposedly unsuitable mother, would be very difficult, if not impossible.

'His Majesty has made a most clever suggestion which would solve all the problems at once, Your Royal Highness,' Rashad announced in a tone of excitement.

Jaspar regarded the older man in polite enquiry but with no great hope for Rashad was his father's yes-man, guaranteed to always agree with and support his royal employer's every spoken word.

'We use our special forces and *snatch* the child...'

Jaspar drew in a very deep and necessary breath of restraint. Sometimes, his father astounded him. A feudal ruler from a young age, his exalted parent had never quite come to terms with the reality that a very different world lurked beyond Quamar's borders.

'There would be no need to negotiate with the foreign Jezebel and the boy would be whisked back to Quamar, renamed and raised as an orphan. Perhaps we could say that he is a distant cousin's child,' Rashad completed with immense enthusiasm.

Only the fond memory of Rashad playing with him when he was a child himself prevented Jaspar from venting his incredulous dismissal of such an outrageous suggestion. Rashad was not a clever man and he was out of his depth, his sole motivation being a desperate desire to tell his ailing royal employer what he most wanted to hear. As for his honoured parent and sovereign, Jaspar reflected in rueful exasperation, illness and grief had evidently temporarily deprived the head of the house of al-Husayn of his usual common sense and caution.

'Please inform His Majesty that the situation will be re-solved without the need for such a dramatic intervention,' Jaspar stated drily.

'His Majesty fears that he will die before he ever lays eyes on the child,' Rashad lamented emotively.

Jaspar was well aware of that fact but also convinced that his father would soon recover his once excellent health if only he would stop fretting himself into pointless rages and thinking of dying. Casting open the file, he expected to see a photo of a leggy brunette of the type his late brother had appeared to find irresistible but there was no photo of either mother or child. So eager had the private detective been to report back on his success in locating the woman that he had wasted no time in gathering supporting evidence.

The child's mother, Erica Sutton, had been christened Frederica, and her own mother had deserted her and her father within weeks of the birth of her twin sisters. At eighteen, Erica had left home with a neighbour's husband in tow but that liaison had soon ended. Becoming a model but rarely working, she had then gone on to enjoy numerous affairs with wealthy married men.

When Erica had given birth to a child, nobody had had the slightest idea who had fathered him, but his mother's newfound financial security had been marked by her purchase of a palatial apartment and the high-spending lifestyle of a party girl in constant search of amusement. As Jaspar read on, his lean, darkly handsome features grew steadily more grave. He was appalled by what he was learning and was no longer surprised by his father's rage and concern. Taking the easy way out of an embarrassing predicament, Adil had left his infant son to the care of a cruelly irresponsible and selfish young woman, who appeared to have not the smallest maternal instinct.

Thrusting aside the file in disgust, Jaspar had not the

slightest doubt that it was his duty to remove his nephew from such an unsuitable home. That a devoted nanny had evidently protected the child from the worst of his mother's excesses was of little consolation, for a nanny was only an employee whose services might be dispensed with at any time. The little boy was at undeniable risk both emotionally and physically in his current environment, Jaspar conceded grimly.

His father had spoken wisely and Jaspar was ashamed that he had set such little store by the older man's outraged condemnation of the child's mother. The only solution *was* for his nephew to be brought out to Quamar. However, and Jaspar allowed himself a wry smile, he would achieve that feat without resorting to springing melodramatic manoeuvres with the army's special forces and causing a diplomatic furore.

Frederica Sutton, known as Freddy since the age of eight and by her own choice, passed the letter from Switzerland over to the grey-haired older woman seated across the table from her. 'What am I going to do now?'

Donning her spectacles and looking very much the retired schoolteacher that she indeed was, Ruth scanned the few lines with a frown. 'Well, that's that, then. You've exhausted every avenue—'

'The *only* avenue.' Freddy's sole lead had been the Swiss bank account from which her late cousin, Erica, had received her generous income.

She had written to the financial institution concerned, explaining the circumstances in some detail. She had hoped that she might somehow establish even third-party contact with whoever had originally set up that payment system. Unfortunately, the cagey response she had received had made it painfully clear that the tenet of client confidentiality forbade any such sharing of information while adding that any more approaches from her or indeed anyone else would be a complete waste of time.

'It's hardly your fault that Ben's father didn't make provision for the reality that at some stage there might be a genuine need for further contact,' Ruth Coulter mused ruefully. 'Possibly he was making it clear that he wanted no more involvement under any circumstances…and who could have dreamt that a woman as young as Erica would die?'

At that reminder, Freddy's aquamarine eyes clouded and she bent her blonde head until she had got her emotions back under control. Her cousin, Erica, had been only twenty-seven when she had met her death on the ski slopes in an accident that could have been avoided. But then Erica had died much as she had lived, Freddy conceded reluctantly, as though every day might be her last, running risk without thought and never, ever thinking of the future.

'I know you miss Erica.' The older woman gave Freddy's hand a brief bracing squeeze. 'But it's been six weeks now and life has to go on, most particularly where Ben is concerned. I doubt if you will ever learn *who* his father is but in the long run that may even be for the best. Your cousin wasn't very choosy about her male friends.'

'She was trying to sort herself out,' Freddy protested.

'Was she?' Ruth raised an unimpressed brow. 'Of course, it's wisest not to dwell on someone's failings once they've gone. Naturally one prefers to remember the good things but one might be challenged in this particular case—'

'Ruth…please!' Freddy was sincerely pained by that frank opinion. 'Surely you remember what a dreadful childhood Erica had?'

'I'm afraid I don't have much faith in the fashionable excuses for downright immoral behaviour. Erica brought that poor child into this world only because it *paid* her to do so.' Ruth grimaced, her distaste palpable. 'She lived like a lottery winner on the child support she received from Ben's father but took not the slightest interest in her own son—'

'She put Ben to bed and read him a story for the first time shortly before she died. They *were* beginning to bond—'

'No doubt you shamed and coaxed her into the effort. If Ben's father had not been an extremely rich and evidently very *scared* married man willing to pay heavily for her discretion, Erica would have had that pregnancy terminated,' Ruth opined without hesitation. 'She had no interest in children.'

Giving up on her attempt to soften Ruth's attitude towards Ben's late mother, Freddy got up and knelt down by the little boy playing on the rug. Ben had his little cars lined up. He was dive-bombing them with a toy aeroplane and all the accompanying noisy sound effects. Aware that her hostess was finding the racket something of an irritation, Freddy directed Ben's interest to a puzzle instead and sat by his side until his attention was fully engaged. He was a very lovable child and she adored him as though he were her own. An affectionate and good-natured little boy with dark curls and enormous brown eyes, Ben had been a premature baby.

Freddy had actually been living with Erica by the time that her cousin had gone into labour. Ben had spent the first few weeks of his life confined to an incubator and Freddy had always blamed that unfortunate fact for her cousin's distressing inability to bond with her baby. Over the months that had followed in her role as nanny to Ben, Freddy had tried everything to encourage that maternal bond to develop and had even taken advice from a psychologist on her cousin's behalf. But nothing had worked. Erica had continued to demonstrate little more interest in Ben than she might have done in a strange child passing her by in the street.

'As you can't contact the father, you need to contact the authorities and notify them about the situation,' Ruth advised. 'It's unfortunate that Erica didn't simplify matters by leaving a will but, naturally, once her solicitor has sorted out her estate, everything will go to Ben as well as that continuing income.'

'Ben's going to be a very rich little boy,' Freddy muttered heavily. 'I expect people will queue up to adopt him and social services are bound to look for a family that are already wealthy in their own right. What hope have I got against that kind of competition? I'm single, currently unemployed *and* I'm only twenty-four—'

'You're also that child's only known relative and you've been with him since birth.' But Ruth Coulter spoke as if neither fact that might support the adoption application that the younger woman was determined to make was a source of satisfaction to her. 'I wish you'd never got involved, Freddy. I can't approve of an unmarried woman of your age taking on such a burden—'

'Ben's *not* a burden.' Freddy's chin took on a stubborn tilt.

'You've had no life of your own since you got tangled up with Erica's problems.' The older woman's disapproval was unconcealed. 'She used you quite shamelessly to take care of *her* responsibilities—'

'I was paid an excellent salary to look after Ben,' Freddy reminded her defensively.

'For weeks on end without a break? Day and night and weekends too?' Ruth enquired drily. 'Your cousin took advantage of your good nature and it's no wonder you're now thinking of that little boy as though he was your son. For the past two years, he might as well have been!'

Studying Freddy's now flushed and guilty face, Ruth

compressed her lips. She had once lived next door to the Sutton family and she had known both Erica and Freddy as children. Children who had been forever joking about the foolish fact that they both had the exact same name— Frederica. Their fathers had been brothers and both had named their daughters in honour of a spinster great-aunt in the forlorn hope that they would eventually be enriched by that piece of flattery. As, at that time, the two families had lost touch with each other, the coincidence had not been discovered until years later. When Erica's parents had been killed in a car accident, Freddy's widowed father had taken in his niece and brought her up with his own daughter.

But who could ever have dreamt that that generous act could have ended up working to Freddy's detriment? In Ruth's opinion, even as a child Erica had been dishonest and precocious, essentially shallow in nature but capable of exercising great charm when it suited her to do so. Ruth had not been impressed by Erica's highly coloured stories of her late parents' cruelty towards her, but a lot of people *had* been impressed even though there had been no proof whatsoever to back up her claims. Within the space of six months, Freddy had been the less favoured child in her own home, for Freddy had never been one to push herself forward or flatter.

Having always been very fond of the younger woman, who had lost her own mother at an early age, Ruth had not been as sorry as she felt she should have been when Erica had run off with a neighbour's husband. Ruth had hoped that without her cousin around to hog the limelight, Freddy would grow in confidence. After all, Freddy was a pretty girl but, having had her self-esteem punctured by Erica at a sensitive age, she regarded herself as plain. Ruth was fond of little Ben as well but she was a pragmatic thinker. She did not want to watch Freddy sacrifice her youth and her freedom just to raise Erica's son. Conscious of Ruth's con-

cerned disapproval and discomfited, Freddy left rather earlier than usual and caught the tube back to her late cousin's
apartment. For an instant, entering the spacious hall which
gave only a tiny taste of the opulence yet to come, Freddy
felt spooked. At any minute she expected Erica to drawl
from the drawing-room, 'Is that you, Freddy darling? I have
the most horrible hangover. My appetite will need tempting
tonight…or do you think I ought to settle for a hair of the
dog that bit me? Do you think sobering up was the mistake?'

Her eyes stung with tears afresh. She had known Erica's
faults, had often despaired over her cousin's self-destructive
habits, but had continued to love her like a sister. In the
right mood, Erica had been tremendous fun to be around
and if she had been around a lot less than Freddy had
wished since Ben's birth, who was to blame for that?

The Arab Prince whom Erica had insisted had fathered
Ben? No, Freddy hadn't believed that particular story, most
especially not when Erica had got *really* carried away and
had added that one day her child's father would be a king!
So she had never shared that colourful tale with Ruth. It
was just possible, however, that Ben's father had been a
rich Arab tycoon, the old geezer with the yacht and the
taste for floating floozies whom Erica had been equally in-
discreet about mentioning. But a royal prince…no way!

'It's time for your bath,' she told Ben, leading him
through to the bathroom off the nursery.

'Boats!' Ben exclaimed with satisfaction, rushing to
gather up the plastic collection of toys in the string bag
hanging from a hook. 'Me play boats.'

'And then we'll have supper.'

'Love you…' Ben wrapped two small arms tight round
Freddy's knees and hugged her with all his might.

Her eyes prickled like mad and she was furious with
herself. She was going to lose Ben. Waiting in hope of a

helpful response coming from that stuffy Swiss bank had been foolish. There was no point kidding herself or trying to avoid the next step of notifying the authorities so that they could make legal decisions on Ben's behalf. But if only it hadn't been for all that wretched money! However, just as swiftly, Freddy told herself off for resenting the existence of the funds that would enable Ben to have the very best of everything as he grew up. Why didn't she just face it? There was no hope of her being allowed to retain custody of Ben.

She was tucking the little boy into his cot when the phone rang and startled her. Once when Erica had been in residence it had rung off the hook at all hours but as word of her cousin's death had slowly spread the phone had grown steadily more silent.

Answering it, she murmured, 'Yes?'

'I wish to speak to Miss Frederica Sutton,' stated a dark masculine voice with an unmistakable foreign accent.

'I'm Miss Sutton, but *which*—?' Miss Sutton are you asking for, she meant to add.

'Please make yourself available at ten tomorrow morning for my visit. I wish to discuss Benedict's future. I warn you that if any other party is present in the apartment prior to my arrival, the visit will not take place.'

'I beg your p-pardon?' Freddy stammered in her astonishment at those instructions, but even as she spoke the caller concluded the call.

Frowning, she began to put together what she had been told. Had she just spoken to Ben's father? Who else would wish to discuss Ben's future with her? But how had he found out that Erica had died? For goodness' sake, he might even be in regular contact with some friend of Erica's! Or possibly her letter to that Swiss bank had discreetly been passed on even though the institution had officially refused to help. Anyway, what did it matter?

By the sound of it, it very likely *was* Ben's father who was coming to speak to her tomorrow. Who else would be so concerned that there should be nobody else present during their meeting? Who else would demand and require such discretion? Although if that arrogant-sounding character who shot out demands without hesitation was a 'scared' married man, she would not have liked to meet a confident one!

Freddy went to bed that evening in a state of growing anxiety as she tried to imagine what plans the man might have for his secret son. She tossed and turned and wondered whether she ought to wear her nanny uniform and parade her excellent credentials in childcare in the hope of making the best possible impression. But in the end she discarded that idea for she wanted to make known her own blood tie with Ben, slender though it was. And with a rich domineering male, there was too much of a risk that her uniform would encourage him to look on her as a mere employee who could have no possible opinion worth hearing.

So she would put on her only suit and *be* suitably humble while listening, rather than attempting to impose any of her own views. She lay frantically trying to plunder her brain for what little Erica had said about the man who had got her pregnant. 'The kindest man I ever met.' Had her cousin been talking about Ben's father or the Argentinian millionaire who had followed him? Or had the Argentinian preceded Ben's conception?

In the darkness, Freddy blushed for her cousin's many affairs. Erica had been very lovely though, and no doubt it had been hard for her to choose one man, especially when they had nearly always seemed to have a wife in the background. Freddy winced, recalling the times when she had tried to preach moral restraint to Erica and Erica would give her a sad look that had just torn at Freddy's heart and say, 'All I want is someone who will really love me.' And then spoil the effect by adding, 'So what if he belongs to some other woman? Do you think she'd think twice in my shoes? It's a hard world out there!'

By nine the following morning, Freddy was ready for her visitor. The apartment shone because she had got up at six to ensure that not a sliver of dust lurked in any corner. Garbed in a navy suit, white blouse and flat court shoes and with her thick curly blonde hair scraped back into an old-fashioned bun, which she felt gave her a much-needed look of greater maturity, Freddy surveyed her reflection with a critical frown. Then, remembering the spectacles she had once worn for eye strain while studying, she went and dug them out and perched them on her nose. Yes, indeed, she thought with satisfaction, she could easily pass for a sensible young woman of thirty, not that she would lie if questioned, but most probably she would not be asked.

'The kindest man I have ever met,' she kept on repeating to herself to ease her nervous tension. If she could just get the opening, she had lots of arguments to make in her own favour. Ben's father would not need to maintain such a hugely expensive apartment for their benefit, nor would her own living expenses with Ben run to a hundredth of Erica's. If he would only agree to her becoming Ben's legal guardian, she would save him an absolute fortune in all sorts of ways! Please, please, please, she prayed, fingers knotted together as she paced up and down.

And then it finally occurred to her to wonder *how* Ben's father had been able to say that he would not show up if there was anyone else in the apartment. A shiver of belated dismay ran down Freddy's taut spine. The only way he could have uttered that warning would have been in the knowledge that he was having the apartment watched in advance of his own arrival and that was a seriously scary thought! Aware that she had disliked the handful of Erica's male friends whom she had actually met, Freddy suddenly felt quite sick with worry. Ben was adorable but his father could well be a creep or a criminal or both!

The bell buzzed. Sucking in a shaky breath, Freddy went to answer the door. As she stood back, three dark-skinned men dressed in suits and built like human tanks strode into the hall. Completely ignoring her, they proceeded to march into every room of the apartment, evidently checking out whether or not she and Ben were on their own. Surging like a frantic mother hen into the lounge where Ben lay asleep on a sofa, Freddy stood over him, muttering, 'Please go away…please don't wake him up…he'll be scared…I'm scared!'

One of the men spoke into a mobile phone and the trio regrouped together out in the hall while still behaving as if she were invisible. Trembling like a leaf, Freddy folded her arms and listened to the lift arrive with a ping on the landing outside the still-open front door: it was *that* quiet. She heard footsteps, a low exchange of masculine voices and then a tall dark male appeared in the lounge doorway.

He did not look like the kindest man she was ever likely to meet, but she kept on staring like an idiot because he was so incredibly good-looking she was knocked for six. She did not know quite what expectations she had had, but certainly she had assumed he would be a much older man. Not a guy who looked as if he wrestled with sharks for fun before breakfast, ran a couple of marathons before lunch, ruled some vast business empire throughout the afternoon and finished off the day by taking some *very* lucky woman to bed and exhausting her. Caught up in dismay by that last far too intimate thought, Freddy reddened to the roots of her hair.

'You are Miss Frederica Sutton?' he demanded, scanning her with brilliant dark deepset eyes that set her heart racing as if she had just heard a fire alarm.

Freddy nodded in slow motion, her entrapped attention

running over his luxuriant blue-black hair, his fabulous bone structure, the delicious hue of bronze to his complexion, his arrogant nose, his *sinfully* beautiful mouth. He was an absolute pin-up, he was totally fantastic, and Erica must have fallen madly in love with him. Just about any woman would, Freddy reflected dizzily, until she recalled that he was a *married* man and strove in shame to rise above all such inappropriate and personal reflections.

'Speak,' he commanded.

It really *was* a command too, Freddy noted, still searching for her lost vocal cords. He spoke like a male who took it for granted that instant obedience to his every wish would follow. 'I'm Frederica Sutton, just like—' my late cousin, the mother of your child, she had been about to say.

'If I wish to enter a conversation with you, I will inform you,' her visitor drawled, running bold and derisive eyes over her taut figure, his highly expressive mouth curling at the corners. 'I am Jaspar al-Husayn, Crown Prince of Quamar, and I stand here in my brother's place as next closest of kin and uncle to your son, Benedict.'

Freddy's hearing and comprehension seized up and slowed to a snail's pace the very instant he mentioned that he was a prince, a Crown Prince moreover. Erica had not been telling entertaining fibs? Ben's father *was* a royal prince? Silenced by sincere shock at that revelation, Freddy stared, eyes wide and shaken behind her spectacle lenses. But had he not also said that he was Ben's uncle and *not* his father?

'Why have you presented yourself to me dressed in that peculiar way? Do you think to impress me with the belief that you are a good mother? Though it must pain me to be so frank, I am well aware of the life that you lead and equally aware that your ugly appearance can only be a pretence calculated to mislead.'

He did not know that Erica was dead, she registered in

dismay. He believed that she was Erica, got up to be ugly, for some strange reason. *Ugly.* Freddy experienced both anger and pain at that label. No, she knew she wasn't pretty, but it was not good news to hear that a plain suit, a dated hairstyle and a pair of spectacles were sufficient to make her worthy of that cruel word: 'ugly'. He looked like a dark angel, talked like an ignorant, unfeeling louse and probably couldn't pass a single mirror without falling in love with his gorgeous reflection! Was it *his* business that she was not Erica? All that nonsense about discretion and here she was being treated like dirt and he wasn't *even* Ben's father!

'Your brother…' Freddy murmured icily while drawing her slender frame taut to reach her full quota of five feet four inches, her back ramrod straight. 'I'm prepared to speak only to your brother, Ben's father.'

'Adil died of a heart attack last month.'

Freddy frowned at him, her mind struggling to compute the reality that Ben truly was an orphan, that not only his mother but also his father was dead. She swallowed hard, seriously troubled by that news. By some awful quirk of fate, Ben had been deprived of the only remaining individual who had had an indisputable right to make caring choices on his behalf.

'It is I who will take charge of Benedict and remove him from your less-than-adequate care.' And having made that utterly devastating announcement, Crown Prince Jaspar strolled over to gaze down with unfathomable dark eyes at the little boy still curled up asleep on the sofa. 'He is very small for an al-Husayn male. We are a tall family,' he remarked critically.

'What do you mean when you say that *you* are planning to take charge of Ben?' Freddy mumbled, her tummy suddenly behaving as though it were a boat in a storm-tossed sea.

Her imagination was already running riot. She didn't like him and she didn't trust him. What did he mean by that comment that Ben was small? Use your brain and think fast, Freddy urged herself. Her shockingly offensive visitor could only be implying that Ben might *not*, after all, have al-Husayn genes. In other words, he was suggesting that Erica might have lied about her son having been fathered by his brother!

And wasn't it perfectly possible that Jaspar al-Husayn might be hoping that Ben would prove not to be a member of his family? Now that Ben's father had passed away, where did Ben come into the scheme of things? Why would this Crown Prince want to take Ben from a woman he believed to be his mother? Yet in contrast, his brother, Adil, had gone to great trouble to keep his illegitimate son a secret and had pledged a great deal of money to the task of ensuring that the child he'd had no intention of acknowledging would have a financially secure future.

'If you value your present lifestyle and income, don't argue with me,' Crown Prince Jaspar murmured, smooth as silk.

And in that moment Freddy decided that it would be far too risky to disabuse him of his assumption that she was Ben's mother. Not yet anyway. How far could she trust a male who had an advance guard of pure-bred thugs? He might well be a most unsavoury character. Certainly he behaved like one with that threat he had just uttered without conscience, announcing that he had the power to set aside the arrangements that his more responsible brother had put in place. What kind of a man spoke like that when a child's needs and security lay in the balance?

And Jaspar al-Husayn needn't bother looking down that classic nose at her as if she were the dust beneath his royal feet. In fact, Freddy, who had a temper that was usually slow to rise, was just about fizzing with rage in her determination to protect Ben. Only if her concerns were put to rest would she dare to concede the dangerous truth that as Ben's uncle *he* had far more rights than *she* could possibly have.

'Can you offer me proof of your identity?' Freddy enquired, unleashing the first volley of what she expected to be a long and bitter defensive battle.

The brilliant dark eyes flashed gold, lush black lashes narrowing over his piercing gaze. 'I have no need to offer such credentials.'

That rich dark drawl carried a note of incredulity that he could not hide. Freddy straightened her shoulders. 'I don't know you from Adam. You could be anybody and I'm not prepared to discuss Ben's future without evidence that you are who you say you are.'

'I am not accustomed to being spoken to in such a discourteous manner,' Crown Prince Jaspar countered in the most lethal tone.

A chill ran down Freddy's rigid spine but she needed time, time to check him out and time to take advice. That it would mean for ever burning her own boats with this arrogant male was unavoidable, for Ben's safety and well-being were of paramount importance.

'Perhaps you could come back tomorrow evening about eight with appropriate references,' Freddy countered unevenly, somewhat intimidated by the aura of sheer blazing disbelief that emanated from him. 'I will then be happy to sit down and discuss in a polite and civilised way what path his future should follow.'

'You have angered me. You will regret it.' Jaspar al-Husayn swore very softly.

Pale as death, Freddy watched him stride from the room and listened to the front door thud shut in his wake. He had given her such a scare that she could hardly breathe. Ben began to wake up, sleepily rubbing his eyes and whimpering a little the way he often did at such times. Freddy gathered him up in her arms and hugged him to her, her heart racing. An orphaned child born of such important lineage and likely to inherit a large amount of money was a very vulnerable child, she reflected fearfully. She needed to make an appointment with a solicitor and check out her legal position.

CHAPTER TWO

LATE afternoon of the following day, Jaspar studied the report from his security team on Erica Sutton's activities since his visit to her apartment. That she had evidently rushed straight to a solicitor for advice came as no surprise to him.

Jaspar was satisfied that he had put Erica Sutton under considerable pressure, which had been precisely his intent. While his late brother had been gracing ceremonial occasions and cruising the Med with his party girls, Jaspar had been acquiring the brilliant business acumen with which he oversaw Quamar's considerable investments abroad. Military school and the tough, fast-moving world of finance had honed Jaspar's natural talents to a fine and ruthless edge. He knew how to negotiate. Once he knew his quarry's weaknesses and the time was right, he moved in for the kill.

Subjecting Erica Sutton to the fear that she might lose all that she had gained by her son's birth had been a deliberate ploy. Doubtless, she imagined that to continue enjoying her present lifestyle she had to retain custody of her son but that was not, in fact, the case. When she learned that she could give up his nephew *without* surrendering her financial security, Jaspar believed that she would rush to do so.

But he was intensely amused to read that Erica had apparently spent two hours in a beauty salon that very afternoon. So the *real* Erica Sutton was about to make herself known! His crack about her unlovely appearance had evidently been more than flesh and blood could stand. Had she imagined when he'd set up that first meeting that he was someone who had power over her finances? Why else would she have gone to such ridiculous lengths to present him with that fake image? How could she have thought that he would be impressed by such a disguise? Adil, connoisseur that he had been, would not have looked twice at a woman with a hideous hairstyle, heavy spectacles and frumpy clothes.

But then, possibly, Erica Sutton was not the brightest spark on the block, Jaspar conceded lazily, recalling the reality that she had telephoned the Consulate of Quamar in an apparent effort to confirm his identity. So naive, so clumsy, he reflected, for naturally even the junior diplomat who had dealt with her call had refused to confirm or deny his presence in London on what was essentially a private trip. But then he was surprised that she had not simply recognised him from the many family photographs on his late brother's yacht, *Beauteous Dreamer*.

Hopefully, he could wrap up the whole unfortunate business by the end of the day for he did not wish to strain his father's non-existent patience. He already had nursery staff standing by to take charge of his nephew. Possibly the arrival of a grandson might distract his parent from the rather more personal goal which Adil's death had sadly made a matter of much greater urgency…Jaspar's *own* marriage.

At thirty years old, he was well aware that he was fortunate to still be single. But then his father had feared that Adil's inability to settle with one woman had been the direct result of having been pressed into marriage while he'd still been too immature to have made that commitment. However, Adil's death had changed the whole picture where Jaspar was concerned. That he marry and produce a son to safeguard the succession was now of great importance.

He would let his father choose his bride. Why not? For

the past two years, the royal household had staged regular social events simply to ensure that he met a great number of young women. On a most discreet basis, innumerable bridal candidates had been served up for Jaspar's perusal, the hope being that he would do what everybody wanted him to do and fall in love. But the knowledge that he was being targeted with every weapon in the feminine armoury had made him extremely critical. And the concept of love left Jaspar colder than Siberian ice. Adil had *always* been falling in love, but Jaspar had only loved once and the experience had been traumatic. Love was a weakness that Jaspar had no intention of falling victim to a second time.

The day before, Freddy had visited the first solicitor able to give her an immediate appointment. Having described Ben's situation without naming names, she had requested an honest opinion of her position.

'An uncle is a close relative and, in this particular case, the authorities would also take into account Ben's inheritance as well as his background,' the older man informed her.

Freddy tensed. 'His…background?'

'Naturally with his father having been of Arabic descent there are cultural aspects which would *have* to be respected in his upbringing.'

Not even having foreseen that likelihood, Freddy paled, but she pressed on regardless to finally reach the climax which she had intended all along. 'But if I was to apply to have Ben made a ward of court…er…to protect him?'

'Protect him?' The solicitor frowned in visible surprise. 'On what grounds? Have you cause to believe that Ben would be at some risk with his uncle?'

'Well, not precisely, but…I didn't like the man *at all*,' Freddy proffered feelingly.

'If necessary, social services would intervene to ensure

the child's well-being but, on the basis of what you've told me about the uncle, I don't see why they should. I also don't think you need to take quite so much responsibility onto your own shoulders,' she was told.

Disconcerted by that quiet rebuke, Freddy left his office, dogged by the depressing suspicion that she had been charging at foolish windmills and refusing to accept the inevitable. *Why* had it not occurred to her that Ben's cultural heritage would weigh heavily in the balance of what was judged best for him? Such an obvious point, yet she had not even recognised it and there was no way on earth that she alone could meet that need.

Arriving back at the apartment, she contacted the Consulate of Quamar to try to verify Jaspar al-Husayn's identity. The man she spoke to was not helpful. However, the internet search she then did on Erica's computer proved more fruitful for the royal family of Quamar had an official website. It contained a small respectful piece on the demise of the former Crown Prince, Adil, and a much lengthier bulletin on King Zafir's precarious state of health. However, her own attention was immediately engaged by the picture of the present heir to the throne, Jaspar al-Husayn, looking impossibly handsome and grave and indisputably the same arrogant male who had visited her.

Totally disheartened by that final confirmation, Freddy went to bed that night and made herself face facts. Jaspar al-Husayn evidently knew enough about her late cousin's lifestyle to have deemed her an unfit parent and could she truly blame him for that? Had she been unfairly biased against him? After all, it had been a considerable shock when Ben's uncle had come out of nowhere to demand him and a hard, hurting blow in terms of her *own* fond hopes of keeping Erica's child, Freddy acknowledged with scrupulous honesty. But it would be very wrong of her to allow selfish personal feelings to blind her to what would be best for Ben.

Ultimately, it seemed, Crown Prince Jaspar would gain custody of Ben and there was nothing she could do about that. However, if she continued, *just* in the short term, to let him believe that she was Ben's mother, she could at least learn what his plans for Ben entailed and try to persuade him to make the break between herself and Ben a gentle one. Then she would have to come clean about only being Ben's nanny and no doubt Crown Prince Jaspar would be absolutely furious with her on that score.

Even as she choked back a sob at the prospect of being parted from Ben, Freddy recognised that it was Jaspar al-Husayn's demand for total discretion that worried her the most. How could he take personal charge of an illegitimate child whose very existence would surely cause an enormous scandal in a conservative Arab country? It was not as though he could adopt Ben: as far as Freddy was aware, Muslim countries did not practise adoption.

Recalling how suspicious the Crown Prince had been of her staid appearance on his first visit, Freddy decided that she had better make what effort she could to look the part she now felt forced to play for a little longer. So the following afternoon she went to get her hair done. Afterwards, she was rather stunned by the foaming mane of eye-catching blonde curls she seemed to have developed.

Freddy had always worn her hair tied back. Indeed, she would have had it cut short had her late father not once remarked on how pretty her hair was. Well, long hair was all very well but not practical during working hours, and long thick curly hair was something else again unless one was talented with a blow-dryer, which Freddy was not.

A couple of early and very wounding experiences with boys had confirmed her conviction that she was a born spinster just as Ruth had once confessed herself to be. In recent years, only amorous drunks or self-pitying types desperate for a sympathetic audience had demonstrated any interest in her. Why? Well, as Erica had said, 'You're a little plump and homely, Freddy.'

Freddy loathed her body and loved to cover it. A mere glimpse of her too ample bosom and curvaceous behind when she was undressing was enough to depress her for the rest of the day. Developing far in advance of her school-mates had been a severe embarrassment in primary school and hiding beneath capacious sweaters and T-shirts had become a necessity when she'd compared her own burgeoning shape to Erica's reed-slender delicacy. No matter how hard she exercised, her full curves remained.

After tucking Ben in, she hovered by his cot, gazing down into his peaceful and sleepy little face. Her throat thickened and she felt as if a giant hand were squeezing her heart and dared not even think of what her life would be like without him. She went for a quick shower and then wound herself into a pink towel. In the cloakroom, she stood at the vanity unit, which had marvellous lighting, and painstakingly applied eye-shadow and mascara. She rarely bothered to use cosmetics yet she knew every trick, lessons learned by watching Erica as both teenager and woman.

The doorbell buzzed just as she was putting on lipstick. She smiled because she had ordered herself a pizza as a treat. Once a week, where was the harm? Taste buds watering, she went to answer the door. It didn't matter that she was only wearing a towel as the take-away employed a woman to deliver in the area.

But when Freddy opened the door, she got a surprise. Jaspar al-Husayn strode into the hall without awaiting an invitation.

'I thought you were my pizza being delivered,' Freddy mumbled, aghast at his early arrival and then shocked all over again by the sheer impact of him in the flesh.

She encountered stunning eyes the colour of pure gold and was dazzled. If I had three wishes, it would be him…and him…and him, she thought dizzily, her heartbeat taking off like a jet plane. Electric tension held her fast and breathing was a challenge. The tall wrought-iron lamp cast shaded light that shimmered over the luxuriant black hair swept back from his brow, accentuated the smooth planes of his hard cheekbones, and lingered on the sculpted curve of his firm male lips.

His lean, tightly muscled frame was sheathed in a dark grey business suit that was exquisitely tailored to his powerful physique. A study in shades of vibrant bronze, he was lethally attractive. And meeting those eyes, those extraordinary eyes that she could not look away from, she felt an enervating charge of tension pulse through her, tautening every tiny muscle. Yet her body was filling with a sensation of liquid, languorous warmth, making her outrageously aware of the heaviness of her breasts and the sudden embarrassing prominence of her nipples.

'Pizza…' Jaspar murmured huskily, rooted to the spot by the sight of her.

Where the hell had his attention been on his previous visit? he asked himself with stark incredulity. Her eyes were the aqua colour of the sea, that curious blending of blue and jade and turquoise that changed according to the light. And she had the kind of hair mermaids had in fairy tales, a wild golden mane that fell round her shoulders in glorious, rippling abundance. But no legendary sea creature could have competed with the luscious swell of her creamy breasts above the towel or that glorious hourglass shape. Even as he hardened in hot-blooded male response to that sensual vision, Jaspar was shifting cool mental gears, knowing that he had severely underestimated the opposition and that was a rare error for him. He wanted to rip the towel off, propel her back against the wall and sink deep

into her, lose himself in the kind of raw, urgent sex he
hadn't fantasised about since he was a teenager. And maybe
he would, once he had got what he wanted.

'P-pizza,' Freddy stammered like a belated echo, dazed
by the throbbing silence, the almost painful tension and
heat inside her, the sheer terrifying emptiness of her own
mind.

'Are you planning to take the towel off?' Jaspar enquired
silkily. 'Or are you just a tease?'

Slow burning colour flushed her throat in a wave and
climbed up into her cheeks as she tore her dilated gaze from
his intent scrutiny and glanced down at herself in dismay,
absorbing the fact that she truly was still hovering a few
feet from him clad only in a towel. With a stifled moan of
embarrassment, she blundered into sudden movement in the
direction of the cloakroom.

Afterwards, she could never work out how it happened,
but as she accidentally brushed against him he caught her
to him, one lean brown hand anchoring into her hair, the
other splaying to her hip. Her startled aqua eyes flared into
mesmeric gold and it was as if fireworks were flaring inside
her, setting every inch of her ablaze.

'The stammer was overkill...' he told her huskily, white,
even teeth flashing as he slanted a mocking smile down at
her, 'but the welcome invitation was *ace*—'

'You've got the wrong idea!' Freddy gasped, all composure crumbling.

'I don't think so...I hate to sound like a jerk, but women
have been throwing themselves at me since I was a teenager.'

And before Freddy could even absorb that unashamed
assurance that wickedly sensual mouth had descended with
devouring heat down onto hers. Intense excitement surged
up inside her in a sheet of multicoloured flame. Reaching
out blindly, she gripped his arm to stay upright. She felt as

if she were falling, falling so fast and furiously that she would burn up before she reached solid earth again. And nothing mattered, nothing mattered but that that connection with him remained. She was in a wonderland of sensual discovery, gasping at the plundering invasion of his tongue inside the tender interior of her mouth, shivering violently, desperately longing for him to pull her close and crush her up against him.

She heard the doorbell buzz with a kind of delayed recognition only as he tensed and then pulled back from her.

'Oh…crumbs…'she framed, blinking rapidly and then shooting into the cloakroom behind him like a scalded cat.

Thrusting home the bolt on the door, Freddy flung herself back against it, shaking like a leaf in a gale. The mirror surrounded with lights opposite confronted her with her own image. Literally cringing with mortification, she studied her swollen mouth, her dilated pupils and the expression of shock and bewilderment still etched there. How are you ever going to go out there again and act as if nothing happened? screamed the first thought to emerge from her reawakening brain.

He thought she had deliberately flaunted herself in the towel too. True brazen hussy stuff. At that realisation, she writhed in even greater embarrassment, but over and above that discomfiture lurked an entire new level of self-knowledge. She honestly *hadn't* known that a man could make her feel like that. There was a sort of shameless fascination still gripping her: that one smouldering kiss could make her forget everything. Who she was, who he was, *everything*. It also seemed especially cruel that she should have made that discovery with Jaspar al-Husayn. In fact, could there be anything more infuriating? All this time she had wondered why most women's magazines raved about sex as though it was a truly exciting pursuit when her own slender experience had taught her otherwise.

And then this guy she hated like poison grabbed her and showed her that the excitement might actually *not* be a giant con practised on the female sex. How dared he have done that to her? What was the point of finding out that a Crown Prince had more than a fighting chance of persuading her out of celibacy? A blasted Crown Prince, she thought afresh, eyes scorching with sudden tears.

He had come to talk about Ben, she reminded herself. Paling, she forced herself to move and unlocked the door sneakily and silently, before pressing down the handle equally quietly and peering out into the hall through a gap barely an inch wide. The coast seemed clear. Had he left? She crept out and then fled down the corridor to her bedroom faster than the speed of light to find some clothes.

Pulling on an oversized T-shirt and a jersey skirt which fell almost to her ankles, she dug her feet into clumpy shoes. The whole time she was dressing, she was rationalising what had happened between them. He had taken her by surprise. She had been temporarily deprived of her wits by the simple fact that he was so gorgeous. But he only had to speak and his mythical attraction vanished, so really she was quite safe from making an even bigger ass of herself. So women were forever throwing themselves at him...oh, the poor love, how did he bear the torment of being so unbearably fanciable? He had the most gigantic ego and she would have done anything to puncture it.

She trudged back down to the main reception rooms, very much hoping he wouldn't be waiting for her. But the guy had no tact, no shame and the kind of self-assurance that would have ensured that the *Titanic* sank the iceberg instead of the other way round. There he was, large as life and twice as bold in the drawing-room, which she had barely entered since Erica's death. But then he had found his natural milieu, hadn't he? He looked more at home there against the elaborate furniture and the curtaining weighed down with excessive swagging, fringing and tassels.

'Your pizza…' Indicating the shallow box parked on the coffee-table, Jaspar al-Husayn sent her a slow, slashing smile that made her heart skip a beat and told her too many things that she didn't want to know.

'Look, I don't fancy you!' Freddy heard herself state with shocking baldness before she could think better of it. 'So you can stop looking so pleased with yourself because what happened out in that hall was just one of those stupid things and there is not the smallest danger that I am going to be tempted to throw myself at you! Not unless I get a brain transplant.'

He said nothing. In the silence that dragged even in the first second, and which was working like a shriek alarm on her nerves by the tenth second, Jaspar gazed back at her with measuring cool.

Freddy could feel her face burning up like a bonfire. While those ten seconds limped past, she went from defensive defiance to shrinking chagrin. What on earth had come over her? Instead of ignoring what had happened, she had dredged it back up again and attacked him like a teenager desperate to save face.

'Let's discuss my nephew,' he finally murmured in his rich, dark drawl. 'Feel free to enjoy your pizza.'

Freddy pictured an imaginary headline: 'Crown Prince battered to death by pizza box'. She hated him, oh, boy, did she hate him. Every time he opened his mouth, he put her down, and only a minute ago he had proved that he didn't even have to speak to achieve that feat. Freddy plonked herself down on an overstuffed sofa. Her tummy gurgled and she stiffened with embarrassment and stared a hole in the pizza box. She had a healthy appetite and she was starving, but she was convinced that if she started eating he would take one scornful look at her and think, No wonder she's that size!

Mind you, he had kissed her, hadn't he? Her downbent head came up a notch. Obviously he hadn't found her that unattractive. There must have been some spark on his side of the fence. Maybe he *liked* women who weren't skin and bone. It was such a seductive thought that Freddy had an instant vision of herself lying in a desert tent being stuffed with sweets by an adoring male, who would *die* if she mentioned going on a diet. What was the matter with her? For goodness' sake, this was probably the most important discussion she would ever hold in her whole life, for Ben *was* her life, and yet her mind was filled with nothing but nonsense!

'I understood that you employed a nanny for my nephew,' Jaspar remarked without warning. 'Where is she?'

Wondering how on earth he could seem to know so much about Erica's life and yet not know that her cousin was no longer alive, Freddy stiffened and then forced herself to look at him. 'She has a family emergency to deal with right now. Look…you said you wanted to take charge of Ben. I'd like to know why.'

Jaspar al-Husayn surveyed her with narrowed golden eyes. 'He is my nephew.'

'But your brother wanted Ben's existence kept a secret. He didn't seem to want anything further to do with him either.' Freddy was choosing her words carefully.

'I will not comment on my late brother's decisions,' Jaspar murmured, his strong jawline clenching. 'It would be inappropriate.'

'But I don't think it's unreasonable of me to ask *why* you have this sudden desire to give Ben a home,' Freddy persisted.

'I have in my possession a recent investigation report into your lifestyle.'

Instinctively resenting that superior tone as much as she disliked the news that a private detective had been snooping into Erica's life without her late cousin's knowledge, Freddy tilted her chin and said with helpless defiance, 'Bully for you!'

Jaspar dealt her a grim appraisal. 'The report made it clear that you are a neglectful mother. You have continually left my nephew to the sole care of an employee, sometimes for periods of six weeks at a time. When you are at home, you throw wild parties for your drunken friends. The police have been called on more than one occasion to settle violent disputes at this address.'

Freddy reddened with sudden shame because it was all true and she turned her head away for a moment, no longer able to meet his challenging gaze. She could still recall lying nervously awake behind a locked door with Ben on the night that Erica had staged her first party since her son's birth. Neighbours had complained to the police about the excessive noise and offensive behaviour of the guests. When, on a subsequent evening, someone had tried to force their way into the bedroom, Freddy had been really scared. After that experience, whenever Erica had decided to throw a party, Freddy had simply taken Ben over to Ruth's and spent the night there with him in peace.

'I...' She swallowed hard, wondering what on earth she could say in her cousin's defence, but on the score of her constant absences and those rowdy parties there was little she *could* say. 'I can see that it looks bad—'

'It looks worse than bad,' Jaspar interposed with cutting contempt. 'It's obvious that you have no taste for being a mother and even less concern for your child's welfare. Adil's son is an al-Husayn. Honour demands that we now acknowledge *our* responsibility towards him.'

'And who does "we" cover?' Freddy prompted, because she knew he was single after looking at that website. In fact there had been some emphasis on the subject of the current heir to the throne of Quamar still being unmarried. Maybe they were subtly advertising him as being up for grabs, hoping that some veiled Middle Eastern princess of unimpeachable virtue and blue-blooded lineage would apply for the privilege of becoming a queen-in-waiting.

'My family,' Jaspar enunciated with pride.

'But you're single and a young child needs a mother figure,' Freddy pointed out with some satisfaction.

His fabulous bone structure tightened. 'I have many relatives within the extended family circle. I hope that some one of them will offer my nephew a caring home.'

'But *not* you,' Freddy noted, angry at the concept of Ben being casually rehomed with the first party willing to take him in.

'As I am unmarried, it would look very suspicious were I suddenly to produce a child out of nowhere and announce that I intended to bring him up. I am not in a position to even consider that possibility.' Jaspar dealt her a look of flaring impatience, his firm mouth compressing. 'Had I had a wife and had she been willing to enter such a pretence, we might have been able to pass him off as an orphaned relative of hers. But, right now, it is not an option.'

So, although he was Ben's uncle, he would not be personally involved in his nephew's future. Freddy was dismayed. Such a proposition was hardly what she had imagined.

'You must understand that our society is not liberal and discretion is a necessity. My nephew's parentage must be concealed for his own sake. Illegitimacy is still a mark of shame in Quamar,' Jaspar al-Husayn continued with gravity. 'Naturally we also wish to avoid creating a scandal which would cause severe embarrassment to Adil's family.'

From beneath her lashes, she noted the brooding tension

of his stance. 'You resent me asking questions…but I love Ben very much and all I want is what is best for him.'

'In the light of what I know about you, I find that claim difficult to credit.' His lean, strong face set hard. 'You have valued your son not for himself but only for his worth in financial terms. I have little taste for this dialogue with you, so let me assure you that your current income will continue at its present level if you give your son into my care.'

'Whatever you think of me, money does not come into this,' Freddy breathed tightly, her tummy giving a sick little somersault at the idea. 'Ben needs to be loved. All children need to be loved and he's an affectionate child. You talk about honour and responsibility but I'm talking about daily love and support—'

'You have no right to question me in this way. Whatever we offer will be immensely superior to the level of care that Ben currently receives,' Jaspar stated with hard finality.

Freddy snatched in a ragged breath. 'But it will take time for Ben to adapt to a new home and new people.'

'I don't have time to waste. My father is at present ill and most eager to meet his grandson. I would like to fly back to Quamar with my nephew tomorrow.'

'*Tomorrow?*' Freddy was aghast. 'Ben hasn't even met you yet and you know nothing about him. He's not a parcel you can just lift and toss onto a plane!'

'I have highly qualified nursery staff waiting to take charge of him.'

Freddy shook her blonde head slowly and looked at him with shaken aquamarine eyes. 'You really don't know anything at all about young children, do you?'

'He is still only a baby and he will soon adapt to a new life with caring people,' Jaspar delivered.

'He would be traumatised if he was suddenly taken away from me. He needs to be eased into that transition,' Freddy told him with spirit. 'It can't be done overnight—'

'If the break must be made, it should be quick and clean. I cannot accept that his attachment to you or your attachment to him is of any true consequence,' Jaspar countered with perceptible derision. 'After all, you have spent most of his short life sunning yourself on tropical shores and partying without him!'

Freddy was thinking frantically fast and she came up with what seemed like a solution on the spur of the moment. 'I'd be willing to come out to Quamar with him and stay in a guesthouse or something until he was able to manage without me for longer periods—'

Brilliant golden eyes shimmered over her. 'You're talking nonsense. This is the same child who had to get by without you for weeks on end, and I have no hesitation in telling you that you won't be welcome in Quamar at any time now or in the future.'

He was a bone-deep stubborn male, Freddy registered, her anxiety on Ben's behalf steadily mounting. He had not a clue about children but it was quite beneath him to admit it. He did indeed believe that he could remove Ben from everything familiar without causing him distress. For the first time, it occurred to her that she had made a cardinal error in allowing Jaspar al-Husayn to continue believing that she was Erica. He was all too well acquainted with her cousin's poor record as a parent and it was hardly surprising that he was impervious to her arguments. So did she now tell him the truth?

If she confessed that she was only his nephew's nanny, he would be outraged. He did not strike her as a forgiving type of male. He might feel that she had tried to make a fool of him. He would be furious that he had discussed what he clearly regarded as very private family matters with a humble employee. Worst of all, he would immediately realise that she had no power to prevent him from removing Ben from her care. He might walk straight into Ben's bedroom and just lift him out of his cot without any further discussion, she thought fearfully.

'Tomorrow morning, I will send the nanny here to collect my nephew so that she can spend the day with him and get to know him. Will that satisfy you?' Jaspar asked drily.

Freddy saw that she was fighting a losing battle. She remembered the solicitor who had suggested that she was taking too much on her own shoulders in seeking to interfere and she lost colour at that recollection. How much was she truly thinking of Ben? And how much was her judgement being influenced by her own wants and wishes? After all, she did not *want* to give Ben up and wasn't that very selfish of her?

'Will Ben have proper parents in Quamar?' she whispered shakily.

'Of course. There is more than one childless couple in the family.'

Freddy hung her head, shame enclosing her. Had there ever been grounds for her to suspect his motives in seeking to change his late brother's arrangements for Ben? Wouldn't it have been much more simple for the al-Husayn family to leave those discreet arrangements in place? Even the investigation report that he had mentioned suggested that his family's most driving concern had been for Ben's welfare.

'If it suits,' Freddy muttered tautly as she stood up, 'I'd like to speak to you again tomorrow evening.'

In the hall, Jaspar al-Husayn gave her a keen appraisal. Perhaps she felt that she had to go through the concerned maternal motions, he reflected. Perhaps she couldn't help herself; perhaps, as was often the case, she could not see herself as the appalling parent that she in fact was. But he had won and he knew it. She would give up her rights to her son on his next visit. He was surprised to feel a faint pang of compassion as he scanned her strained face and the tense downcurve of her ripe mouth.

As the apartment door closed behind him a painful shuddering sob broke from Freddy. Ben was as good as gone. When she admitted that she was merely his nanny, who knew what Jaspar al-Husayn would do? He would certainly never accept the strength of the bond between her and Ben. 'If the break must be made, it should be quick and clean.' No, had she confessed her true identity, Ben might have been removed from her care even sooner.

CHAPTER THREE

AFTER a sleepless night, Freddy rose early the next morning.

Every last minute she had to spend with Ben now seemed so impossibly precious. She sat watching him eat his favourite breakfast of a boiled egg with toast soldiers for dipping and her throat closed up so much, it physically hurt. She studied his rounded little face below his dark fluffy curls, the twin crescents of his long lashes, the smooth baby skin still flushed from sleep, and she honestly thought that her heart was going to break.

The night before, she had let herself get all worked up about a stupid kiss probably because it had been easier to concentrate on that foolishness than to face and deal with the loss of the child she loved. But Ben wasn't hers and he never would be hers and somehow she had to learn to accept that and step back. The pain she was feeling now was entirely her own fault. During her training, she had been warned not to make the mistake of forgetting that the child in her care had a mother and that she was only a temporary carer who would inevitably move on to another family. But she had not been able to abide by that rule. Ben had looked to her for love and she had given it to him, rationalising that in Erica's absence, Erica's very unwillingness to make that commitment, someone had to compensate Ben and give him what he needed to thrive.

It had been Freddy who had sat by Ben's incubator hour after hour during the first worrying weeks of his life, Freddy who had ultimately named him after their paternal grandfather when Erica had said she couldn't care less what her son was called. Eyes watering as she forced a smile for Ben's benefit and washed his face and hands, she found herself thinking back to her earliest memories of Erica.

When her widowed father had taken her orphaned cousin into their home, Freddy had been a lonely eight year old. Even then, Erica had been an incredibly pretty girl with an elfin face, catlike eyes and silky dark brown hair. She had had enormous charm as well. She had had the power to make Freddy's dour father laugh and had been wonderful at teasing him out of his bad moods. Admiring Erica for her vivacity and confidence, Freddy had been happy to take a back seat. She had had to get much older before she'd appreciated that, beneath all that superficial sparkle, Erica was quite incapable of being happy for more than a couple of hours or of ever feeling truly secure.

Seven years later, there had been a huge scandal when Erica had run away with a neighbour's husband. Freddy's father had raged at the embarrassment of it all for days on end. Only weeks later, the erring husband had slunk back home again and Erica had attempted the same feat, only to have the door slammed in her face by her uncle. Freddy had been heartbroken that awful night. She had seen the shock and disbelief on Erica's face, Erica who had never ever thought of consequences or of how her actions might have impacted on other lives.

But the following year, Erica had come to see them again. Looking very glamorous and impossibly penitent, she had soon won her uncle's forgiveness and had told them stories about her exciting life as a successful model in London. Stories full of whopping fibs, Freddy had later appreciated, for the truth that Erica had depended on her lovers to keep her would scarcely have been acceptable.

At nineteen, Freddy had gone to college to train as a nanny and, for some time afterwards, contact with her cousin had dwindled to the occasional phone call. However, when Freddy's father had died, Erica had come to the funeral, wan and pregnant and indeed looking anything but well. The cousins had had an emotional reunion and Erica had asked Freddy to come and live with her in London and help her get through the remainder of her pregnancy.

Freddy had not had to think twice about that decision. At the time she had just completed her first job as a nanny and, in the wake of her father's death, she had been ready for a change. Erica had been genuinely ill, suffering from continual nausea and the constant threat of a miscarriage. Her cousin had spent the last weeks preceding her son's birth lying flat on her back in a hospital bed, her only visitor, Freddy.

So, to some degree, Freddy had understood Erica's refusal to relate to her tiny child in his incubator. In so many ways, Erica had never really grown up. Like a kid just let loose from school, Erica's only thought after her delivery had been to regain her figure and reward herself for all those months of sick and joyless boredom. In her mind, Ben had already had too big a slice of her life.

'Why do you think I brought you down here to look after me?' Erica had asked when Freddy had tried to remonstrate with her cousin. 'I know you'll do what I ought to do. You can be his substitute mum.'

'But he needs *you* to love him.'

'I think the only person I have ever loved is you,' Erica had quipped.

Freddy was dredged from her painful memories by the buzz of the doorbell. It was barely nine in the morning and the nanny had arrived to collect Ben much earlier than Freddy had hoped she would. The young woman introduced herself in perfect English as Alula. A slim brunette in her twenties, constrained in her manner and reluctant it seemed to even look Freddy in the face, Alula immediately centred her attention on Ben.

Freddy hovered and answered questions about Ben's dietary preferences and routines that were asked with reassuring professionalism. She scolded herself for feeling uneasy at the brunette's total lack of friendliness. 'Where are you taking Ben?' she asked, trying to sound casual.

'I haven't yet received instructions.' Alula knelt down on the floor to study Ben much as if he were one step narrowly removed from divinity and practically begged for the toy he was holding. 'He is a most beautiful child.'

Ben was by no means untouched by the tidal wave of almost reverential appreciation coming his way. Beaming, he bestowed the toy on his admirer. Freddy felt like a fly on the wall and tried to tell herself that she was delighted that Alula was so marvellous with children. Some time later when she had gained Ben's trust, Alula turned and opened the front door again for herself. 'Goodbye,' she said, holding Ben's hand in hers. 'Say goodbye, Ben.'

'Bye…' Ben breezed and then he suddenly pulled free of the brunette, startling her as he ran back to Freddy to demand, 'Kiss Ben!'

Swallowing hard, Freddy hugged his warm, squirming little body close. 'If he's upset, please call me. I can advise you,' she said unevenly.

With a nod that might have signified agreement, Alula walked out onto the landing. Freddy stared out at the two tough-looking men with the cropped haircuts who must have been standing out of view when the other woman had arrived. Bodyguards, she assumed, and they already had the lift open and waiting. As Ben stepped into the lift, he glanced back over his shoulder and grinned at her, patently proud of his own independence.

How trusting a confident child was, Freddy thought wretchedly as he disappeared from view and she retreated back into the apartment, almost blinded by the tears swimming in her eyes. She ought to be proud of herself. She had taught him to be confident, taken him to a playgroup from an early age and encouraged him to mix with other children as well as the nannies she had met up with from time to time.

It was the slowest, longest day of her life. She kept on trying to concentrate on how she could best explain her brief masquerade as Erica to Jaspar al-Husayn. Would he understand the shock and anxiety which had initially persuaded her into that pretence? Would he recognise and radically disapprove of the special bond between her and his nephew? And would he be reasonable? Or would he walk right back out again with Ben, shorn of any fear of her interference?

As the afternoon crept on, a tight knot began to form in Freddy's hollow stomach. She had only eaten a morsel of toast at breakfast and had not been able to face lunch. Well, Jaspar al-Husayn had said that his nanny would be spending the day with Ben and it seemed that the entire day was going to run its course. In her heart she was glad that Ben had not become upset and had not had to be brought home early, but she was also surprised. He was not accustomed to doing without her and as he got tired he usually became very clingy. But then no doubt Alula had laid on a feast of attractions to keep him distracted, or possibly Ben was being allowed to enjoy a lengthy nap.

When the bell sounded just after five, Freddy nearly broke her neck in her haste to open the door, only to fall back a step in surprise when she saw Jaspar al-Husayn poised with only his bodyguards behind him. 'Is Ben waiting in your car?' she asked. 'He must be awfully tired by now.'

'Erica...'

'Freddy,' Freddy corrected without even thinking about it, for as she stepped back automatically to allow him entrance she was too busy noting the screened darkness of his eyes, the tautness of his superb bone structure and the pronounced tension he exuded.

As his security men filed in past her Jaspar watched her peer out the door again, patently still on the watch for the little boy, who was already many thousands of miles away. He could feel her eagerness, see her distraction and he averted his attention from her with a sense of shame entirely new to him and far from welcome to a male who prided himself on his principles. Indeed, his heart sank at the task facing him: how to present an inexcusable act in terms that might even be passably acceptable. For if he did *not* contrive to placate her, the biggest scandal that had ever hit Quamar was about to break and it would be impossible to protect his people or his family from an international storm of opprobrium. She had not given legal consent to surrendering her child.

At that instant, Jaspar did not believe he would ever respect his father again. To make such an order without thought of the consequences! To issue a command like the feudal king he was in a world with media that would label him a lawless tyrant and judge Quamar as backward and uncivilised. The newspapers would inevitably expose Adil's sordid double life and cover every Quamari citizen with deep shame and dishonour. The country that Jaspar loved with every breath in his body would suffer. Right was right and wrong was wrong.

Erica or Freddy Sutton or whatever odd name she chose to call herself might be a lousy parent, but she *did* have feelings for her son. He had not initially wished to concede that, but on later appraisal he had appreciated that her every question regarding his nephew's future had been based on concern for the boy. A proper agreement had been *just* within reach. Had he not seen the defeat in her eyes and interpreted it as her sad acceptance that she was not the mother that her son deserved? But now the balance of power had changed and Jaspar was deeply conscious of that reality.

Freddy hovered as one of the bodyguards closed the front door. The hall seemed extraordinarily full of large intimidating men. Obviously, Ben wasn't coming home just yet. As the tension in the atmosphere began to tug at her awareness, a sense of foreboding assailed her. She turned to lead the way into the drawing-room, saying in an unnaturally flat voice that got nowhere near the assured tone she had hoped to strike, 'You know, Ben really should be home for his usual bedtime. That's seven, by the way.'

She turned round to face Jaspar al-Husayn, aquamarine eyes troubled, her hands knotting together in front of her.

'I have come here to ask your pardon,' he murmured in a constrained tone.

Freddy blinked, a frownline forming between her brows. That note of humility was so strikingly unexpected that she stared.

'Please sit down so that I may explain what has happened,' he continued, his grave expression and the stamp of pallor around his compressed lips betraying a tension that she could no longer pass off as the result of her own imagination.

Ben had had some kind of an accident, Freddy thought in horror, and so sick was she at that idea that her legs literally wobbled beneath her and she stumbled down onto the seat behind her. 'He's not dead…' she mumbled sickly.

'*No*. He is in good health,' Jaspar surged to assert, seemingly gaining strength from his ability to make that assurance. 'Indeed, you need have no concern at all for his physical well-being.'

'Then…then why are you asking my pardon?'

Faint dark colour scored his high cheekbones.

'This morning at half-past nine, the nanny, Alula, brought Ben to me so that we might become acquainted. It was most successful. He is a very *friendly* child,' Jaspar said with charged emphasis. 'I then went out to attend a business meeting and, when I returned late this afternoon, I received a phone call from my father…'

Freddy sat forward on the edge of the seat. 'Your…father? King Zafi?'

'Zafir…' Jaspar corrected not quite levelly, his lean brown hands clenching into fists before he lifted his proud dark head high, dark golden eyes grim. 'As soon as I had left the consulate, Alula and the individuals with her conveyed Ben to the airport. By utilising a forged Quamari passport, they were able to take your son onto the private jet awaiting them. Ben is now within an hour of landing in Quamar.'

Freddy gazed at him with wide enquiring eyes. He had wound her up too much before he had even commenced an explanation and words like 'passport' and 'consulate' were failing to connect to make sense inside her head. 'Ben is…?'

'Ben is no longer in this country,' Jaspar delivered with the curtness of stress.

No longer in this country? A frown of incomprehension drew her brows together as she struggled to come to terms with that staggering announcement. 'That can't be…'

'This covers me with shame…'

What was he talking about shame for? He had to be involved right up to his royal throat. Ben had been kidnapped by that creepy nanny! Ben had been snatched, *stolen*! Freddy's head began to whirl and her stomach to churn. A pounding pulse thumped behind her temples as she struggled to think. But it was as if her brain were suddenly wrapped in dense fog. She could not get past that first terrifying realisation that Ben might not be coming home, that all the while she had been trustingly waiting for his return he had been up in the sky in a plane that was taking him further and further away from her.

'Say goodbye…' Alula had said sweetly.

Freddy shuddered, perspiration beading her short upper lip as she wrapped her arms round herself, suddenly cold to the marrow with horror. For an instant she felt like a shocked child, incapable of imagining such cruelty. What sort of savages were these people? Jaspar al-Husayn had come here demanding her trust and she had finally given it, believing that there was no point in her even *trying* to apply for custody of Erica's son.

'You can't do it…you can't take him like that,' Freddy framed in a faraway voice, her waxen face glazed with complete shock. 'He hasn't even got his pyjamas. These things need to be planned.'

Jaspar launched himself at the decanter set sited on top of the ornate drinks cabinet, extracted a glass from within and proceeded to pour a very large brandy. It would help her, he told himself, help her through the shock. He addressed the bodyguard, poised just outside the door, in low-pitched Arabic and instructed him to call the consulate doctor. Whatever transpired, he had to contain the fallout until she had calmed down and he had had a chance to reason with her and to lie through his teeth and persuade her that really a quick and clean break was ultimately for the best. Bitter distaste and raw frustration at the prospect filled him. Freddy wondered why he was curling her numb fingers round a bulbous brandy goblet. She had stood up without even realising it. She could see that he had spilt liquid on the top of the wood cabinet. 'I need to wipe that up,' she told him. 'It'll wreck the surface.'

'I'm sorry…I'm not used to pouring drinks.' Jaspar curved long fingers round her other hand and urged her to hold the goblet with both. The goblet was shaking.

She looked up into his darkly handsome face, marvelling

at his perfection that close, and she had not a single thought beyond that for she was still refusing to accept what he had told her. As long as she refused to believe, it wouldn't be real. For if she had to accept that it *was* real…no, no, it could not be. It was some mistake, some stupid crazy mis-understanding. He wouldn't be here saying humble words like sorry that sounded alien on his lips if there was not a explanation and if things were not soon to be sorted out, she told herself doggedly, and sipped her brandy.

The spirit raced like fire down her throat and she coughed, but then discovered that there was something cu-riously comforting about the warmth now spreading through her chilled insides and so she kept on sipping.

'We will make restitution. Anything that you want,' Jaspar murmured tautly.

'I want Ben…' Freddy did not even have to think. 'I want Ben. You're a Crown Prince. You recall that plane.'

'Though I would give much to do so, I cannot counter-mand my father's orders. He is the head of the armed forces.'

Freddy tilted her buzzing head back and blinked slowly. 'Armed forces?'

Jaspar al-Husayn loosed a ragged sigh. 'The personnel on the plane are not civilian and they will complete their mission. I am powerless to intervene but I did *try*.'

Freddy trembled. Almost everything he said was just words flying about like crazed birds dive-bombing her ears. But her mind was finally coming to grips with what he had first told her and she was being flooded with the unbearable realisation that Ben was truly gone. *Gone!* Taken without any form of agreement even from the authorities. How had she ever given her trust to such a male? How had she ever been stupid enough to let Ben leave her care for even an hour? A crime had been committed. Why had she not yet phoned the police? Letting the empty goblet fall with a crash from a nerveless hand, not even pausing to take account of the shattered glass, Freddy crunched over the shards to reach for the phone.

'What are you doing?'

And that was when it happened, when automatic pilot suddenly switched into violent reaction. As Jaspar al-Husayn lodged his big powerful frame between Freddy and the phone, which now beckoned to her much like a lifebelt to a drowning swimmer, she just exploded back into feeling and agonised awareness.

'Get out of my way!' she launched at him between gritted teeth, giving him a forceful push out of her path in a move that took him sufficiently aback to propel him sideways. 'I'm calling the police. You've broken the law. People aren't allowed to steal British citizens and I don't need a solicitor to tell me that! I'm going to create the biggest stink over this filthy business that your wretched tinpot country has ever heard! For all I know, you're planning to *kill* Ben!'

General mayhem broke out in the midst of her outburst. Suddenly his bodyguards were surrounding him as if he were being threatened by a terrorist, but not looking awfully comfortable about carrying out their duty and studying the floor with painstaking determination.

'You're such a coward…' Freddy snarled at him in disgust. 'I wish I'd punched you in the mouth!'

Hissing an outraged command in his own language, Jaspar broke through the human wall. His men shot back out of the room again at speed and closed the door behind them into the bargain. 'I am *no* coward but until you are in a state to listen to me I will not allow you to make a phone call. It pains me greatly to deny you what you have clear justification to demand but, for the moment, this appalling affair must be contained.'

As Jaspar was now between her and the phone again,

Freddy landed a kick on his shins, thinking that now he could be *genuinely* pained, and threw herself at the phone. He caught her within inches of her objective and whirled her round to face him, both hands closing over hers to restrain her. 'Though you assault me, I will not hurt you. But you *must* calm down—'

'Calm down?' Freddy shrieked, struggling wildly to escape hands that felt as strong as tempered steel. 'You can't do this to me...you can't stop me ringing the police and having you arrested as a kidnapper!'

His shimmering golden eyes clashed with hers. 'The phone lines have been disconnected.'

Freddy gazed back at him in horror. She could not use the phone? The phones were dead. Four very large men in the apartment? She was virtually a prisoner! White as a sheet at that acknowledgement, she swayed and he loosed her hands to close long, sure fingers over her upper arms and gently ease her down onto the nearest sofa.

'I mean you no harm and Ben is safe from harm as well,' Jaspar intoned, dropping down into an athletic crouch in an effort to appear unthreatening and put their eyes on a level, but he was sincerely shaken by the events of the past few minutes and the extent of her fierce protectiveness toward her child. 'I *swear* that I was not involved in any way in this disgraceful affair. I urge you to think before you act and to allow me to describe the consequences of informing the authorities. Consequences which will not only damage Ben but many other innocent people.'

CHAPTER FOUR

'MY FATHER'S phone call was brief,' Jaspar divulged, lean, powerful features taut as he lowered himself down in one sleek, fluid movement onto the sofa opposite Freddy. 'He required medical attention during the call.'

Thinking that ill health could be a very convenient excuse, Freddy was silent. Having come to the brink of hysteria, she was fighting to retain control of herself. Ben was currently out of her reach and she could not allow herself to think about that lest she break down again and lose her focus. She was recognising that the status quo had changed. Jaspar al-Husayn was afraid of what *she* might do. He had abandoned his formal royal reserve because he had no choice. The news of the disconnected phones had grounded her as nothing else could have done. He was desperate to hush up the whole matter and, in *his* desperation, she would find a way to get Ben back.

Trust and faith had been broken. No longer was she prepared to credit that Ben could find a safe and loving home in Quamar. Decent civilised people did not engage in snatching innocent children, utilising force, power and wealth to take what they wanted, regardless of the distress that would result. Her fingers bit into her palms. To think that she had been ashamed of her own small pretence! When that sin was set next to theirs, all shame evaporated and she knew that she would do whatever it took to regain Ben.

'Freddy…please listen to me.' She met the stunning dark golden eyes wholly intent on her, sensed the strong will focusing his energies on the problem. He is *very* clever, she

55

found herself thinking, the consummate diplomat and negotiator. He will run rings round you if you let him.

Evidently unperturbed by her silence, Jaspar continued, 'After what my father has done, I *don't* expect you to have compassion for him, but Adil's death hit him very hard. From the minute he learned of your son's existence, all his thoughts have centred on him. He longs to meet his grandson. He fears that he will die before that can come about.'

He looked so concerned, sounded so incredibly sincere that Freddy wanted to hit him again. Sitting there talking, lean, bronzed face expressing just the right amount of solicitous sympathy, the rich, dark drawl full of level and reasonable appeal. It made her want to stand up and scream and attack again, smash that brilliant façade of his, for how did she know that he was even telling her the truth? How did she know that this outcome had not for some reason been planned all along? What did she really know about *their* motivations?

'I'm afraid that my admission yesterday that it would take somewhat longer than my father had hoped for me to gain custody of Ben may have caused Ben's removal without your permission,' Jaspar admitted in a tone of considerable regret.

Freddy tilted her chin. 'Talking at me won't get you anywhere. I want Ben returned and if you don't do that, you're in trouble. I bet you have diplomatic status but you're not above British law and Ben is a British citizen—'

'If this matter becomes public, Adil's family will suffer greatly. The press will dig into my late brother's private life and create a scandal that will taint every al-Husayn for many years to come.'

'Obviously someone should have had the guts to make your brother live a different life. That's not my problem,' Freddy responded without hesitation. 'I don't care about your family or your country or anything but Ben.'

'I believe that you were willing to hand him over anyway,' Jaspar countered. 'What has happened is very wrong but Ben is now in Quamar and my father will not surrender him again.'

Her small hands clenched and unclenched round each other. 'Then you take me out there to *be* with him!'

His darkly handsome features shadowed, brilliant eyes veiling. 'My father would have you deported. He would consider you a pernicious influence on the child. That investigation report on your lifestyle and your treatment of Ben appalled him.'

'What are you still sitting here for, then? You haven't got any power. You're telling me that you can do nothing, so you might as well take yourself off,' Freddy stated in a voice that, in spite of all her efforts, was starting to shake with the rising force of her emotions again. 'You have two options. Either you bring Ben back or you take me to him—'

'In time, I will be able to prevail upon my father to allow you some access to your son, but I cannot achieve that sea change overnight,' Jaspar reasoned, spreading lean brown hands in a graceful motion of appeal that utterly fascinated her.

He had been tutored in body language, she thought bitterly. How to act open and honest and human. But he needn't think she was being taken in…behind those eyes he was out-thinking and out-talking her, endeavouring to make her accept that what had happened could not be changed for the present, but that he would work on her behalf to reason with his tyrannical old father.

'I don't believe anything you say. I want Ben. I'll go to the police, and if the police don't listen because you're royal and powerful and rich, I'll go to the newspapers and you had *better* believe that the press will listen!' Freddy warned him between chattering teeth for she was breaking up inside herself, her hard-won composure refusing to hold up any longer for every time she said Ben's name she was engulfed in pain.

'Do you think that your son will some day thank you for revealing that you went to bed with his father solely to enrich yourself? Are you prepared to tell the world that you conceived a child only for profit and neglected him?'

Her aquamarine eyes focused on him in shaken horror. She shut her eyes tight. She was trying so hard not to think of how Ben's day must have gone. He would have enjoyed meeting Jaspar. The airport and the plane would probably have been a thrill, but during the long flight his confidence would've begun to dip for too many strange events would have been forced on him in too short a space of time. He would have begun asking for her, needing contact with familiar faces and surroundings to feel safe. As time went on, he would've become increasingly bewildered and unhappy because he was only a baby and so far his life had taught him that what he wanted, be it food, cuddles or Freddy, he would always receive. When she failed to appear, he would be frightened and he would cry...and was that creepy nanny, Alula, likely to be much consolation?

Silent tears were trickling down Freddy's face. Momentarily Jaspar shut his own eyes. As she suddenly twisted and flung herself down into the tumbled cushions as if she felt forced to try and hide her grief from him, he could stand the distance between them no longer.

'I swear on my honour something will be done, no matter what it takes,' he breathed, sinking down on the sofa to one side of her shaking body to smooth her hair back from her brow in an almost awkward movement.

'Go away...you bastard!' Freddy sobbed brokenly and wept all the harder.

The dam-burst of distress she had fought to contain for so long could be contained no longer.

'Freddy…'

'Your sick father has just taken a two-year-old on a whim and what's g-going to happen when he loses interest in Ben or he dies? Who's likely to want Ben after there's been a ghastly scandal and all your hateful family have suffered because of him?' Freddy condemned on another wave of gasping sobs.

Jaspar found himself facing an angle he had not yet considered because his whole being was bent on persuading her to remain silent. He swore under his breath and at that point the consulate doctor crept in and bowed very low.

Freddy could not stop crying. All she could think about was Ben's distress and her own complete inability to help him. No matter how big a fuss she might make, it was unlikely to bring Ben home. Kings did not grovel to public opinion beyond their borders, not an old tyrant capable of having his grandson snatched, anyway. She suspected that King Zafir was as stubborn as a pig and would go to his deathbed without admitting that he had done wrong. Why had she thought she had power, for the power to threaten was *not* enough, was it? Not if it ultimately damaged Ben and his prospects in Quamar.

How could she gain power in such a situation? Freddy wondered frantically. How could she go out to Quamar and be there for Ben without being threatened with deportation? If only she were someone important, someone who had status, someone who could not be written off as a nobody and ignored and refused entry to their precious country! And then in a flash it came to her.

She felt the slight prick of the injection in her arm but was much too deep in her desperate ruminations to pay proper heed. It was insane but hadn't Jaspar offered her, 'Anything that you want' and didn't she have him over a barrel? But she needed to protect herself too, didn't she? The price of her silence would be a wedding ring. He could marry her…secretly, put her in a veil or something and smuggle her into Quamar. Surely that wouldn't be beyond his power? She could look after Ben then and live in some rural, underpopulated spot until the old king had got fed up with his two-year-old grandson or died. Then Jaspar could divorce her and she could bring Ben home again. Nobody need ever know.

'You could marry me…' Freddy said dizzily, opening eyes with dilated pupils and registering that she was lying on her back looking up at Jaspar without any recollection of having moved.

Stunning golden eyes enhanced by spiky ebony lashes widened as they gazed down into hers with transfixed attention.

'Secretly…' Freddy added, sounding rather smug and feeling oddly euphoric, noting that the ceiling above was shiny and reflective without wondering why. 'Hide me. I'd keep quiet and look after Ben and then when the time's right, you divorce me.'

Jaspar watched her big aquamarine eyes drift closed and a vague sphinx-like smile curve her lush mouth. He emerged from the lift and tightened his hold on her as he strode out to the waiting limousine. She had been given a very mild sedative yet her mind was wandering. The doctor had been unhappy when Jaspar had admitted administering brandy, but he had assumed a woman who threw wild drunken parties on a regular basis would require a *large* brandy to feel any beneficial soothing effects. Perhaps she was hallucinating.

Marry her in secret and hide her? She had an incredibly colourful imagination. In the rear of the limo, he cradled her limp body. He had not liked that smile. She could not demand such an act of insanity and personal sacrifice from him. Every nerve fibre rebelled at the mere mention of his marrying a woman of her character and reputation. A drunken and promiscuous gold-digger...yet, in spite of all those men, she still tried to kiss with her mouth sealed shut like a teeny-bopper who didn't know any better.

Freddy wakened slowly, stretching in glorious comfort before opening her sleepy eyes.

But it only took one look at her unfamiliar surroundings for her to thrust herself up against the pillows in shaken disconcertion. Dim dawn light was filtering through a chink in the curtains. Scanning the grand bedroom, she glanced down in equal confusion at the nightdress she wore, an opulent blue satin and lace affair with a low neck. A slight sound made her jerk in dismay and she was even more unnerved by the sight of the tall dark shape unfolding from a chair in a shadowy corner. A muffled gasp of fright escaped her.

'It is only I...' Jaspar al-Husayn's familiar drawl sounded.

'Where on earth am I?' Freddy demanded, sufficiently reassured to give vent to her angry bewilderment.

He touched a wall switch and the tall lamps on either side of the bed came on. Pools of soft light illuminated the taut set of his bronzed features and the brightness of his incisive gaze, but also delineated the strained line of his sculpted mouth and the shadow of dark stubble now roughening his strong jawline. 'You're in the Consulate of Quamar. To be within reach of a secure phone line, I had to return here last night and I couldn't leave you alone in the state that you were in.'

Still attempting to come to terms with having woken up in a totally strange environment, Freddy protested. 'But I've been asleep for hours. I remember someone giving me an injection—'

'A doctor and it was a very mild sedative,' Jaspar qualified in the same maddeningly even tone. 'Please do not accuse me of having kidnapped you as well. I could not abandon you as you were, nor could I remain in that apartment—'

'*Ben*…' Momentarily, Freddy was rocked by the memory of the previous day's events and the pain of recollection pierced her deep. 'Have you heard anything yet?'

Jaspar straightened his wide shoulders. 'That the flight landed safely and that Ben was put straight to bed when he arrived at the palace. He's fine.'

On the brink of arguing with that optimistic statement, Freddy became conscious of the manner in which his lion-gold gaze was resting on her. The silence hummed. Her mouth ran dry, her pulses quickening. Within the satin bodice, her breasts stirred, making her embarrassingly aware not only of the straining sensitivity of her nipples, but also that she was distinctly underdressed. Her cheeks flaming, Freddy yanked the sheet clumsily higher and anchored it beneath her arms. 'Who put me to bed?'

'The maids.'

'And what are you doing in here?'

'I knew you would be frightened when you woke up in a strange place. Do you remember what you suggested to me last night?' Jaspar enquired softly, poised at the foot of the bed, brilliant golden eyes intent on her.

Freddy lost colour. So it had not been a crazy dream that she had told him he ought to marry her to get her into Quamar and a position where she could be reunited with Ben. She could see that he was expecting her to be embarrassed but she found herself lifting her chin, something odd and unfamiliar but decidedly aggressive powering her. 'Perfectly.'

'But it could only have been the brandy talking. To demand that I should marry you? What could be more ridiculous?' Jaspar asked, smooth as silk.

Her taut fingers dug into the sheet she was clutching. 'A

nasty old tyrant of a king kidnapping his grandson with army personnel? Them acting like a bunch of terrorists on foreign soil? Your late brother's taste for sleazy sex on the ocean waves? Well, perhaps not ridiculous but, let's face it, royal you may be…but where your family's concerned, you've got nothing to be proud of. And certainly no good reason to think you're one bit better than I am!'

Jaspar was outraged by her abuse of his family. Paling as though she had struck him, he flung his proud dark head back, a current of rage unlike anything he had ever experienced shooting up through his lean, powerful frame. In all his life he had never had to withstand such an attack and the unhappy grains of truth within the content only further inflamed him. Only hours earlier, he had had a violent argument with his father on the phone on *her* behalf, the father whom he had been brought up to respect as both sovereign and parent, the father whose will he had been taught never ever to question.

But there she sat unafraid and defying him, like some Lorelei on the rocks, draped in a wild tangle of blonde curls, a siren in human form but pure cutting steel beneath the alluring femininity. And he promised himself then that, no matter what happened or what it cost him, there would be a reckoning for her attempt to soil him with the same dirt that clung to her.

Freddy raised an unsteady hand to her pounding brow. She was shocked at what she had thrown at him, amazed that such venom had come so readily to her usually gentle tongue. Jaspar might be the unacceptable face of the al-Husayn royal family, every one of whom she now loathed sight unseen, but she *did* recognise that he had drawn the short straw. His brother, Adil, had got off scot-free with his excesses and his sick father was pretty much untouchable, for who was likely to tell home truths to an absolute monarch, who enjoyed unfettered power?

'Are you telling me that the matrimonial proposition was serious?' Jaspar demanded, his wrathful incredulity unconcealed.

Freddy froze. She had been half out of her mind with grief when she had come up with that wild idea. Thinking of it afresh, she still saw it as a wild idea, but *not* necessarily the wrong idea if it was her only hope of influencing events and reclaiming Ben from what she now viewed as the lawless hell-hole of Quamar. Right now, she knew that she had the most power that she would ever have. He did not want the police or the press to get wind of what had happened, but he could not prevent her from informing them.

'Unless you can come up with something better than you offered me last night,' Freddy muttered tightly. 'Yes, I was serious. I want Ben home. But, failing that, I want to be with him.'

'I refuse to marry you,' Jaspar growled. 'You're trying to blackmail me—'

Freddy considered that angle and then nodded with an apologetic light in her anxious aquamarine eyes. 'Yes, I suppose I am, but I'm only concerned with Ben's happiness and I can't trust your promises—'

Jaspar shot her a scorching look of raw incredulity. 'Yet you are willing to *marry* me?'

'I don't think even your father could get away with throwing me out of the country if I was your wife,' Freddy pointed out. 'After all, if he did that, I would have an even bigger story to tell the newspapers when I came home, so the need to keep me quiet and reasonably content would be an ongoing necessity.'

'Oh, I could do that…I could do that easily,' Jaspar murmured throatily, his rich, dark drawl rousing a curious little twist of heat deep in her pelvis as he braced lean brown hands on the high footboard of the antique bed.

As the silence pulsed like the quiet before a volcanic eruption, Freddy stared into vibrant golden eyes. Dizzy and enervated, she opened her mouth so that the tip of her tongue could sneak out to moisten her dry lips. She watched his gaze lower there and her lips tingled in response as she struggled to recapture her focus. 'Marriage would protect me…'

'Would it?' Jaspar prompted, indolent in tone as a prowling jungle cat.

'Nobody need ever know and you would just go on with your life as if I didn't exist. It would only be a sign of good faith on your part…that's all.'

'A sign of good faith,' Jaspar ground out. 'And this you truly demand of me? It *is* blackmail…have you no shame?'

'Not where Ben's concerned.' Freddy cast her eyes down because she refused to retreat from what she saw as her only hope of seeing Ben again.

Unimpressed by the evident emotional pang now assailing her, Jaspar withdrew his hands from the footboard to curl them into fists of restraint. 'OK…since shame doesn't come into this equation—how much cash do you want to keep this whole affair quiet?'

Freddy's head came up in shock and she gave him a look of horror. 'Ben isn't for sale. How can you even *suggest* that I would accept money from you?'

Jaspar backed off to the wall, no longer trusting himself that close to his tormentor. 'You took it from Adil—'

Freddy flushed. 'That was different.'

'But with me…it's marriage or nothing, right?' Jaspar's dark drawl was raw-edged as he moved with fluid grace round to the side of the bed.

'All I want is access to Ben. Don't forget that option,' Freddy hurried to remind him, for really he was going on as though marrying him might be her sole objective and it was becoming rather embarrassing.

Jaspar came down on the bed so slowly she was mesmerised into the belief that he actually wasn't doing what he was doing. 'And what do you think I'm going to get out of this deal?'

Freddy gazed at him with huge aquamarine eyes and stopped breathing like a fawn trying to blend into woodland, scared that a sudden movement might provoke the hunter. And that was exactly how she felt. That close to Jaspar al-Hussayn, she was on the edge of such an electrifying charge of fevered anticipation that she could barely think straight, but she could feel the danger all right.

'You think I want you,' Jaspar murmured thickly.

''Course I don't,' Freddy mumbled, feeling the buzz in the air, the enervating high of awareness of his virile masculinity that close. But while even the most basic caution urged retreat, she did not move a muscle.

'You *know* I do.'

Freddy's heart skipped a beat in sheer shock. *He* wanted *her*? She studied him with fascination, helplessly thrilled by that admission. He was sober. He didn't look like he was about to unload the story of how his last girlfriend had made his life a living hell either. He found her attractive? A guy who looked like her every fantasy come true actually found her attractive. 'You do…*honestly*?' she prompted breathlessly, leaning forward, keen to hear him tell her that all over again.

Jaspar reached out and slowly laced long brown fingers into the tumbling fall of blonde waves and drew her down against the pillows. In shock at that bold move, her heartbeat hit earthquake mode and she opened her mouth to protest but somehow said nothing. Locked to that scorching golden gaze, she was mesmerised, deliciously aware of every fibre of her own feminine body. An almost painful ache stirred low in her stomach, making her shiver.

He took her mouth in an exploratory foray and she felt

as if she were flying, only not fast enough, and seemingly of their own volition her hands rose and her fingers dug into his silky black hair, dragging him down to her. She felt engulfed by him then, the lean, hard weight and heat and strength of him, and excitement raced through her like a shooting star. His tongue plunged into the tender interior of her mouth and she gasped, her spine arching as he cupped her breast, teased the distended pink nipple with expert fingers. A moan was torn from deep in her throat. Sensation flooded her in a wave of response so strong, it brought her crashing back to awareness.

As she jerked, aquamarine eyes flying wide, Jaspar was already snaking back from her to snatch up the bedside phone. Freddy had never been more mortified in her life and was very grateful that he was paying attention only to his call. Feverishly flushed and overheated, she gazed down in dismay at the gaping neckline, the sight of her own bare breast crowned by a wanton peak. Hurriedly covering herself, she hauled the sheet up to her chin, shut her eyes tight and snatched in a ragged breath.

Jaspar was talking in his own language, dark drawl cool, clipped and level. She cringed beneath the sheet, rolled over, pushed her burning face into the pillow. There was just no excuse for her behaviour. She hardly knew him, nor was she in the habit of rolling about beds and allowing such liberties. How that passion had erupted in the midst of what had been a virtual argument, she had no idea, but she was seriously shaken by her own behaviour.

'We'll get married tomorrow morning.'

Having tensed at the sound of him tossing down the phone, Freddy blinked, hearing literally on full alert. Slowly she raised her head, unable to immediately absorb that startling announcement, couched in the coldest of tones. *'Tomorrow?'*

'Here within the consulate, the laws of my own country

prevail. The ceremony must take place as soon as possible because I want to be back in Quamar by tomorrow evening.' Lean, powerful face grim, Jaspar surveyed her with glittering golden eyes that had the oddest chilling effect on her.

'You're...you're actually prepared to go through with this and marry me?' Ironically, Freddy was shattered by her own victory.

'As you are well aware, I have little choice. I must pay the price of your silence.'

And then *she* would pay the price for her blackmail and the greed and ambition which had prompted such a preposterous demand, Jaspar reflected with grim satisfaction. By marrying him, she would become a Quamari citizen and, as a member of the royal family, much less fortunate than the rest of the populace in terms of personal freedom. Marooned in the desert, she would find precious little to amuse her, but then he was thinking more of his *own* amusement. Presumably, her son would also benefit from her presence until he had forged other relationships. Once that feat had been achieved and his nephew seemed secure and content, Jaspar planned to dispense with her services. By that stage, he would probably be pretty tired of her in any case.

As he studied her with veiled eyes a faint smile curved his handsome mouth. She was as luscious as a peach and he was entranced by the air of utter innocence that she had perfected. Had he not known what he did know about her shallow, avaricious nature, he might even have been taken in, just as the night before he had been genuinely disturbed by her apparent anguish at being parted from her son. But he need have no finer sensibilities about teaching her a lesson.

Stealing a glance at him, her eyes full of guilty discomfiture, Freddy wondered what he had found to smile about, for she could not have raised a smile should her life have depended on it. *The price of your silence.* He was prepared to meet her demand to save his precious family from public embarrassment. But those words, those cold and unforgiving words so redolent of blackmail shamed her. However, it was Ben she was concerned about, *only* Ben, and he would eventually recognise that, wouldn't he?

'All I care about is Ben...' Freddy muttered almost pleadingly.

'I'll order breakfast for you. I suggest that you return to your apartment and pack. I'll send a car to pick you up tomorrow at eight,' Jaspar informed her.

'You can't possibly go through with marrying him...' Ruth Coulter said with an amount of disbelief that unnerved Freddy that evening.

Freddy bent her blonde head even lower over the case she was packing and suppressed a groan. Ruth had come over to the apartment as soon as Freddy had called her. Although aghast at the manner in which the al-Husayn family had taken possession of Ben, she was very much more shocked by Freddy's solution to that crisis.

'It's the only way I can get to see Ben and have some influence over what happens to him out there,' Freddy muttered defensively.

'For goodness' sake...by forcing the Crown Prince to make you his wife?'

'Only on paper. I mean, it's going to be a secret, nobody's ever likely to know about it. But if I hadn't played that card, there was no way I was *ever* going to get into Quamar!' Freddy protested feelingly. 'The marriage bit is only to ensure that Jaspar has good reason to help me and he wasn't planning to help me otherwise, just fob me off with vague promises. Really, the marriage angle will be very short-lived—'

'How?'

Freddy breathed in deep. 'Well, Ben's grandfather will probably lose interest in him and of course by that stage I'll have come clean about who I am and then I'd be able to bring Ben home...or...' Freddy trailed out the word in desperation as the older woman's frown simply deepened. '...or maybe, there'll be a couple...as Jaspar suggested...who want to make Ben their son. If that happens, I swear that I'll accept the situation and bow out.'

'If you'd told the Crown Prince that you were only Erica's cousin and Ben's nanny at the beginning, would any of this have even happened?' Ruth demanded. 'You might well have found yourself invited out to Quamar *with* Ben!'

Freddy stiffened. 'I don't think so. He already had a nanny organised and he talked about a clean break being the best thing for Ben, which just shows how much *he* knows about children!'

'You haven't thought this through,' the older woman warned her in growing frustration. 'All you're thinking about is Ben.'

'Yes,' Freddy affirmed. 'But it's my job to look out for him because there's nobody else to do it. The least I can do is be there for him until he doesn't need me any more.'

'I've never seen you like this before. If only Erica had left a will.' Ruth sighed, studying the younger woman's unusually set and stubborn expression. 'I'm surprised she didn't because she said she was planning to have one drawn up.'

'She also said she'd have to find a gorgeous solicitor first.' A sad smile curved Freddy's lips at that recollection. 'But a will wouldn't have changed this situation.'

'It might well have done. Erica may not have been a good mother but she *did* recognise that you were,' Ruth replied thoughtfully.

Paying little heed to that opinion, Freddy closed her suit-case and hauled it out to the hall to sit beside the other case she had already packed for Ben.

'Freddy…you simply *can't* blackmail Ben's uncle into marrying you,' Ruth emphasised even more forcefully. 'A man who despises you won't help you and may even go out of his way to punish you for putting him in an impossible position. Let me go and talk to him and tell him who you really are…'

On the drive to the Consulate of Quamar early the following morning, Freddy was still thinking back with regret to that conversation, for she was more used to taking Ruth's advice than flying in the face of it. But admitting her real identity was too dangerous and she was not prepared to risk sacrificing any prospect of seeing Ben again. Ben needed her and whatever it took she would go to him.

Although she had hoped that the blue three-piece designer suit she wore would make her feel more confident, she was uncomfortable in such finery. The skirt felt too short and neat fitting for relaxation and she felt too bare in the thin strappy top she wore below the neat little jacket. Always generous, Erica had often bought Freddy identical outfits to those she had worn herself, but Freddy had only ever worn them to please on an occasional basis. The contrast between Erica's extreme slenderness and her own greater abundance in the same garments had always been too painful a reminder to Freddy of her own failings.

But then from adolescence on, people had often made thoughtless comparisons between the two girls, for Erica had neither gone through the embarrassing puppy-fat stage which had once tormented Freddy, nor suffered from tongue-tied shyness in the company of others. Frequent criticism from her father for her awkwardness had caused Freddy's self-esteem to sink low and she had taken refuge in sweatshirts and trousers, determined not to compete in any way with Erica's ultra-feminine appearance.

When Freddy was fifteen, Erica had persuaded one of her friends to invite Freddy out on a date. Unaware that her cousin had been busy behind the scenes, Freddy had been thrilled. Her pleasure, however, had been short-lived. Returning from the cloakroom after seeing the film that evening, she had heard her date saying to a mate, ''Course, I *don't* fancy her! Erica gave me twenty quid to take her out.'

Freddy had wept long and hard that night but she had never told Erica that she had found out the truth. And when, four years later, Erica had stolen Freddy's first serious boyfriend while home on a weekend visit, Freddy had been a really good sport about it. After all, Steve had been very attractive and Freddy had felt that it had been all too good to be true from the minute he'd shown an interest in her.

'I'm sorry,' Erica had groaned guiltily on the phone the following week. 'I was only testing him out for you.'

'Steve wasn't important to me,' Freddy had insisted valiantly, wiping her streaming swollen eyes dry with her sleeve, fighting to retain a little dignity after having been dumped like a hot potato.

And within a couple of years of that experience Freddy had stopped actively trying to attract the opposite sex and based her social life on interest shared solely with female friends. Life had seemed very much smoother and simpler. Joking that when a man approached her he only wanted a sympathetic shoulder to cry on had become second nature to her. But staying home in recent years had also become a necessity with Erica away so much and Freddy reluctant to hire a babysitter.

If only she hadn't kissed Jaspar, Freddy reflected in guilty discomfiture. Not just once but twice and what an idiot she had made of herself! Only, *he* didn't know that, though, did he? He probably just thought she was as loose as her apparent reputation, which was of some comfort. But, nonetheless, that unfortunate intimacy brought in a more personal and embarrassing dimension and made maintaining a dignified distance more difficult. Well, there would be no more nonsense in that line, she told herself squarely.

At the consulate, Freddy was shown into a room which contained two grave-faced men, who introduced themselves as lawyers. She was totally taken aback and intimidated by that development and within minutes was tied in knots of shamefaced mortification while she wondered how much they knew about the situation between herself and Jaspar. A document described as a marriage and confidentiality contract was set in front of her.

With an unsteady hand and burning cheeks, Freddy made a play of glancing through the document, which stretched to forty-three pages of clauses and sub-clauses couched in almost impenetrable legalese. Nowhere could she see a mention of Ben. Reassured, she sighed, recognising that it had been foolish of her not to expect such a demand. Evidently having expected some argument, her companions looked rather nonplussed.

For a while she was left alone in the room. Then Jaspar arrived, accompanied by the lawyers and an imposing white-bearded clergyman wearing a long robe. Colliding with Jaspar's grim dark eyes, Freddy paled. For the first time, she acknowledged that entering a marriage on such terms went against everything she had ever been brought up to respect. Her tummy twisted with guilt and unease and she averted her attention from him. Yet still his image and the impression he made on her remained stamped in her mind's eye; the taut gravity of his lean, handsome features, his commanding height and breadth in a tailored light grey suit, his striking self-command in a challenging situation.

It was, somewhat to Freddy's surprise, a Christian ceremony, which made her feel even worse. At the end of it, nothing was said. Their companions filed back out again, leaving her alone with Jaspar.

'Are you satisfied now?' he breathed almost indolently.

Freddy gave him a harried nod. 'This wouldn't have happened if you'd given me another option,' she muttered uncomfortably.

Jaspar appraised her with glittering eyes the colour of pure gold. Without the smallest warning, he reached for her with complete cool and pulled her close, one lean hand curving to her hip in the most disconcertingly intimate fashion. Freddy reddened and attempted to step back, but he held her fast.

'What are you doing?'

'Handling the merchandise I just acquired,' Jaspar murmured softly.

'I beg your pardon?' Freddy gasped.

'I don't like your hair up like that.' Long fingers swooped up to the clip holding her hair tight to the back of her skull and tossed it away so that a tangled thicket of pale blonde curls descended *en masse* to her shoulders.

'Do you really think that I don't plan to profit in some way from this deal too?' Jaspar surveyed her bewildered and beautiful face with hard amusement and freed her when she least expected it, leaving her standing there trembling and disconcerted.

'What are you talking about?' Freddy stooped to retrieve her hair clip with as much defiance as she could muster and, throwing back her head, she wound her hair up into a twisted coil, restoring it to order.

'You'll find out. By the way, you got the ring but you didn't acquire a title. Only my father can make you a princess and, if I were you, I wouldn't hold my breath on that score.'

'What would I want to be a princess for?' Freddy snapped, that angle not even having occurred to her.

'By the time our paths separate, you might just feel that you've earned the privilege,' Jaspar quipped, smooth as silk.

He was trying to scare her out of flying back to Quamar with him, Freddy decided, and her chin came up. One thing he needed to learn about her, she thought, she was no quitter. As far as she was concerned, that marriage ceremony had brought her one giant step closer to Ben and that was all that need concern her.

CHAPTER FIVE

SECURE in the knowledge that she would soon see Ben, Freddy assumed that her stress level would return to normal.

However, the sight of the entire flight crew dropping to their knees to greet Jaspar when they boarded the private jet shook Freddy a great deal. Until that moment, his royal status had not seemed quite real to her, but the solemn respect he commanded was striking. The luxurious interior of the jet and a main cabin the size of her late cousin's drawing-room impressed her to death. Settled in a leather reclining seat and besieged with magazines, refreshments and an array of movies by the attendants, she felt as though she were a lottery winner on the holiday of a lifetime.

As the flight progressed Freddy found herself watching Jaspar almost continually. The longer she spent in his radius, the more he fascinated her. While he worked on his notebook computer, she noted the extraordinary length of his lush ebony lashes, the smooth, sculpted line of his high cheekbones, the narrow-boned perfection of his nose and the passionate curve of that mobile mouth.

He was drop-dead gorgeous and when he talked on his satellite phone, chatting first in French and later in Spanish with easy fluency, and she caught a glimpse of his vibrant dark golden eyes alive with intelligence and energy, her attention was engaged even more.

She watched him move a lean hand in fluid expressiveness, proud dark head angled to one side. Then he shot a glance in her direction and caught her staring. She felt the blood rise beneath her fair skin, the tight clenching sensation low in her pelvis, the surge of instantaneous heat that followed, but was powerless to control her own physical response. In haste, she wrenched her dismayed gaze from the hard grip of his, her heart racing frantically fast.

Why did she have to be so wretchedly, pointlessly attracted to him? Freddy's teeth gritted. She was furious with herself and mortified. Why did she have to act like a silly daydreaming schoolkid around him? Was she suddenly turning into a sex-starved woman desperate for a man? Assailed by that lowering suspicion, she felt her colour rise even higher. How often had Ruth chided her for steering clear of men? But then, it was all very well for Ruth to talk, but times had changed in the dating game. Freddy did not believe in casual sex but, when she had dated, she had been put on the spot time and time again, forced to defend her views and laughed at and scorned on more than one occasion.

Jaspar sank back down into his seat, stretched out in one long, measured movement and contemplated his blushing bride with cynical amusement. Had she been his acknowledged wife, he would have taken her to the big bed in the main sleeping compartment and eased the ache of his throbbing sex without hesitation, for rarely had he received a more blatant unspoken invitation. However, discretion was the name of the game and such a flagrant act would be unwise. Many of his people would soon be aware that he was keeping a woman in his desert palace for gossip was food and drink to the Quamaris. But what he did not flaunt would be acceptable as long as he still appeared to be single.

In addition, the rumour of her existence would serve to keep Sabirah at bay, Jaspar mused, a rather cruel light gleaming in his reflective gaze. Sabirah, whom he had once hoped to marry. Sabirah, whom he had adored with passionate idealism and who had appeared to return his feelings right up until the moment that Adil's wandering eye had fallen on her. Ambition had triumphed. Though she had barely been half his brother's age, Sabirah had disdained the younger son and had chosen to become the heir to the throne's third wife. But since Adil's untimely death Sabirah had been behaving with dangerous impropriety.

Was he for ever condemned to pay for his elder brother's sins? Jaspar wondered with sudden fierce bitterness. Here he was with yet another of Adil's cast-offs, forced to link his proud name with that of a female unfit to breathe the same air as the women in his family, a heartless gold-digger who had not batted an eyelash at the news that the father of her child was dead. Lean, powerful face taut, he surveyed her. She had spirit, though. He *liked* women with spirit. If he had to tell the staff to destroy every hair ornament in the Anhara, she would wear that glorious blonde mane loose for his pleasure. The prospect of spreading her across his bed and driving her wild with desire filled him with more hungry impatience than he had felt in a long time. Adil might have bought her favours but *he* would be the one who truly possessed her.

As the jet juddered to a final halt and the steps were rushed to the exit door, Freddy sat very stiff in her leather seat, staring out at the superb ultra-modern airport. Never before had she been in company with a male so polished at simply ignoring her existence. True, Jaspar seemed to be an exceptionally busy male, but surely a little casual conversation would not have killed him?

She felt extremely foolish when he moved to disembark without even looking in her direction. Rushing to catch up with him, she whispered urgently, 'Have you a veil or something so that I can cover myself up?'

'Were you hoping for one?' Over one broad shoulder, Jaspar slanted her a gleaming golden glance of mockery.

'Sorry. A veil would cause more of a sensation than your face. Quamari women don't shroud themselves because we are not Muslim. This *is* a Christian country.'

Freddy went scarlet at that unexpected revelation and wished she had had the opportunity to learn more about the country that was to be her home for at least the next few weeks. It was hot and nervous tension made her feel even more flustered. It was not a pleasant surprise either when Jaspar headed for the helicopter a few yards away instead of continuing on towards the airport building.

'We're travelling on from here?'

'Yes.' While the pilot was bowing low to the ground, Jaspar closed strong hands round her waist and lifted her up into the helicopter.

Freddy did up the seat belt with anxious hands. 'When will I *see*—?'

'I hope to bring him home with me late this evening but you will have to practise patience,' Jaspar imparted. 'I must speak to my father first'

'But what if he says no?' Freddy prompted fearfully.

Jaspar flashed her an exasperated look. Was she downright stupid or something? Of course, his father would say *no*! But the announcement that he had married Ben's mother would take precedence at that meeting for he would not lie to his father. Such a secret could not be kept from the older man and, unless he was very much mistaken, his father would immediately attempt to have the marriage set aside on the grounds that it had taken place without his permission. A divorce would not be necessary. Nor would it be necessary to tell his bride that within the space of weeks, and without her consent, she would almost inevitably be dispossessed of him again.

The craft rose into the air and tilted into a turn, churning up Freddy's stomach with a panoramic view of the city skyscrapers beyond the airport. As the helicopter flew out over the desert, she stared out initially in dismay at the emptiness. But almost as soon she began to see with a keener eye and note the strange rock formations and the green valleys scattered with flat-roofed houses before the rippling sand in shades of ochre and cinnamon and gold took over again for miles.

It was a relief to step out onto solid ground again.

'This is the Anhara, my private home,' Jaspar murmured.

Standing on the edge of the heli-pad, Freddy gazed in wonderment at the lush gardens full of mature trees and colourful shrubs that stretched as far as the eye could see. No building was even visible. 'What a beautiful place.'

'It was once a Moorish fortress. I had the gardens restored some years ago.' Jaspar's strong jawline clenched as he recalled why.

A paved almost secret path led below the trees to a glorious arched entrance built of ancient stone and etched with intricate carving. With the sensation that she had wandered into another world and one of pure enchantment, Freddy followed in his wake, barely noticing the rank of servants on their knees, more interested in the fabulous interior that just shrieked antiquity. She was going to live in this wonderful building? My goodness, she ought to be paying him for the privilege!

'Freddy…' Waiting for her to negotiate the magnificent stone staircase, Jaspar extended an impatient hand to hurry her on. A sudden smile flashed across his bronzed features as he watched her caress the worn carved balustrade with gentle fingers, her awestruck appreciation touching him for he took his surroundings entirely for granted. But then a lesson in good taste would do her no harm. He almost shuddered at the memory of her over-gilded and flashy apartment.

Freddy looked up into that smile and was as dazzled as if Jaspar had turned a spotlight on her in darkness. Shaken and dizzy, she felt the warmth of his hand close over hers and she trembled, the breath tripping in her throat, her mouth running dry. His eyes roved over her with an intensity that sent a wicked shard of excitement flaring through her.

Jaspar removed the hair clip with pronounced care for the second time in two days, flung it aside with an arrogant hand. 'Now I will take you to my bed and pleasure you.'

Her aquamarine eyes widened in direct proportion to her shock. It was one thing looking, another thing for her to be dreaming in that line, but altogether something else again for him to threaten to turn safe if risqué fantasy into very dangerous reality. 'I b-beg—?'

'Yes, you *will*,' Jaspar husked in throaty and undeniable promise, swooping down to sweep her off her startled feet and lift her into his arms before she had the slightest conception of what he was doing.

'Put me down this minute!' Freddy spluttered.

'It's safe to drop the blushing *ingénue* act now,' Jaspar delivered with amused superiority as he strode towards the double doors set below an arch across the vast upper landing. 'Before it becomes a bore.'

'A…bore?' Freddy whispered shakily.

'I prefer an honest passion in my women,' Jaspar divulged in the tone of one set on educating. 'You're hot as hell for me and I for you—'

'No, I'm not!' Freddy slung at him a full octave higher as he shouldered his way through one of the doors with complete cool. 'You've got the wrong idea—'

'I do hope not,' Jaspar murmured in a sizzling undertone that shimmied down her spine like a storm warning of sensual threat.

But as he crossed the anteroom into the spacious bedroom beyond, Freddy was quite incapable of responding for the most extraordinary sight had seized her attention and closed up her vocal cords simultaneously. A stark naked and very beautiful brunette was reclining across the vast bed like some seductive houri in an oil painting, every stunning angle of her exquisite body posed to attract and about three feet of silken hair draped over one shoulder to fall into an elaborate coil down onto the pale sheet.

Appalled by all that rampant nudity on display, Freddy flushed scarlet. Jaspar froze, uttered what sounded like a stifled oath and then literally dumped Freddy down onto the chaise longue just over the threshold. Gaping, Freddy watched as the now infuriated brunette rose up on her knees and let out a screech that would have shattered glass. Bee-stung red lips no longer arranged in a sensual smile, slanted dark eyes flashing with incredulous fury, the female flew off the bed like a tigress ready to claw.

Jaspar, who was strikingly pale, loosed a volley of freezing Arabic and snatched up the bedspread to fling it at the woman.

'Excuse me...' he murmured with unearthly cool to Freddy, striding back out of the room again.

'Who are you?' the brunette shrieked at Freddy, struggling to wrap the spread round her lissom curves. 'Jaspar spoke to you in English. You foreign slut!'

Aghast, Freddy shrank her shoulders in and averted her attention, thinking that her companion really shouldn't be hurling insults of that nature at anybody else. Who was she? His discarded mistress? My goodness, he had had no compunction about rejecting her, had he? A trio of female servants rushed in and began to urge the woman from the room. Before she got out of earshot, she was sobbing noisily.

At last, silence fell. Freddy snatched in a shaken breath as the door onto the landing thudded shut again and steps sounded on the tiled floor of the anteroom. Well, he had said women threw themselves at him, but she had not realised he'd meant it quite so literally, and what on earth he could possibly want with *her* when that *femme fatale* had been lying in eager wait for him, she could not begin to imagine.

'Now where were we…?' Jaspar enquired lazily.

Shattered by that proof of his indestructible self-assurance, Freddy glanced up at him in frank wonderment. 'We weren't anywhere,' she mumbled. 'Nor are we going to be.'

'This is our wedding night.' His brilliant tawny eyes shimmied over her in the most familiar fashion imaginable and left her feeling hugely self-conscious. 'You're my wife and I intend to enjoy you.'

Aquamarine eyes wide, Freddy stared back at him, bereft of words for she could see that he was serious. '*Enjoy* you.' It was a very revealing phrase. One enjoyed a meal, a sport, an experience. Where she came from, the average male did not talk about *enjoying* a woman as though her body were a service on offer. But then she was not in England now, she was in Quamar and she did not think his usually wonderful grasp of English was at fault. She believed that that choice of words had been quite deliberate.

'Surprised?' Jaspar elevated a winged ebony brow, a derisive light in his incisive gaze. 'I hardly think so. Forcing me to marry you was not the act of a sensitive woman. Though you knew that I was solely concerned with your son's well-being and that I had not been involved in his removal from London, you insisted that I go through with that mockery of a ceremony. Was that just?'

Was that just? That simple question devastated Freddy and made her squirm where she sat. Frantic with fear for Ben, motivated only by her fierce need to go to his aid, she had closed her eyes to the injustice of what she was doing to Jaspar al-Husayn. Shame had touched her but she had refused to surrender to that prompting or to pause and consider what her demand might mean to him. Now colliding with scorching dark golden eyes that glittered like flames, she saw the tough masculine pride she had dented.

'You're an intelligent man. You can't tell me you want to sleep with me just to level the score,' Freddy muttered in an awkward rush, tense fingers locked together and flexing and unflexing. 'I mean…that would just be silly and not at all sensible.'

'Sensible…' Jaspar flung back his darkly handsome head and laughed outright, making her flinch. In a lithe movement, he shrugged out of his jacket and tossed it carelessly on the inlaid chest at the foot of the bed. He undid his collar and cast his tie aside as well.

'I don't feel…*sensible*,' Jaspar imparted in his accented drawl, turning that single word into a mocking retaliation.

Freddy tried and failed to swallow. Transfixed where she sat, she stared at him. Her speech about not being silly and being sensible had been an infallible passion killer on all the hopeful men preceding him, but he had shrugged it off without hesitation. Standing there, long brown fingers engaged in slowly unbuttoning his silk shirt, he challenged her with his stunning eyes, all earthy masculinity and raw sex appeal backed by rock-solid confidence. No, not sensible, she thought abstractedly, mesmerised involuntarily by the aura of the untamed that he emanated. He was of a breed of male utterly unknown to her.

'You hardly know me…' Freddy reasoned weakly.

'I know *too* much.' Strolling forward, light as a big cat on his feet, Jaspar made that wry quip and reached down to raise her upright. He eased the jacket from her slight shoulders, let it drop to the floor and feasted his attention on the burgeoning swell of her lush breasts beneath the taut fabric of her camisole. She backed away, almost tripped over the chaise longue in her haste, a tiny pulse flickering like mad in the hollow of her collar-bone and pounding out her tension.

He was poised several feet away, from his wide shoulders to his taut stomach and long, powerful thighs, incredibly male. Her breath was coming in choppy little bursts from her lungs, her heart hammering, for she could feel her own weakness threatening to break like a dam inside her. He only had to look at her and she wanted him with a deep, fierce craving that terrified her. He made her want what she had never wanted, made her feel as she had never felt. For the first time in her life she felt wildly feminine and desirable and that was a shockingly seductive sensation.

'What are you afraid of?' he asked lazily.

She tensed even more, unnerved by his perception, afraid he might see that she was afraid of herself, of the power he had over her, of the lure of sexual hunger and curiosity. But, worst of all, the frightening urge she had to simply surrender to her own darkest urges, disregarding everything she had always held dear. Freddy had always thought she was a very sensible young woman, but somehow she had roved wildly off course the instant Jaspar had come into her life. Over the past couple of days, she had done crazy things, things she had never dreamt she might do, and now there was a very strong part of her just longing to live out the sheer fantasy of being wanted by such a male.

'Nothing.' The silence seemed to eddy around her like a rippling pool.

He tugged his shirt from the waistband of his tailored trousers and it fell open on a bronzed slice of muscular hair-roughened chest.

'It is only sex…' Jaspar mused with magnificent nonchalance.

'Only sex…' Her voice shook a little, mouth dry, throat tight, her entire being achingly aware of him and of the tightly beaded tingling peaks of her breasts.

'Live a little,' Ruth had once urged her in exasperation but Freddy did not think that Jaspar quite fell within that category. Jaspar was in a major category all of his own, labelled wicked temptation, a moral challenge to be denied. *Only sex?* A mental chasm wider than the Arabian Gulf divided them. Who is ever likely to find out? a sneaky little voice whispered inside her head. Maybe she could just enjoy *him* as an experience. After all, they were married, she found herself suddenly thinking, clinging to a technicality that just minutes earlier she would have scorned.

Jaspar stretched out a lean hand, an expectant look in his imperious gaze that just sent every pulse she possessed crazy. Her resistance crumbled as she meshed dizzily with his glorious eyes and later she had not the smallest memory of her feet carrying her over to his side, only of the devastating kiss that engulfed her in an erotic fire of anticipation.

'I like the zip,' he remarked, settling her back from him to score a considering fingertip along the zip that was straining over her breasts. 'Very tantalising. If you'd removed the jacket when we were airborne, I do believe I would have succumbed to the invitation.'

She was naked beneath the top for she had found it impossible to get the zip done up over a bra. 'Too many pizzas...' she mumbled in guilty disarray. 'Or maybe it was the fudge.'

Jaspar's inky, spiky lashes swept up on bemused golden eyes. 'Fudge?'

In her mind's eye, she saw herself hovering there muttering a confessional like a woman who had cheated on a diet and she cringed for herself, but she just could not think straight that close to him. Not with her mouth still swollen from his, her mind in free fall and her knees wobbling under her. He was like fudge, she thought helplessly. She could still *taste* him, warm and sexy and the last word in mind-bending pleasure.

'Fudge…' Jaspar repeated afresh and, laughing huskily, he backed her towards the bed.

As she rested back against the edge he caught her against his lean, hard, muscular frame and slid down the zip on her skirt. In haste she sucked her tummy in and prayed for the skirt to fall and not linger round her hips like a betrayal. She craved the cover of the sheet. She wanted the curtains closed lest he get too close a look at her flaws and change his mind. She had a sudden image of the phenomenally slight brunette he had thrown out of his bedroom and stopped breathing altogether. The skirt shimmied down in merciful obedience, but then she started thinking about the size of her *derrière* and she was onto that bed so fast, casting off her shoes in haste and seated, she was jet-propelled.

'You are *so* skittish,' Jaspar mused, well-defined brows rising.

Already secure beneath the shield of the sheet, Freddy leant back against the pillows, striving to look amused, cool, woman-of-the-worldish. It was only sex, she reminded herself doggedly. She was twenty-four and a certain scientific interest was as natural as her nerves. But ought she really to be considering sharing a bed with a male whose bedding was still warm from the occupation of her extremely recent predecessor?

In dismay at the reality that she had inexplicably contrived to forget that shattering scene, Freddy asked jerkily. 'Who was that woman?'

Silence stretched.

'Nobody who need concern you,' Jaspar drawled smoothly, but faint dark colour scored his fabulous cheekbones, his expressive mouth hardening. 'She is not and has never been my lover.'

Deeply relieved by that assurance, Freddy could not help thinking that desperation drove Quamari women to serious outer limits in their pursuit of a man. She had been very much shocked by what she had seen, would have been shaken in any circumstances, but had been all the more so at such a scene occurring in a conservative country such as he had sworn Quamar to be. And what might have happened, she wondered grudgingly, had he entered his bedroom alone as the brunette had so evidently expected him to do? Maybe he would have been a pushover for her considerable but slender attractions.

Jaspar shed his shirt in a graceful movement. Freddy was mesmerised by the lean, flexing ripple of his muscles as he moved, the powerful pectorals defined by a triangle of dark, curling hair, his hard, flat stomach. He was like a film unfolding fascinating scene by scene for her. Until she had seen him, she had not believed that a man could be beautiful, but she could not tear her attention from him.

'Do you often get into bed with your clothes on?' Jaspar enquired teasingly.

Rudely reclaimed from her dreaming appraisal, Freddy reddened to the roots of her hair and shrugged and rearranged the sheet. 'It's a little cold up here,' she said in a small voice.

'I'll switch off the air-conditioning.'

Now she was going to roast alive for her foolishness. Below the sheet she began to shimmy by covert degrees out of her tights and shame at her own wanton eagerness engulfed her then. How could she do this? Just give way to lust? That was what it was. She was behaving like a tramp and she was not one whit better than the houri who had greeted him naked on his bed. Beneath the concealment of her lashes, she stole a glance back at him, her nervous tension rising as she noticed, really could not avoid noticing, the definitive cling of his boxer shorts to the aggressive bulge of his masculine arousal.

'Your ears have turned bright red,' Jaspar commented.

Freddy raised frantic hands and buried the offending parts below her tumbling curls, cringing at the recollection of the teasing she had once suffered at school for that same telling symptom of embarrassment. 'Really?'

Shedding his boxer shorts without an audience at that point, Jaspar added to his crimes by throwing back the sheet, but as at that same moment he laced one sure hand into her hair and brought his hot mouth down with devouring hunger onto hers she failed to notice.

'I am so hot for you, *ma belle*,' he husked, his breath fanning her cheekbone.

He was calling her beautiful in French. Wholly entranced, Freddy sunk back into her dream state, laced two daring hands into his thick black hair and looked up at him with rapt eyes of dazed appreciation. 'Kiss me again.'

He kissed her breathless. She was drowning in the hot musky male scent of him, exulting in the seductive weight of him as he rested against her thigh. He undid the camisole zip inch by inch until she was in an agony of fevered anticipation. He slid a hand beneath the parted edges and even before he made contact with her flesh she was on a high, so that when he actually moulded his hand to the full, firm thrust of her swollen breast, the pent-up breath hissed from her parted lips in a long, sighing moan.

'Oh...' Freddy gasped, spine arching as he stroked the sensitised mound and lingered to toy with a distended rosy nipple.

Sweet sensation made her ache. He captured a throbbing tip between his lips, lashed the straining peak with his tongue, teased with his teeth. Within seconds of that tormenting rush of exquisite feeling, Freddy was lost.

'You have delectable breasts,' Jaspar muttered hungrily.

If this was a dream, she didn't want to wake up, Freddy reasoned feverishly. Hot and self-conscious as he scanned her ripe curves with apparent male appreciation, she raised herself from the pillows to let him remove the camisole. And all the time *she* savoured *him*: the silken crescent of his black lashes, the hard slant of his cheekbones, the stubborn thrust of his jawline, the silky feel of his hair below her fingers, the smooth satin skin of his wide shoulders. As his lashes lifted, she drowned in the smouldering heat of his appraisal and never wanted to breathe ordinary oxygenated air again.

'I think you're gorgeous,' Freddy heard herself whisper in reward.

Jaspar gave her a slashing wolfish smile that made her heart jump like a jack-in-the-box. The strangest swell of emotion filled her to overflowing. He probably said that kind of stuff to all his lovers, but he spoke with such sincerity that she just wanted to wrap her arms round him and hug him tight. For the very first time in her life, she was feeling beautiful and sexy and nothing had ever felt so good.

Jaspar readdressed his attention to the creamy swell of her breasts, letting the tip of his tongue trace the tempting valley between while rolling the quivering pink buds, already damp from his ministrations, between expert fingers. And she flung her head back, giving herself up to a kind of enraptured torment she had not even known existed, her breath wrung from her in tortured little gasps.

'You're exquisite,' Jaspar savoured, claiming a passionate and provocative kiss, reacting to the wildness of her response with a hungry, driving urgency that sent her arching mindlessly up to him. 'Blackmail pays unexpected dividends, *ma belle*.'

Blackmail. The word trickled into a mind shut down on an overload of pleasure: 'Jaspar...' she moaned, hauling him back down to her again.

He laughed against her seeking lips, teased her with his tongue, plunging and then withdrawing with erotic mastery, sending the feverish hunger inside her climbing higher and higher until she twisted and squirmed beneath the onslaught. He leant back from her, drew up her knees, slid a hand beneath her hips and skimmed off her panties. She tensed, momentarily dredged back to the real world, suddenly conscious of her own nudity, what she was doing and an incipient flare of panic.

'You match my passion.' Like a sleek predator in vibrant bronze, Jaspar leant over her, fading light gleaming over his tousled hair and illuminating his eyes to a drugging gold intoxication that she was defenceless against. 'I *knew* you would,' he growled with raw satisfaction.

She was melted honey again, going with the flow, lost in the depths of those extraordinary eyes, every inch of her on a high of sensitised awareness so that when he skimmed his fingertips over her stomach to the cluster of pale curls below, her thighs parted on an instinct as old as time. She was achingly conscious of the slick wet heat at the heart of her, the thrumming pulse of almost unbearable tension and craving.

And when he found the tender bud in that secret place, a wave of sensation flooded her in a surge of excitement so powerful, she went out of control. Any sense of time or space vanished. She writhed beneath an exploration that plunged her into sensual abandonment, conscious of nothing but him and the breathless, glorious, agonising pleasure of what he was doing to her frantic body.

'Please…' she whimpered, arching like a cat up to him, unable to stay still, wanting, needing, but totally unable to find the words.

Eyes ablaze with molten hunger, Jaspar slid over her and tipped her up to receive him. She tensed as she felt the hot, hard probe of his shaft against her warm, damp entrance, but white-hot need controlled her, vanquished that flash of fear of the unknown. He drove into her with all the forceful passion she had invited and the sharp stab of pain as he penetrated her tender sheath startled her into a cry.

Jaspar stilled to frown down at her in surprise. 'I'm hurting you?'

'No…' Freddy gasped, eyes tight shut against the threat

of his, in dismay and embarrassment at that unexpected hurt.

He shifted over her. 'You're very small,' he muttered on a sensual groan of combined pleasure and concern. 'But I burn for you, *ma belle*.'

'Don't stop…' She was all shaken up, but the banked-up excitement was still rippling through her in a desperate driving wave of craving.

He didn't stop. He eased further into her with a lithe but controlled undulation of his lean hips and she was entranced by that new sensation, shamelessly hungry for more. He set up a fluid rhythm that sent her heart rate to a thunder in her own eardrums, the explosive passion seizing her again. She angled up to him, helplessly urging him on, wanting, wanting…*wanting* and then finally, when she could bear the suspense no longer and when every nerve-ending was screaming, he sent her flying to a peak of ecstatic release. Glorious splintering sensation cascaded through her convulsed body. He shuddered over her with a harsh cry of male satisfaction and she closed round him like a cocoon, in the grip of wondering contentment.

Jaspar raised his dark head and studied her with crystal-clear tawny eyes. 'I'm sorry I was so rough. I've never hurt a woman like that before—'

'No…no,' Freddy muttered, raising her fingertips like a gentle silencer to his beautiful mouth. 'It was nothing—'

He pushed straying curls back from her brow in a gesture that squeezed her all too susceptible heart. *'But—'*

'Shush.' Unable to continue meeting his gaze lest he recognise her intense mortification, Freddy kissed the only bit of him within reasonable reach, his stubborn jawline. For a split second he tensed beneath that affectionate salutation, and then he laughed huskily and threw himself back against the pillows in a careless sprawl, carrying her with him.

'Now I can face an audience with my father. Sex is a wonderful release for tension, *ma belle*.' Jaspar informed her indolently, lean fingers idly toying with a long blonde curl. 'We will have a good time together while you are here.'

That fast, Freddy wanted to hit him. *A wonderful release for tension?* How could he so degrade what they had shared? As if he had had a strenuous stress-busting game of squash or something? That lovely addictive sense of intimacy and warmth felt totally destroyed in the wake of such casual, unfeeling dismissal. And, that quickly, she began sinking back into her normal self, only to be almost exploded back out of that no-longer safe shell by a true appreciation of what she had just done. About then she also recalled his comment about blackmail paying unexpected dividends and shame settled like a lump of lead in her tummy and expanded exponentially.

Supremely impervious to such sensitivity, Jaspar shifted her off his sprawled length with easy strength, threw back the sheet on his side and sprang off the bed. He vanished into an adjoining room and within the space of minutes she heard a shower running. She rolled onto her tummy. It was much, much too late to be having second thoughts, she told herself unhappily, but, even so, she was in turmoil. Every confused emotion felt ragged and magnified and tears threatened far too close to the surface. She had feelings for *him* that until that moment she had refused to recognise, but she shrank from examining what those feelings were.

She listened to the sound of drawers and cupboard doors opening and shutting from yet another room. He was getting dressed.

'Freddy…?'

Biting her lip, she turned over and sat up, trying to behave normally but with absolutely no idea of what was normal in such a situation.

Damp black hair brushed back from his brow, freshly shaven and dressed in a light grey pinstriped suit, Jaspar looked almost depressingly spectacular and like a Crown

Prince again. It occurred to her that she very much preferred him undressed, shorn of reserve.

'I will see Ben and at the very least get a report on how he has been managing,' Jaspar imparted, grave dark golden eyes resting on her as though willing her to be strong. 'I will try to bring him back here. More than that I cannot promise.'

Her mouth wobbled and she compressed her lips and nodded in mute acceptance.

As Jaspar began to turn away, he suddenly stilled to glance back at the bed. With a sudden imprecation, he flipped the sheet fully back from her.

'What's wrong?' Freddy began, knees raised to her breasts, the ease of sensual oblivion no longer available to her and discomfited shyness gripping her.

Jaspar lifted shaken eyes from the bloodstain on the sheet where he had lain with her.

Belatedly, Freddy registered the same view and she froze in stricken discomfiture. She tried to reclaim the sheet, but with one opposing pull Jaspar hauled it right off the bed.

'I don't believe this but the evidence is hard to ignore,' Jaspar breathed not quite levelly, his dark accented drawl fracturing round the edges. 'If you were a virgin, you *cannot* be my nephew's mother.'

The awful silence felt like a giant weight pressing down on Freddy.

CHAPTER SIX

SHORN of even the top sheet for cover, Freddy was frozen to the mattress and pale as death.

Jaspar's commanding gaze demanded answers but, foolishly, she just wanted to vanish and never ever be forced to see him again. How stupid she had been not to appreciate that, if she became intimate with him, he might realise that she was not the experienced lover he would naturally have expected. She had not foreseen the start of pain that had first betrayed her when they had made love or the possibility of physical proof of her virginity. After all, hadn't she once read that men could often not tell the difference and that certain sports made an actual barrier less likely?

'Who are you?' Jaspar demanded, so low and raw in tone that she shivered in the ghastly quiet that awaited her explanation.

And Freddy knew that she had no option but to tell the truth for nothing else would suffice, and she could have wept at the humiliation she had brought down on herself. Sitting naked on his bed was not the most conducive of positions from which to confess to a guy who was going to be, quite understandably, *very* angry with her.

'Answer me,' Jaspar urged with lethal force.

Freddy trembled, her damp skin chilling even in the warmth of the room. 'Can I get dressed first?'

'No.'

Freddy's eyes stung and glistened as she stared a hole in the offending sheet.

'Before I lose my temper, start talking,' Jaspar advised.

'Erica…Ben's mother died on the ski slopes in an accident nearly two months ago,' Freddy whispered brokenly and she twisted her restive fingers together round her knees. 'She was my cousin. We had the same name—'

'The same name? What nonsense is this?' Jaspar cut in with savage impatience.

'Our fathers were brothers so we were both Suttons and we were also both christened Frederica. It's a family name. When I was eight, Erica lost her parents and came to live with us—'

'You are trying to tell me that there were *two* of you?' Jaspar launched at her with ringing incredulity. 'Look at me before I haul you out of that bed and force the truth from you!'

Freddy flinched and looked up, clashing with flaming golden eyes that struck her like a whiplash scoring tender skin. 'I lived with Erica. The apartment and everything was hers…but I've been looking after Ben since the day he was born,' she hastened to tell him, her strained voice shaking. 'I'm Ben's nanny.'

'You're the…*nanny*?' Jaspar stared at her with blistering disbelief. 'You were your cousin's servant?'

Freddy's face flamed and she bowed her head down over knees, slowly tightening and closing up into a smaller and smaller ever-shrinking ball. So that was how he regarded her standing as a nanny. A servant. Well, how else had she imagined he might look on her? From the vantage point of his own very superior status, what else could a nanny be on his terms?

'Yet you made me marry you,' Jaspar continued in thunderous continuance, striding to the foot of the bed to snatch up the sheet and toss it in a contemptuous heap at her curling toes. 'Don't try to make me feel sorry for you. I'm not impressed for you didn't shrink from lying deceit and blackmail. If I threw you naked from my home in disgust, who would blame me?'

Her head shot up, panic stamped in her ashen face.

'But if you're telling me the truth and you did share your cousin's name, you are still my wife. Yet you are an impostor and a cheat for you are *not* Ben's mother and can have had no rights over him!' Jaspar decreed in dark fury. 'But I will deal with you later. At this moment, my father awaits me.'

Jaspar strode out to the landing and fought a powerful desire to go back and wrench a fuller confession from her. Though at least she had not belonged to Adil first and indeed was unlikely ever to have met his late brother. Yet that was irrelevant, Jaspar decided, furious that that single point in her favour should have even entered his mind. The real Erica Sutton had had many flaws, but the one sin that could not be laid at the door of Ben's true mother had been that of pretending to be anything other than she was. Relying on that investigative report, he had allowed himself to be trapped into marriage by a scheming, opportunistic liar. The 'devoted' nanny. Sabirah and then *this* in the same day. Fierce anger hardened in him.

As the sun went down an hour later, Freddy stood in the air-conditioned cool of a spacious reception room on the ground floor and watched the cascade of peach, scarlet and gold radiating in a glorious starburst across the horizon. Showered and clad in a light summer dress that had no pretension towards fashion, she was thinking that she had only herself to blame for her present predicament. Jaspar would not even consider reuniting her with Ben now. She was Ben's nanny, not his mother and, what was more, Jaspar was absolutely disgusted with her. She had seen the cold distance slot into his dark eyes like a door slamming shut in her shaken face.

Well, what more had she expected from him? In pursuit of what she had seen as being in Ben's benefit, she had played a rotten devious trick on Jaspar. It was bad enough that she had given him no choice other than to marry her. But for him to discover that she was not even the woman he had believed she was, and that she had had no right whatsoever to have made such a demand on Ben's behalf, had to have been the absolute last straw. Never had Freddy hit a lower ebb or fought harder to hold back tears, for she did not feel right then that she deserved to wallow in self-pity.

She was so ashamed of herself. So much grief and regret but all to what purpose? Why hadn't she appreciated that when the truth came out she would make an enemy of the one individual in Quamar who might have helped her? But then she had refused even to think about *when* she might finally have told the truth. For she had known that her only strength had lain in her masquerade and that, bereft of that pretence, she was powerless to engage Jaspar's compassion. And, that very evening, she had seen his sympathy over her enforced separation from the child that she loved. But she would not see that again, would she?

How could she have gone to bed with him? The dulled intimate ache at the heart of her body was a mortifying reminder of that ultimate and least forgivable mistake. Even knowing that she had to get a grip on her response to Jaspar al-Husayn, at the first challenge she had given way to temptation. Given way so fast too that she burned all over just thinking about how *easily* she had talked herself out of her own principles. Being used as a release for tension seemed a just reward for such cheap behaviour. Furthermore, engaging in that intimacy while still pretending to be Ben's mother could only have worsened her offence in his eyes and would act as another nail in her lying, deceitful coffin.

At eight the following morning, Jaspar emerged from the helicopter with his nephew clinging to him like a limpet.

'Feddy?' Ben prompted anxiously for about the hundredth time since he had wakened earlier, 'Ben want Feddy.'

'Freddy...' Jaspar corrected for at least the fiftieth time. 'She's here.'

The royal nursery staff had conducted an exhaustive enquiry into what a 'Feddy' might be, so that it might be supplied to soothe Ben, but had naturally drawn a blank in their attempt to identify what they had assumed was a much-loved toy. Of course, had his nephew asked repeatedly for his mother, there would have been no such misunderstanding, but no such word had emerged from the little boy since his arrival.

'Feddy...' Ben's bottom lip trembled, huge brown eyes misting with disappointed tears, his lack of trust that the person he wanted would appear patent.

His strong face clenching at the recollection of his nephew's innocent, trusting confidence barely forty-eight hours earlier in London and the obvious damage that had resulted from his sudden loss of all that was familiar to him, Jaspar's arms tightened round his brother's child. That same day in London, he had known the minute that Ben had smiled at him that, without a shadow of a doubt, the child was an al-Husayn for when Ben smiled, it was Adil's smile.

Freddy had not heard the helicopter for the walls of the Anhara palace were thick. Having fallen asleep on a sofa in the early hours while she'd sat up awaiting Jaspar's return and news of Ben, all she had had from the breakfast tray brought to her was a cup of tea. As she paced the beautiful mosaic-tiled floor, she was wondering fearfully why Jaspar had been away for the whole night. Was he even *coming* back?

Pale and drawn, she glanced towards the door when she heard steps echoing in the vast hallway beyond. And then Jaspar appeared on the threshold. His lean, powerful face taut, his hard dark eyes struck hers in a look as physically arresting as a blow. Only as she evaded that grave appraisal that judged and found her wanting did she have the space to notice the little boy he was lowering to the floor.

Her throat burned and she couldn't breathe. For a split second she was paralysed to the spot for she had been fully convinced that, after what Jaspar had discovered about her, he would make no effort at all to reunite her with Ben.

'Feddy...?' Ben whimpered on the back of a doubting sob.

And Freddy just ran, covered twenty feet in seconds to come down on her knees and scoop Ben up into her arms and hold him tight. She could hardly keep her voice under control as she muttered inarticulate things in her eagerness to comfort him. His tiny fingers gripped her tight, his sturdy little body trembling against her. She kissed and hugged him over and over again, held him back from her with overflowing eyes just to look at him, even managing to bring a watery smile to her lips for his benefit. As he squirmed back into closer contact, she looked over the top of his curly head, her face wet with tears of relief.

'I'll never be able to thank you enough...I'm really grateful. I know I don't deserve this but, for *his* sake, thank you from the bottom of my heart,' Freddy told Jaspar shakily.

'I don't want your gratitude,' Jaspar breathed, his grim dark-as-night gaze stinging hot pink into her cheeks. 'My nephew is here only because he needs you.'

Freddy dropped her blonde head. 'I accept that.'

'Don't play the martyr,' Jaspar derided. 'You never had the smallest intention of giving him up.'

At that accusation, her head flew up again, aquamarine eyes bright with disagreement. 'I *did*—'

'No, I will not accept that,' Jaspar cut in with ruthless bite. 'You put your own priorities ahead of his needs.'

Stabbed to the heart by that charge, Freddy said painfully, 'That's not how it was.'

'You were his nanny, not his guardian. In comparison with his father's family, what did you have to offer? Security? You were a young, single woman without the independent means necessary even to support him,' Jaspar pointed out with scorn.

'I know but—' She loved Ben so much, she wanted to plead, a sob catching in her convulsed throat.

'He is only two years old but he belongs to a dynasty that has six hundred years of proud heritage to share with him,' Jaspar delivered. 'He needs and deserves far more than you could *ever* have hoped to give him. His birthright is here in Quamar. He will never live in England again.'

'I just love him,' Freddy muttered chokily, struggling to keep her voice level as Ben looked up at her, but she was chilled by that assurance that Erica's son would never return to England.

'Yet when you could have told me that you were his nanny, you chose instead to *lie*—'

'I never actually—'

'A lie of omission is no less a lie,' Jaspar interrupted, one step ahead of her to squash that potential excuse. 'Had you admitted your real identity, I would have brought you to Quamar to ease his path.'

Her strained face tightened. 'I think you'd have been far too angry with me to even consider doing that.'

'Emotion never gets in the way of my intelligence. Nor, it seems, in the way of yours.' His brilliant dark golden eyes were filled with contempt. 'You used my nephew just as much as his neglectful mother did. You saw the chance to advance yourself through him and you grabbed it.'

Cut to the bone by that condemnation, Freddy gasped. 'That's not true!'

Jaspar elevated an ebony brow, his challenging gaze hard

as granite. 'Then why else did you blackmail me into marrying you? And why else were you so willing for that marriage to be consummated?'

Arms cradling Ben, who was demonstrating a contented desire to drift off to sleep, Freddy stared back at Jaspar, painful colour climbing in her cheeks and then draining slowly away again.

'Don't tell me you spread yourself on my bed for greater love of Ben as well,' Jaspar drawled with cutting clarity, eloquent mouth slanting with derision. 'The ultimate sacrifice? Surely not? No, I think you had far less presentable and more ambitious motives for allowing me access to that glorious body of yours. And not one of those motives related to my nephew's welfare.'

Only the knowledge that if she spoke up in her own defence she would inevitably provoke an argument that would disturb and upset Ben kept Freddy silent. But there was now a mutinous curve to her soft mouth and an angry light in her aquamarine eyes. He was twisting events. Who had carried her into that bedroom? Who had been the last word in seductive persuasion? Who had been ruthlessly set on taking advantage of that ceremony at the consulate and consummating their marriage? Who had reminded her that she was his wife, thereby lessening her resistance at the worst possible moment? Him, him, him and *him* again!

'I'm not fighting with you in front of Ben,' Freddy stated tightly.

His strong jawline clenched. 'I don't fight with women.'

But she had no doubt that, should the opportunity arise, he would be a fast learner. Without another word, Jaspar swung round and strode away and, gradually, Freddy started to breathe again.

There had been so much she had wanted to ask him. Was Ben only visiting for a few hours? When did he have to go back to wherever he had come from? Was she likely to see him again? Or was this a single meeting during which she was expected to say goodbye? Sobered by that fear, Freddy no longer felt like arguing about anything. She was lucky she was seeing Ben at all, she conceded wretchedly. Jaspar had said that he had only brought Ben to her because he needed her, which meant that Ben had been unhappy. Her heart sank at that knowledge.

She spent what remained of the morning reuniting Ben with his favourite toys and pursuits. Ben was very clingy and quiet. She caused a stir in the household by personally cooking lunch for him in the vast basement kitchen, which seemed to her next door to medieval although every inch of it was scrupulously clean. After Ben had eaten, she sat with him until he had fallen asleep in the bedroom where she had had their luggage placed. While there, she reflected uneasily on Jaspar's accusations.

He had not yet given her the chance to explain herself, but he was utterly convinced that greed had influenced all her dealings with him. And could she really blame him for his conviction that she was a gold-digging adventuress willing to use even sex as a means of placation? After all, Erica had been free with her favours and very fond of money. Indeed, her cousin had been downright mercenary with her lovers, even boasting about how generous a settlement she had won in return for her silence about her son's parentage, and Jaspar could well be aware of that fact. So, when Freddy had concealed her identity and had then demanded that he marry her, well, he wasn't likely to think of her as a pleasant, trustworthy or morally upright person, was he?

About twenty minutes later, leaving one of the maids to sit with Ben, she went off in reluctant search of Jaspar. She caught a glimpse of herself in a tall mirror and stopped to stare. Her hair was a riot of curls, her face was bare of make-up and her print dress was pretty shapeless. She found herself wanting to go and do herself up and she shook her head in bewildered impatience at the vagaries of her own mind. *He* wouldn't care what she looked like and she had no business caring. Since when had she been worried about her appearance? Only since a dark accented drawl had murmured, *'ma belle,'* she acknowledged, ashamed of her own weakness.

Finally having to ask for assistance from the manservant who seemed to be in charge of the staff and who spoke excellent English, Freddy was led to a door and abandoned there. She knocked, waited and, not receiving an answer, she went in.

Jaspar swung round from the window where he had been poised, a questioning look of anger burnishing his eyes, accentuating the set of his fabulous bone structure. It was obvious that he had had no intention of answering that knock on the door.

'I'm sorry…I thought it was OK just to come in,' Freddy said awkwardly.

Since his return, Jaspar had changed into a casual white shirt and beautifully tailored beige chinos. She was trying very hard not to look at him direct, but, from the instant she saw him without Ben's presence as a distraction, it was as if he were a giant magnet and she could not resist the pull. His breathtaking dark good looks made the breath catch in her throat. From the hard, angular set of his features to the leashed, muscular power of his lean, well-built frame, he was overwhelmingly male.

Assailed by a compulsive tide of memories from the day before, Freddy was plunged into an agony of tongue-tied discomfiture. One after another those images came at her: the lean, tensile strength of him against her, the excitement of his mouth and his hands on her, the wild, terrifying intensity of her own pleasure. Feverishly flushed, she felt her body quicken and heat in direct response to what was in her own mind and perspiration filmed her short upper lip as she tore her attention from him, appalled that she could have so little control over herself.

'I came here to talk to you,' Freddy mumbled in a stifled voice. 'But now that I'm on the spot, I don't know where to start.'

'What have we left to discuss?' Jaspar murmured low and deep, setting up a chain reaction down her taut spine with the dark, evocative timbre of his drawl. 'Ben? He stays here with us. Eventually he will visit my father several times a week but not until he has settled down again.'

Wondering how on earth he could have managed to extract such a far-reaching agreement from the ruthless older man, Freddy muttered in confusion, 'That sounds great but…well, how is that kind of arrangement going to be possible?'

'For Ben's sake, it *has* to be possible. He is unhappy in my father's household and you cannot be with him there because you are my wife.'

'You could just let me say that I'm his English nanny,' Freddy pointed out in a tentative tone. 'Then… er…perhaps, I could go back there with him.'

'It's too late for that now. My father is aware of our marriage and also that Ben's mother is dead. Naturally, he is displeased that you have become my wife, but, had you been your cousin he would have been outraged.'

Listening to him, Freddy's lips parted and she said in horror. 'You told him…*everything*?'

Jaspar dealt her a grim smile. 'What I tell my father is no concern of yours.'

In receipt of that unapologetic snub, Freddy reddened, but since she hoped he had massaged the truth more than a little it was not a subject on which she was inclined to linger. 'I never dreamt this would all get so complicated—'

'You're not that naive. You didn't care.' His strong jaw-line taut, Jaspar spoke with harsh clarity. 'I'm not ashamed to admit that I did not feel the need to personally shoulder responsibility for my brother's child yet you have forced me to do so. Had I not insisted that your presence was necessary to Ben and that *I* would raise him, I could not have brought him back here today.'

By the time that Jaspar had completed that revealing speech, Freddy was in shock and very pale. She was appalled. She did not know what to say for she had not thought of that kind of consequence, indeed had never really thought beyond her longing to hold Ben in her arms again or her determination to ensure that he had a secure future.

'Ben was miserable without you and, although he would eventually have forgotten you, I could not stand by and watch him suffer. He is Adil's son and I *loved* my brother,' Jaspar breathed in a driven undertone, dark golden eyes glittering a warning as though he was waiting for her to make some comment likely to offend. 'Adil would have taken my child without thought and brought him up. He had a huge heart. I'm afraid I'm not quite so big in the heart department.'

'I didn't mean to do *anything* that would make you feel that you had to bring up Ben yourself.' The most awful feeling of guilt was closing in on Freddy for she both understood his feelings and respected his honesty. There was no reason why he should have felt otherwise. By all accounts, Adil had been a hopeless womaniser and it was hardly fair that Jaspar should find himself having to deal with the consequences. After all, Ben's own father had made no such sacrifices on his child's behalf and Jaspar was a young, single male—well, he would be single again soon, she reminded herself uneasily.

Jaspar vented a humourless laugh. 'I planted the very seed that prompted you to demand that I marry you.'

She blinked. 'What are you talking about?'

'I told you that if I *had* been married, Ben might've been passed off as a relative from my wife's side of the family, thereby enabling me and my then non-existent wife to give him a home,' Jaspar reminded her with dark derision. 'Don't tell me that it's a miracle that we are now in that exact position.'

'That wasn't what gave me the idea,' Freddy protested tautly. 'In London, I felt powerless...and after Ben vanished, how could I trust that you or your family had decent and caring intentions towards him? Right-thinking people don't behave like that. When your father had him snatched, I thought he had to be an absolute monster—'

'He doesn't regard removing Ben from London in that light. He believed that he was rescuing his grandson from neglect, and had you admitted that Ben's mother was dead my nephew would not have been taken. Secure in the knowledge that we were Ben's closest relatives and that he was safe from harm in your care, my father would have been content to wait a few days longer.'

Her face fell, her troubled eyes dropping from the cold condemnation in his for she had explained herself to the best of her ability but failed to make the smallest impression on him. 'I'm sorry...but I don't think I really follow what's happening now,' she confided truthfully, the band of tightening tension round her temples threatening the onset of a headache. 'When do we get a divorce?'

'We *don't*...at least not in the foreseeable future,' Jaspar delivered with a stark bitterness that he made no attempt to hide. 'I must keep you as my wife.'

Freddy frowned. 'I don't understand.'

'My father could have set our marriage aside because I married you without his consent,' Jaspar admitted grittily. 'But if he did so, you would have to return to England. Ben would then be deprived of you again. As at this mo-

ment in time that would break the child's heart, I had no
choice but to argue that I wanted our marriage to stand.'

'Oh…' Freddy was bereft of any words of consolation
as she finally appreciated the ironic and galling position in
which Jaspar had found himself placed. Yet even feeling
as he did about her, he had put Ben's happiness first and
that made her eyes prickle with tears. She felt so horribly
guilty because it really was all her fault.

'My father is now talking in terms of making a public
announcement about our marriage,' Jaspar stated flatly.

'You mean…your father's w-willing to accept me?'
Freddy stammered in a wobbly voice of disbelief.

'He was and is very keen to see me married and produce
an heir.' His expressive mouth compressed to a hard line.
'I said you were pure. That was all he needed to hear—'

Freddy gave him an aghast look. 'You let your father
know I was a virgin?'

'You have nothing else in your favour,' Jaspar informed
her drily. 'Although I suppose you will be wonderfully pho-
togenic.'

'Well, don't you bother agreeing to any public announce-
ments,' Freddy urged him angrily, her temper finally spark-
ing. 'And stop blaming me for everything that's gone
wrong! If Ben hadn't been kidnapped, none of this would
have happened!'

'But now that it has, recriminations are pointless and, if
I have no choice other than to remain married to you, I
intend to make use of the situation.' Jaspar sent her a winging glance that had sufficient cool challenge within it to
make her tense even more.

Freddy folded her arms, her chin coming up. 'How?'

'You are going to give me a son.'

'Sorry…?' Freddy said with a look of uncertainty, thinking that obviously he could not mean that as it had sounded.

'And I warn you,' Jaspar murmured lazily, his dark drawl

tasting each word with silken precision, 'my brother's wives had a whole string of daughters, so it could take quite some time for us to strike lucky.'

Freddy turned hot pink, opened her mouth, closed it again and then snatched in a ragged breath. 'OK…you've had your joke. Ha ha and all that, but I'm really not in the mood to laugh.'

'That's good, because I'm not joking. You wanted to be my wife and you *are* my wife. Producing heirs to the throne goes with royal territory.' Silent on his feet as a prowling tiger, Jaspar strolled across the distance that separated them and rested reflective dark golden eyes on her bemused face. 'You can bet that I will be home every night this week.'

Freddy retreated a step. 'That's not funny, Jaspar.'

'It wasn't meant to be. My once excellent sense of humour *died* last night while my father was pontificating on whether or not we ought to have a church blessing to mark our union,' Jaspar admitted flatly.

'Oh…my goodness,' Freddy mumbled in the stretched-tight and screaming silence, registering that that discussion had been the ultimate last straw on his terms. 'But surely we can get out of this mess some way—'

'Not while we have Ben to consider—'

'But that doesn't mean it has to be a *real* marriage—'

Jaspar tracked her over to the wall to which she had backed. 'I won't settle for anything less, *ma belle*.'

'But you've been acting like you hate me!' Freddy slung in desperation, her taut shoulder blades finally making contact with the wall.

'Did that stop me taking you to bed yesterday?' Jaspar enquired.

Her cheeks burned. 'No, but—'

'Did you enjoy yourself?' Jaspar incised in a velvet purr.

Her hands knotted into fists by her side and she could no longer look him in the eye. 'That's not the point—'

'It's exactly the point. For a woman who went to shameless lengths to capture me, you're acting very oddly—'

'It wasn't you I wanted to capture…it was Ben!' Freddy snapped between gritted teeth of chagrin. '*Ben* from start to finish—'

Jaspar curved his hands to her waist, drawing her away from the wall.

Her breath tripped in her throat. The sizzle of awareness was in the atmosphere, tensing her muscles, rousing a tiny twisting sensation low in her pelvis. 'Don't you dare,' she warned him nonetheless.

'I always dare,' Jaspar mused, lion gold eyes resting on her soft full mouth until she literally felt them tingle. 'In fact a dare is a challenge—'

'Well, in this case it wasn't.' Freddy backtracked fast, deciding that, with her level of resistance, caution was wiser than foolish valour.

'Tell me you don't want me—'

'I don't want you—'

'And I'll call you a liar.' Jaspar let his hands slide down to the feminine fullness of her hips, easing her inexorably into contact with his hard, muscular frame.

She was trembling, mouth dry, heart hammering. The scent of him was in her nostrils. Warm male overlaid with a faint trace of some aromatic lotion and an extra dimension of something that was uniquely him, something that made her just want to drink him in like an addictive drug, she discovered in dismay.

'Please let go of me…'

Jaspar raised a hand and let his long fingers slowly lace into the fall of her blonde hair. The whole time he kept his striking dark golden eyes nailed to hers. He lowered his dark head, angled her mouth under his and she closed her eyes and swore to herself that she would stand there like an ice sculpture.

A roughened sound of amusement escaping low in his throat, he let the tip of his tongue tease her lips and she jerked, feeling the peaks of her breasts tighten and throb, the sudden surge of heat inside her. As his tongue darted deeper into the tender interior of her mouth, excitement flared like a betrayal inside her and mind over matter was no longer sufficient to restrain her. A stifled moan of frustration was torn from her.

'I desire you,' Jaspar muttered thickly, long fingers gathering up the skirt of her dress, caressing the curve of her hipbone, the shapely length of her thigh as with his other hand he tugged her head back and claimed a devouring kiss that made her dizzy with longing.

She did not want him to stop. She was quivering, pushing herself against him, the damp, hot pulse at the heart of her spurring her on. Hands dropping to below her hips, he lifted her off her feet, crushed her to him, let her feel the unmistakable thrust of his erection, tipped her head back with the passionate urgency of his plundering mouth.

'I want to be inside you, *ma belle*,' Jaspar groaned and on some level she knew that he was bringing her down on a cool, hard surface but she was beyond all thought of intervention.

Sliding her thighs apart, he hauled her back into connection with him. She was burning up, loosing little whimpering sounds low in her throat. With every plunge of his tongue, she wanted more and her skin felt tight and hot, her breasts were aching and her fingers were digging into his luxuriant black hair. And then a sound from the outside world she had forgotten penetrated: the loud, urgent ring of a phone. Her eyes opened and suddenly she was questioning what she was doing and, in instant rejection, pushing herself back from him.

Drawing back, Jaspar breathed unsteadily. 'For once, you are right. This is not the place for this.'

In stricken silence, she stared at him, noting the line of feverish colour accentuating his hard cheekbones, the smouldering blaze of his eyes, and then the frown slowly darkening his lean, bronzed features as though he too was taken aback. Her heart was still pounding as though she had run a three-minute mile. Lowering her head, throat suddenly thick with tears, she slid off his desk and brushed down the skirt of her dress with trembling hands. What had got into her? How could she just lose herself in him the minute he touched her? It was as if a wild, wanton stranger had taken her body over. The force of her own passion shocked her.

Jaspar was speaking on the phone. She would have fled had he not been lounging back against the door. As her attention lingered on him in the most covert of appraisals, she noticed that he was still visibly aroused and her face burned hot. Looking away, she lifted an unsteady hand to her swollen mouth.

Jaspar slung the phone aside again, lean, strong face taut. 'It seems I have a business meeting to attend in New York. My deputy has come down with appendicitis and I'll have to leave immediately. I'll be away for several days.'

'Perhaps you could think over your plans for us while you're away' Freddy muttered unevenly.

Jaspar sent her a penetrating glance and his lean face hardened. 'Was it so conceited of me to imagine that your primary objective was to become my wife and *share* my life?'

Surprised by that question though she was, Freddy was quick to say. 'Yes.'

'Naturally all you were looking forward to was becoming a very wealthy divorcee and duplicating your cousin's success without having to go to the trouble of producing a child,' Jaspar continued with raw derision.

'I've been doing no such thing!' Freddy was disconcerted by the fresh slant his cynical suspicions had taken.

His dark golden eyes arrowed over her unimpressed, his beautiful mouth curling. 'No wonder you're complaining. Instead of shopping until you drop all over Europe and partying, you're going to be my wife—'

'Just how could I have planned to carry on like that when I have Ben to look after?'

'I imagine you'd have hired a nanny as Ben's mother did. You were all set to follow in the family footsteps and why not? What else have you known and what other example would you follow?' Jaspar demanded. 'Your mother deserted you and your father for a richer man and your cousin was equally mercenary in her choice of lovers!'

Freddy looked back at him, aghast at that offensive allegation about her mother coming at her out of nowhere. What on earth was he trying to suggest? What he had just said had no basis in fact whatsoever.

'How dare you insult my mother's memory like that?' Freddy condemned with stricken force. 'My mother did *not* desert my father. She died of pneumonia when I was only two years old!'

Recognising her genuine distress, Jaspar had stilled. His eyes veiled. 'I'm sorry. I should not have descended to that level. That report must have confused your background with your cousin's—'

'No. If you ask me, the idiot that wrote that stupid investigation report just sat in his office and *dreamt* all the dirt of the day up sooner than go and make proper enquiries!' Freddy hurled, far from mollified by that apology. 'Erica's parents were killed in a car crash and were as happily married as my own were. In fact my aunt and uncle were so devoted to each other that they had no time at all to spare for their own daughter.'

'That is as may be—'

'I have very little recollection of my mother.' Freddy breathed painfully, a sob catching in her throat. 'But what I do remember, I *cherish*. Don't you ever dare to say such a thing about her again.'

In a sudden but entirely natural movement, Jaspar reached for her hand as though he would have comforted her, but Freddy snatched her fingers angrily free of his again.

'Do you know what's wrong with you?' she asked fiercely.

Jaspar veiled his eyes. 'I feel sure you're about to tell me.'

'Your life's been too easy and you're judgemental, selfish and insensitive!' Freddy threw at him as she dragged open the door. 'You'll be a lousy king! People make mistakes but sometimes they make them for good reasons as I did and I'm not one bit sorry I'm going to be here for Ben...because you have about as much heart as a stone! And you practically told me that *yourself*!'

And with that final unarguable word on the subject, Freddy stalked out, leaving Jaspar with a very strong urge to smash something.

'You will find great happiness in marriage,' Jaspar's father had been assuring him with galling good humour by the early hours of the morning. 'I had only spoken to your mother twice in the presence of her parents before our wedding but what a joy it was for us to discover each other as man and wife afterwards.'

His wife was finding joy pretty thin on the ground, Jaspar acknowledged, and for some reason that annoyed the hell out of him.

CHAPTER SEVEN

THREE days later, Freddy received her first visit in her role as Jaspar's wife.

In the midst of sorting out the entire wardrobe of little boy's clothes, which had been sent over from the royal palace that morning, Freddy glanced up to see Basmun, the head of the household staff, hovering.

'Yes?' Freddy prompted, reflecting that as news of the fact that she was *married* to Jaspar had spread through the Anhara palace the staff had demonstrated a very different attitude towards her. They no longer avoided looking at her and indeed awarded her an embarrassing degree of respectful attention. She suspected that when she had first arrived they had believed that she was Jaspar's mistress and had been extremely uncomfortable and unsure of how to behave around her.

'Princess Hasna has called, my lady. Refreshments are being prepared,' Basmun said with a low bow.

And who on earth *is* Princess Hasna? Freddy wondered in lively dismay as she tidied her hair and scrutinised her blue cotton skirt and top, deciding that they would have to do for to keep an important guest waiting would be unwise. Presumably the princess was a member of Jaspar's family.

Descending the superb stone staircase, Freddy passed by a gigantic arrangement of pale yellow roses on the lower landing. The beautiful bouquet had arrived for her only the day before. Why Jaspar should have sent her flowers she had no idea, any more than she had yet managed to work out why he had so far phoned her on four separate occasions. He would ask about Ben, enquire about what she was doing, run through his entire daily schedule with her and then assure her that he was looking forward to coming home. Had she not had experience of it four times over, she would have sworn that someone must have had a gun to his head to make him talk in such a civil way to her. If only he had employed some of that time telling her a few facts about his family…

Family, a subject that continually returned to haunt Freddy's own thoughts. Ever since Jaspar had upset her with his mistaken belief that her late mother had deserted her father for another man, Freddy had been feeling uneasy. The allegation niggled at the back of her mind, reminding her of just how little she *did* know about the woman who had brought her into the world. She wanted to see that investigation report for herself and discover how such a crazy misapprehension could have come about. Having made that resolve, Freddy went to meet her important visitor with a lighter heart.

A very attractive girl clad in a fashionable trouser suit rose to greet Freddy with a friendly smile. 'I'm your husband's niece, Hasna, and you are Freddy…or ''Feddy'' as I hear little Ben likes to call you.'

'He still can't get the r sound quite right,' Freddy confided, the worst of her tension evaporating.

'I couldn't wait to meet you.' Hasna's bright blue eyes inspected Freddy with open curiosity. 'But now that I have, I'm not surprised that my uncle Jaspar fell madly in love with you at your first meeting. You're very pretty.'

Somewhat thrown by that speech, Freddy managed to thank her for the compliment but was grateful for the diversion of mint tea and a spectacular array of tiny cakes arriving. Where on earth had Hasna got such a story from? Jaspar madly in love with her? He would cringe if he heard that sort of talk within his own family circle.

'You have certainly put Sabirah's nose out of joint.' Her

visitor grinned. 'She couldn't believe that Jaspar could go off and marry another woman now that she is free.'

'Free?' Freddy prompted, deciding just to plant in the odd encouraging word for it seemed that the youthful Hasna promised to be a mine of information.

'Free to marry again…since my father died.' Hasna's animated face shadowed. 'I miss him very much.'

'I'm sure you do.' And a princess surely had to have a prince for a father. Was Hasna one of Adil's daughters? Freddy paled. Unsettled by Hasna's cheerful reference to Ben and keen to avoid sensitive issues, she murmured hastily, 'You were telling me about this…er…Sabirah.'

Hasna gave her a mischievous smile. 'I think you know very little about our family. Sabirah is my father's widow and only twenty-six years old. He married her five years ago when everybody was expecting Jaspar to marry her.'

'My goodness…' muttered Freddy, no longer so sure she wanted to tap into the mine of information on offer, her tummy giving a nauseous little flip at the concept of Jaspar having *wanted* to marry any woman, for he had definitely not wanted to marry *her*.

'She didn't love my father and, of course, he had no idea that she had been making up to Jaspar too,' Hasna informed her with gathering steam. 'Of course, we hate her. Even though my father passed away only recently, Sabirah immediately began chasing after Jaspar again!'

Still very uncomfortable with the odd feeling of stark hurt that had surfaced a minute earlier, Freddy swallowed back the lump in her throat. She was very much afraid that she had discovered the identity of the naked seductress in Jaspar's bed.

'We were all scared that Jaspar might end up marrying her,' Hasna continued with a grimace. 'Even my grandfather was worried. After all, Jaspar used to be crazy about her and she *is* gorgeous.'

Freddy felt as if someone had put a large foot on top of her lungs for she was finding it hard to breathe. Jaspar had been crazy about Sabirah? Why on earth was she thinking in such an inappropriate way? Hadn't she herself forced Jaspar into what should only have been a marriage on paper? Why was she trying to forget *how* and *why* they had married? Why was she reacting to Hasna's revelations like a normal wife under threat?

'So it's wonderful that you came along and he fell passionately in love with you instead,' Hasna completed with a dreamy expression. 'Some day I want to fall in love like that. How does it feel?'

'Blissful,' Freddy mumbled not quite steadily.

'Can I ask you something?' Hasna leant forward eagerly. 'Is there any truth in the rumour that when Jaspar brought you home on your wedding day, Sabirah was here lying in wait for him?'

'Where on earth did you hear that?' Freddy heard herself ask, her voice sounding to her as though it were coming from the end of a long dark tunnel because she had just had her own worst fears confirmed.

Hasna sighed with patent disappointment. 'You mean…it's not true?'

'Not true.' Freddy preferred to remain sensibly silent on that dangerous subject.

'I suppose that Sabirah getting her comeuppance like that *was* too good to be true,' her visitor conceded with unashamed regret. 'We were all dying to find out.'

'Who's…"we"?' Freddy was keen to leave the entire topic of Sabirah behind.

'Well, there's Medina, my older sister. She's married and her mother was my father's first wife,' Hasna explained. 'After the divorce, he married my mother and she's English just like you and I have two sisters, Taruh and Nura… Sabirah was his third wife.'

Freddy was amazed that Jaspar's late brother had been married three times over but her companion's easy manner with her and her colloquial English were no longer a surprise, particularly when Hasna went on to confide that she and her sisters attended an English boarding-school. An hour later, Hasna's departure left Freddy deep in thought.

Evidently Jaspar's family believed he had succumbed to a whirlwind romance and things that had not made any sense to Freddy were finally falling into place.

Jaspar had been in love with Sabirah before she'd married his brother and presumably Sabirah must have had feelings for Jaspar too. Hasna might well be prejudiced against her stepmother. Perhaps Sabirah had had little choice but to marry Adil: it had to be pretty hard to say no to the heir to the throne when he proposed. But what an appalling situation Jaspar must have found himself in, forced to watch his philandering brother marry the woman that he himself loved. Adil had even fathered Ben while married to Sabirah.

Did that excuse Sabirah for literally throwing herself at Jaspar's head? Could Jaspar have carried on a secret affair with his brother's neglected wife? Freddy doubted that. There was something intrinsically straight and upright about Jaspar. Furthermore, he had been shocked by the sight of Sabirah artistically arranged on his bed and he had gone right ahead and made love to Freddy afterwards, which did not suggest to her much in the way of tortured masculine sensitivity.

However, unless Freddy was very much mistaken, the threat of Sabirah lay behind King Zafir's astonishing acceptance of his son's sudden marriage to a woman he had never even met. She might be a very inferior match for the Crown Prince of Quamar but, as Hasna had confided, her grandfather had been afraid that his son would want to marry his brother's widow and a nobody of an English nanny was obviously considered a lesser evil.

Two days later, Jaspar arrived back earlier than expected.

Without ever admitting the fact to herself, Freddy had spent hours preparing for the event. By seven that evening, her nails were painted blush-pink and her wayward curls had been conditioned into subjection, but she had no make-up on and she had been engaged in trying on every garment that Erica had ever given her. The helicopter came in to land when she was halfway into a short lilac dress with a frilled hem and struggling to get the zip up.

'Oh, no...' she groaned, knowing that she was over-dressed and that she most liked the very first outfit she had previewed. However, cramming her feet into mules, she gathered up Ben, who was already in his pyjamas, and headed for the stairs.

She saw Jaspar first: he was crossing the hall below, lean dark features serious. He looked gorgeous and her heartbeat quickened, her mouth running dry. He tipped his head back and stilled to look up at them. She turned hot pink.

Brilliant dark golden eyes roamed over her and he mounted the stairs to greet them. 'Let me take Ben,' he urged.

Ben went to him without hesitation and started chatting away, excited words tumbling over each other and incomprehensible. Jaspar smiled down at his nephew and the effect of that warm, charismatic smile made her breath catch in her throat.

'He's back to normal already. Just the way I remember him in London, full of life and fearless again,' Jaspar commented with satisfaction.

'Yes...'

'You've worked a real miracle with him.'

'I just play with him and cuddle him...and that's about

it, really,' Freddy muttered, brain as empty as a yawning crater at the moment when she most longed to come off with something if not witty, at least intelligent.

Jaspar strolled down the stairs again and as she drew level with him he turned to study her. 'You look fantastic in that dress,' he murmured with husky appreciation.

'Erica gave it to me but I haven't worn it before…I didn't go to the sort of places where people dress like this,' Freddy muttered in an even more breathless rush, closing her damp palms in on themselves, feeling as if she were on a first date and so awkward her nerves were screaming. So now he was free to wonder why she was parading around in a dress more suited to a flashy nightclub than his home.

'I'll take you shopping. You have no need to wear your cousin's cast-offs now.'

'It's not a cast-off. She bought it for me. She was always very generous and I know you think that she was a hateful person but I cared about her.' Having fired off that heated little speech, Freddy could have bitten her tongue out for right there in front of her his lean, strong face froze.

The silence lay heavy.

'You have a point.' Jaspar took her aback with that sudden agreement. 'If you don't abuse Adil, I'll endeavour to match your generosity where Erica is concerned. Some day we'll have to talk to Ben about his natural parents and we need to take a less emotive view of his past.'

Freddy nodded, the anxious light in her aquamarine eyes clearing. He was talking as though they were likely to be together for a very long time, she was thinking dizzily. But then no other arrangement made sense, did it? Where had her wits been over the past few days? When Jaspar had been talking about her having his children, he would hardly be expecting her to abandon them at some future stage.

His decision to put Ben's needs first and to bring up his

nephew with her meant that their marriage *had* to become a real marriage. Jaspar had had no choice on that score. No more choice than he had had in telling her that she would have to try and give him a son. He needed an heir, whether he liked it or not, whether he wanted to be married to her or not.

Jaspar, she registered, had moved on faster than she had and accepted the inevitable. The beautiful roses and the phone calls had all been part of the same parcel. He was trying to act like a normal husband. Only a normal newly married man might have grabbed his wife after five days away rather than reaching straight for the toddler. Unfortunately, Jaspar was married to a woman whom he would not even have asked out on a date had he ever had the opportunity and practising restraint could hardly be a challenge for him. He had probably hauled her into bed on their wedding night more out of sheer bloody-mindedness than anything else, Freddy decided wretchedly.

Basmun served coffee with great ceremony in the main salon. Jaspar had brought a toy train back from New York for Ben: a motorised engine large enough for Ben to sit on and complete with its own track. Freddy watched Jaspar putting the track together while Basmun strained at the leash to come to his royal employer's assistance, clearly regarding the task as beneath Jaspar's dignity. But Freddy could see for herself that Jaspar was enjoying himself and she was touched by the sight of Ben clumsily attempting to copy his uncle's every move.

'No, not there,' Jaspar told Ben and Ben gave him a hurt look and Jaspar groaned and let the little boy continue to get in his way.

As she watched them together Freddy could see the faint family resemblance between man and boy. When Ben lost the last of his toddler chubbiness he would have much the same nose as his uncle, and the colour of his eyes, if not the set of them, was almost identical. Jaspar would be a great role model for him too.

Her throat tightened. Fate might have put them on opposing sides when they'd first met but she saw so much to admire in Jaspar. His intelligence, his strength, his honesty and family loyalty, not to mention the powerful sense of responsibility that had made him place the needs of a child he barely knew ahead of his own. He didn't lose his cool in a crisis either but had he known the ultimate price that he would pay, she was sure he would never have agreed to marry her.

How could her conscience do anything other than claw at her? She had deprived him of the right to choose his own wife and he was stuck with her. Finally, just at the point where she was beginning to realise that she was falling in love with Jaspar al-Husayn, she was recognising what a humiliating trap she had fashioned for herself. Never would she be able to think that she was wanted for herself or even that he had chosen to be with her. The narrow loveless boundaries of the marriage she had foolishly forced on him would *always* be with them.

Ben fell asleep on top of the toy train. With Freddy leading the way, Jaspar lifted his nephew and carried him upstairs. Having tucked the little boy in for the night, Freddy turned to find Jaspar watching her with a grim light in his gaze.

'I gather you've been sleeping in here as well.' Having thrown a meaningful glance at the less than seductive T-shirt nightwear with its English logo lying on the other single bed in the room, Jaspar strode back out into the corridor.

Freddy was very tense. 'Yes.'

'Didn't you listen to *anything* I said before I left for New York?' Jaspar demanded with considerable impatience.

'You can't share Ben's room like a nursemaid. I've already instructed Basmun to hire a nanny—'

'But that's not necessary—'

'Yes, it is. Ben must learn Arabic as well as English and there will be many occasions when it won't be convenient for you to look after him,' Jaspar retorted levelly. 'Do I really have to spell out to you that a wife shares her husband's bed?'

On the galleried landing, he snapped lean brown fingers in imperious command and issued a clipped instruction to a servant passing through the hall below.

'I shared Ben's room because I thought it would help to make him feel more at home here,' Freddy argued.

'Overkill,' Jaspar pronounced with conviction. 'Did you share his accommodation in London?'

Freddy flushed. 'Occasionally.'

'A maid can sleep in the nursery until a nanny is hired. I'm going for a shower before dinner,' Jaspar completed with icy finality.

'For goodness' sake, after you'd gone, I didn't know *where* I was supposed to sleep!'

Jaspar cast her a gleaming dark golden glance empty of any hint of apology. 'Well, *now* you do.'

Furious with him for making such an issue of the matter, Freddy followed him. 'I'm only just getting used to the idea that we're really married.'

'How strange. That married feeling hit me like a lightning bolt on our wedding day!'

'I don't think you need to be so sarcastic,' Freddy snapped.

'You think not?'

As Freddy entered the bedroom Jaspar swung round, sent the door behind her slamming shut and before she had the slightest idea of his intention he had backed her up against the still-juddering wood. He brought his mouth down with explosive driving heat on hers, strong arms closing round her as he hauled her up to him and melded her slighter length to the hard, muscular power of his own.

He might as well have set off fireworks inside her. She went from angry stiffness to encouraging pliancy, the hunger he unleashed flaming into passionate union with her own. Her head fell back, allowing him to deepen the connection, her lips parting to the erotic penetration of his tongue, a shaken moan dredged from her in response. Sweeping her up into his arms, Jaspar laid her down on the bed and gazed down at her with molten eyes of appreciation for a moment before straightening again.

'Don't worry,' he breathed in a tone of intimate amusement. 'Even a cold shower and a four-course meal couldn't take me off the boil, *ma belle.*'

Mortified by the response he had wrung from her with the barest minimum of effort, Freddy stared up at him while struggling to catch her breath again. 'You can't just expect me to—'

His lean powerful face set taut, brilliant eyes shimmering a warning. 'I expect nothing but a modicum of common sense from you. While the servants believed you were my mistress, they would've vied with each other to be discreet for my benefit, but you're now my acknowledged wife and everything you do is likely to be talked about.'

At that news, Freddy paled. 'Really?'

'What else did you expect when you married a man in my position?' Jaspar demanded in exasperation. 'And if a rumour that our marriage is already so troubled that we occupy separate bedrooms spreads beyond these walls, we have no hope of convincing anybody, least of all my father, that this is the love-match I said it was!'

'Love-match?' Freddy repeated unevenly.

His narrowed gaze darkened, his strong jawline clenching. 'How else do you think I persuaded him to accept our marriage? With the *truth*?'

Pale as milk, Freddy dragged her guilty eyes from him. In that harsh intonation, she recognised his angry regret at the necessity of having had to voice such a lie. She should have had greater faith in what Hasna had said on the same subject.

'It was the only argument I could use,' Jaspar admitted half under his breath, his anger having spent itself. 'His honest pleasure on my behalf shamed me.'

It shamed Freddy too.

'There's really nothing I can say to make things right,' she muttered shakily.

'But I too made mistakes,' Jaspar murmured flatly. 'I didn't want to trawl through the murky secrets of Adil's life and I resented the necessity. I did indeed think of Ben as a parcel who might be tossed on a plane. But, all that is behind us now.'

'How can it be?' Freddy muttered uncomfortably.

'It *has* to be,' Jaspar countered with a level of self-assurance that disconcerted her. 'We have to live together and make a success of our marriage...and why not?'

Disconcerted, Freddy raised her head. A good half-dozen reasons why not were heaped on the tip of her tongue but she remained silent, all too willing to be persuaded otherwise.

'You look surprised.' Jaspar shed his jacket in an indolent, very masculine movement and loosened his tie. 'We'll discuss it over dinner.'

They dined in the formal splendour of a room so large it could have handled a state banquet. Freddy could not help thinking that, with so many other rooms available, a dining-room where their voices did not echo and the servants did not have to trek sixty feet from the door to the table might have been rather more relaxing. Not that Jaspar seemed remotely uncomfortable with his surroundings, however. But then from birth he must have been accustomed to acres of space around him, Freddy thought ruefully, and it was she, rather than Jaspar, who had to adapt to a challenging new environment and a pronounced change in status.

When the coffee was brought, Jaspar lounged back in his carved chair, the very epitome of male relaxation. 'While I was in New York, I looked at our situation from a business point of view…'

'A *business* point of view?' Freddy parroted helplessly.

'Sometimes it's a good idea to examine a problem from a different perspective,' Jaspar informed her. 'I came to the conclusion that marriage has a lot in common with a business deal.'

Barely recovering from the cut inherent in being labelled a problem in his life, Freddy was forced to swallow even more pride in receipt of that concluding statement.. 'How can you say that?'

'In the usual scenario, a man and a woman fall in love and marry, each of them armed with an entirely separate set of expectations, and then they either compromise or break up,' Jaspar contended, dark golden eyes lit with supreme cynicism. 'But we're *not* in love and I already know the worst that you are capable of. That has to be an advantage.'

By the time he had finished speaking, Freddy had lost colour. 'Is it?'

'Naturally it is. We have a marriage of convenience, a practical, unemotional arrangement which can satisfy us both in different ways. You will have Ben and the lifestyle that you wanted in return for which—'

'You get…you hope…a son and heir,' Freddy completed doggedly for him, struggling to conceal the tide of angry pain assailing her. After all, if he could sit there discussing their relationship in the most appalling cold-blooded terms, far be it from her to betray any sentimental or sensitive weakness.

'*And* a beautiful and very sexy wife,' Jaspar traded huskily, sensual appreciation lighting his stunning eyes as he surveyed her. 'I see no reason why we shouldn't establish a mutually beneficial relationship. We leave the past behind us and make the most we can of the present.'

Below the level of the table, Freddy's taut fingers were biting into the fine linen napkin on her lap. 'I would need more than that to be happy—'

'You should have thought of that aspect before you married me,' Jaspar countered with lethal cool.

'I didn't know I was going to end up *living* with you, did I?' Freddy snapped, her fragile composure splintering to give vent to the churning emotions she had been fighting to suppress while she listened to him. 'And do you know what I see? Just one more wimpy male who got hurt *once* in his wretched life—'

Jaspar dealt her an incredulous look. 'I beg your pardon?'

'And felt so damned sorry for himself and his wounded pride that he's been taking it out on every woman he's been with since by acting like an absolute four-letter word!' Freddy condemned fiercely, thrusting back her chair to stand up. 'Well, you're not taking it out on me! So if and when you're willing to offer me something other than the *business* blueprint for the marriage from hell, tell me. In the meantime, don't you dare lay a finger on me. I'm out of bounds—'

'You're damned right you are,' Jaspar grated, rising to his full commanding height, a level of scorching anger that shook her blazing in his lean, hard-boned features. 'What is this talk of wimpy males and wounded pride? Where has all this nonsense come from?'

'It's not nonsense,' Freddy told him, her strained voice shaking with the force of her disturbed emotions. 'I wish it was but I honestly believe that you dislike women. I thought it was just me but I don't think it is—'

'Answer the question. To what were you referring? And to whom have you been talking?' Jaspar demanded with charged force.

At that repetition, Freddy paled, for she was already aware that in giving way to her temper she had lost control of her tongue and said far too much, and she certainly did not want to name the source of her information as being a member of his own family. 'I'm sorry if I was offensive…I don't think we should get into that,' she said in a small, tight voice.

'You were referring to Sabirah.' His jawline rock-hard, Jaspar studied her now-reddening face with raw derision.

'What I was trying to say…clumsily,' Freddy conceded in deep discomfiture, 'is that I couldn't face having a baby with someone who talks about us having an *unemotional* arrangement. I do have feelings—'

'Then respect *mine*,' Jaspar breathed in seething condemnation.

As he strode out of the room Freddy braced trembling hands on the table and snatched in a ragged breath. He got much angrier than she did but stayed in control, she thought sickly, running back over her own thoughtless attack on him and the resentment that had prompted it. She winced for herself. There he had been telling her that there was no prospect of him ever developing a warmer attachment to her and, in her hurt and disappointment, she had lashed out at him on a subject she should not have broached. Reminding him about Sabirah had been a downright nasty thing to do and, in doing so, she had got exactly what she deserved, hadn't she? For in his volatile reaction, she had seen much that she would sooner not have seen: a pain and bitterness that still lingered five years on. Sabirah had hurt Jaspar a great deal.

A couple of hours later, long after the sun had gone down in a blaze of glory and she had given up hope of Jaspar reappearing, Freddy went upstairs. And on the bed in what she was striving to regard as *their* bedroom, what did she find? A large pile of exquisitely wrapped gifts with a card on top that was inscribed with her name in Jaspar's bold black scrawl.

Her heart sank as if weights had been anchored to it. The first and smallest parcel contained her favourite perfume, which she always wore. She breathed in deep. The second was an opulent jewel case containing a delicate gold watch studded with diamonds. Swallowing hard, she fingered her stainless steel watch that had a bracelet that was forever working itself loose. The third and largest parcel opened to disclose a glorious antique rosewood vanity case filled with gleaming silver-topped containers and a whole array of fascinating items. She gazed at it in frank disbelief. The fourth gift was a designer handbag, similar in style to the bag she used but infinitely superior. And the fifth was an elaborate gilded coffer filled to the brim with…mouth-watering fudge.

Legs feeling wobbly, registering that she was married to a guy with meteoric grasp on the principles of one-upmanship, Freddy folded down in a heap on the soft thick rug beside the bed and stuffed herself with the fudge. If she had been paranoid she might have thought he had bought her all those presents just to make her feel that she was the most hateful woman alive. But she wasn't paranoid. However, she *was* striving to understand why the male who had talked about marriage being on a par with a business deal should have confounded her every expectation and left her reeling.

Those gifts told her so much about Jaspar, she reflected,

still in a daze at his extravagance while she worked her way steadily through the fudge. He was incredibly obser-vant. He must have noticed her fiddling with the faulty catch on her watch and he had identified her perfume, even recalled the colour and shape of her handbag yet he had only seen her with it once that she could recall. However, she had no idea how he had found out that she adored Victorian things and collected little bits and pieces like but-ton hooks. He had been so generous, so thoughtful in choosing presents that would please her that she was touched to the heart, but also shamed into considerable dis-comfiture.

A man who disliked women would not have exercised that degree of care or consideration. No, she was dealing with a male who simply distrusted women and not without good reason. A male who had learned to hide his true na-ture behind a cold front of reserve and a stinging talent in the field of put-downs. But still a guy who had sent her roses, phoned her every day and done a heck of a lot of shopping on her behalf. She smiled through the tears trick-ling down her cheeks.

A marriage of convenience? Well, considering that she had blackmailed him into marrying her and then left him feeling that he had to *stay* married to her for Ben's sake, she had no right to talk about wanting more. He had had to settle for less than what he wanted, so she would have to as well. She wondered how long it would be before she heard him call her, 'ma belle' once more and even if he would ever use those words around her again…

CHAPTER EIGHT

JASPAR eased the bedroom door closed in his wake and then stilled in surprise.

In the moonlight flooding through the windows he could see that Freddy had fallen asleep on the floor. A ring of fudge wrappers and crumpled tissues surrounded her like a statement and he could see that her nose was pink and her eyelashes still clogged together. An unexpected shard of tenderness stirred in him: she looked so small and forlorn. Gathering her up, he laid her down on the bed and unzipped her dress to ease her free of its crumpled folds.

She was so tactless, so utterly lacking in the more subtle feminine wiles of persuasion, that she fascinated him. From an early age Jaspar had been taught never to speak without thought, never to relax his guard and never ever to lose control of his temper. But until Freddy and her towel had exploded into his once smooth and organised existence, his self-discipline had rarely been challenged. After all, people didn't criticise him or argue with him and women had always been eager to please him.

Only Freddy had dared to make demands. Standing there at the dining table ranting and raving at him quite unaware that an aghast Basmun was striving to hurry backwards out of the room again with a heavy tray. She had a lot to learn. Although his father was already testily demanding to know when he could expect to meet his new daughter-in-law, Jaspar felt that he could not risk the potential conflagration. Freddy was a firebrand and his parent's concept of contemporary womanhood was a good half-century out of date.

Freddy came awake with a sleepy sigh and focused on

Jaspar. Moonlight gleamed over his black hair, mirrored the sheen of his dark eyes, marked the bold angles of his hard cheekbones and shaded the hollows. She sat up with a start. 'Where have you been?'

'Working in my office—'

'I didn't even think of looking there for you. I thought you'd gone out—'

'There's not a lot in the immediate radius of the Anhara.' Stretching out a lean hand, Jaspar switched on the lamps by the bed.

Blinking in the sudden light, registering that he must have removed her dress and that she was only wearing a lacy bra and panties, Freddy coloured in confusion. She studied his darkly handsome face and the faint smile curving his mouth and her heart skipped a beat. She was relieved that he was no longer angry, that her thoughtless words had done no lasting damage. 'I'm sorry about what I said. I don't know what gets into me around you. I don't say nasty things to other people,' she muttered defensively.

'It's forgotten.' Tipping his proud dark head back, Jaspar gazed down at her, eyes a stunning lambent gold beneath dense black lashes. 'In certain moods, I love to provoke.'

As her mouth ran dry her breath feathered in her throat. She was electrified by the look in his eyes, the hungry male appreciation that he made no attempt to hide. 'I have a quick temper.'

'At least you didn't kick me this time,' Jaspar said huskily, reaching behind her with lethal cool to release the catch on her bra.

As he eased the straps down her arms her face flamed, but a hot, tight twist of excitement was unfurling like a dark flower in the pit of her stomach. Her full creamy breasts with their taut rosy peaks spilled from the bra cups, brazenly bare for his appraisal. In the humming silence, she sucked in a quick shallow breath to sustain herself.

'You are magnificent, *ma belle*,' Jaspar rasped in a roughened undertone.

She tingled all over, feeling so aware of him, so suddenly desperate for his touch but, at the same time, wonderfully aware of her own femininity and confident of her power to attract. Obeying a wanton prompting that she could not resist, she found herself tipping back her shoulders and arching her spine so that her shapely curves were all the more prominent.

A driven groan escaped Jaspar and he succumbed to the temptation of that tantalising movement by closing a hand into her hair and dragging her down onto the pillows, following her there with unconcealed impatience to close his mouth with devastating urgency to first one straining nipple and then the other. All the breath in her was drawn out of her in one long keening moan of startled response.

'I am hopelessly in love with your glorious body,' Jaspar confided with ragged fervour.

'Hmm…' Words were beyond her. Her whole being was bound up in the hot provocation of the male fingers kneading her lush breasts and toying with their tender, throbbing peaks. Her hand laced into the silky depths of his thick hair, her hips shifting on the mattress, the thrum of rising heat spreading through her with electrifying intensity. He lashed the rigid tips to tormenting sensitivity with the tip of his tongue and she was gasping for breath, neck arching as she thrust herself helplessly up to him.

'You have a volcanic effect on my libido.' In a lithe movement, Jaspar pulled back from her and sprang off the bed to undress.

'Really?' A dazed sense of achievement assailing her, Freddy watched him rip off his beautifully tailored suit with the kind of impatience that struck her as a considerable compliment. He wanted her. He wanted her something fierce. Never had she dreamt that she could have that kind of effect on a man. Never had she suspected that that knowledge might enable her to lie half naked and unashamed, accepting the burning gold admiration of his eyes on her.

'You are a very sensual woman,' Jaspar told her with husky appreciation.

And he was an incredibly sexy guy, Freddy thought dizzily, losing the lingering remnants of concentration to discover that she could not take her eyes from his lean, well-proportioned physique either. He was all power and potency, all dominant male and muscles from his wide, strong shoulders to his long masculine thighs and so very different from her, for where she was all soft and yielding he was all taut angles and hard, virile promise. 'I don't know what I am,' she confessed. 'I'm only just finding out—'

'Let me show you…' Jaspar breathed, urging her round to face him so that he could slide his hands beneath her hips to skim off the last garment that concealed her from him. 'I've thought of this moment every day I've been away from you, *ma belle*.'

Wholly naked then, she blushed rosily, shy as she had not been seconds earlier, but he came down beside her and claimed her lips with an explicit need that fired her every skincell with passionate response. She reached up to him, holding him to her, glorying in the hair-roughened abrasion of his muscular chest against her tightly beaded nipples, drinking in the familiar male scent of him with heady recognition and rejoicing in the need he made no attempt to hide from her.

He rearranged her on the mattress and plotted an increasingly provocative and tormenting path down over her trembling body. She closed her eyes, head falling back as she gave herself up to the stream of intoxicating sensation, feeling the tightening knot of ever-increasing tension build at the very heart of her where she was hot with helpless long-ing. And then he eased her thighs apart, found the hottest point of all with his knowing mouth. He sent shellshocked tremors travelling through both her mind and her body and her aquamarine eyes flew wide in dismay.

'No, you can't…' she mumbled.

'Yes, I can,' Jaspar countered thickly. 'I want to drive you out of your mind with pleasure.'

As suggestions went, she considered that one fairly se-ductive, but inhibition fought with desire until he took de-cision from her. Just as quickly, what he was doing to her all-too-willing and rebellious body wiped every other con-sideration from her mind. She hadn't known, indeed could never have dreamt, that she had such a capacity for enjoy-ment and, having had that fact discovered for her, had no control over the strength of her own response.

'Oh…' She was all liquid heat and burning, her heart hammering so hard that she was panting for breath. A mer-ciless craving for satisfaction was twisting through her writhing length like a tightening red-hot wire.

Just when she was on the quivering brink of that peak, her whole being centred on his every move, Jaspar hauled her under him, tipped her up and sunk into her in one driv-ing thrust. A shocked moan of delight was wrenched from her and then there was only the hot, aching pleasure of his pagan rhythm, the urgent surge of his maleness over and inside her in the mindless union of frantic desire. She rose to meet his every thrust in fevered response until her hunger peaked at an unbearable height and she splintered into what felt like a thousand shining pieces and drowned in the floodtide of exquisite pleasure that followed.

There was something to be said for 'only sex', Freddy conceded in a daze as the tremors of sweet ecstasy only slowly receded from her quivering body. But if he used that phrase again, she would kill him, she *knew* she would.

Yet even as he shuddered over her with an uninhibited groan of fulfilment she was smiling and closing herself round him in a cocoon of loving intimacy. She had blessings to count. He had bought her fudge and he was great with Ben. He loved her body, truly loved her body. He had been made for her; he just didn't know it yet. She let possessive fingers idly thread through the damp, tousled strands of hair at the nape of his neck and skirt round to skim down one angular cheekbone.

Closing his arms round her, Jaspar rolled over so that she lay on top of him. Pushing the tangled blonde curls back from her face with surprising gentleness, he smiled at the feverish flush that merely enhanced the brightness of her aquamarine gaze and traced the reddened curve of her full lower lip with a reflective fingertip. 'Next time you come to New York too, *ma belle*.'

'To help you shop?' Freddy teased.

Reclining back against the banked-up pillows, Jaspar shrugged a broad brown shoulder. 'When I'm in the city, I like to get out for some fresh air between meetings.'

'Oh, I'm not complaining.' Freddy was entranced by the faint defensive air he exuded as if he was just a little self-conscious about having bought so much for her. 'I was just knocked flat by all those pressies and I haven't even said thank you yet.'

'I've had all the thanks I required.' Jaspar gave her a wolfish grin that made her heart tilt on its axis. 'Glad you liked the fudge.'

'I ate the whole box…don't remind me!' Freddy groaned in embarrassment.

Jaspar laughed and shifted her back onto the mattress beside him so that he could gaze down at her discomfited face. His dazzling golden eyes narrowed to a slumbrous level and he lowered his dark head and captured her mouth with a slow, searching sensuality that made her head spin.

A long time later, he carried her into the shower with him. She had not a clue what hour of the night it was by then, but the water cooling her heated skin woke her out of her satiated daze and she remembered the niggling curiosity that had troubled her while he had been abroad. 'That report…that private detective's report that was done on Erica,' she told him. 'I want to see it.'

Jaspar tensed in the loose circle of her arms. 'Why?'

'Nothing in it is likely to shock me,' Freddy pointed out ruefully. 'I did *live* with Erica. But it's really the bit purporting to be about either my mother or hers that I'd like to get a look at.'

'But you said that your mother died when you were a baby. You can hardly doubt such a fact.'

'I *don't* doubt it.' Reluctant to reveal just how uninformative her late father had been on the subject of her mother, Freddy struggled to explain her feelings. 'But naturally I'm curious when something odd like that comes up and it relates to my family.'

Tugging her out of the shower cubicle, Jaspar lifted a big fleecy towel and wrapped her into its folds. 'You should just forget about it. I very much regret having mentioned the matter. In any case, I had the report destroyed.'

'But why?' Freddy gasped.

'I was thinking of Ben. I felt that it would be unwise to retain a document that vilified his mother.'

Seeing his point, Freddy sighed. 'I really did want to see it.'

'But that report was full of errors.' In the midst of towelling his lithe, sun-darkened body dry, Jaspar regarded her in some bewilderment. 'I could have fresh inquiries made by a different agent but I really *don't* see—'

'Yes, I'd like that,' Freddy rushed in to assure him with a vigorous nod of pleased confirmation, her determination to pursue the matter unhidden. 'My pet theory is that my uncle, Erica's father, may have been married before he met her mother and that that first marriage broke up.'

'This long after the event, does it really matter?'

'It does to me.'

'Then it will be done, *ma belle*,' Jaspar asserted levelly.

A warm smile curved her lips. 'How did you know I would like that vanity box?'

Jaspar grimaced and then laughed. 'That report. Your life and your cousin's were blended into one but, once I knew the truth about you, it was easy to work out what related to you rather than to her.'

'Yes. Erica collected miniature alcohol bottles.'

His appreciative golden gaze rested on her twinkling aquamarine eyes and the cheeky smile on her face set between the torrent of wild damp curls tumbling round her shoulders. 'Do you know that the first time I saw you in a towel, I started thinking about mermaids?'

Freddy blinked. 'Mermaids?'

'There's a place in the mountains not too far from here where I used to swim as a boy. Some day I must take you there…' As his roughened drawl dropped in tone to send a responsive shiver down her spine, and she met the smouldering intensity of his stunning eyes, Freddy found herself surging back into his arms at the exact same time as he reached out for her again.

Over four weeks later, Freddy lay on a gorgeous silk woven rug on a grassy bank beneath the spreading shade of a graceful plane tree. It was a glorious spot. Far above a hawk wheeled and dipped against the cloudless blue sky. Rocky hills sheltered the fertile valley floor and spring flowers and vegetation grew all around the lake.

Freddy watched Jaspar dive in a lithe curve into the dappled water, the sunlight turning his wet skin to shimmering bronze. He was so hopelessly energetic, she thought, and she smiled for Jaspar did everything with energy and commitment. Fulfilling his duties as Crown Prince of Quamar might sentence him to listening for hours to the often petty disputes between ordinary Quamaris that were brought to him for settlement in preference to the courts, but he never betrayed any sign of impatience or exasperation.

'I have to be accessible and approachable,' Jaspar had pointed out ruefully only the day before when a particularly complex quarrel over grazing boundaries had been laid before him and had dragged on so long that their afternoon out had had to be cancelled. 'Our people have a great respect for the old ways and so must we.'

Although she was feeling languid and lazy from the heat, she was thirsty and, pushing herself up on one elbow, she dug into the cool-box which was disguised as a giant picnic basket and withdrew a bottle of mineral water and a glass. As she sat up a faint sensation of dizziness made her head swim and she blinked. That was the second time in a matter of days that she had felt woozy and she was conscious that her period was a little overdue. But then in the past her cycle had been disturbed before by foreign travel and even by emotional upsets and there was no denying that her life had changed out of all recognition over the past six weeks. She wondered if it was too soon to do a pregnancy test, but also felt that the chances of her having conceived the very first month of their marriage were slim.

Although Jaspar *did* make love to her just about every day of the week, she conceded, watching him work off his surplus energy in the water, her gaze possessive and tender. She was head over heels in love and the past month had been a revelation to her for she had simply never been so happy. As each sunlit day melted into another beautiful sunset, she felt more secure in that happiness. No matter what other demands were made on him, Jaspar devoted a great deal of time to her and Ben.

Of course, he had said that they would have to make a success of their marriage. But the way he talked to her and sought her out to share little things with her had made Freddy hope that there was rather less hard work involved in making a go of things than those warning words of his had originally made her fear. Jaspar genuinely seemed to *want* to be with her and his affection for Ben was patent. However, when it came to more personal feelings, Jaspar was very much more reserved.

Oh, he told her she was beautiful so often that she was almost beginning to think that she might be, she reflected with helpless amusement. And he laughed when she joked, and in turn he teased her, and they had a wonderful easy camaraderie that was nonetheless equally given to erotic interludes because he was a very passionate guy. So he found her desirable and he enjoyed her company. He was fond of her but he would never love her and she could hardly blame him for that. Love either happened or it didn't and if it hadn't happened yet, it would never happen.

Stark naked and magnificent, Jaspar padded up to lift a towel. 'Some mermaid,' he chided with vibrantly amused eyes. 'Lying here in sloth on the bank.'

'One dip a day is enough for me and, after eating so much, I feel totally lazy,' Freddy confided, mouth running dry at the sight of him, heartbeat quickening in concert.

'You're still tired? But you had a nap—'

'I didn't. I was just lying with my eyes closed—'

'I walked over here and spoke to you. You were *fast* asleep.' Jaspar pulled on khaki chinos.

Her gaze rested on his powerful torso, the whipcord ripple of muscle as his arms flexed. The tantalising little furrow of dark hair that dissected his flat stomach was visible for he had not yet zipped up his chinos. A wicked little spiral of heat twisted up from her pelvis. He was just so breathtakingly fanciable at every moment of the day.

Without any thought of what she was doing, she got up on her knees and pressed her lips to his stomach.

His hands came down in her hair and then he dropped down in front of her, eyes flashing molten gold over her pink face for she was embarrassed by her own boldness. He spread his fingers to her cheekbones ensuring she met his challenging gaze. 'Don't stop there, *ma belle*,' he murmured in a throaty tone of intimacy.

On the jolting journey back to the Anhara across the rough gravel plain that ringed the hills before the desert sands took over again, she was aware of the satisfied ache of her body and the indolent after-effects of their lovemaking, but even more conscious of the intense strength of her feelings for him. As he drove she rested a hand on his long, powerful thigh and occasionally he would cover her fingers with his own in an acknowledgement of her need to retain that closeness.

'We're happy,' she said softly.

'So we are,' Jaspar conceded lazily.

'Was it like this with you and Sabirah?' she heard herself ask, and she could have sworn that no thought of asking such a question had occurred to her, yet those impulsive words emerged from her lips nonetheless.

The silence fell like a curtain.

His surprised withdrawal was palpable in that brief silence and she could have kicked herself.

'Naturally not,' Jaspar finally responded with a perceptible lack of expression. 'We only met in company.'

In actuality, Freddy had not been referring to anything that related to physical intimacy for he had already told her that he and Sabirah had not been lovers. She had been referring to the sense of closeness and understanding that she herself felt with him and asking rather foolishly if he had felt the same with Sabirah. However, as he appeared only to think of *their* bonds in the most primitive of male sexual terms, yammering on about her own far more highflown sensations would be like laying her love at his wretched feet! She was furious with herself and with him.

'But times are changing. Career women in the city are beginning to go out in mixed social groups, but in rural areas and in conservative families parents are still very careful of their daughters' reputations.'

'When you want to change the subject, you don't need to give me a cultural lecture to do it!' Freddy snatched her hand from his muscular thigh as though he had slapped her.

'What's the matter?' Jaspar demanded.

'Nothing.' Face rigid, two high spots of hurt and chagrined colour marking her cheekbones, Freddy stared out through the dusty windscreen, watching the blinding sunlight begin to drain the desert sands of all colour and life. The hottest part of the day was approaching, which was why they had come out early and enjoyed brunch rather than lunch, for in another hour the temperature would scorch even in the shade.

Yet she still loved Quamar. It was a really beautiful country and the people were wonderfully friendly and welcoming. Jaspar had taken her out on lots of tours and tagging along with a male whom the Quamaris seemed to regard as being next door to a divinity had been educational. She had drunk goat's milk in nomadic tents, cheered at an impromptu horse race out in the desert and enjoyed chilled mint tea in the fashionable villas belonging to Jaspar's friends. And everywhere, no matter whom he was with and no matter how rich or humble his host, Jaspar was the same relaxed, courteous and charming guest, who always said and did the right thing.

'You're my wife. You have no reason to be jealous of my past,' Jaspar murmured drily.

'When your past arranges herself naked on your bed, I

have *every* reason!' Freddy flared, losing her temper with a suddenness that shook even her.

'It's unworthy of you to mention that episode. I hope you didn't gossip about that with Hasna as well,' Jaspar delivered in icy reproof, finally revealing that he had known all along that his niece had been the source of her identification of Sabirah.

'I didn't gossip with Hasna at all!' Freddy launched back furiously.

'But you *listened*,' Jaspar countered without skipping a beat.

She wanted to hit him for facing her with that unarguable point. 'Just stop this blasted car and let me out!'

'Don't be foolish. We're in the desert,' Jaspar murmured in the most infuriatingly superior tone.

Recognising that Jaspar wanted to protect Sabirah from the consequences of her escapade hurt Freddy and hardened her attitude. Surely the servants must have talked about the brunette's behaviour? How else had Hasna known that her father's widow had come to the Anhara that day to wait for Jaspar? So how dared Jaspar tell her that she shouldn't even mention that episode? Had theirs been a normal marriage from the outset, he would have had to give her a much more extensive explanation at the time.

'I would still like to know what you're arguing with me about,' Jaspar stated about fifteen minutes of unbroken silence later.

'You don't *want* to know.' And Freddy said not one more word during that drive.

Ben, who had spent the morning with his grandfather at the royal palace, was waiting in the hall to greet them, eager to show off his new drum set. He never returned without a gift and was generally overtired, overexcited and stuffed far too full of sweets as well. But Freddy had had to rethink her assumption that King Zafir's interest in his grandson might only be a whim for the older man spent time with Ben every week. Yet King Zafir had made no effort whatsoever to meet his son's new wife, Freddy reflected uneasily, wounded by that obvious and deliberate oversight.

As Ben ran to Jaspar, Jaspar swept him up and asked him in slow, distinct Arabic if he had had a good time. His nephew responded quite naturally in the same language and Freddy was unable to follow every word for she was learning at the slower rate of an adult. Although she had asked the staff to correct her mistakes, Jaspar had explained to her that all Quamaris would regard such an act as discourteous and that only a teacher would be relaxed in such a role with her, so Basmun had since been looking out for someone to instruct her in Arabic.

'I have a meeting. I must change,' Jaspar murmured.

Retrieving Ben, Freddy went off with Basmun to see how the work on the design for the new kitchens was coming on. She had learned a lot about historic buildings over the past month, not least that the Anhara might be their home and in the private ownership of the royal family but that Jaspar believed that no major changes should be considered without full consultation with the Department of National Monuments. Freddy had soon grasped that the best solution was simply to create new kitchens in some less historic part of the Anhara.

She checked over the plans with the architect and made an adjustment or two on Basmun's shyly proffered advice. By then it was lunchtime, but Ben was not hungry and moreover he was ready for a nap, so Freddy took him upstairs to his nanny. She was a lovely young woman with a bubbly sense of humour and not quite as given to spoiling Ben as the maids were. Ben cried for his teddy bear which was missing from his cot and Freddy realised that it must have been left in the gardens first thing that morning when she had seen Ben off on his visit to his grandfather.

'I'll get it. I know where it is,' Freddy assured the younger woman.

As she walked below the beautiful trees outside, sheltering from the heat of the sun, she thought over the silly argument she had had with Jaspar. It *had* been silly for she would have been disgusted had Jaspar been the sort of male who wanted the world to know that a woman had given him the kind of invitation that Sabirah had. And, furthermore, hadn't she herself been rather lacking in compassion over that whole episode? Wasn't it possible that, while grieving for her husband and feeling lonely and isolated within a family that did not seem to like her very much, Sabirah had done something crazy that she had just as swiftly regretted?

Having retrieved the missing teddy, Freddy had reached the junction of two paths when she saw an elderly white-bearded man standing below the trees. Clad in the sombre traditional dark blue robes worn by the desert herdsmen, he was leaning heavily on a stick and struggling with some difficulty to catch his breath in the hot, still air. He looked as if he was about to collapse and as she hurried towards him she noticed his lined features were grey and damp with perspiration.

'Come and sit down,' Freddy indicated the bench nearby and she cupped his elbow to demonstrate her meaning with action for she had little hope that he would understand English.

Taken aback, the older man protested in Arabic, which only increased his breathing difficulties. 'Please don't get upset,' Freddy begged. 'I'm only trying to help. You're not well and you really must rest. Did you walk all the way up the steps from the entrance gates? Those steps are very steep. I can hardly manage them myself.'

Freddy pressed him with determined hands down onto the seat. 'Breathe slowly,' she urged anxiously. 'I'm going to run indoors and fetch you a nice cold drink. Now, don't you dare move an inch or I'll be very cross with you.'

He gave her a shaken look from beneath his beetling white brows. His mouth opened.

'No, don't try to speak. Just rest until I come back.' Freddy sped back indoors. Finding Basmun hovering in the foyer, she told him that a doctor might be required because an elderly man had taken ill in the gardens. She then poured a glass of water from the cooler kept in a side porch for the benefit of thirsty staff and visitors and hurried back outside again.

On her breathless return, she was relieved to find the old man still seated where she had left him. With his hair and his beard and his quaint air of stately calm, he might have walked right out of the pages of the Bible. He accepted the glass of water and drank with appreciation before saying, 'Thank you. You are kind.'

'You look better,' Freddy remarked before it dawned on her that he had responded in her own language, and then she smiled in relief. 'I'm glad you speak English. I'm afraid I still only have a few words of Arabic, and when I first saw you I forgot every one of them! Are you here alone?'

'My...' he hesitated '...companions await me at the gates.'

'I think you should see a doctor.' Feeling very hot and bothered on her own account, Freddy waved a cooling hand in front of her face.

'I have seen too many doctors,' he complained, his fiercely intelligent dark eyes revealing his frustration. 'I am tired of being told to rest.'

'But resting is part of the healing process and you really ought to do as you're told. You mustn't neglect your health,' Freddy persisted gently.

'Are you in the habit of issuing orders to your visitors?'

'Only the stubborn ones.' But her usual bright smile was

weak for she was beginning to appreciate that she was not feeling at all well herself. 'I'm sorry…' she began, rising upright on legs that felt like wobbly sticks, her head swimming with sick dizziness, and a split second later she did something that she had never done before: she fainted.

CHAPTER NINE

FREDDY surfaced feeling woozy. She was lying on the bed in the air-conditioned cool of their room and Jaspar was staring down at her, his lean, dark features taut with concern.

He gripped her hand. 'My father's personal physician, Dr Kasim, is waiting outside to see you.'

'But I don't need to see a doctor,' Freddy muttered in embarrassment. 'I was silly. I went running about in that awful heat—'

'Fetching drinks of water for an obstinate man, who should have known better,' Jaspar interposed with a distinct lack of charity. 'My father is as anxious as I am to be assured that you have received a proper medical examination. You may have picked up a fever.'

While Freddy was striving dizzily to work out what possible connection King Zafir could have to the drink of water she had delivered to the old man in the gardens, Jaspar was already opening the door to another even more elderly gentleman with a clipped goatee beard. Jaspar looked inclined to hover, but Freddy raised a suggestive brow and he took the hint and left the room. She could see that he was really worried about her and she was touched, but she was mortified by the fuss that was being made.

Dr Kasim was the last word in tact. After answering his stream of questions and submitting to a minor examination, Freddy watched him write out his notes with punctilious care. He was so ancient, so stooped with venerable age, that she believed that she could hear his finger bones creaking.

'There's nothing wrong with me…is there?' she prompted.

'No, nothing wrong.' He looked up with a reassuring smile. 'You are in the early stages of pregnancy. I'm honoured to make that diagnosis and to be the first to give you that news.'

Freddy's soft lips parted and then slowly closed again. She was going to have a baby? Yes, that possibility had crossed her mind, but not in any serious way, more in a daydreaming fashion of what might be at some time in the future. Yet already their child had stolen a march on her expectations and taken life inside her. A wondering smile curved her mouth.

Dr Kasim cleared his throat. 'When you have engaged a gynaecologist, he will naturally advise you, but as you are at present my patient I would urge you to be very careful. Avoid exercise and anything which tires you. Drink only bottled water, eat only fresh food. Avoid spices and late nights and rest morning and afternoon…'

As his flood of instructions continued on beyond that point and included a pointed suggestion that all activity in the marital bed ought to cease forthwith as well, Freddy surveyed the wizened little doctor in growing disbelief. She was a healthy lump who rarely even caught a cold and he was talking to her as if she were a frail little flower. She found herself hoping that his strictures would ultimately prove to be several decades out of date.

'You cannot be too cautious when you carry a potential heir to the throne,' Dr Kasim informed her with great gravity. 'But as I am sure you wish to be discreet about that fact at present, be assured of my confidentiality.'

The joy of conception was a little dimmed for Freddy by the prospect of the sexless, spiceless eight months of early nights ahead of her, but she scolded herself for doubting the doctor's advice. After all, she thought mournfully,

Erica had not had an easy pregnancy. Her cousin had suffered from constant nausea. Freddy suppressed that unwelcome recollection and chose to concentrate instead on more uplifting images of an adorable little baby boy or girl with Jaspar's hair and Jaspar's wonderful smile…

He would be really pleased when she told him, yet she found herself reluctant to immediately share the news of her pregnancy. She would see a gynaecologist before she risked telling Jaspar that she was to be an untouchable couch potato for the foreseeable future. She was sure he would adhere to all such advice for Dr Kasim's sober words had impressed on her that the tiny being inside her womb could well end up being a king some day. But the more she considered the doctor's strictures, the more she wondered fearfully if he had noticed something during his examination that had suggested that she might be at risk of a miscarriage.

Yet here she and Jaspar were in the virtual honeymoon phase of their marriage and suddenly all that free and easy self-indulgence would have to stop… There would be no more nude bathing in the hills, no more wildly exciting encounters in the bed or the shower or on picnic rugs. Yes, she wanted their baby, but she was very much afraid that such severe limitations would damage their relationship.

'Why are you crying?' Jaspar's dark drawl startled her out of her frantic ruminations. He came down on the side of the bed and lifted her into his arms. 'Dr Kasim says you're fine…'

'Yes…' Freddy said in a wobbly voice, burying her damp, discomfited face in his shoulder, drinking in the familiar soothing scent of him and loving the feel of his arms around her. 'What age is he?'

'Must be eighty if he's a day, but my father has a great regard for him. A couple of younger doctors do make up his team. I thought you'd prefer an older man, *ma belle*,'

Jaspar murmured gently, smoothing the curly hair tumbling down her taut spine. 'Was I wrong?'

'He was very nice,' she conceded.

'You should be smiling. With a simple glass of water you have won my father's approbation. He is downstairs quoting the story of the Good Samaritan to the entire staff. I understand that you bullied him into sitting down and scolded him,' Jaspar drawled in a slightly charged undertone.

Freddy emerged from the cover she had taken against his shoulder, aquamarine eyes shattered. 'Are you telling me that that elderly man outside was your father...the *King*?'

'He doesn't like helicopters and he was driven here. At the gates, he told his attendants that he would manage the steps up through the gardens without assistance and of course they dared not disobey him. I gather that he was in some distress when you spotted him—'

'Yes...' Freddy was aghast at the familiar way in which she had behaved towards his royal parent. 'Jaspar, I had no idea! He was dressed just like one of the tribesmen, like a shepherd—'

'He would soon tell you that he does not consider himself in any way superior to the most humble of his subjects.' Jaspar's dark golden eyes were brimming with vibrant amusement. 'He is so accustomed to being recognised that it didn't occur to him that such a misapprehension might arise.'

'My goodness, what a dreadful impression I must have made on him!' Freddy groaned in despair.

'Far from it. He was *very* impressed. Instead of calling for the servants, you took personal care of him and put yourself out on his behalf. He said you were a plain-speaking and charitable young woman and full of good sense. From him that is the highest of accolades. That you also look like a live angel may have helped him to swallow his loss of dignity.'

Colouring at that reference to angels, Freddy shook her blonde head for she was still in shock. 'I'm so grateful that I didn't offend him. But you don't expect to find a king wandering about all on his own in a garden and dressed just like he was anybody!'

Jaspar burst out laughing. 'I'll warn him to wear his crown on his next visit!'

'Stop it…' Freddy said, hot-cheeked with chagrin.

'My father has a great fondness for the Anhara because he once lived here with my mother. As you know she died when I was eighteen, but he misses her almost as much now as he did then. I suspect that he dismissed his attendants today because he wished to spend a few moments of private reflection in the gardens.'

'He must've loved her a great deal.'

'She was French on her mother's side and always spoke French in preference to Arabic. They were very well matched. She had a very definite personality.' Jaspar paused and gave her strained face a concerned appraisal. 'I *should* have taken you to meet my father weeks ago. But his moods have been so uncertain of late that I was afraid—'

'You were afraid that I might offend him.' Her throat closed over.

'I underestimated *both* of you and for that I owe you an apology. Do you think you will be feeling well enough to join us for dinner?'

Freddy gave him a valiant nod of confirmation for she was actually fighting to conceal the fact that she was on the brink of tears. She knew that she was in an over-sensitive mood and that her emotions were swimming about far too close to the surface, but she could not prevent herself from reading deeper meanings into what he had said:

they were *not* well matched as his parents had been. He had backed off from the challenge of letting her even meet his father…he had been ashamed of her.

And why shouldn't he be? Wasn't it time she faced up to a painful fact or two? Jaspar *should* have married a princess, an aristocrat or at the very least a well-born Quamari woman, who would have instinctively known how to behave in all sorts of situations. Freddy was painfully convinced that, but for King Zafir whimsically deciding to be impressed rather than insulted by her attitude towards him, she might have offended the older man for life and caused Jaspar great embarrassment and discomfiture.

Jaspar caught her coiled fingers in his and slowly unlaced them. 'I'm grateful that my father had the opportunity to meet you as your natural self.'

Her natural self? Outspoken, thoughtless, bossily barging in where angels feared to tread, Freddy translated, in no mood to be comforted by such words of support. She was a walking disaster and she had better hope that if their baby was a boy he took after Jaspar rather than her. 'We're together for ever, aren't we?' she muttered tightly.

Jaspar settled her carefully back against the pillows and stared down at her with a questioning intensity that she could feel, his stunning eyes narrowed. He looked distinctly pale at the prospect.

'Stuck together like salt and pepper…Ben and sex the only glue,' she framed chokily and stuffed her face in the pillows.

'That's *not* how I feel.' Jaspar swore in a raw undertone to her rigidly turned back. 'Don't talk like that. What's wrong? Did Dr Kasim upset you in some way?'

Silence answered him.

'I'm sorry I was sarcastic earlier,' Jaspar breathed abruptly, rather like a male mentally fingering through all potential sins.

'Why shouldn't you have been?'

'I hurt your feelings, *ma belle*.'

Now who was being tactless? Freddy's body language took on an even closer resemblance to a graven image carved in solid stone.

'Yet you only asked a harmless question,' Jaspar conceded flatly. 'But I'm willing to talk about Sabirah if you want. If I was uncomfortable before, it was only because I have never discussed that period of my life with anybody.'

The original man of steel and he was ready to tell all. But was she strong enough to hear the story of how much he had adored Sabirah without succumbing to an attack of low self-esteem that could take her a lifetime to recover from? It would make her feel insecure, encourage her to indulge in pointless comparisons between herself and the love of his life. *He* was the love of *her* life and dwelling on the past and what could not be changed was unhealthy and immature.

'I don't want to know about her...not *anything*,' Freddy told him with gloom-laden emphasis.

Silence lay again for several seconds while he attempted to comprehend her sudden change of heart.

'But—'

'I don't care in the slightest,' Freddy added thinly. 'Listening to blokes moaning about how they would never love again used to be one of the most tedious aspects of being single. I really don't think I ought to encourage you along the same path—'

'Freddy...' Jaspar growled, settling his hands to her waist to turn her over to face him again.

'Just you keep your inner feelings and thoughts to yourself. A stiff upper lip, we call it in England,' Freddy informed him with dogged conviction. 'Much the best attitude. Take your regrets to the grave with you, don't share them with me.'

Shimmering dark golden eyes clashed with hers. 'Message received.'

It was extraordinary. The minute she removed the pressure for him to talk about what he had most definitely not wanted to talk about, he behaved as if he had been rudely denied a welcome opportunity. He was furious with her volte-face. But Freddy was really grateful that she had seen the error of her ways. If Jaspar got talking about Sabirah, he would be *thinking* of the beautiful brunette and reliving the powerful emotions of the past. Did she really want to encourage such dangerous recollections? No, she did not indeed. Particularly not when it came to a female ready to strip off to capture him.

'But that won't prevent me from questioning you about every boyfriend you have ever had,' Jaspar announced, smooth as silk, rising up to his full height.

'The first one took me out because Erica bribed him to do it and the second one dumped me for her. After that, I was more cautious. There were a couple of brief entanglements. There was the guy who burst out crying over dinner talking about his ex-wife...' Freddy recalled, beyond all embarrassment. 'There was the one who brought his ex-girlfriend to visit so that she could explain that his talking to *me* about his feelings for *her* had helped them to get back together again—'

Jaspar was nailed to the spot, fascination stamped in his darkly handsome features. 'You're not serious, *ma belle*.'

'The virtually empty pages of my past experience with men contain few funny punchlines,' Freddy informed him flatly. 'They all without exception told me I was a very nice person but either they bored me to death or they were forever talking about the woman they really wanted who *didn't* want them.'

'That is not the case with us—'

'You had no choice, Jaspar. I blackmailed you into marrying me.'

'I can't say that there haven't been compensations.' Jaspar shot her a gleaming look of pure erotic recollection, his beautiful mouth curving into a wicked smile.

Her heart jumped up and down behind her breastbone and the little flame that never quite went out in his radius surged but, although she reddened, she looked stonily back at him.

'I think I should bale out of this conversation before I crash and burn beyond recovery,' Jaspar murmured drily.

The door closed behind him. Her mouth trembled but she buttoned it flat again. Had she mentioned the baby, how different things might have been, but once again she would have known that something other than her own self was keeping him with her. Not just Ben any more, but their own child as well. She loved Jaspar more than she had known she could ever love anybody, but she could not bear the idea that, in spite of all his caring gestures, she was so very much less than he had wanted in a wife. Even so, she knew that she would have to come to terms with the hurt to her pride and learn to appreciate what she did have.

An early dinner staged with King Zafir at the head of the imposing dining table and his entire entourage encamped on their knees in the hall beyond was something of a strain. He shot a string of questions at her without hesitation, established that she had a good working knowledge of the Bible and commented freely on her less detailed answers. In an effort to shield her, Jaspar stepped in once or twice, only to be told that he ought not to get into the habit of being a domineering husband who imagined his wife could not speak up for herself. A short and pithy lecture on the most important aspects of a successful marriage followed and Freddy marvelled at Jaspar's ability to sit through it with a straight face.

She was able to relax more and observe when the dialogue between father and son moved to more official matters, and she decided then that the older man was not quite as advanced in years as she had thought and was probably only in his late sixties. He was a strong character, not the type to suffer fools or indeed ill health with patience, but, in spite of his crusty and critical nature, he seemed to have an essentially kind heart. However, just listening, she was discovering where Jaspar had learned his rock-solid self-discipline: it had been forged in the fire of personal experience.

At the end of the meal, she read Jaspar's almost imperceptible signal that she ought to leave them alone and she wandered across the hall into the library, which had a large selection of English books, and sat down to read. Only forty minutes later, Jaspar appeared in the doorway, tall and dark and breathtakingly handsome in his tailored suit.

'I'm sorry I was in such a natty mood earlier,' she said straight off. 'Has your father left?'

'Yes. He was tired. I was proud of you,' he murmured levelly. 'You didn't allow him to intimidate you. He means well but his manner can be...'

'Abrasive?' she slotted in with her ready smile.

'Yes.' Stunning dark golden eyes rested on her, his lean, strong face rather taut. 'A month ago you asked me to make enquiries on your behalf and I did so. This afternoon, I received a report on your background that clarifies the matters which had concerned you.'

Freddy's eyes had widened and then she moved forward with eagerness. 'Oh, let me see it.'

'I took the liberty of reading it and I should warn you that it contains information which will upset you,' Jaspar advanced with measured care.

Freddy stilled in bewilderment. Upset her? Jaspar settled a folded document down on the coffee-table. Freddy stared at it and then in a sudden movement she stooped and snatched it up, shaking it open with visible impatience. Within the space of a minute, however, she was fumbling her way dizzily down onto the sofa behind her while she read and re-read only the first couple of sentences.

'This can't be true…this says that my mother died only ten years ago,' Freddy whispered incredulously.

'There is no question of a mistake this time. A copy of your mother's death certificate came with the report,' Jaspar informed her ruefully. 'But I don't understand *how* your late father found it possible to maintain the fiction that she had died when you were a baby.'

'He hated talking about her, but I put that down to his grief over her death, so I felt guilty when I asked him questions,' Freddy said unevenly. 'I'm so shocked that he lied to me…but it wasn't really that difficult for him to fool me—'

'How wasn't it difficult?' Jaspar prompted.

'He changed jobs and moved to the other end of the country soon after her supposed death. He said Mum had had no relatives left alive. In all my life, I never met anyone who had known her. When I asked for photographs and things like that…' her voice quivered '…Dad said the box containing the albums had gone missing during the house move. Ruth suspected that he'd been so devastated by my mother's death that he had burnt everything in a fit of grief.'

'He was a middle-aged bachelor when he met and married your mother and she was a good deal younger. Such inequal marriages often run into trouble.'

Freddy was reading the report but already foreseeing what was coming next. It *had* been her mother who had run off with another man. Yet she could hardly concentrate. Her mind was stuck on the awful realisation that her mother had not only abandoned her as a baby, but had also failed to make any attempt to regain contact with her daughter in all the years that had followed.

'She could never have loved me…she must have been like Erica…detached…' Freddy's strained voice petered out entirely as she absorbed the next section of the report. Indeed, so great was her disbelief, a strangled gasp escaped her. Her mother had given birth to twin girls shortly before she had left her father!

'I have sisters…that's not possible!' Freddy exclaimed vehemently.

Jaspar removed the document she was crushing between her fingers and came down beside her, enclosing a supportive arm to her rigid spine. 'Your father was convinced that the little girls were not his and when your mother took off with her latest lover he refused to accept responsibility for them. The babies were still in hospital at the time and the authorities took charge of them.'

'My s-sisters…' Freddy mumbled shakily. 'I have sisters and I never knew. How could Dad keep that from me?'

'Enquiries are still being made, but it won't be a simple matter to trace your sisters if they were adopted, as such very young children most likely were.' Jaspar expelled his breath in a rueful hiss.

'Mum deserted all of us. Cuckoos do that,' Freddy muttered with a shaken little laugh of acknowledgement. 'They leave their eggs in other bird's nests so that they don't have to be bothered with the work of raising them. Dad would have felt so humiliated. No wonder he moved hundreds of miles away afterwards. He would've hated people knowing the truth.'

'It's clear that your mother was a rather unstable personality—'

'You mean she had mental problems?' Freddy snatched up the report again and scanned the remaining information. 'There's no need to take refuge in euphemisms, Jaspar. She liked men a lot, by the looks of it, and there's nothing at all here about how she lived for the last twelve years of her life—'

'The enquiries are continuing. The agent believes that she may have changed her name or remarried at some stage, but by the time of her death she was living alone.'

'I suppose that's how you end up when you keep on abandoning other people.' Her face pale and stiff, Freddy tossed the report aside as if it meant nothing to her and stood up. 'I'm tired. Thank you for getting that information for me.'

'Freddy…don't be too hard on your father for keeping you in the dark. He probably believed that he was protecting you,' Jaspar murmured.

Freddy compressed her lips. 'Maybe.'

'Don't beat yourself up about this, *ma belle*.' He tugged her into the circle of his arms. 'What bearing does your background really have on your life now?'

Freddy looked up at him with helpless hostility. Jaspar with his six hundred years of ancestral history and the solid family tree that the whole al-Husayn family revered. There was no chance that he would ever suffer the sense of deep humiliation and betrayal that she was attempting to conceal from him.

'I appreciate that you think it's easy for me to make such a statement,' Jaspar persisted, his fabulous cheekbones scored with faint colour. 'But you are who you are.'

As unloved by her mother as her poor sisters had been from birth. And the father she had trusted had thought too much of his own pride to tell her the truth. She turned her head away, swallowing hard.

'We'll find your sisters. It may take a while but it *can* be done,' Jaspar asserted.

'Yeah…' Freddy nodded jerkily and broke away from

him before the tears thickening her throat got the upper hand.

Upstairs, she locked herself in the bathroom, ran a bath and had a good cry while the water was running. She was reeling in shock from what she had learned and it was little wonder that she felt gutted for she had had a very idealised image of her mother. Now that innocent image had been smashed for all time.

She pretended to be asleep when Jaspar came to bed.

'I'll be leaving tomorrow for three days. I have to attend a meeting in Dubai in my father's stead,' Jaspar announced as he undressed in the darkness, evidently unimpressed by her efforts to fake slumber. 'I wish you could have accompanied me but the last thing you need right now is the stress of making polite chit-chat to complete strangers—'

'And then you doubt I could even manage that,' Freddy put in thinly.

'If you can cope with my father, you are more than equal to any challenge.'

'Tell me…are you always this relentlessly charming in the face of adversity?'

'I know you're hurting right now and that there is really nothing I can do to alter that. I was tempted to destroy that report and tell you that the agent had come up with nothing of a new or mysterious nature…but you had the right to know the truth and I honour my promises.'

'I married a saint.'

The mattress gave with his weight and almost simultaneously he reached for her. He stole the breath from her body with a hungry kiss. 'Stop trying to fight with me.'

He was strong and warm against her, the heat of his lean, muscular frame defrosting the lonely chill inside her heart. And when he kissed her, her rebellious body came alive with feeling and longing and love. She could have bitten out her tongue for being so ungracious and unpleasant to him. Why she should continually attack him when he had shown her only understanding she had no idea, but she was ashamed. She shifted into him, adoring the scent and the touch of him.

'I get irritated with you being so perfect all the time,' she muttered in a small voice.

Jaspar laughed huskily. 'I'm far from perfect and you know it—'

'You're a darned sight more perfect than I am...' He was extracting her from the nightdress she had donned as something of a statement with the kind of smooth expertise that took her breath away. 'I mean, when and where did you learn to do this, for a start?'

'No comment. Sometimes you ask the craziest questions, *ma belle*,' Jaspar muttered thickly, running an explorative hand over the swell of her full breasts, lingering to tease at a straining peak and provoking a low moan from deep in her throat.

Her back arched, a dulled ache throbbing between her thighs, and she was instantly, wantonly and irretrievably on fire for him. All the stress she had endured seemed to find a vent in that fierce surge of desire. But a moment later she recalled the doctor's advice and, dismayed that she could have so easily forgotten that warning, she jerked back from Jaspar as if she had been burnt.

'No...we can't...'

Jaspar uttered a short succinct word that she had never heard before, but she needed no translation to know that it was a curse word.

'Jaspar...'

'I've had enough,' Jaspar breathed with thunderous quietness, and he tossed back the sheet and got out of bed again.

In the moonlight, he was a lithe silvered shadow. Aghast

at his departure, Freddy sat up and exclaimed, 'I'm sorry, I—'

'Forget it,' he said with dark satire as he pulled on a pair of jeans.

'Where are you going?'

'Freddy—'

'Can I come too?'

'That would rather defeat the point, wouldn't it?'

'I just don't want you to go,' she admitted chokily.

'Give me a break. One minute you're pushing me away as if I'm assaulting you, and the next you're begging me to stay?'

'*Please…*'

The silence buzzed with his fierce reluctance; she could feel it.

'Sorry…' Jaspar opened the door. 'I just want a good night's sleep.'

'It wasn't that I didn't want you,' she began in a rush. 'It's just that I'm…I'm pregnant!'

But the door closed with a thud at the exact same time as she spoke and there was no way he could have heard her. For a whole hour afterwards, she hated herself. Of course, he didn't understand why she had reacted like that, but she had inflicted too many of her see-sawing emotions on him and he had reached saturation point. She got out of bed, retrieved her nightdress and went off to look for him. He was fast asleep in a bedroom two doors down from their own, no sheet over him, no air-conditioning on, not even the curtains closed.

From the foot of the bed she surveyed him and tears made her eyes feel all hot and prickly. She had never really understood how vulnerable love would make her until she looked at Jaspar asleep and her heart just threatened to break inside her because she was terrified of losing what they had. Crowding him, she decided ruefully, was not a good idea. With a last lingering look at the bold profile etched against the pale linen and the long elegant sweep of his brown back, she tiptoed back out again.

She rose early the next morning to have breakfast with him before he left and found Ben, beaming and still in his pyjamas, keeping Jaspar company. Sheathed in a charcoal-grey business suit of exquisite cut, he looked breathtakingly handsome.

'If it's any consolation,' Jaspar confided with his charismatic smile, 'I had a lousy night's sleep.'

'I didn't do so well myself,' Freddy confided, heart singing that the awkwardness of the night before was behind them.

In the shelter of the outside porch, he drew her close to his lean, powerful body, stunning dark golden eyes intent on her, and claimed her mouth in a slow, searching kiss that left her every skincell humming.

'To be continued,' he murmured with husky sensuality.

Two days later, Freddy emerged smiling from her appointment with a consultant gynaecologist. She had been told that she was in excellent health and all her fears had been set to rest. Dr Kasim's strictures had indeed been judged rather too stringent. Her bodyguards awaited her on the ground floor of the ultra-modern hospital and as soon as the lift doors opened they moved forward, looking relieved by her reappearance. She suspected that Jaspar had instructed them to stick to her like superglue but, appreciating the amount of attention their presence would attract, she had asked them to stay downstairs. In about twelve hours, she thought happily, Jaspar would be with her again and she could hardly wait to tell him about their baby.

The limousine travelled through the wide tree-lined streets of the city and on to the royal palace. Jaspar had informed her that they had a large apartment within the massive palace complex and she was keen to see it. The palace was a sprawling weathered sandstone collection of buildings, the earliest of which dated back to the thirteenth century. As her visit had been prearranged, she was greeted at the main door by a little man who introduced himself as Rashad and who bowed so low to her that she was afraid that he might topple over.

It was soon evident that Rashad was acting on her father-in-law, King Zafir's instructions and that merely showing her the way to Jaspar's apartment was the least of them. Rashad had been asked to give her an official tour of the palace and instruct her on the history of the al-Husayn family. He was a very nice man, but after two solid hours of trekking up and down stairs, along endless corridors and through innumerable courtyards, Freddy began to feel rather tired. Catching a glimpse of her own wan face in a mirror, she suggested to her companion that perhaps they could continue the tour another day.

Rashad delivered her to the sunlit outer courtyard of what Jaspar had airily described as an apartment. Sheltering behind a glorious fountain and a very beautiful casuarina tree lay what Freddy would have described as a most substantial house. She smiled at the fabulous arrangement of yellow roses in the spacious hall, relished the air-conditioned cool and was taken aback when she was informed that a visitor already awaited her.

'A visitor?' she questioned, her heart sinking, for there was nothing she wanted more than to kick off her shoes, sit down and enjoy a relaxing cup of tea.

The senior manservant lowered his gaze. 'Princess Sabirah has been waiting for some time.'

Freddy tensed. Well, she supposed that, whether she liked it or not, the meeting was overdue. In recent weeks, she had received visits from Adil's eldest daughter, Medina, as well as Hasna's English mother, Genette, and her younger sisters. Each and every one of them had been charming and she had got on like a house on fire with Genette, who was very good-natured and friendly. Perhaps she herself had been remiss in not extending a polite invitation to Sabirah, she thought ruefully, for that ghastly embarrassing scene in which they had initially met at the Anhara *had* to be got over and sensibly forgotten: Sabirah was a member of Jaspar's family and could not be ignored.

In the sunlit drawing-room, which was furnished with mellow antiques, Sabirah rose to greet her and for a moment Freddy could do nothing but stare for Sabirah was *so* beautiful, far more stunning than Freddy had allowed herself to recall. The brunette had the perfection of an exquisite china doll and her fitted blue designer suit was a superb frame for her slender, elegant figure.

Instantly Freddy felt *huge* in comparison and she said awkwardly, 'I'm sorry I wasn't here when you arrived.'

'I'm relieved that you're willing to speak to me after the unfortunate way in which we first learnt of each other's existence.' Sabirah's smooth and unembarrassed reference to her own bold presence in Jaspar's bedroom on the same day that Freddy had married Jaspar increased rather than defused Freddy's tension. 'I'm willing to surrender my pride for Jaspar's sake.'

Freddy frowned. 'I beg your pardon?'

Exotic slanted dark eyes rested on her. 'I've come here to ask you to set Jaspar free.'

Freddy stared at the gorgeous brunette, her natural colour ebbing, her heart rate speeding up. 'That's…that's quite a major demand.'

'Jaspar loves me and I love him.' Sabirah spoke with daunting confidence. 'Perhaps that doesn't matter to you. Perhaps you don't care that he will never be happy with you. But Jaspar doesn't deserve to lose his one chance of happiness just because Adil fathered an illegitimate child.'

Freddy tensed even more. So Sabirah knew about Ben.

'You have no need to look dismayed. I don't resent the child. Why should I? I didn't love my husband,' Sabirah told her without hesitation. 'I only want to talk about Jaspar—'

'But I don't *want* to discuss Jaspar,' Freddy cut in tautly.

Sabirah's lustrous dark eyes hardened. 'I'm only asking you to *listen*.'

'Maybe I don't want to listen either,' Freddy could sit still no longer. Getting up, she walked across to the window and then looked back with pronounced reluctance at her unwelcome visitor, wondering if she could just ask her to leave. Part of her wanted to listen but the other part of her was more afraid of what she might hear.

'Jaspar and I fell in love almost six years ago,' Sabirah proclaimed. 'But we were discreet about our feelings for neither of us was in a hurry to marry.'

So Jaspar had never actually got as far as proposing to the brunette, Freddy interpreted from that statement. Strengthened by that suspicion, she said quietly, 'I'm not trying to rain on your parade but all this happened an awfully long time ago.'

Sabirah ignored that comment and Freddy flushed.

'As soon as Adil decided that *he* was in love with me, Jaspar and I were forced apart,' Sabirah stated emotively. 'My family put enormous pressure on me to accept Adil's proposal. As far as they were concerned it was a great honour and one day I would become queen of Quamar.'

As that scenario was exactly what Freddy had once imagined, she was dismayed for she did not want to think of Jaspar and Sabirah as star-crossed lovers, separated through no fault of their own.

'Only imagine my feelings when I later discovered that not only was my husband an appalling womaniser but also that he had *never* been destined to become king!' Sabirah acknowledged Freddy's look of surprise at that news with a grim little smile. 'During our honeymoon, Adil admitted that his father had informed him when Jaspar was only fifteen that Jaspar would succeed to the throne.'

'But Adil was Crown Prince,' Freddy muttered in disconcertion.

'His title was merely a convenient screen to allow Jaspar to grow up with greater freedom. Adil was content with the pretence,' Sabirah asserted with a shrug. 'He accepted that Jaspar had many fine qualities that he himself didn't have and he was not an ambitious man.'

Of course, it made much greater sense that Jaspar should all along have been the son intended for the throne, Freddy conceded inwardly. Adil with his three marriages and his taste for party girls would not have been a wise choice of ruler for a conservative country and her father-in-law was not a foolish man.

Sabirah leant forward in a confiding way. 'That's what I'm trying to explain to you. Jaspar will never be selfish. Jaspar will always put family loyalty before his own personal feelings.'

Freddy could not argue with that assessment and her heart sank right down to her toes for she knew exactly what Sabirah was building up to telling her.

'But don't you think that Jaspar deserves to be happy?' Sabirah demanded pointedly.

'Yes, of course I do, *but*—'

'Do you realise that Jaspar has not spoken one private word to me since the day I agreed to marry his brother? That's how loyal he was to his brother even though he loved me himself! I went to the Anhara that day in an effort to force him to declare his feelings for me—'

'Jaspar doesn't respond very well to force,' Freddy slotted in tightly, her tummy churning. If there was a word of truth in Sabirah's passionate argument, it meant that she herself was hanging onto a marriage that was doomed, for with Sabirah on the sidelines how could her own relationship with Jaspar ever grow? He would always be thinking back to what might have been and eventually bitterness would set in.

'Jaspar adores me but he is too conscious of his position to ask you for a divorce. But if *you* were to leave *him*, he would be granted a divorce and he would then be free to marry me without attracting criticism.'

'I wouldn't marry you if you were the last woman left alive in Quamar,' Jaspar imparted with stinging derision from the doorway, startling both Sabirah and Freddy to such an extent that they spun round to gape at him.

Sabirah went rigid. 'Of course you will say that in your wife's presence, for you don't want to hurt her, but—'

'Do you realise how long I've been standing outside this room listening?' Jaspar demanded, brilliant golden eyes shimmering, lean, dark face clenched hard as he studied the woman proclaiming herself to be the one and only love of his life. 'Let me tell you that I found the Romeo and Juliet slant to your colourful tale nauseous!'

While wondering what on earth Jaspar was doing back a full ten hours ahead of what he had assured her to be a most rigid schedule, Freddy had never been more relieved to hear so blunt a speech of rebuttal. Two high spots of red now burned over Sabirah's cheekbones. Aghast at Jaspar's inopportune appearance, Sabirah had been silenced. But what shook Freddy the most was her recognition of the icy rage barely leashed in Jaspar's lancing appraisal of the tiny brunette. Even the most disinterested observer would have realised that Jaspar had the utmost contempt for the other woman.

'Your own father *begged* you not to marry Adil. He thought the age gap between you was too great and, in despair at your determination to become a Crown Princess, your father finally told you that my brother would be an unfaithful husband.' Jaspar's evident inside knowledge of those facts made Sabirah shoot him a look of dismay. 'But your own ambition triumphed over all the warnings. How dare you try to destroy my marriage, which is as happy as your own was miserable?'

'How can you speak to me like this after what we were to each other?' Sabirah demanded shrilly, outraged pride stamped in her stunning face.

'I have long been grateful that Adil saved me from making the biggest mistake of my life. Now leave us,' Jaspar commanded. 'I suggest you enjoy a long vacation at your parents' country house—'

'I don't want to go home to my parents!' the brunette launched at him with unconcealed horror at the suggestion.

'It is my father's command and if you prefer to wait until he summons you to tell you *why* that is his wish, feel free to do so,' Jaspar advised silkily.

Sabirah paled to the colour of parchment and averted her eyes. She hurried out of the room without another word.

'I doubt if she will even stop to pack,' Jaspar murmured with grim satisfaction. 'She has only recently ended a rampant affair with a city businessman whose wife discovered them *in flagrante delicto*. Rumours are already circulating. Naturally she wishes to put a few thousand miles between herself and my father for he has lost all patience with her.'

'Sabirah's been having an affair?' Freddy exclaimed in sharp disconcertion. 'Even while she's been chasing after you?'

'Sabirah craves status and position above all else. How on earth she managed to convince herself that I would ever look at her with favour again, I have no idea.' Jaspar shook his dark head. 'She has a very much exaggerated concept of her own attraction.'

'She's incredibly beautiful...and you were awfully

shocked that day when you saw her on your bed. I'm sure that must have…er…upset you,' Freddy muttered tautly.

'Indeed it did. I was as embarrassed as a teenage boy. One doesn't want to see one's sister-in-law naked,' Jaspar countered with a grimace that was very eloquent. 'In my eyes, she will always be Adil's wife and I was appalled that she could be that shameless.'

'But you didn't want me gossiping about her. I assure you that I never breathed a word about that episode.'

'Freddy…I didn't want *anyone* gossiping,' Jaspar responded with an unexpected laugh. 'If any more wild rumours about Sabirah escape she will never attract a second husband. My whole family is praying that she will eventually remarry so that we will be free of her and what hope have we got if she destroys her reputation?'

Freddy surveyed him with bemused eyes. 'You don't feel anything at all for her…do you? I thought that she was supposed to be the love of your life.'

'She hurt my pride most. In my own way I was quite conceited five years ago,' Jaspar confided with deadly seriousness and a look of regret that squeezed her heart, for she suspected that her idea of conceit and his would not tally. 'Adil was twice her age and a very large man but she married him without hesitation.'

'But you loved her—'

'I *thought* I loved her but I now believe that it was more of a lust to possess than love. I didn't understand the difference then. I was humiliated by the discovery that she would sacrifice everything for ambition. I then had the very great advantage of seeing how she conducted herself as my brother's wife.' His strong jawline hardened. 'Watching her snub the family members whom she outranked and encourage malicious gossip for her own amusement killed any lingering regrets I had pretty fast.'

'Were you aware that your father *always* planned for you

to be his successor?' Freddy asked, yielding to her considerable curiosity on that point.

'I had not the faintest idea until he told me so last week. I marvel that Adil did not hate me for it,' Jaspar confessed. 'I finally understand why my brother made no effort to reform his lifestyle. I also believe that the disappointment of learning that she would never become queen twisted Sabirah into the hard, bitter woman that she has since become.'

Recognising his faint pity for the brunette, Freddy let go of her last fear that he still cherished Sabirah in some corner of his heart, and so intense was her relief that she felt a little dizzy and she sank down heavily onto a sofa.

Jaspar crossed the room so fast that he might have been a bullet fired from a gun. Crouching down by her side, he breathed in a driven undertone, 'We have wasted all this time talking about Sabirah but tell me now without further delay, what is the matter with you?'

Her brows pleated. She studied him, read the strain in his lean, darkly handsome features, the pallor stamped beneath his bronzed skin, the clear anxiety in his searching dark golden gaze. 'I don't know what you're talking about.'

'I know you were at the hospital this morning and that when your bodyguards saw you again you were very pale and serious,' Jaspar recounted tautly.

Freddy's frown increased. 'You've been spying on me!'

'I just *need* to know what's wrong with you. I cancelled my last meeting in Dubai and flew home. I've been worried sick. And then I arrived back and find that witch telling you a pack of nonsensical lies!' Jaspar groaned.

'I'm not ill. I can tell you that much.' Freddy veiled her dancing eyes but she was touched by the level of concern he was making no attempt to hide from her.

Jaspar studied her in bewilderment. 'If you weren't ill, why were you at the hospital?'

'I'm pregnant.'

'You're not ill?' Jaspar prompted like a record stuck in a groove.

'Well, if I'd listened to Dr Kasim I would probably be considering myself next door to being a bedridden invalid,' Freddy said cheerfully. 'But I saw a consultant gynaecologist today and he was very reassuring. He says I'm a healthy pregnant woman.'

'You're expecting a baby...*already*?' Jaspar studied her with wondering dark golden eyes. 'But we've only been married a few weeks. That possibility didn't even cross my mind. You're actually going to have a baby.'

'Yes, I believe we've established that fact.' Freddy was tickled pink by his shock and the sort of reverent light beginning to glow in his gaze as he began to finally absorb what he was being told.

Jaspar scooped her bodily off the sofa and sank down with her on his lap, both arms wrapped round her. 'You've known since Dr Kasim saw you at the Anhara? Why didn't you tell me?'

'I wanted a second opinion. He told me we oughtn't even to sleep together any more,' Freddy admitted in a rueful rush. 'That's why I said no that night—'

'You can say no whenever you like. I acted like a fool.' Jaspar swore, closing one lean hand tightly over hers. 'I was trying to comfort you and, of course, making love was the last thing you felt like. Unfortunately, I couldn't resist my own urge to express my feelings for you in a more physical way. I'm sure I seemed insensitive to you, but it was not meant in that way.'

Freddy was quite flabbergasted by that confessional speech.

'Until this moment this has been a dreadful day, *ma belle*,' Jaspar admitted with a ragged edge to his dark, deep drawl. 'First I received the news of your mysterious hospital visit—'

'I don't see why that should have bothered you so much—'

'Initially it didn't, but then fear started to build at the back of my mind and I could not concentrate no matter how hard I tried. I began to imagine that all sorts of things might be wrong with you and I had to be with you, I *had* to come home.'

Freddy toyed with his silk tie. 'Silly,' she said, while loving every word he had spoken for his description of his mounting anxiety touched her heart to its core.

'So forgive me if I have not yet shown my pleasure at the news of our child's conception,' Jaspar urged. 'I'm still in shock. Are you sure you're in good health?'

'I'm *very* healthy,' Freddy told him with gentle emphasis.

His arms tightened round her. He bowed his proud dark head over hers and pressed her close. 'I was sick with worry. Our baby…that is wonderful news, but the knowledge that you are well still feels like the best news of all.'

She smoothed her fingertips over one strong cheekbone. He turned his mouth into her hand and kissed her palm.

'Three months before my mother died, she went for a simple check-up at the hospital and learned that she was terminally ill. She did not tell us until her condition could no longer be concealed and by then she had little time left to share with us. We always regretted that she couldn't trust us to be strong for her…' Jaspar muttered rather thickly. 'I have had a most irrational fear of hospitals ever since.'

Tears stung Freddy's eyes. She hugged him close, loving him all the more for sharing that sad little story with her and finally understanding why her intelligent and usually very sensible husband had overreacted to such an extent to the discovery that she had kept an appointment at the hospital.

'I can have the baby at home,' she told him soothingly.

'But that might not be safe and above all your safety is what counts, *ma belle*,' Jaspar intoned huskily. 'You know, I love you very much…'

As he lifted his head and she tipped up hers, she collided with a look more open and more intense than any she had yet received from him, and her heart jumped and she ran out of breath.

'At first, it was lust of the lowest order,' Jaspar confessed a little shamefacedly. 'And then it became obsessional lust. I never wanted any woman as much as I wanted you, but I was initially so angry at being pushed into marrying you that I did not recognise my own feelings.'

'You don't need to apologise for that.' Joy was spreading through Freddy in a heady flood.

'Even when I didn't want to be drawn to you, I was. I was intrigued when you stood up to me and I began to appreciate that you *did* love Ben. But I wasn't as generous as I ought to have been about the extent of your love for my nephew,' Jaspar murmured gruffly. 'By then, I wanted you to want me for myself, not because I was your ticket to possessing Ben. Initially that made me feel bitter and used.'

Freddy was stricken by that admission. 'I never dreamt that you felt like that—'

'But I couldn't stop thinking about you the whole time I was in New York and then I came home to discover that you were sleeping in the nursery and it was like a red rag to a bull!' Jaspar loosed a reluctant laugh. 'Ben seemed to have much more pulling power with you than I had, *ma belle*.'

'No, you always had pulling power,' Freddy assured him

feverishly, wrapping both arms round him to emphasise the point. 'I just started—'

A loud knock on the door finally penetrated their cocoon of mutual absorption.

'What the hell?' Jaspar groaned, setting her down more sedately on the seat beside him.

It was Rashad who entered with much apologetic bowing. He spoke in Arabic and Jaspar instantly rose to his feet looking puzzled.

'Your friend, Ruth, has phoned several times. I believe she has some urgent news she wishes to share with you,' he explained as Rashad withdrew again. 'I'm sorry. If I hadn't instructed the staff that we were not to be disturbed her call would have been put straight through to you.'

Freddy was perplexed. 'I can't imagine what Ruth could possibly have to tell me that would qualify as urgent.'

'You had better call her immediately.'

Freddy got up to do so, anxiously wondering what was wrong, for Ruth was not the kind of woman likely to employ the word urgent without good reason. She had written twice to the other woman, rather awkward communications for she had not yet managed to bring herself to the point of admitting that her marriage to Jaspar had become a real marriage.

'Freddy?' Ruth sounded unusually excited. 'Is that you?'

'Yes, it's me—'

'I have fantastic news for you!' the older woman asserted with satisfaction. 'You have the right to take Ben and come back to London with him.'

'Come back to London with Ben?' Freddy echoed, wide-eyed.

'I searched your cousin's apartment from top to bottom and I finally found her will—'

'Erica really *did* write a will?' Freddy queried in some surprise.

'I would've found it a lot sooner had I not foolishly assumed that *you* had done a thorough search of her personal effects!' Ruth stated in frank reproof. 'Had you done so, you could have saved yourself all this grief. Erica left you *everything*!'

'Erica left me…what?'

'Everything she possessed as well as full legal guardianship of Ben. Have you nothing to say, Freddy?'

'I'm so shocked…' Meeting Jaspar's narrowed stare, Freddy pressed the phone to her shoulder and murmured shakily. 'Ruth's found Erica's will and my cousin left me everything including guardianship of Ben…'

Tears thickened Freddy's voice and then overflowed, dampening her cheeks. The knowledge that Erica had trusted her to that extent *and* had taken the trouble to have such a will drawn up had shaken her. Erica might not have taken to motherhood, but she had cared enough about her son to consider Ben's future in the event of anything happening to her.

'If I were you, I would just sneak back home with Ben the minute you get the chance,' Ruth suggested. 'Legally, the al-Husayn family can do nothing to prevent you from keeping him.'

Freddy's thoughts were straying as she watched Jaspar leave the room, his sculpted profile clenched and pale. 'I'm pregnant, Ruth—'

'Say that again—'

'I fell madly in love with Jaspar and we're having a baby,' Freddy extended in an apologetic tone. 'He's absolutely wonderful. I'm sorry I wasn't more honest in my letters…and when you've made such an effort on my behalf and found Erica's will, I feel awful.'

Freddy listened anxiously to the humming silence on the line.

'I presume I can now look forward to regular holidays in a royal palace?' Ruth enquired.

'Oh, yes. We'd love to have you!'

'I'll forgive you.' Ruth laughed, but she sounded shattered for all that.

Finishing the call with a promise of phoning back later, Freddy went off to look for Jaspar. Why on earth had he left the room? His seeming pallor must have been a trick of the light, she decided, for Jaspar must surely have guessed that she had been on the very brink of telling him that she loved him before Rashad had interrupted them.

Jaspar had not gone far. He was pacing up and down the hall like a prowling tiger, every movement betraying his high-voltage tension. As soon as he heard her steps, he swung round, lean, powerful face clenched taut, dark golden eyes filled with pain. 'The minute I saw your tears of relief, I realised what was coming next. Now that you have a legal right to Ben and adequate resources, you want me to let you go because I have nothing further to offer you...'

Comprehension sank in on Freddy then.

'I *can't* do it. I can't let you go,' Jaspar swore vehemently. 'I can't imagine my life without you and Ben. These last weeks we have shared have been very precious to me. What must I do to convince you that if you give me enough time I can make you happy here in Quamar?'

'Jaspar—'

But Jaspar was too wound up to be silenced. 'I know you've been making the best of things for Ben's sake—'

'That's not true—'

'The last few weeks, I didn't care...it was enough for me—'

'Jaspar, will you let me get a word in and will you calm down?' Freddy launched at him in frustration. 'I love you! I haven't the slightest intention of asking you to let me go.

As for me having made the best of things with you…well, in one sense that *is* true. You're the best thing that ever happened to me and I fancied you like mad the minute I laid eyes on you.'

'Keep talking…' Jaspar encouraged, giving every impression of a male locked into her every word as he moved forward.

'I felt so guilty about having blackmailed you into marriage and then…well, being so *happy* with you seemed wicked and self-serving.'

'But I'm glad you blackmailed me into marriage—'

'You were ripping about it at the start,' Freddy reminded him helplessly.

'But I adapted fast,' Jaspar pointed out as he bent and swept her with great care up into his arms. 'I soon saw that you were the woman for me—'

'In bed, first of all,' Freddy slotted in.

'Are you telling me that you knew you *loved* me the first time we got between the sheets?'

Meeting that dubious downward look, Freddy reddened fiercely. 'No, but at least I didn't yammer on about it *only* being sex!'

'I knew those words would return to haunt me.' Shouldering shut the door of a spacious bedroom, Jaspar gave her a wolfish grin and settled her down on the canopied bed. 'But while I still believed that you had been my brother's woman first, I couldn't concede that the attraction was any stronger. You would have laughed yourself sick had you heard me only a couple of hours later fighting to *stay* married to you!'

'Fighting?'

'With my father. The first thing he said to me on the score of our marriage was that if I had married you on a foolish impulse, he would be doing me a kindness in having it set aside.' His dark golden eyes gleamed as he gazed down at her with a warmth that felt like sunshine on her rapt face. 'And no sooner had he spoken than I was gripped by the most powerful need to hold onto you and it had precious little to do with Ben—'

'Honestly?' Freddy prompted.

'Honestly.' Jaspar swept her carefully up into his arms. 'We've both used Ben as our excuse to be together. We hid behind him when we weren't yet ready to face our feelings for each other.'

'I knew pretty soon how I felt about you,' Freddy whispered.

'Tell me that you love me again,' Jaspar urged.

A glorious smile lit her face at his eagerness to hear those words again for she wanted the exact same words. 'I love you loads—'

'I adore you. How could you not realise how I felt about you?'

'Because you're kind of a special person anyway,' she told him feelingly. 'I just thought you were making a real effort to ensure that our marriage worked.'

'I wanted you to love me—'

'Not when I called you a wimp, you didn't. That was such an awful thing for me to throw at you.' Freddy sighed with an excessive lack of tact.

'I *had* decided that I didn't want to fall in love again,' Jaspar admitted rather grittily, colour demarcating his fabulous cheekbones. 'There was some grounds for you to accuse me of using Sabirah as an excuse to think all women were untrustworthy and out to get me—'

'Oh, they probably *were* out to get you.'

'But I have never treated any woman badly,' Jaspar intoned steadily. 'Except you—'

'If these last few wonderful weeks have been what you call treating me badly, what is *good* treatment like? I can hardly wait.' Freddy was quite unable to be serious. She was so happy, she was on an unstoppable high. The man of her dreams, the father of her baby and her husband was studying her as though she was the most precious being in his world. For the first time, she felt that Jaspar was truly hers to love and her conscience troubled her no longer.

'I have the rest of my life to show you, *ma belle*,' Jaspar told her, smoothing a wondering hand over her still-flat tummy and splaying his long, lean fingers. 'Are we really going to have a baby?'

'Yes.'

'You're fantastic…'

'So are you.' She dragged him down to her and he took the hint and crushed her readily parted lips beneath his own with all the hunger she craved.

'Are you sure we should be doing this?' Jaspar surfaced to ask at one point, passion and concern mingled in his possessive gaze as he lay over her literally rigid with the effort self-control was demanding from him. 'I love you so much and I could not stand to risk your health in any way. Are you *really* sure?'

Freddy was awfully glad she had not let Dr Kasim within an inch of her impressionable husband. 'You can come and see the consultant with me the next time.'

Jaspar gave her his wonderful smile. 'That would make me feel better. But right now, all I need is to hold you and show you my love, *ma belle*.'

Freddy had no objections to that plan whatsoever and the rest of the afternoon melted away without either of them thinking about anything but their joy in each other.

In his own apartments a good quarter-mile away, King Zafir waited in vain for his son and his daughter-in-law to join him for lunch. Rashad insisted that he had passed on the invitation. His royal employer fretted and fumed at Jaspar and Freddy's lack of punctuality and wondered what on earth had got into Jaspar. Around then, the older man began recalling the first months of his own happy marriage. An abstracted smile on his lined features, he ate his lunch and uttered not another word of complaint.

Just over a year later, Freddy strolled through the gardens of the Anhara with her younger son, Kareem, in his pram and her elder son, Ben, riding his bike.

Ben was now entitled to call himself an al-Husayn as well for she and Jaspar had adopted him the previous year. She still thrilled to the knowledge that Ben was now truly their little boy. Ben might have lost out by the manner of his birth on being a prince but, as Jaspar had pointed out, the position carried many restrictions and a great deal of responsibility. Ben would grow up free to make choices that their younger son, Kareem, was unlikely to ever enjoy. Named in honour of the very first King of Quamar, Kareem would be raised just as Jaspar had been, to put his country first, his family second and his own personal wishes last of all.

Kareem was such an easy baby to look after, Freddy thought as she looked proudly down at her infant son whose little inner time clock already seemed to suggest a certain natural discipline. Kareem slept within minutes of being placed in his cot *and* through most of the night. One of Jaspar's aunts had told her that Jaspar had been like that as a baby too: calm and uncomplaining. But Freddy reckoned that some babies instinctively knew and appreciated when they were secure and loved.

Ben paused on his bike to peer down into the pram. 'Kareem's sleeping again,' he lamented. 'When will he play with me?'

'Another couple of months and he'll be sitting up and a little more fun—'

'Will he be talking?' Ben asked hopefully.

'Making little talky noises…but not words.'

'I'll help him with his words,' Ben said solemnly. 'I'm his big brother.'

Slowly they wended their way back indoors. Freddy let their nanny take charge of the children and as she went upstairs to change for dinner she was thinking about what an eventful year it had been.

Just a month after she had discovered that she was expecting Kareem, she and Jaspar had enjoyed a full church blessing of their marriage and her father-in-law had officially bestowed the title of Princess on her. She had been very relieved that she'd been still able to fit herself into a beautiful wedding dress for the blessing ceremony and the service, which had been attended by so many people.

Six months ago, Sabirah had married a wealthy Lebanese tycoon and had left the country. All of Jaspar's relatives had issued a collective sigh of relief at the knowledge that the power-hungry brunette would not be returning to the royal household.

Ruth had come to stay with Freddy and Jaspar several times and she and Jaspar got on very well. Freddy had particularly appreciated the older woman's calm while she'd been carrying Kareem for Jaspar had been maddeningly prone to panicking at her every minor twinge during her pregnancy. However, her husband had got over his aversion to hospitals fast once he'd realised that the only person he trusted to reassure him about his wife's health was her gynaecologist. But Kareem had been born at the royal palace with a full complement of medical staff and every piece of emergency equipment known to man standing by. Jaspar had suffered a great deal more during Freddy's brief labour than she felt she herself had.

'That I should have put you through *that*…' he had groaned, wrung out in the aftermath and clinging to her hand as though she had come through a near-death experience. 'Never again, never ever again. I had no idea what it would entail.'

It had been very hard not to laugh and hurt his feelings, but it was pretty fabulous to be loved and needed and appreciated to that extent. But then she loved him every bit as much, she thought tenderly as she dressed for dinner, donning a turquoise designer gown with an off-the-shoulder neckline. She picked through her collection of jewellery. Some of it dated back hundreds of years and other more delicate pieces were gifts from Jaspar. Her father-in-law, who had recovered his health rapidly over the past year, was equally generous to her and she had become very fond of the older man. She liked the fact that Jaspar's family was close and had begun to think of his family as being her own.

Her aquamarine gaze shadowed on the awareness that the twin sisters she had learned existed a year earlier were still as lost to her as they had ever been. Time moved on, but with it Freddy's longing to be reunited with the only relatives she had left alive grew stronger. She would find herself dreaming about her sisters as she imagined them to be and then waking up feeling foolish, for how could she picture sisters she had never seen? As far as had been established, the twins appeared to have been adopted. However, the adoption agency used had been a private one that no longer existed and the stored records that had at first seemed to offer some hope had proved to be incomplete.

'I've got a surprise for you. Close your eyes,' Jaspar murmured huskily from the doorway.

Freddy stole an appreciative glance at him in the mirror. He was lounging back against the door and looking dropdead gorgeous.

'You're cheating.'

'I haven't seen you all day but if you've got me more fudge, I'll kill you,' she muttered, lowering her lashes.

'Is it my fault you can't resist temptation, *ma belle*?'

Even his voice still sent little shivers through her in certain moods. Yes, it *was* his fault that she found him quite irresistible, not that she had any quarrel with that. Going to bed with an irresistible guy every night was not the stuff of complaint.

'Keep on smiling like that and we might never make it downstairs to dinner,' Jaspar warned.

Her smiled just got bigger and bigger and bigger.

'You shameless hussy, you,' Jaspar muttered raggedly as he spun her round to face him and claimed a hungrily sensual kiss, only to set him back from her again with a rueful groan. 'But this is important.'

Surfacing from that far too brief embrace, Freddy gazed up at him in bemused enquiry. 'What is?'

'One of your sisters has been identified...now, don't get too excited,' Jaspar warned her levelly, dark golden eyes serious. 'This is old information and we might have a name but we don't have an address or anything else.'

Totally ignoring his initial warning, Freddy gasped joyously. 'What's her name?'

'Melissa. She's the elder twin and she goes by your mother's maiden name, Carlton. We know where she was living at the age of five but, so far, nothing further has been established.'

'But if we've got her name...that's a great start!'

'So it is,' Jaspar agreed, his brilliant gaze nailed to her excited face and his arms tightened possessively and protectively round her, for she had such high hopes.

'I love you so much,' Freddy told him with her heart in her eyes. 'I can feel in my bones that we're going to find her!'

Jaspar anchored long fingers into her tumbling blonde

mane. 'I love you too. I also tucked Ben into bed on the way in here and Kareem is fast asleep.'

'You're so organised.' Freddy turned pink.

'And you are so willing to *be* organised, *ma belle*,' Jaspar teased with a husky laugh of appreciation. 'Did I ever tell you how wonderful you are?'

'You can't tell me often enough.' Freddy quivered against his tall, well-built frame as he extracted a lingering kiss that sent her temperature rocketing, and dinner was very, very late that evening.

THE DISOBEDIENT MISTRESS

by

Lynne Graham

CHAPTER ONE

LEONE ANDRACCHI lounged back in his comfortable leather chair and surveyed the woman whom he would use as a weapon in his quest for revenge.

Across the busy room, Misty Carlton was keeping her catering staff hard at work dispensing refreshments. She wore her copper hair in a no-nonsense style. Her grey suit and sensible shoes were neither feminine nor flattering and her pale face was unadorned by make-up. Her whole appearance suggested a businesslike and serious young woman keen not to draw attention to her sex, and her cover seemed to work for Leone had yet to see a single one of his executives attempt to flirt with her.

Was every man in the room with the exception of himself blind? Did only *he* see the promise of those silvergrey eyes and the voluptuous fullness of that lush pink mouth? Dressed in appropriate clothing, she would be stunning, far more arresting than any conventional beauty for her colouring gave her a fey, sensual quality that was unusual. He was already picturing her slender curves embellished by silk lingerie and her long, slim, coltish legs sheathed in cobweb-fine stockings and complemented by very high heels. She was tall but he was taller still and she would not need to wear flat shoes around him. A selfmocking smile lurked in the depths of Leone's dark-asnight eyes as he conceded that he had yet to mentally clothe her beyond the level of her undergarments. But then he was a Sicilian to the backbone and all Sicilian men knew how to truly appreciate an attractive woman.

Within a couple of weeks at most, Misty Carlton would

be one of the most talked-about women in London. As his mistress, she'd find her name would hit the gossip columns and the paparazzi would go digging into her background and if their quest was inefficient, he would ensure that a tip was dropped in the right quarter. Having established her identity to his own satisfaction, he had left the reveal-ing links in place. Indeed, everything that would happen in the near future had been decided almost six months earlier when he had first found her and worked out how best to lure her into the position of a sitting duck waiting for him to take aim and fire. Which was right where she was at this particular moment, Leone savoured.

Misty Carlton was the illegitimate daughter of the man against whom Leone had sworn vengeance in his sister's name: Oliver Sargent. The smooth-talking politician, who had founded his reputation as a respectable family man by preaching moral standards and who lived an exceedingly nice life on his inherited wealth. Oliver Sargent, who was a hypocrite, a seducer of teenagers and ultimately little better than a murderer. Oliver Sargent, who had left Battista to die alone in the shattered remnants of her car sooner than call the emergency services and risk a scandal.

Leone's dark, chiselled face was sombre. Though it was almost a year since his sister's funeral, Leone's gut still twisted with pain whenever he allowed himself to remem-ber how Battista's life had been wilfully, cruelly and mer-cilessly sacrificed. The doctors had told him that had she been discovered sooner she might have survived the crash. That summer, she had only been nineteen years old, a pol-itics student doing research work on Sargent's staff.

A beautiful, idealistic girl with bright brown eyes, long black curly hair and a very trusting nature. Within weeks of her beginning her volunteer placement, Leone had been heartily sick of the sound of Sargent's name but it had not occurred to him that a bad case of hero worship might put

Battista at risk. After all, Oliver Sargent was a married man and a quarter of a century older than his kid sister. He had overlooked the fact that Sargent was a handsome charmer, who could easily pass for being a great deal younger than he actually was.

'Mr Andracchi…?'

Unaware of quite how intimidating his grim expression was, Leone focused in some surprise on the pastries being offered to him, for the almond biscuits and custard tarts were traditional Sicilian treats. The slender hand holding the plate was shaking almost imperceptibly but his gaze was keen. He glanced up into Misty Carlton's drawn face, recognising the marks of strain there in the bluish shadows beneath her eyes and the tense set of her delicate jawbone. She had brown lashes as long as a child's and she was trembling. But then she was desperate. He *knew* that for he had planned it that way. She was on the very brink of losing the business that she had worked so hard to build up. He held her in the palm of his hand.

'Thank you,' Leone murmured, dark deep drawl rather mocking for if she fondly imagined that he was likely to be impressed by so unsubtle an attempt at downright flattery, she was very much mistaken. Contracts were awarded on the basis of price, efficiency and reliability and, whether she liked it or not and through no fault of his, she had broken more than one of the basic rules of setting up a new business. '*Nucatoli* and *pasta ciotti*. What a pleasant surprise. You are spoiling me.'

A tiny betraying pulse was flickering like mad just below her fragile collar-bone, drawing his attention to the fine, delicate skin of her throat. 'I like to experiment…that's all,' Misty said breathlessly.

She was all of a quiver and her body language screamed at him: the dilated dark pupils, the flush on her cheeks, the moist pink of her parted lips. He turned her on and, had he not known what he *did* know about her, he might have believed that she was too innocent to hide those sexual signals of availability. But he knew better, felt free to assume that, had the room been empty, he might have pulled her down onto his lap and explored that quivering, slender body so hot and eager for his with her willing encouragement. His own sex threatened to betray him with primitive male urgency but he thought about revenge instead and his blood cooled fast. He had no intention of bedding Oliver Sargent's daughter. She would be his mistress in name only.

'Don't we all?' Leone quipped with husky suggestiveness and bit into a tiny custard tart that melted in his mouth, while she hovered like a submissive handmaiden to one side of him. A faint sardonic smile curved his masculine lips. He liked her stance. He was an old-fashioned guy and the pastry was delicious. Maybe in her spare time she would be able to occupy herself in his kitchen. Eager to please, she certainly was. Though someone ought to have warned her that even a hint of nervous desperation was likely to alert clients to an unsound business.

'It's good,' Leone told her softly.

The big silver-grey eyes lit up with a surge of relief and pride. He had an erotic image of her spread across his bed in the drowsing heat of a Sicilian afternoon, glorious red hair cascading in a tangle, lush pink mouth begging for his while she writhed and moaned with pleasure beneath his expert hands. Sadly, it was not to be, he reminded himself, exasperated by the predictable effects of his own powerful libido.

She poured his coffee with her own hands. He wondered if her rock-star lover had appreciated those little touches of essential femininity calculated to make even the wimpiest male feel as though he could go out and club a lion to death before dragging it back to the connubial cave to impress her in turn. She was no fragile little flower, though. The file on her had turned up quite a few surprises for she might be only twenty-two, but she had led a chequered life and one that might have inspired his compassion had she not, it seemed, been guilty of fleecing a little old lady out of her savings. Behind those mist-coloured eyes lurked a greedy little schemer with a heart of stone.

Blood will out, Leone thought fatalistically as he accepted the coffee already sugared to his preference. She might not have the foggiest idea of who her father was and she might never have met him but he already saw a similarity between Oliver Sargent and his natural daughter in the way that she seemed to use people and reinvent herself to turn situations to her own advantage.

Melissa Carlton had grown up in a series of foster homes and trouble seemed to follow her around. She had once been engaged to a prosperous landowner and her former fiancé's mother was *still* congratulating herself on her success in seeing off a young woman whom she had deemed to be both mercenary and calculating. The rock-star lover had followed: an unwashed-looking yob with spiky bleach-blond hair given to screaming indecipherable lyrics into microphones while Misty had danced wildly on one side of the stage. That had not lasted long either.

'May I have a word with you, Mr Andracchi?' Misty asked tautly.

'Not just at present,' Leone said, watching her flinch and pale without an ounce of remorse.

She could stew a little longer. And why not? Ultimately, she was going to get the deal of the century and profit very nicely indeed from their arrangement. Saving her skin stuck in his throat but what else could he do? She was Oliver Sargent's Achilles heel and he needed her co-operation to bring the bastard down. Not that she would know how she was helping him until it was too late. But then even the best deals came at a price and she was not a sensitive woman. Sensitive women did not rip off old ladies and leave them struggling to make ends meet while continuing to pose as a caring pseudo-daughter.

When the press identified Misty Carlton as Sargent's illegitimate child, her father's political career would go down the tubes for no man had been more sanctimonious about his moral principles than Oliver Sargent. His good-living childless wife might well pull the plug on him too but Leone had no interest in that possibility. He already knew what Sargent valued most: his power, his ambitious hopes of higher office in government, his adoring coterie of female supporters. And when the scandal broke, Oliver Sargent was going to be stripped bare of his pride and his power and his influence. It would be a brutal punishment for a man who revelled in his own importance and lived for admiration. Once Sargent's cover was blown all the other dirt would eventually surface too: his financial dou-ble-dealing and questionable friendships with dishonest businessmen. He would be ruined beyond all hope of po-litical recovery.

It wasn't enough, though, it wasn't nearly enough to compensate for Battista's sweet life cut off in its prime, but when the axe fell Leone would be sure to let his victim know *why* he had destroyed him. Sargent was already ner-vous around him although the older man did not yet sus-pect that Leone knew that he had been in that car the night his kid sister had died. But then Battista's sleazy seducer had covered his tracks too well and, no matter how hard Leone had tried, proof of that fact had been impossible to obtain.

He watched Misty Carlton, who was the very picture of her late mother, marshal her staff. Unless he was very much mistaken, Oliver Sargent would begin sweating and fearing exposure the very *instant* he saw her and heard her name…

Misty wondered if she had ever hated anyone as much as she hated Leone Andracchi.

He had dismissed her as though she were a servant speaking up out of turn but this was the last day but one of her temporary contract and she had yet to be told whether or not it was going to be renewed for the next year. If it wasn't, she would be bankrupted. Perspiration beading her short upper lip, Misty got on with her work but, no matter where she was in the gracious room with its oppressive clubby male atmosphere, she was conscious of Leone Andracchi's brooding presence.

A real Sicilian tycoon, fabulously wealthy and famously devious and unpredictable to deal with. He dominated the room like a big black storm cloud within which lurked the threat of a lightning strike. His own executives were nervous as cats around him, eager to defer to him, keen to impress, paling if he even began to frown. Yet he was only thirty years old, young indeed to wield such enormous power. But then he was supposed to be absolutely brilliant in business.

Shame about the personality, Misty thought bitterly. It was just her luck that she should be forced to kowtow to a sexist dinosaur, who had taken her attentions quite as his due. My goodness, he had *loved* it when she'd brought him those special pastries and had practically purred like a jungle cat while she'd sugared his blasted coffee for him. Her strong pride had stung with every obsequious move, for boot-licking did not come naturally to her. Perhaps the Sicilian baking had been overkill but, really, what did she have left to lose? Beggars couldn't be choosers. She had crawled for Birdie's sake, Birdie who was going to lose her home if Misty didn't manage to pull her own irons out of the fire and get that contract confirmed. And when it came to Birdie, there was no limit to the efforts Misty was willing to make.

'That Andracchi guy is *so* gorgeous,' her friend and employee, Clarice, groaned in a die-away voice as she stacked cups into containers by Misty's side. 'Every time I look at him I feel like I've just died and gone to heaven.'

'Shh.' Misty reddened with annoyance, for a waitress casting languishing lustful glances at the big chief would hardly qualify as professional behaviour.

'You're always looking at him out of the corner of your eye,' the chirpy and curvaceous brunette whispered back cheekily before she walked away.

All right, so she looked, but not because she was a mug for those serious dark good looks of his! No, she looked the way one looked to check a lion was still in a cage with the door safely locked. Leone Andracchi unnerved her. It had to be her imagination that she felt that *he* was always watching *her* for she had yet to catch those brooding dark golden eyes doing so, but in his radius she felt hideously self-conscious.

And yet in any normal business empire the size of Andracchi Industries, she would never even have got to meet a male as hugely important as Leone Andracchi. After all, she was only a caterer on a short trial contract to just *one* of his companies and surely far beneath his lofty notice. Furthermore, Brewsters was not in London but based on the outskirts of a country town in Norfolk. Yet, on a visit to Brewsters, Leone Andracchi had taken the trouble to interview her personally. He had also sent her jumping through a line of mental hoops like a circus animal he was training for his own nasty amusement.

As her wan face stiffened at the recollection, she scolded herself for the resentment that lingered. In accepting her bid for the contract and very much surprising her in so doing, Leone Andracchi had given her what had seemed to be the opportunity of a lifetime. It was hardly his fault that that opportunity had turned sour or that she had bitten off more than she could chew.

'Andracchi is what I call a *real* man,' Clarice stressed in a feeling sigh of infuriating appreciation as she shoved past again. 'All muscles and rampant energy. He just reeks of sex in the raw. You know he'd be a wicked fantasy in bed—'

'He has love rat written all over him and a lousy reputation with women!' Misty gritted in a driven undertone. 'Will you *please* drop the subject?'

'I was only trying to give you a laugh.' Her friend pulled a surprised grimace. 'Lighten up, Misty.'

Feeling guilty, Misty reddened, aware her nerves were jumping like electrified beans. But even her friend had no idea just how precarious her business, Carlton Catering, had become. It was ready to crash and go to the wall. If she did not get that all important contract from Andracchi Industries, the bank would refuse to extend her loan and she would not even have sufficient funds left to pay her employees at the end of the month, never mind her suppliers. Shame drenched her in a tidal wave. How had she got into such a mess?

A blond male in a smart suit approached her. 'Mr Andracchi will see you now in his office.'

She could see the man's barely concealed surprise that Leone Andracchi should be involving himself yet again in such a minor matter. But then as the great man himself had drawled in explanation almost four months earlier, 'Lunch is an art to a Sicilian and I want the executives here to benefit from a new experience. I'm tired of watching people scoff sandwiches at their desks. I believe that a proper meal will increase productivity throughout the afternoon.'

So every day she had provided a light lunch in the executive dining room that had been set up and on afternoons like this, when a major business powwow concluded, she had been asked to stay on to serve refreshments as well. Visiting the cloakroom first, she washed her hands and checked that she was still tidy. She wasn't looking her best and she knew it, which didn't help. Sleepless nights and constant worry had left their mark.

Her own fault, she told herself bitterly. She had taken a risk on Leone Andracchi's whim and on what might yet prove to be an experiment he had no intention of even continuing. Furthermore, even if he had decided to retain the lunches, there was no guarantee whatsoever that her business would win the contract. He was going to kiss her off. She knew it, could *feel* it in her bones. Her punishment for borrowing from the bank to expand was coming. What was it to him if her piffling little firm went into receivership? He would probably like to see her beg. Could she do it for Birdie? Beg that big, muscle-bound, arrogant jerk for mercy? She shuddered at the prospect but her only alternative was even less appetizing: Flash would haul her out of trouble without hesitation. Only it would be for a price this time and the price would be her body and she hoped to heaven that she would never, ever sink that low...

A secretary who looked suitably cowed by the effect of a week-long visit from the tycoon boss of Andracchi Industries opened the door of a big office for her. Straightening her slight shoulders, Misty breathed in deep and walked in, striving for a look of calm confidence, which was in no way echoed by her churning tummy and her damp palms. Please, please don't let him try to shake hands, she prayed inwardly.

'Sit down, Miss Carlton.'

Leone Andracchi was on the phone, standing by the sunlit windows of the spacious office. She listened to him talking in soft, liquid Italian, the way a real smoothie talked to a lover. Phone sex, sleazebag, Misty thought loftily and her upper lip curled in disgust. But, unfortunately, Clarice was right on one score. He *was* drop-dead fantastic to look at. Luxuriant black hair that just begged to be disarranged by a woman's fingers, stunning high cheekbones, stunning everything, really, she conceded grudgingly. Classic arrogant nose, well-defined ebony brows, really masculine strong jaw, beautifully shaped mouth. As for the eyes, those eyes of his were a revelation on their own. Black as pitch in certain moods, all lustrous, dazzling, sexy gold in another. And he knew how to use them all right to signify just about everything that other people used words to convey.

She had seen those eyes, in bully mode, freeze employees in their tracks. Send female office staff fluttering with the same sense of threat as hens scenting a fox. He got off on women fussing round him. He was the 'Me Tarzan, you Jane' type and he went for fluffy busty little blondes who giggled and gasped and clung. Pathetic, really. In her opinion, a *real* man would have wanted a *real* woman, one with a brain, one capable of fighting back and putting him in his place. And if ever a guy had needed putting in his place, it was Leone Andracchi. He was so full of himself he set her teeth on edge.

Finishing his call, Leone flicked a glance at his waiting victim, wondered why she had that curious little scornful smile hovering on her lips and that faraway, almost smug look in her eyes. He strolled with fluid grace over to the desk and realised that she was genuinely miles away, one of those individuals whose imagination was strong enough to blank out all sense of time and surroundings.

Misty was acquainted with that old chestnut about imagining intimidating people naked to bring them down to human size, only she wasn't even a little tempted to picture Leone Andracchi shorn of his exquisitely tailored suit. But just as suddenly she was seeing Leone Andracchi in her mind's eye and her mind had developed a dismaying life all of its own, imagination running riot on that tall, well-built physique of his. Her own embarrassing thoughts shocked her rigid, shocked her right back to awareness again, cheeks hot, skin tight over her bones.

'Welcome back, Miss Carlton,' Leone Andracchi murmured with sardonic bite.

'Mr Andracchi…' Heart beating so fast, she felt as if it were banging at the foot of her throat, Misty forced herself to raise her head high.

'I'm sorry I kept you waiting,' he added.

No, he wasn't. She didn't know how she knew that, for that lean dark angel face was uniquely uninformative, but she sensed it. He lounged back in galling relaxation against the desk, the indolent angle of his sleek, taut, muscular frame pronounced. He had to be about six feet four at least, she calculated, and not for the first time.

'Naturally you want to know my thoughts on the contract due to be awarded. Although I'm really not obligated to give you that information,' Leone Andracchi pointed out smoothly. 'However, in the light of the excellent standard of service you have pioneered over the past eight weeks, I feel it's only fair to tell you *why* your bid has been unsuccessful.'

Her tummy flipped at the confirmation of the refusal that she had most feared. The blood drained from her set features and her hands laced together on her lap. 'I don't need empty compliments,' she said tightly. 'If Carlton Catering hasn't been awarded the contract, then you obviously weren't satisfied with the service at all.'

'It's not that simple,' Leone drawled. 'You're over-extended and it would be very unwise to take the risk that

your business will stay afloat for the duration of a year
long agreement.'

Her silvery grey eyes were now widened to their fullest
extent. For the first time she ditched her caution and connected direct with his brilliant dark golden eyes. 'May I
ask you where you received that information?'

'My sources are private.'

Meeting that steady, fathomless gaze, she could feel her
head beginning to swim and the breath catching in her
throat. 'It's quite untrue.'

'Don't lie to me. I have no time for lies,' Leone told
her smoothly. 'My information is always accurate. I know
that the only way your bank will extend your loan is if
you bring them the contract for the next year's catering
here signed, sealed and delivered.'

'If someone at the bank has been making allegations
about the viability of my business, I will be sure to make
an official complaint.' Misty threw her head back, silver
eyes blazing challenge. 'I assure you that were you to give
me that contract I would deliver the service required for
the period specified and I would not have any problems in
doing so.'

'I'm impressed by your optimism,' Leone countered levelly, 'but let's cut to the chase. You have talent and you're
great at organisation but you fell down when it came to
the bid for the first contract. Your price was ludicrously
low. Yet you're in a labour-intensive industry, saddled
with high staff turnover, crippling insurance costs and public health regulations that are very expensive for a small
business to meet. As a result, you have barely recouped
your costs.'

'I wanted the job. I priced that bid to win in the obvious
hope of recouping costs over the next year,' Misty informed him. 'You said you liked to support new local busi-
nesses—'

'Not when the captain at the helm is a woman who refuses to acknowledge when she's in over her head. How you can sit there and argue with me when I know for a fact that you're behind with the rent on your business premises, behind with your bank loan *and* up to your pretty throat in debt—'

'Leave my throat…pretty or otherwise…out of this, please.' Misty rose to her feet, no longer able to tolerate being looked down on by him. How dared he speak to her in such a way? How *dared* he? It was bad enough learning that the contract on which she had placed all her hopes was to be awarded elsewhere, but that he should add insult to injury by enumerating what he deemed to be her mistakes was more than flesh and blood could bear.

'And losing your temper with me will impress me even less,' Leone informed her with a derisive look at her aggressive stance. She might be around five feet ten tall, but she was as slender as a willow wand. What on earth was the matter with her? She was useless at bluffing. Her eyes gave her away every time. Did she really expect him to waste time listening to her trying to convince him that she *wasn't* on the edge of a financial abyss?

In the space of a second, rage almost ate Misty alive. The temper that she had long since mastered threatened to overflow like lava. She wanted to take a swing at him. She wanted to wipe that derisive slant off his lean, strong face with a well-placed fist and that simple awareness disconcerted her enough to put a brake on her anger.

'You've brought me in here, given me the bad news, but you *didn't* need to personalise the issue,' Misty stated with curt dignity. 'So why would you think I want to impress you now?'

An ebony brow elevated. 'I could be thinking of throwing you a lifeline.'

A shaken and involuntary laugh escaped Misty. She was

grateful that he had not given her an opening in which to beg. She was even grateful that he had made her furious. For if she were forced to stop and consider the appalling consequences of losing that contract, she might well come apart at the seams and embarrass herself. He liked playing games with people, she decided. Or maybe it was only women he liked toying with.

'Is that really a possibility?' The tip of her tongue came out to moisten her dry lower lip as she wondered if it was remotely likely that, in spite of what he had so far said about her business acumen, he might have some other job to offer her.

The silence hummed like a circular saw on her straining nerves. His attention had dropped to her lips, the too wide, too full mouth she hated. No doubt he was noticing that it was out of proportion to her face. Men were supposed to think about sex, what was it…at least once every five minutes? She reckoned he would be challenged to keep his mind clean for sixty seconds. He had an aura of potent virility that no woman could avoid noticing. She studied him, the lush black lashes screening his gleaming scrutiny, and her lips actually tingled with her awareness of him, her rebellious body stirring with the sensations she had grown to fiercely resent experiencing in his vicinity. The sudden tense, full sensation lifting her breasts inside her cotton bra cups, the utterly demeaning throb of her nipples tightening.

Never had Misty been so grateful for the concealment of her jacket. Imagine him *seeing* that physical evidence, imagine him *knowing* that he could make her stupid body react like that with one charged glance! Ever since she had met him, she had recognised that cruel Old Mother nature was reminding her that she had hormones, but it meant nothing. She had been hurt too much to risk herself again with any man and she need hardly worry that this particular male was likely to make a pass, for Leone Andracchi was just doing what came naturally to a sexual animal of his appetites: considering every passing woman of a certain age on her merits. And she knew her merits to be few and far between.

'Anything's possible. Didn't anyone ever tell you that?' Leone murmured, smooth as velvet.

Flash had told her that when he'd been trying to talk her into his bed. Try it, you might find you like it. *Not* the seduction line of the century, but another week or two of his determined siege and she might have succumbed out of gratitude and love, for she did love him, would always love him, only not the way he had wanted her to love him. But sometimes in low moments she would think that she should have snatched at his offer and made the best of it.

'It's my motto.' Misty was careful to keep Leone Andracchi out of focus, determined to blank him out as a man, get her foolish physical self back under control and let those taunting sensations subside.

'Sit down,' Leone Andracchi told her.

Obviously *something* was in the offing. She dropped back down into the seat, thought that maybe, after all, it had been worth staying up half the night to produce those wretched Sicilian recipes for his benefit. Major egos liked being stroked. Honey went far further than vinegar, she reminded herself doggedly. What had happened to her belief that she could make herself beg? Why did the prospect of speaking even one humble word to Leone Andracchi clog up her throat like a threatened dose of poison?

'I have a role that I would like you to fulfil for me over the next two months.' Leone surveyed her steadily. 'In return I would rescue your business, and at the end of our agreement I would ensure that you had sufficent work to survive. What do you think?'

'The last time I looked there wasn't two blue moons hanging out there in that sky,' Misty quipped with helpless bluntness.

CHAPTER TWO

LEONE ANDRACCHI dealt Misty a look of hauteur, his wide mouth tightening with perceptible exasperation.

Having immediately recognised her mistake in making such a facetious response, Misty had turned hot pink with discomfiture. She could not work out where those inappropriate words of doubt had emerged from. It was the effect of *him* again, she decided. He spooked her, put her on edge, knocked her out of the cautious business mode which she had no problem maintaining around other clients.

'I'm sorry,' Misty said flatly, 'but what you just said sounded too good to be true.'

'So you're now willing to concede that you're facing bankruptcy?' Leone probed.

A chill at the very sound of that terrifying word sank into Misty's bones and she shifted uneasily in her chair. 'Mr Andracchi—'

'Until you admit that reality, I will go no further,' he warned her.

Her earlier argument to the contrary had evidently offended. She would have loved to have known what he would have done in the same position. Announced to his one last hope that his back was up against the wall? No way, he was far too clever for that, so why was he judging her for her attempt to regain his confidence? Just because he refused to credit that she could have fulfilled that contract for a year! But she *knew* she could have, had done the figures over and over again, had been ready to go on living like a church mouse to have done so.

21

'Or leave my office,' Leone Andracchi added with lethal cool.

'I'm…facing…bankruptcy,' Misty framed like a clock-work toy with a battery about to run flat. The admission hurt, made real what she had until then refused to contemplate and she hated him all the more for forcing her to that brink.

'Thank you. As I said I have a promising proposition to offer you. It's nothing to do with catering, although if you find yourself overcome with the urge to cook Sicilian cuisine in your spare time, I will have no objection,' Leone imparted with a sardonic smile.

The offer had nothing to do with catering? *Nothing?* She hoped that swallowing his sarcasm in silence would prove to be worth her while.

'First, I want your assurance that nothing I now say will be repeated beyond this office.'

Since the first rule of any business was respecting client confidentiality, Misty bridled at that statement. 'Of course. I'm no gossip and I'd be a fool if I was.'

'I need a woman to pretend that she's my mistress.'

She heard an imaginary crash as her jaw metaphorically hit the floor. She waited on the punchline, certain he was mocking her in some way and determined not to rise prematurely to the bait.

'You will note that word, "pretend,"' Leone Andracchi stressed with unblemished cool. 'I'm not into sexual harassment of my employees and you would be, in effect, my employee for I would insist that you signed a legal agreement to maintain the fiction until *I* say that your role is at an end.'

Misty sucked in a ragged breath and continued to stare at him, utterly silenced by that second speech. He was actually serious, yet she could not credit that he was addressing her with such an offer. What reason could he have for asking *any* woman to pretend to be his mistress? He had to have a little black book the size of an entire library. For goodness' sake, wasn't he dating an actress from a television show at present? Jassy something or other? A pneumatic blonde with the kind of curves that even other women stole a shaken second glance at?

'I'm afraid I don't understand,' Misty framed very slowly and succinctly while she wondered if he were a brick short of the full load in the mental department or drunk as a skunk and just not showing physical signs of his condition.

'You're not required to understand. I have my own reasons and I don't intend to share them. I know women don't like mysteries but, in this case, discretion is necessary.'

'If you do have some…er…need to hire a woman for such a novel role, I can't think why you should approach me,' Misty reasoned with enormous care.

'Can't you?' A faint smile momentarily softened the tough line of his mouth.

She had no intention of lowering herself to the level of spelling out the obvious. But she wasn't beautiful or glamorous, nor did she have the high public profile of the kind of women he was usually associated with.

'Is this some kind of a joke?'

'It's on the level.'

'But you must know hundreds of women,' Misty protested, intimidated by his persistence. 'Why me?'

'I prefer to hire and fire rather than coax and trust,' Leone countered without hesitation. 'Why are you trying to dissuade me from rescuing you from your financial problems?'

Put like that, keeping quiet seemed more sensible, but she could not accept that he was serious without some idea of his motivation for such a weird offer. 'This is very strange.'

Leone shrugged a broad shoulder in unconcerned acknowledgement.

'I mean…*seriously*,' Misty emphasised.

'I am serious and the position wouldn't be that easy to fill. You'd have to act the part, dress the part and convince people that we're lovers.'

Warm colour inched up beneath her fine complexion and she glanced away from her studious scrutiny of his exquisitely tailored suit jacket. 'I don't think I'd be a great hit in that department.'

'You just need the right props and the ability to do exactly as I tell you at all times. It would definitely be a case of when I say jump…you say how high?'

Misty could see herself being a major disappointment in that field too. But it was dawning on her that, peculiar as his proposition was, he was not pulling her leg. He wanted a fake mistress. What did being a fake mistress entail?

'We are talking….*fake* mistress here?' Misty prompted in a strained undertone.

'Do you really think that I need to pay for sex?'

Her even white teeth gritted. If she said jump to him and he said how high, she would direct him to the nearest lift shaft, but with that ego of his he would bounce back out of the fall. 'There's no need to get that personal, Mr Andracchi. Your private life is your business but my safety is mine.'

'Are you trying to suggest that I might be some sort of pervert?' Leone shot back at her in an incredulous growl.

'How would I know? This is not a common or garden offer. Like, I don't have rich Sicilian tycoons offering me the moon just to pretend to be their mistresses every day, do I?' Misty snapped out in bewilderment and embarrassment.

'And if you take that tone and attitude, you are unlikely to have even *one* Sicilian tycoon still interested.'

Legs cramped by the rigidity of her posture in the chair, Misty got up again and walked across the office before spinning round to face him, wide grey eyes frowning. 'Just tell me why you're asking me to do this…why me?'

'You couldn't afford to welch on any deal we would make or change the terms to suit yourself.' He stood straight and tall, eyes hard gold and direct.

Misty flinched. Mr Mean and Tough, who, it seemed, knew exactly how she was placed and that was between a rock and a hard place. He had no shame about reminding her of that unpalatable fact. Perhaps it was a timely reminder too. Any alternative to bankruptcy and Birdie losing her home ought to be considered. But how could she possibly consider taking on a role in which she would be less than convincing? Didn't he see that? People wouldn't believe that she was his mistress for one minute! He specialised in beautiful women. Yes, he liked women, but why did she judge him for that?

'I couldn't do it…' she muttered. 'We mix like oil and water. I wouldn't be at home in the sort of social life you must have. And I couldn't possibly convince anyone that we were…lovers.'

'Oh, I think you underestimate yourself on that score,' Leone breathed in a different timbre, rich, dark drawl snaking round her like a husky, mesmeric spell.

Nibbling at the soft underside of her full lower lip, Misty was entrapped by the intensity of his narrowed golden stare. Gorgeous eyes, undeniably gorgeous eyes. Her mouth ran dry, her muscles tightening in response. Even his voice, liquid dark enticement of the most dangerous kind, yet another enhancement to his magnetic masculine presence. The gene pool had not been stingy when he'd been born.

Entirely against her own will, she wanted to smile, soften, be a woman in all the ways she had once allowed herself to be even if it put her at risk of getting hurt again. The atmosphere was buzzing with the sensual vibes he could put out. He could whip up the tension without effort. And no matter how hard she tried to remain impervious, excitement nibbled at her every nerve ending and she quivered as a taunting flame lit low in her pelvis and forced her to press her thighs together in shamed disconcertion.

'Just say the word and sign on the dotted line and all your troubles are at an end.'

'What would playing your pretend mistress involve?' Misty heard herself ask and surprised herself.

'Living in the apartment I would supply, wearing the clothes I buy, going where I ask when I ask without question.'

Mistress as in mindless *slave*, she translated with a secret little shard of amusement. He was a real domineering louse. But it was interesting to note that he wasn't suggesting any type of shared accommodation. The masquerade would only be of the public variety and would require no greater intimacy. He wanted a dressed-up doll to play a stupid role for some reason he refused to reveal. Maybe it was another Andracchi whim like the executive lunches. Or maybe it had some business purpose…which would make it an unusual job but still a job like any other.

It wasn't as though he would be expecting her to hop into bed with him. Of course, he wouldn't. Her face burned that she had even suspected he might. After all, he had much more attractive possibilities than her available: women who had probably forgotten more than she had even learned about bedroom pursuits. She would be as safe as houses with him but she would be selling herself, handing over her pride and her independence in return for cold hard cash support. That was cheap and nasty and the thought of it left an unpleasant taste in her mouth, but she had Birdie and her employees to think about and pride didn't pay the bills.

'What would you do for me?' she whispered chokily, the humiliating request for greater clarity on that point hurting her.

'Settle your debts, put your business back on an even keel, cover the wages of your staff while you're working for me. Anything else, name it. I'm prepared to negotiate.' Leone Andracchi gazed back at her, cool as ice.

Her tummy churned. She loathed him for issuing that unvarnished bribe of greater remuneration. He had it all worked out. He believed that he could buy her and it shamed her to acknowledge that she had put herself in a position where he could think that and act on it.

'I'll think it over this evening.' That admission cut through Misty's pride like the first wounding slash of a knife.

'What do you have to think over?'

'I think you're underestimating my side of what you call the deal.'

His strong jawline hardened. 'I don't see a problem or a conflict of interests. You get to wear fabulous clothes, live in a superb apartment and enjoy the high life for a couple of months.'

'I can see that you believe that that should be a big draw, but it's not.' Lifting her head with determined composure, Misty walked to the door.

'What more did you expect?'

'Respect…for a start.' Misty pushed out that admission between gritted teeth.

'That has to be earned…and I doubt your ability to earn mine.'

Did having bad luck in business make her so much a lesser person? Did he only respect successful people with big bank balances and social pedigrees? He really was obnoxious. He had had no need to make that last comment. It suggested a prejudice against her that both shook and mortified her, for he might have enquired into the state of her catering business but surely he could know very little else about her?

'I shouldn't have said that. I'm sorry,' Leone Andracchi drawled flatly.

'Don't let it worry you,' Misty advised, registering that he was merely concerned that he might have overplayed his hand and not truly regretful. 'You're self-satisfied, arrogant, manipulative and ruthless. You could have given me that contract, for I believe you're well aware that I would've worked my socks off to fulfil it. However, you prefer to use my problems as a weapon against me. You have very little conscience and even less compassion. Do you really think I'm surprised that you should also be very rude?'

And with that concluding accolade Misty skimmed him a flashing glance from her silver grey eyes. He was very still. Pretty much gobsmacked by that retaliation. Hard dark eyes assailed hers in a seering look that was pure naked intimidation.

'I shouldn't have said that. I'm so sorry,' Misty told him with an insincerity that more than equalled his own a minute earlier, and with that she left his office at speed.

Hit and run? Was that all she was good for? She had been scared that he might have a temper the size of his powerful personality. But biting the hand that she might end up having to feed from was real insanity. Right this very minute, he would be comforting himself with that superior awareness and thinking how stupid she had been to risk alienating him to that extent. And it was surely paranoiac of her to believe that he might have deliberately withheld that contract to put her under more pressure to agree?

In fact it was most likely that he had turned to her because some other woman had refused. A fake mistress? Why? What was Leone Andracchi up to? Such an extraordinary proposition *and* an expensive one if he was planning to put her in some fancy apartment and furnish her with an appropriate wardrobe. So somehow it would have to profit him. But as she went down in the lift, still shell-shocked by their interview, she could not work out how setting up a pretend mistress could possibly benefit him.

She pictured that lean dark face, breathtakingly good-looking, devastatingly cool and unrevealing. Nobody would ever accuse of Leone Andracchi of wearing his thoughts on his sleeve. A shiver of foreboding ran down her spine. As she crossed the spacious foyer on the ground floor her steps slowed. What was she doing walking away from his rescue bid?

In return for her playing some ridiculous role as his mistress, he would save her business and enable her to continue paying the mortgage on Birdie's home as well as ensure the ongoing employment of her staff. When the rewards were so great and so many other people would suffer if her business failed, what was a couple of months out of her life? What had been the point of walking out on Leone Andracchi when in reality she had no choice but to accept his terms? She had no other options, had she?

Misty had to make herself walk back into the lift; the prospect of eating humble pie had no appeal. In the short corridor which led to Leone's office on the top floor, she was disconcerted to see him standing outside the door in conversation with two men. She came to an awkward halt a good ten feet away, two high spots of pink forming over her cheekbones. It took her just two seconds to decide that he was deliberately ignoring her, a lowering impression only increased by the sight of him looking so infuriatingly at ease. Arrogant dark head held at an angle, his jacket pushed back by the lean hand he had thrust in the pocket of his tailored trousers, he emanated relaxation. Angry resentment stiffened her to stone.

Finally, Leone turned his head and lifted an enquiring ebony brow, lean strong face urbane.

'The answer's...*yes*,' Misty framed with flat emphasis.

His brilliant dark eyes gleamed and he stretched out a hand. In the very act of turning away to make good her escape while he was occupied, for she really had had enough of him for one afternoon, Misty stilled. With frozen reluctance, she moved forward, horribly conscious of his companions' curiosity as they stepped back out of her path.

His wide sensual mouth curved into a slow, charismatic smile that made her mouth run dry. He caught her fingers in his and closed an arm round her.

'Excuse me...' he murmured huskily to their audience, pressing open the door of his office to back her over the threshold.

'What on—?' earth are you playing at, Misty began to say.

Warning dark golden eyes assailed hers and before she could utter one more syllable he had whirled her round and brought his mouth crashing down on hers with devouring sexual hunger. An inarticulate moan of shock was dragged from her but, in the split second in which she was incredulously aware that the wretched door wasn't even closed to conceal them, his passionate intensity scorched her into sensual awakening. As he banded his hands round the curve of her hips and pressed her into intimate connection with every muscular line of his big, powerful body, raw excitement flamed through her quivering length like a forest fire licking out of control.

His tongue plundered the moist, tender interior of her mouth in a devastatingly erotic invasion, every explicit probe of that lancing exploration driving her sensation-starved body crazy. Her heart hammering, she was fighting for oxygen but clinging to him, conscious of the unmistakable thrust of his arousal, inflamed rather than repelled by that evidence of his masculine hunger.

A febrile line of colour accentuating his superb cheekbones, Leone released her and snatched in a ragged breath. 'I think that was an impressive enough statement of our intentions.'

Less quick to recover, Misty pulled in a lungful of air like a drowning swimmer, her legs feeling barely strong enough to support her as she instinctively fell back against the wall for support. She couldn't credit what had just happened between them. It wasn't just that he had grabbed and kissed her; it was the infinitely more disturbing truth that she had revelled like a wanton in that passionate embrace. She was shattered by the betrayal of her own body, the response that he had demanded and extracted without her volition.

'Our intentions?' Misty framed unevenly, noting that the corridor was now empty, face burning at the appalling awareness that she, who prided herself on behaving in a professional manner in a business environment, had just committed the ultimate unforgivable sin.

'Too good an opportunity to miss,' Leone quipped, slumbrous dark eyes veiled by his lush black lashes.

She was so enraged by that explanation that she wanted to slap him into the middle of the next week. 'You *said* that you weren't into sexually harassing employees.'

'If you think that we're likely to convince anyone that we're intimately involved without an occasional demonstration of lover-like enthusiasm, you must be very naive,' Leone countered drily. 'But it will only be for public consumption. In private the act dies.'

'You don't need to tell me that.' Not trusting her temper

in his vicinity and bitterly conscious that she had burnt her boats without taking the time to consider the potential costs of such a role, Misty compressed her lips hard. 'May I leave now?'

Leone flicked her a considering glance. 'Yes. I'll see you at my hotel tonight at nine and we'll get the remaining details ironed out. I'm staying at the Belstone House hotel—'

'Tonight doesn't suit me,' Misty said facetiously, unable to resist the temptation.

'*Make* it suit,' he advised. 'I'm returning to London tomorrow.'

With a rigid little nod of grudging agreement, Misty walked back out again, her slender spine ramrod straight. But she was even more angry with herself than she was with him. How could she have lost herself like that in his arms? But then she had never felt like that before with a man, no, not even with Philip in the first fine flush of love. She paled, suppressing that unfortunate thought. What she had felt at nineteen was hard to recall three years on. Leone Andracchi had caught her off guard. Self-evidently, he possessed great technique in the kissing department, but why hadn't her loathing for the man triumphed?

Colouring and confused by what she could not explain to her own satisfaction, Misty climbed into the van in Brewsters' car park and drove to the premises she rented on the outskirts of town. There she joined her three staff in the clean-up operation that concluded every working day. It was after five by the time she locked up and all she could think about was how her business had become so vulnerable that one lost contract could finish it off.

Carlton Catering was just over a year old. She had started out small, doing private dinner parties and the occasional wedding. Nothing too fancy, nothing too big and her overheads had been low. But when, five months ago, her supplier had mentioned that there was a tender coming out for providing lunches at Brewsters, the biggest, swankiest company on the industrial estate, she had been eager to put in a bid and expand. On the strength of that trial contract, she had borrowed to buy another van and upgrade her equipment.

However, disaster had struck soon afterwards. Her premises had been vandalised and the damage had been extensive but her insurance company had refused to pay out, arguing that her security precautions had been inadequate. That had been a bitter and unexpected blow, for the repairs had wiped out her cash reserve and from that point on she had been struggling to stay afloat.

'Your need to reduce your personal expenditure to offset that loss,' her bank manager had warned her only six weeks earlier. 'In spite of your cash-flow problems, you're continuing to pay the mortgage on a house that doesn't belong to you. I respect your generosity towards Mrs Pearce, but you *must* be realistic about the extent of the drain on your own resources.'

But sometimes being realistic utterly failed to take account of circumstances and emotional ties like love and loyalty, Misty reflected painfully as she drove home. Birdie Pearce lived in a rambling old country house called Fossetts, which had belonged to her late husband Robin's family for generations. Unable to have children of their own, Robin and Birdie had chosen to become foster parents instead. For over thirty years the kindly couple had opened their home and devoted their lives to helping countless difficult and disturbed children.

Misty had been one of those foster kids and she too had been unhappy, bitter and distrustful when she had first gone to Fossetts. She had been twelve years old, hiding behind a tough front of not caring where she lived or who looked after her, but Birdie and Robin had worked hard to gain her trust and affection. They had transformed her life by giving her security and having faith in her, and that was a debt she knew that she could never repay but, above all, it was a *loving* debt, not a burden.

For the past fourteen months, a fair proportion of Misty's earnings had gone towards ensuring that Birdie could remain in her own home. Not that Birdie knew that even yet, for her husband had once managed their finances and Misty had taken over that task after the older man's death. Misty had been shocked to discover that Fossetts was mortgaged to the hilt. When Robin's investments had failed and money had become tight, he had borrowed on the house without mentioning the matter to anyone.

Now over seventy, Birdie had a bad heart and she was on the waiting list for the surgery that would hopefully ensure that she lived well into old age. But in the short term, without that surgery, Birdie was very vulnerable and her consultant had emphasised how important it was that Birdie should enjoy a stress-free existence. Birdie loved her home and it was also her last link with Robin, whom she had adored. From the outset, Misty's objective had been to protect the older woman from the financial worry that might bring on another heart attack. But even Misty had not appreciated just how much it would cost to keep Fossetts running for Birdie's sake.

It was a tall, rather Gothic house with a steep pitched roof and quaint attic windows. Built in the nineteen twenties, it sat in a grove of stately beech trees fronted by a rough meadow. Parking the van, Misty suppressed a troubled sigh. Fossetts was beginning to look neglected. The grounds no longer rejoiced in a gardener. The windows needed to be replaced and the walls were crying out for fresh paint. Although it was far from being a mansion, it was still too big a house to be maintained on a shoestring.

Yet the minute Misty stepped into the wood-panelled

front hall, she felt for a moment as though all the troubles of the day had slipped from her shoulders. On a worn side table an arrangement of overblown roses filled the air with their sweet scent and dropped their petals. She walked down to the kitchen, which was original to the house and furnished with built-in pine dressers and a big white china sink.

Nancy was making salad sandwiches for tea. A plump woman in her late fifties, Nancy was a cousin of Robin's, who had come to live at Fossetts and help out with the children almost twenty years earlier. These days, she looked after Birdie.

'Birdie's in the summer house,' Nancy said cheerfully. 'We're going to have tea outside.'

Misty managed to smile. 'Sounds lovely. Can I help?'

'No. Go and keep Birdie company.'

It was a beautiful warm June evening but Birdie was wrapped in a blanket, for she felt the cold no matter how good the weather. She was a tiny woman, only four feet eleven inches tall and very slight in build. Her weathered face was embellished by a pair of still-lively blue eyes. 'Isn't the garden beautiful?' she sighed appreciatively.

Misty surveyed the dappled shade cast by the trees, the lush green grass of early summer and the soft pink fading show of the rhododendron blooms. It was indeed a tranquil scene. 'How have you been today?'

Birdie, who hated talking about her health, ignored the question. 'I had visitors. The new vicar and his wife. They've hardly been living here five minutes and already they've heard those silly rumours about how I've been reduced to genteel poverty by some greedy former foster child.' Birdie tilted her greying head to one side, bright eyes exasperated. 'Such nonsense and so I pointed out. Where on earth are these stories coming from?'

'That business with Dawn, I expect. Someone's heard

something about that and got the wrong end of the stick.'
Misty neglected to add that the more curious of the locals
had evidently noted the visible decline in the Pearce for-
tunes and put the worst possible interpretation on it. But
then over the years that the Pearces had fostered, more
than one pessimistic neighbour had forecast that they
would live to regret taking on such 'bad' children.

And sadly, the previous year, Dawn, who *had* once been
fostered by the Pearces, had come to visit and had stolen
all Birdie's jewellery. Birdie had refused to prosecute because Dawn had been a drug addict in a pitiful state. Since
then, yielding to Birdie's persuasions and her own longing
to reclaim her life, Dawn had completed a successful re-
habilitation programme but none of the jewellery had been
recovered.

'Why do people always want to think the worst?' Birdie
looked genuinely pained for she herself always liked to
think the very best of others.

'No, they don't,' Misty soothed.

'Well, what have you got to tell me today about that
handsome Sicilian at Brewsters? I would love to get a peek
at a genuine business tycoon. I've never seen one except
on television,' Birdie said naively, for all the world as
though Leone Andracchi were on a level with a rare animal.

Misty smiled at the little woman, but a great surge of
loving tenderness made her eyes prickle and she had to
look away. She told herself that she ought to be copying
Birdie's sunny optimism, turning her problems round until
a silver lining appeared in the clouds. And, lo and behold,
Leone Andracchi began looking more like their saviour!
So why the heck was she still festering with anguished
loathing over one stupid kiss? Was she turning into an
appalling prude?

'Actually...Mr Andracchi's offered me work in London.'

Misty's gaze was veiled, for she could not have looked Birdie in the eye and told that partial truth. 'How would you feel about me going away for a month or two?'

'To work for a handsome millionaire? Ecstatic!' Birdie teased after she had recovered from her surprise at that sudden announcement.

After tea, Misty went upstairs and opened the wardrobe which contained the clothing that Flash had insisted on buying her in an effort to lift her out of her depression after Philip had broken off their engagement. Fancy frivolous designer garments that had not seen the light of day in over two years. She selected a turquoise *faux* snakeskin skirt and top and a pair of spiky-heeled shoes. After a quick bath, she dug out her cosmetics, which dated from the same period and which had been similiarly shelved after she had said goodbye to her brief foray into Flash's glitzy, unreal world.

Flash had transformed her into a rock-star chick and she had learned how to make the best of her looks. Not that it had been much comfort then to see a sexy, daring image in the mirror when the man that she had loved had rejected her. It had wrecked things between her and Flash too, she acknowledged with pained regret. The day Flash had made her fanciable on his own terms had seemed to be the beginning of the end of their friendship. He had stopped thinking of her as a sister, stopped seeing her as the skinny little kid who had shared the same foster home with him for almost five years and had decided that he wanted more.

Making use of the elderly car that only Nancy used now, Misty drove over to the country house hotel where Leone Andracchi was staying. The gracious foyer exuded expensive exclusivity, and when she enquired at the desk she was informed that Leone was in the dining room.

While she hovered, working out whether she ought to wait or seek him out in the midst of his meal, a fair-haired male emerged from the lounge bar and stopped dead at the sight of her, reacting in a similiar vein to the doorman, who had surged to open the door for her, and the male receptionist, who had tripped over a waste-paper basket in his haste to attend to her.

'Misty…?'

For a split second, Misty thought she was dreaming for, even though it had been three years since she had heard it, she recognised that hesitant, well-bred voice immediately and she spun round in shock. *'Philip?'*

'It's been so long since I've seen you.' Philip Redding stared at her; indeed, his inability to stop staring was marked. 'How a-are you?' he stammered.

'Fine…' Her lips barely moved as her silver-grey eyes lingered on him for, although they still lived within miles of each other, she had been careful to avoid places where they had been likely to meet and, apart from seeing his car on the road occasionally, had been very successful in ensuring that they had not run into each other again.

'You look…you look quite incredible.' His colour heightened as he found himself forced to tilt his head back to meet her gaze. 'I've often thought of calling in at Fossetts—'

'With your wife and children?' Misty enquired in brittle disbelief.

Philip paled and stiffened. 'Just the one child…Helen and I are getting a divorce, actually…it didn't work out.'

Twenty feet away, Leone Andracchi stilled, stunned by the vision of Misty Carlton shorn of her shapeless grey suit. With her wealth of copper hair tumbling loose, eyes that gleamed like polished silver were soft on the face of the man she was regarding, her wide peach tinted mouth parted to show pearly teeth. Leone could not quite work out what she was wearing. The top seemed to be held up by the narrow chains bisecting her slight shoulders. The rich fabric gleamed beneath the lights accentuating the thrust of her breasts, the slender indent of her waist, and screeched to a death-defying halt above long, long, endless legs capable of stopping traffic.

'Misty…?'

Taken aback by Philip's blunt admission that his marriage was heading for the divorce courts, Misty shifted her attention to the tall dark male poised several feet away. Leone Andracchi. She collided with sizzling golden eyes that seemed to burn up all the available oxygen in the atmosphere and instantly she tensed, butterflies fluttering in her tummy. But even as she reacted to his vibrant presence her mind was marching on to make uneasy comparisons between the two men. Leone was much taller, more powerfully built and strikingly dark next to Philip with his boyish fair good looks.

'Sorry if I've kept you waiting, *amore*,' Leone murmured smooth as silk, moving to her side to place an infuriatingly possessive hand on her spine.

'Philip Redding…' Philip shot out a hand with all the easy friendliness that was natural to him. 'Misty and I are old friends.'

'How fascinating,' Leone drawled in a tone of crushing boredom that made the younger man flush. 'Unfortunately, Misty and I are running late.'

'Look, I'll call you,' Philip told Misty, giving Leone a bewildered look, quite out of his depth when faced with such a complete lack of answering courtesy.

'Don't waste your time,' Leone advised before Misty could respond, shooting Philip a derisive glance of cold menace as he pressed her over to the lift and hit the call button with one stab of a punitive finger. 'She won't be available.'

Her face flaming but her lips sealed, for she could not intervene when she did not *want* Philip to phone Fossetts

and upset Birdie, Misty stalked into the lift while listening
to Philip mutter in disconcerted response, 'Well, I must
say...really, for goodness' sake...'

'Do you like behaving like the playground bully?'
Misty enquired dulcetly as the lift doors whirred shut.

'While you're with me, you don't talk to other
men...you don't even *look* at other men,' Leone delivered
with simmering emphasis.

Misty clashed head-on with brilliant golden eyes that
went straight for the jugular and a bone-deep charge of
grateful excitement surged through her long, slender length
for the very last thing she wanted to think about just then
was Philip, whose rejection had torn her apart with grief
and despair for longer than she cared to recall. 'Is that a
fact?'

'Particularly old flames...' Leone decreed, impervious
to sarcasm.

Misty tilted her copper head back and shrugged a slim
shoulder, glorious silver eyes wide and mocking, the knot
of sexual tension he had already awakened licking through
her like a dangerous drug in her bloodstream. 'Then you
had better watch me well.'

'No. I'm paying for total fidelity and the illusion that
you have eyes for no other man,' Leone imparted without
hesitation. 'Flirting with Redding was out of line.'

'Flirting...?' An involuntary laugh empty of humour
was wrenched from Misty, the emotions roused by that
unfortunate encounter with her ex-fiancé breaking loose of
her control. 'Philip's the last man alive I'd flirt with!'

'I saw the way you looked at him,' Leone said with
grim clarity.

'And how was that?' Misty queried unevenly, curious
in spite of herself.

'Do I need to draw pictures?'

Her silver-grey eyes darkened as a shard of bitter pain

from the past assailed her but she veiled her gaze in self-protection. So for an instant she had recalled happier times when Philip had meant the world to her, but those days were very far behind her. And why was she so sure of that reality? Three years earlier, she had only been engaged to Philip for six weeks when a drunk driver had crashed into Philip's car. Although Philip had sustained only a concussion, Misty had suffered internal injuries and had required surgery. Afterwards she had learned that she might never be able to conceive a child and Philip had found the threat of a childless future impossible to accept. But never let it be said that Philip was unfeeling: after all, he had had tears in his eyes when he'd ditched her, when he'd told her that he'd still loved her but that she wasn't really a *proper* woman any more...

'Redding was all over you like a rash—'

'He didn't even touch me!'

'He didn't get the chance.'

As Leone rested a lean hand on Misty's spine to prompt her out of the lift again, she jerked away and flung her bright head high, sending him a warning look from bright silver eyes. 'I don't see an audience, so keep your hands to yourself!'

CHAPTER THREE

MISTY'S eyes leapt in skittish mode round the luxurious
hotel suite while she struggled to disguise the fact that her
whole body wanted to shake as if she were a leaf in a high
wind.

She could not credit that that brief meeting with Philip
should have brought so many wounding memories to the
surface and destabilised her to such an extent. But then
she had worked long and hard to bury all that pain, to rise
above the cruel concept that fertility was the sole measure
of femininity, and had learned to focus on another future
other than that of a husband and a family.

'Would you like a drink?' Leone Andracchi enquired.

'No, thanks.'

'Possibly it might calm your nerves—'

Misty whirled round in a surge of fury that erupted so
suddenly it made her feel dizzy with the strength of it.
'There's nothing wrong with my nerves! Stop trying to put
me down—'

Brilliant dark golden eyes rested on her. 'So the wimp
upset you—'

'Don't talk about Philip like that...you don't know
him.'

'I don't need to,' Leone purred, surveying her with sardonic amusement. 'He showed himself up.'

Misty threw back her head, copper hair flying back from
her flushed cheekbones. 'No, I think *you* did. I don't like
aggressive men.'

A slow, winging smile slanted his wide, sensual mouth.
She had the maddening suspicion that, far from her draw-

ing blood with her retaliation, he was actually enjoying the exchange. 'I'm not aggressive...I'm strong and you like that.'

'I don't know what you're talking about.'

A winged ebony brow quirked. 'Don't you?'

She could feel the tense silence buzzing around her. Her mouth had run dry and her heart was thumping like a trapped bird against her ribs. She looked at him: so very tall and lean with the sleek, honed, muscular build and grace of a natural athlete. His cropped, slightly curly black hair gleamed in the lamp light that picked out every fabulous angle of his bone structure, accentuating the carved cheekbones, the hollows beneath, the firm, sensual line of his mouth. Drop-dead gorgeous, as she had been refusing to acknowledge from the moment he'd appeared in the downstairs foyer and shadowed Philip like Everest looming over a bump in the lawn.

Entrapped by those smouldering dark golden eyes, she could look nowhere else and every breath that quivered through her felt like a huge effort. The taut peaks of her breasts ached and a sliding, curling sensation low in her pelvis made her tighten her thighs. Her knees had developed a slight tremor and all the time she was aware only of the almost terrifying rise of anticipation that took account of nothing but the fierce longing gripping her.

'You want me...I want you, but it's not going to happen,' Leone breathed in a charged undertone that rasped down her sensitive spine like a roughened caress. 'This is strictly business and we don't need to make it complicated.'

Stark disconcertion rippled through Misty. She felt stripped naked, exposed. Urgent words of proud denial brimmed on her lips until she saw the way his burning gaze was homed in on her mouth and she trembled, the excitement climbing again, mindless and without conscience.

'Business…' Leone repeated thickly.

Someone rapped on the door and, although the knock was light, Misty flinched, dredged from her fever with a sense of guilty embarrassment. As the door opened and a young man appeared with a file in his hand she turned to stare out the window, breathing in slow and deep, fighting to still the nervous tremors currenting through her. Nobody had ever had so powerful an effect on her and it was starting to scare her: it was as if she had no control over herself around him, as if her brain went walkabout. But *he* was feeling that pull too. That shook her, surprised her, made her feel a little less mortified. Although she knew that the worst thing she could do would be to lower her guard around a male like Leone Andracchi, the knowledge that the attraction was mutual still made her feel better about herself, better than she had felt in a long time.

The door snapped shut and she turned back.

'This is the agreement I mentioned.' Leone extended a document. 'Read it and then sign.'

Misty accepted the document. 'And if I don't sign?'

'We don't have a deal.'

She sat down and began to read. It was typical employment contract stuff, no mention of her pretending to be his mistress or of clothes or apartments either. However, there was a clause that said she would forfeit all benefits and payments if she tried to walk out before he considered the job complete. She didn't like, that but her attention was caught by the sum of cash he was offering in return and that amount bereft her of breath. Enough money to keep the mortgage on Fossetts ticking over for the next year and more, as well as allowing sufficient funds to settle her outstanding bills and cover staff salaries during her absence.

Cheeks burning, Misty swallowed hard and looked up. 'You're being very generous…but what am I supposed to think about this bit that says I can't walk out on this without your agreement?'

'You may think what you like,' Leone murmured levelly, 'but I assure you that the position won't entail anything either immoral, illegal or dangerous.'

None the wiser, but still troubled that he saw the necessity of making that stipulation, Misty lifted the pen from the table in front of her. He wasn't going to explain himself and she couldn't afford to throw away the only lifebelt on offer.

'Wait…' Striding back to the door, Leone called the young man back in to witness her signature and his own.

Such devotion to legal detail rather unnerved Misty. When the document was duly removed, she smoothed her damp palms down over her skirt. 'Now what?'

'Just a few details. I'll send a car to pick you up at nine on Monday—'

'This Monday coming?' Misty questioned. 'That's only six days from now—'

'I want this show up and running for the following weekend.' Leone settled a notepad down on the coffee-table. 'Make a note of your measurements. You need a new wardrobe.'

Misty bridled at both the instruction and that announcement. 'I already have quite a few presentable outfits—'

'But maybe I'm not into the rock-chick look.' Leone dealt her startled face a sardonic appraisal. 'Maybe I prefer a more elegant and subtle image.'

Rock chick? Misty coloured with annoyance and chagrin, for her top only bared her arms and her skirt was not that short. However, she was more concerned by what his choice of that particular label had revealed. 'You know about Flash, don't you? How?'

'Don't be so naive. Do you really think I would've offered you this role without knowing anything about you?'

When he put it like that, he did make her sound naive, but she didn't like the idea that he had run some sort of a check on her background. He had contrived to make a connection known to precious few and, after her time with Flash, Misty had soon learned that just about everybody who *did* know assumed that she had slept with her former foster brother and that arguing otherwise made little impression.

'There's nothing wrong with what I'm wearing,' Misty said defensively.

Leone surveyed her with exasperated dark golden eyes. 'Tell me, is it your special mission in life to argue with my every simple request?'

'You don't request, you *order*, but bearing in mind that this is supposed to be a job, I'll try to be more receptive.'

'Thank you *so* much.'

Misty drew in a deep steadying breath. Tight-lipped, she filled in her measurements on the notepad, tossed it aside and said equally drily, 'Anything else?'

'Have you always found it this difficult to follow instructions?'

Misty nodded in grudging acknowledgement.

Leone shifted a fluid and expressive hand. 'It's very irritating.'

Misty folded her arms with a jerk. 'Anything else happening next Monday?'

'You get a complete make-over and move into the apartment. We'll go out in the evening—'

'Where?'

'I haven't decided yet. Any questions?'

None that Misty thought that he would answer, and she stood up. 'Is that it, then?'

'I'll see you out to your car—'

'No need,' Misty said in surprise.

Leone swung open the door for her exit and said nothing.

Teeth gritting, Misty stood in the lift with him in silence.

Head high, she crossed the foyer and stalked out onto the steps where a lean hand caught hold of hers.

'*What?*' Misty snapped, forced to swing back.

Leone closed her other hand into his too. She connected with smouldering golden eyes that sent her heartbeat racing and her tummy gave an apprehensive somersault. 'Don't…'

Black lashes low over his slumbrous gaze, Leone stared down at her with vibrant amusement. 'Stop trying to pretend it's a punishment, *amore*.'

Her colour heightened and her slender body quivered as he drew her closer. His sensual mouth drifted down onto hers with an aching sweetness that took her wholly by surprise. She trembled and almost without her own volition pressed forward into the hard, muscular heat of him, every skincell in her body leaping in excited reaction. It was an intoxicating kiss—searching, erotic, teasing, and she could not get enough of that sensual exploration. A low moan sounded deep in her throat.

Leone set her back from him. 'A very convincing pretence,' he murmured with roughened satisfaction.

Her fingers jerked in the grip of his, her anger provoked by an intense sense of embarrassment. 'You—!'

'Temper, temper.' A wry smile slashed his lean, strong face.

Misty dragged her hands free of his and said icily, 'Goodnight.'

Halfway across the car park, she glanced over her shoulder and saw that he had moved to the foot of the steps to watch her progress. Not quite as confident in dark car parks as she liked to pretend, Misty was relieved. She was digging into her bag for her keys when a male figure appeared from behind Birdie's car and a gasp of fright broke from her lips.

'It's only me, Misty,' Philip groaned. 'I recognised Birdie's old car and parked behind it—'

'You scared the life out of me!' Misty settled her bag on the bonnet of the car to better enable her search for her keys, furious that she hadn't got them out before leaving the hotel and rigid with discomfiture in Philip's radius.

'I'm sorry, but I thought it would be easier to talk to you here rather than at Fossetts where I'm sure I'm not very popular—'

'We don't have anything to talk about. I'm sorry that your marriage has run into trouble…*genuinely* sorry,' Misty stressed awkwardly without looking at him. 'But it's not as though we're even friends any more, is it?'

'Just listen to me. I never got over you,' Philip swore emotively. 'I was crazy to rush off and marry Helen—'

'I don't want to hear that kind of stuff from you.' Keys in her shaking hand, Misty struggled to find the lock and make good her escape. 'Please go home.'

'You heard her. Back off.' It was Leone, his dark, deep, accented drawl as welcome at that moment as a rescue squad, his shadow blocking out Philip's, his long, sure fingers removing the keys from hers to unlock the door of the car. In her surprise and relief, she glanced up at him, noting how the aggression he had earlier denied was stamped into every line of his lean, powerful face, but not one atom of that aggression was aimed at her. Philip was the unhappy recipient and Philip, she saw out of the corner of her eye, had already backed off so far that he would need a loud hailer to continue their dialogue.

'Thanks,' Misty said raggedly, diving into Birdie's ancient car at supersonic speed.

'No problem. Did that idiot scare you?' Leone demanded.

'No...' Misty lied, attention nervously lodged to the clenched fist within view. 'No, not at all.'

Without another glance at either man, she drove off, but she stopped a mile down the road to wipe her tear-wet face dry with a tissue. No, she no longer cared about Philip, but her memories hurt terribly. How could Philip even think that his interest might still be welcome after the way he had treated her?

Within six months of ditching her, he had married a well-bred blonde with a cut-glass accent and a double-barrelled surname—exactly the sort of young woman his snobbish mother had always wanted him to marry. And within a year he had become father to a beautiful baby boy. Misty might not have seen Philip in recent years but she *had* seen his wife and child out shopping on several occasions. She would never forget the pain of first seeing their baby and knowing that that special joy was unlikely ever to be hers. It seemed all wrong too that the son that Philip had sworn he could not live without having some day should now be caught up in the miseries of a divorce.

Sucking in a steadying breath, Misty drove home. After she had got over Philip, she had forced herself out on dates purely to please Birdie. But when she had casually encouraged those men to share their aspirations, she had discovered that they too took it for granted that their future would hold children and paled at the gills at the mere mention of a woman with fertility problems.

It was one thing for a man to marry a woman unaware that there might be a problem in that department, another thing entirely for him to do so armed with that knowledge. That took either a very special love or a male who didn't want kids. So to protect herself from that horrible sinking feeling of inadequacy, of seeing herself as something less than other women and of having to ultimately face confiding the consequences of that car smash in any more lasting relationship, she had given up on dating and had concentrated on setting up her business instead.

And she had been perfectly happy and content until Leone Andracchi had come along and reminded her that she was still a woman and still susceptible to all the feelings and fancies that she had foolishly assumed she could shut out and ignore. In his vicinity she had all the resistance of a schoolgirl with a bad crush and that hammered her pride hard. But what worried her most was the awareness that Leone Andracchi fascinated her: his every move fascinated her, even though he infuriated her.

Had he insisted on seeing her out to the car park because he'd suspected that Philip might still have been hanging around? Or had that just been coincidence? Surely it must have been coincidence. Yet why was she receiving the impression that, even when Leone was faking a caring role, he was a very possessive guy with the women in his life? After all, he seemed prone to standing over her like a Rottweiler guarding a bone!

But obviously she had picked up the wrong impression and Leone was simply a good actor, for Clarice had brought in a couple of glossy gossip magazines in which he had featured with various beauties and Misty had formed a picture of a very different male. A guy so cool in relationships that ice might be cosy in comparison. A guy who got bored very easily and without apology, generous to a fault but ungiven to commitment or romantic gestures, indeed the guy most likely to forget your birthday, overlook St Valentine's Day and cancel dates last minute in favour of work. A guy whose lovers always looked nervous, as if at any moment they awaited the news that they were no longer flavour of the month. In short, an absolute rat, whom any sensible woman would avoid like the plague…as would she to the best of her ability.

On the day that Leone had arranged, Misty arrived in London. While the chauffeur removed her two bulging suitcases from the boot of the opulent limousine that had collected her from Fossetts, Misty stared up at the massive ultra-modern apartment building shadowing the pavement.

Over the last week, while she had closed up her business premises and made a dozen last minute arrangements to take care of various matters, she had been conscious of a positively childish little glow of growing excitement. She was embarrassed by that reality but had been forced to concede that her life had been pretty uneventful for a long while. Although she would hate seeing less of Birdie, the change of scene was especially welcome after the stress and worry she had suffered in recent months.

Travelling up in the lift, she studied her reflection in the mirrored wall and frowned. All anxious eyes and mouth, she thought ruefully, no alteration there, nothing very special either, although Leone must have seen something to have behaved as he had. Unfortunately, her self-esteem had sunk to an all-time low after Philip and had never really recovered. After all, that self-esteem had been a hard-won achievement even *before* Philip had entered her life.

So many people had broken promises to Misty that it had taken a very long time for her to learn to trust anyone. She could still recall her mother clear as day: a beautiful redhead with lovely clothes and a constant embattled air of uneasy apology.

'As soon as I get organised, you can come and live with me,' her mother had promised repeatedly when Misty had been living in care. 'I gave your sister up for adoption…you know she was sickly and I could never have managed her…but I couldn't bring myself to give you up as well.'

But Misty had lived from birth to adulthood in foster care and by the time she was five her mother's occasional visits had become only a memory. Years later, it had been a shock to discover that her parent had remarried within eighteen months of her birth and that there had never been any question of her bringing her illegitimate daughter into the marital home when her second husband was not even aware of Misty's existence.

A trim older man in a steward's jacket introduced himself as Alfredo at the door of the apartment. She stepped into a very large hall floored in marble and glanced into a reception room, which rejoiced in minimal modern furniture and a decor of white on white. The only colour she could see came from the artworks on display. It was fashionable and elegant but cold and unappealing, she reflected in some disappointment.

Well, what had she expected? she asked herself ruefully. Cosy clutter? Having shown her into a spacious bedroom complete with dressing room and *en suite* facilities, Alfredo passed her a sheet of paper headed, 'Appointments.' At that point, Misty realised that a busy afternoon lay ahead of her at various beauty establishments and she grimaced. Evidently, Leone was of the opinion that in the looks department she needed all the professional help she could get!

By the end of those appointments some hours later, her hair coaxed into a streaming mane and her practical short nails disguised by fake perfection, Misty had decided that being a mistress, pretend or otherwise, promised to be the most boring existence imaginable.

The limousine was on the way back to the apartment and stuck in the teatime traffic when Leone called her on the car phone. 'I'll pick you up at seven,' he informed her, the rich timbre of his dark, deep drawl making her spine tingle.

She breathed in deep. 'Where are we going?'

'A movie première.'

'Oh…' Misty was disconcerted, not having expected anything like such a grand public occasion.

'Wear the jewellery,' he told her huskily. 'I chose diamonds for you.'

Back at the apartment she went straight to her bedroom. A shallow heart-shaped case sat on the dressing table and she clicked it open to a breathtaking diamond necklace and drop earrings. Dragging her attention from them in astonishment, she noted that her suitcases had disappeared. An examination of the dressing room not only revealed that her luggage had been unpacked but also revealed a large selection of new garments in her size. In addition, a long slinky silvery gown with slender straps hung in apparent readiness for her and it carried the label of one of the world's most exclusive designers.

At half-past seven, Misty strolled into the vast lounge where Leone was poised by the floor-deep windows. Even from the back he looked spectacular: sunlight gleaming on his proud dark head, wide shoulders tapering to narrow hips and long, powerful legs.

'I don't like being kept waiting,' Leone delivered before he even turned round.

'You didn't give me much warning.' Misty stilled, copper head high, slim body taut as she waited for him to look at her.

He swung round. '*Dio mio*…you spent the entire afternoon getting ready!'

Dark golden eyes glinting with impatience zeroed in on her and then narrowed to stare.

Misty knew that she had never looked better. The shimmer of the silver and the glitter of the diamonds flattered

her copper hair and fair complexion and the dress was a
dream of deceptive simplicity cut to enhance her slender
curves. A fashionable frilled split ran to high above her
knee and revealed one slim, shapely leg shod in a kitten-
heeled diamanté shoe.

The silence was electric.

'You look fantastic,' Leone breathed in another voice
entirely, his rich drawl roughening. His screened gaze
roamed from her silvery eyes and the glow in her triangular face to linger on the ripe pout of her burgundy tinted
mouth before travelling on downward to absorb the full
effect of the dress.

Beneath that intent scrutiny Misty's mouth had run dry
and she was alarmingly short of breath. Aware of his vibrant masculinity with every skincell in her thrumming
body, she fought to get a grip on a sudden inexplicable
sense of euphoria. 'Thank you.'

'That doesn't mean that you're forgiven for keeping me
waiting,' Leone asserted in the hall.

'You might as well get used to it,' Misty dared. 'Outside
business hours, I'm always running late—'

'This *is* business,' Leone reminded her drily.

As he stood back for her to enter the lift colour lit her
taut cheekbones. 'Then don't look at me the way you do.'

'Looking's not touching,' Leone murmured, smooth as
silk.

Her teeth ground together. He had, it seemed, an answer
for *everything*. She climbed into the limousine with frustration currenting through her. The whole time she had
been getting dressed, she had marvelled at the lengths to
which he was willing to go to establish their masquerade.
The apartment, the clothes, the fabulous jewellery, not to
mention the cost of winning her agreement—it had all
come at a high price. What could he hope to achieve from
such a pretence? Her imagination had run riot. She had

even wondered if he was having an affair with a married woman and attempting to establish a mistress as a cover story.

'I wish that you would tell me what this is all about,' she said tightly. 'I swear that I would keep it quiet.'

Leone stretched his long, powerful length into an indolent attitude of relaxation. He surveyed her from below dense ebony lashes. 'By the time this finishes, you will no longer be in the dark as to my motivation.'

Something in his voice sent a shiver down Misty's spine. 'I don't think I like the sound of that.'

'I'm paying you well for your services,' Leone countered with crushing cool.

Her temper sparked. 'Courtesy costs nothing,'

'You're too proud for your own good.' Leone rested measuring eyes on her, lean dark features impassive.

Misty stared back at him, her facial bones tight. 'I feel like a doll you've dressed up!'

'Worry if I start trying to *un*dress you,' Leone advised in a jungle-cat purr.

She couldn't help it: her face flamed and, although she had been dying to ask what the film was, she said nothing for the remainder of the drive.

Even before they emerged from the limo, she saw the press cameras and the crash barriers holding back the crowds waiting to see celebrities arrive. Her nervous tension started to rise. Cool as ice, Leone walked her between the barriers with a light arm at her spine. She was quite unprepared for the sudden question shouted by a journalist.

'Who's the new lady, Leone?'

And without the smallest warning, the cameras were turned on them along with a whole new barrage of questions, which Leone ignored. A smile stuck to her numb mouth like paint, perspiration dewing her short upper lip, Misty was intimidated by the surge of interest and the photos being taken. What on earth would Birdie think if she opened a newspaper and saw Misty, who had supposedly come to London to *work*, attending a film première with diamonds hanging from her ears? How was she to explain that development? Why the heck hadn't it occurred to her before now that a male who made regular appearances in the gossip columns was likely to attract that kind of media attention?

'You should've warned me it would be like this,' Misty muttered minutes later, her low-pitched voice full of reproach. 'I had no idea that my being with you was going to be such a public event.'

Leone dealt her a sardonic appraisal. 'Ditch the artless routine. Why do you think you're looking so good? Only married men hide their mistresses.'

'Well, I can tell you right now that being *your* mistress stinks!' Misty hissed furiously out of the corner of her mouth.

'If we were playing this for real, you wouldn't be talking like that,' Leone drawled in purring provocation, his breath fanning her cheek, and she coloured furiously as she caught an older woman watching them and realised how intimate his pose must seem.

Before the lights went down, Misty engaged in looking out for famous faces and spotted several. Her self-consciousness only returned when she realised that she was under examination too by several sets of curious eyes. The film was an edge-of-the-seat thriller and she thoroughly enjoyed it. Before the credits were rolling down the screen, Leone whisked her out again. Emerging into the brightly lit street, she froze at the sight of the waiting cameras.

'Ignore them and smile,' Leone murmured as he felt her stiffen in discomfiture.

As the limo door closed on them he flashed her a look of exasperation. 'Why the shrinking-violet act?'

'I don't want my photo in the newspapers!' Misty protested. 'I don't like people talking about me!'

'You...*don't*?' Leone queried in a tone of mockery.

The silence buzzed.

Leone leant forward, extracted a DVD from a storage unit and fed it into the player below the built in television. He zapped the control and lounged back in the corner. 'I just want to remind myself of how shy you are in public...'

Misty frowned in bewilderment as the television screen came to life to show Flash on stage at one of his concerts, and then a split second later her heart sank as she realised *which* concert it was. There she was dancing like a wanton show-off, hair everywhere, wild-eyed, skimpy little dress showing far too much thigh. She broke out in nervous perspiration. Her fingers knotted, nails scoring welts into her palms. Her lowest moment...and somehow *he* had discovered that that ghastly performance of hers had been captured for posterity on film, which was more than she had known herself. In all her life, she did not believe she had ever felt more humiliated or embarrassed than she did at that instant.

'Switch it off!' Misty pleaded in a desperate rush.

'I'm looking hard for signs of timidity,' Leone confided. 'There you are in front of thousands of people—'

'*Please* switch it off!' Misty gritted feverishly.

'Don't be so selfish,' Leone scolded her with a slow, mocking smile that made her face burn even hotter with squirming chagrin. 'The camera loves you and I'm sure the guys in the audience loved you too. You're very sexy.'

Misty made a wild grab at the remote he held in one lean hand, but he stretched it out of reach. 'If you don't give me that control, I'll-'

'You'll...what?' Leone prompted with amusement.

'You don't understand...Flash *dared* me! I'd been drinking, I didn't care about anything that night...'

Registering that she was telling him things he had no right to know and merely increasing her own mortification, and recognising that the cynical glint in his dark golden eyes had merely heightened, Misty lost what remained of her hold on her temper and threw herself at him to retrieve the control.

'*Accidenti!*' Leone exclaimed, finding himself engaged in a physical struggle with something of his bemusement showing in his lean, strong face. 'Are you crazy?'

'Give it to me!' Misty raked at him, straining over him to stretch a hand up to his.

'When I pictured you on my lap,' Leone savoured with roughened intensity as he dropped the remote and closed both lean hands round her slender forearms at speed, 'this isn't quite the way it was, *amore*.'

Infuriated at the position he had trapped her in, Misty snapped, 'Let *go* of me!'

Instead he drew her fully down on him. Smouldering dark golden eyes lodged on her startled face. 'You should think twice before you climb on top of a guy and ask him to give it to you...'

Belatedly she realised that her dress had ridden up and that the most sensitive part of her whole body was pressed to the hard, surging masculine arousal of his. Her breath caught in her throat, heat flaring through her in an accelerated surge of sexual awareness. 'You know I didn't mean—'

'And right now,' Leone murmured with mesmeric huskiness, his brilliant eyes holding hers as he anchored one hand into the fall of her copper hair to ease her forward. 'I am very tempted to satisfy your request.'

He locked his hot mouth to the tiny pulse flickering like crazy below her collar-bone and a shudder of response hotter than any fire raked through her. Her head tipped back, one hand grabbing at his shoulder to steady herself,

a strangled little moan torn from her throat. Her breasts
were taut and full, her nipples straining. He bent her back
over one strong arm and let his sensual mouth rove over
her exposed cleavage, driving her mad with frustrated
longing for more. Shock was leaping through her in waves
for her own hunger had surged so fast in response to his
that she was breathless and her heart was beating so fast
she was afraid it would burst.

'*Dio…*' Leone growled, gathering her up in his arms
and laying her down full length on the smooth cream
leather seat. 'I don't want to stop…'

CHAPTER FOUR

MISTY clashed with Leone's burning golden eyes and just lay there, every inch of her drawn tight with screaming anticipation.

He hit a button and the flickering lights of the city streets showing through the tinted windows were screened out, locking them into greater privacy. He shed his jacket in a fluid but purposeful movement. He plucked off her shoes, cast them aside and then he reached for her again.

'I...' she began, nervous second thoughts prompting her at the exact same moment as Leone's carnal lips locked to hers with urgent hunger.

It was like going to heaven on a rocket. The explosion of passion jolted her. His tongue plundered the tender interior of her mouth, setting up a chain reaction through her quivering body. He slid a hand beneath her hip, lifting her to him, and she locked her arms round his neck, letting that wild kiss deepen to the brink of cutting off her own oxygen supply.

With a harsh rush of breath, Leone lifted his dark head, colour scoring his superb cheekbones, golden eyes shimmering over her. Unclasping her hands, he drew the straps of her dress down over her arms. 'I want to rip that dress off you and the silk would tear like paper, but we *do* have to vacate the car at some stage,' he pointed out with audible regret.

Shock shrilled through her as he unzipped her dress and cooler air hit her exposed flesh. She was breathing in rapid, irregular little gasps, striving not to think of what he had just said, but her brain had begun to turn again. They were in a car. Did she want to lose her virginity on the back seat of a car? All right, so it was a limo, but right now his chauffeur probably had a very good idea of what his passengers were doing and she would have to walk out past the man and pretend she didn't mind him thinking she was a real little…a real little slut…

'You have gorgeous breasts…' Appreciative golden eyes scorched over the pert, pouting mounds now bared for his appraisal.

In thrall to the conviction that she was behaving like a wanton, she glanced down at her own nakedness and almost had a heart attack. But her immediate effort to cover herself with her hands was thwarted by the simple fact that he was holding them.

'In fact, I don't think a brief sortie is likely to satisfy me.' Leone lowered his head to run the tip of his tongue over a quivering pink nipple and her spine arched in an involuntary spasm of response, an ache stirring with powerful effect between her thighs.

'No…?' she gasped, too controlled by tormenting sensation to catch her breath.

He closed his mouth round a lush rosy peak and caught her sensitive flesh between his teeth in a teasing, sensual assault. She could not restrain the low, keening cry that escaped her parted lips. A knot of unbearable tension was tightening low in her pelvis. She wanted him, she wanted him as she had never wanted any male. Somewhere in the background she was dimly conscious of the faint sound of music, familiar music that tugged at her memory. Then Leone let his fingers tug at her distended nipples and thought was snatched from her again with a vengeance. Excitement had her in its tenacious hold. She was lost in the fierce hunger of her own body

'I'm going to screw you senseless, *amore*,' Leone intoned with raw sensual force, sinking his hands beneath her hips to tug her dress out of his path. 'And then I'm going to take you into my bed tonight and do it all over again.'

A combination of shock, excitement and shame hit her all at once. But even as that threat excited her to an embarrassing degree the words jarred on her: too raw, too realistic. And in the background she finally recognised the melodic sound of the song that Flash had written for her and inwardly cringed at her own weakness with Leone Andracchi. How could she have been so stupid as to allow matters to get so far? Leone would just be using her for sex. He didn't care about her, he didn't even *like* her, for goodness' sake! That she found him sheer, tormenting temptation was no excuse. And letting him have her on the back seat of his limo would be the ultimate in tarty behaviour. Surely she had more respect for herself?

'What's wrong?'

It shook Misty that he had noted her withdrawal that fast. She snaked back from him and sat up in an awkward movement, frantically wrenching at her dress in an effort to yank it up and cover her breasts at speed. There was a ghastly ripping sound that made her squeeze her stinging eyes shut in despair. But the electric silence that stretched was even tougher on her nerves.

'You've changed your mind,' Leone breathed not quite steadily.

'I'm sorry,' she mumbled shakily. 'I wish I'd changed it sooner but this...*us*...well, it's a really bad idea. As you said yourself, strictly business is wiser.'

'You want me to make a deal that includes access to your body as well?' Leone derided in a tone that stung her sensitive nerves like a whiplash.

In a sudden motion, she turned round and hit him so hard with her open palm that a shuddering sensation ran up her arm and her hand went numb. 'Don't you dare talk to me like that! I'm not some whore available for a price!'

A silence that left the previous silence behind in the starting stakes had fallen. A perfect imprint of her finger-tips was burned into the olive skin above his aggressive jawline and his golden eyes were molten with outrage and shock.

'I'm not going to apologise for hitting you either,' Misty framed on the back of an overwrought sob. 'It's a pity someone didn't thump the hell out of you a long time ago! Just because you're not used to a woman saying no.'

'I didn't argue. I freed you immediately,' Leone grated in a ferocious undertone. 'There is no excuse for you strik-ing me when you know that I can't hit back.'

Misty was trembling. She sat up, dragging at the dress until it stretched back over her breasts. She was scared to look to see where the delicate silk had torn. She dived into the shoulder straps and began to struggle to do up the zip.

'Let me,' Leone said icily, turning her round to run up the zip with the merest touch, as though he were risking radioactive contamination.

'Thanks.'

He sent the blinds flying back from the windows with the stab of one lean finger. She wanted to open the pas-senger door beside her and throw herself out even though the limo was still moving. His wounding words had bitten deep and sent her careening into the kind of loss of control she had not surrendered to since childhood, and in the aftermath she was in shock and ashamed but she couldn't bring herself to apologise for slapping him after what he had said.

The limousine drew up. The chauffeur opened the pas-senger door. As she sat there, frozen with knowledge that her once-beautiful gown was now ripped right up to her waist, something warm and heavy was draped round her shoulders: his jacket. She drew in a quivering breath and began to climb out. An arm curved round her, keeping the jacket in place, Leone walked her into the well-lit foyer and exchanged a word with the unctuous doorman, who went to call the lift for them.

Inside the lift the silence was so profound that it buzzed in her ears. She couldn't bring herself to look at him until it occurred to her to wonder why he was accompanying her. Just to get his jacket back? She glanced up. His lean, powerful face was set in forbidding lines, stunning eyes veiled and dark.

He used a key on the apartment door and tossed it on a side table. She slid out of his jacket and extended it.

He hooked it with one lean brown hand. 'Goodnight,' he said without any expression at all.

As he strode in the direction of the bedroom corridor, Misty cleared her throat. 'Where are you going?'

'To have a long cold shower,' Leone framed in a gritty tone. 'You have a problem with that too?'

Her face flamed. 'I meant...you're staying the night *here*?'

'I don't sleepwalk,' Leone assured her very drily.

Finally she added two and two and made four for herself. Her full mouth compressed. 'You're staying because I'm supposed to be your mistress. So I'm a put-out-on-the-first-date girl now as well as everything else...'

'I beg your pardon?' Leone had swung back.

Misty surveyed him with silver-grey eyes awash with resentment. He was a visual joy and she was questioning now if her susceptibility to those stunning dark good looks of his had dulled her wits a week earlier. She had not foreseen the costs she would pay in terms of her own reputation, but she *should* have done. In a small business like hers, the reputation of a female owner was all important. Nobody was ever likely to take her seriously again after she had been seen draped round Leone Andracchi wearing diamonds and designer garments. That was bimbo territory. The few who had accepted that Flash was just a very good friend would now suspect otherwise. People would decide she was a gold-digging tart who threw herself at any rich man who came within her reach and female clients would be none too keen to hire her services.

'You heard me.' She folded her arms with a jerk. 'If you stay tonight, you're making me look like a tramp.'

'I'm so grateful that you're *not* my mistress.' Thrusting lean brown fingers through his tousled black hair, Leone surveyed her with an aura of sardonic satisfaction. 'You saved us both from making a serious error of judgement this evening. Feel free to hit me any time I get too close in the future.'

Anger stiffened her. 'I really am starting to *hate* you—'

'Hold the feeling, nourish it,' Leone advised with silken mockery. 'Because if you ever end up in bed with me, life as you know it will end.'

Misty flung her head back, lustrous copper coils of hair falling back from her slanted cheekbones, grey eyes silver with rage. 'Oh yeah?'

A wolfish grin of appreciation slashed his lean dark features. For a split second all the charisma he had bent over backwards to conceal from her flashed out full force and she found herself staring, hooked like a fish on a line. 'Oh, *yeah*,' he emphasised huskily. 'I'll be gone before you get up tomorrow. I'll see you Friday. We're heading up to Scotland for the weekend.'

And with that concluding assurance he strolled with fluid grace down the corridor, leaving her standing there like a woman who had just seen exactly what she did not want to see. A male genuinely capable of fascinating her, a male who could shift within the space of minutes from icy reserve to sardonic humour to that self-mocking smile, which had made her stupid heart sing and bang like a drum.

Snatching in a ragged breath, Misty walked down to her own room, closed the door and leant back against it for a moment, feeling oddly empty. She lay awake in the moonlight and was shaken to discover her mind wandering to an imaginary vision of Leone having a cold shower. Feeling the heat of a self-loathing blush, she rolled over and stuffed her face in a pillow. She relived her own wild, wanton craving for him in the limo and squirmed with discomfiture.

When she had heard other women talking about not being able to resist some guy, she had never been too impressed. After all, she had not even found Philip irresistible. In her teens, she had had to come to terms with the cautionary tale of her own mother's mistakes and deep down inside, although she had never admitted it even to Birdie, she had been afraid that she might turn out to be the same as her mother, Carrie, who had mistaken lust for love. Carrie had flitted from one relationship to the next and left a trail of destruction and abandoned children in her wake.

Misty had been studying at catering college when she'd met Philip. From that first week, they had been inseparable and he had seemed so romantic and caring that she could never, ever have guessed what the future had held for them both.

Right from the start, however, Philip's mother had been cold with Misty, and one afternoon the older woman had said with revealing distaste, 'You really don't know what's in your background, do you?'

And, sadly, that had been true for it said 'father unknown' on Misty's birth certificate. She was illegitimate and had no relatives to offer even on the maternal side. Philip had had to stand firm against his mother's efforts to break them up and Misty had believed that he'd truly had to love her to have withstood that pressure. Once they had become engaged, Misty had begun feeling more secure in their relationship and, although until that point she had always called an anxious halt to their lovemaking, she had finally agreed to go away for the weekend with him. A dream weekend in a historic country hotel. But they had never arrived: on the way there, they had had the car accident and that had been that as far as she and Philip had been concerned.

After falling into an uneasy dose, Misty wakened soon after dawn feeling thirsty. Rolling out of bed, she freshened up in the *en suite* and, having tugged on her wrap over her nightie, she padded out into the corridor to go in search of the kitchen. As she walked past the dining room, she almost cannoned into Alfredo, who was carrying a coffee pot.

'Misty?' It was Leone's dark drawl.

Misty hovered awkwardly in the doorway. He looked gorgeous. Having risen from the breakfast table in courteous acknowledgement of her appearance, immaculate in a grey business suit worn with a snazzy dull gold tie, Leone shifted an inviting hand. 'Join me.'

Slowly she shook her copper head in wonderment.

'Why are you staring at me?' Leone asked.

'You're such a contradiction. I walk into the room and you stand up. Someone taught you very good manners—'

'My mother,' Leone slotted in drily.

'But it was such a waste of time when you can hardly open your mouth around me without being offensive.' Misty sighed, settling down into a seat opposite and reaching for the jug of orange juice.

Disconcerted, Leone breathed in deep, brilliant dark golden eyes shimmering as he sank back down again. In the electric silence, broken only by the manservant's reappearance, Misty poured herself a glass of pure orange and sipped. Alfredo poured Leone's coffee and, grey eyes dancing with amusement, Misty sugared it for him with a teasing hand.

'So where are you off to at this early hour?' she asked brightly as she pounced on a warm croissant and began to eat it.

'Paris…'

'I was there once but I didn't really see it. I was with Flash. Either we were in the hotel hiding from his horde of screaming fans or I was backstage.'

Leone's intent scrutiny was lodged on her lush pink lips as the tip of her tongue snaked out to retrieve a stray crumb. As she noted the path of his attention, a slow burning curl of heat ignited in her pelvis and she shifted on her seat. Cold shower time, she thought guiltily, horribly conscious of her own vulnerability. In a frantic attempt to distract herself, she focused on the portrait on the wall. She had noted it the day before. It was the sole piece of traditional art she had so far seen in the apartment: an oil of a young girl with a dreamy expression in her dark eyes.

'That's a lovely painting,' she remarked brittly. 'Anyone you know?'

Right before her eyes, Leone froze, lean, strong face clenching hard. 'My sister…she's dead.'

Misty paled, lips parting and then sealing again before she made a desperate effort at recovery. 'Well, at least you had her for a while.'

His forbidding frown would have silenced a lesser woman. 'And what's that supposed to mean?'

Misty sucked in a steadying breath and wished that she had stuck to muttering conventional regrets. 'I…er…well, I have a twin sister that—'

Fortunately that sudden announcement seemed to grab his attention. 'You *know* that you have a twin?'

'We're not identical…that's about all I do know about her.' Misty shrugged, regretting having raised so personal a subject yet grateful that they had moved on from the too sensitive topic of his own sister's death. 'She was adopted and I wasn't.'

'One would've assumed that twins would have been kept together,' Leone remarked with veiled eyes.

'When it came to my sister and I, our mother was willing to sign away her rights to her but not to me as well. I tried to establish contact with my twin through the private adoption agency when I was a teenager but she wasn't interested. I just got a letter back saying that her adoptive parents were all the family she needed and that she didn't want to meet me. Birdie thinks that she may change her mind when she's older.' Misty forced an accepting smile, as if that negative response hadn't been any big deal, but the fierce disappointment and hurt of that rejection still lingered. She had had such high hopes and those hopes had been shattered by that chilly little letter bare of even an address lest she make a nuisance of herself by arriving on the doorstep.

'Birdie…your foster mother,' Leone answered for himself.

'You know a lot about me.' Before she had slept the night before, Misty had mulled over that little scene in his limo and his cruelly manipulative playing of that recording of Flash's concert in Germany. 'I think you could've been more up front about that.'

'I was *very* up front on that score last night. You struck me,' Leone reminded her.

Misty reddened to the roots of her hair. 'All right, I shouldn't have done that but you provoked me!'

Stunning dark golden eyes nailed to her with relentless force, Leone lounged back in his chair. 'That's not an excuse.'

'I lost my temper.'

'Try again.'

Misty could feel that forbidden anger mushrooming all over again. 'I'm sorry…I'm *sorry*…I'm sorry…OK?' she reeled off on a rising note.

'Who says you can't take a horse to water and *make* it drink?' Leone murmured with cool satisfaction.

Misty drew in a deep shaken breath and counted steadily to ten.

'I have to leave.' Tossing down his napkin, Leone rose to his full intimidating height. He strode away and then paused and wheeled back round again, lean, strong face taut. 'If anyone contacts you or visits you during my absence, you tell them absolutely nothing about our relationship and you stay in role. Agreed?'

Disconcerted, Misty nodded slowly. Was he expecting someone to call on her?

As he strode out into the hall she leapt off her chair and hurried in pursuit, determined to ask the question that had niggled at her the evening before. 'Leone…?'

His screened gaze ran from the crown of her tousled copper head, down over her simple white nightshirt and wrap and the long, slender legs beneath, before running back up to rest on her pink cheeks. 'Did anyone ever tell you that you look luscious at six in the morning?'

'Do you ever think of anything but the obvious around a woman?' Misty asked ruefully.

'Did no one ever teach you how to receive a compliment?' Leone demanded.

'Look, I have this question I want to ask…' She linked her hands together. 'Are you having an affair with a married woman and trying to set me up as your cover story?'

'I don't have affairs with married women. Sharing a woman would never come naturally to me.'

She reddened but continued, 'So this *is* a business thing—'

'Sicilian business,' Leone qualified, smooth as black velvet. 'You wouldn't understand the nuances.'

'I suppose not...' Misty watched him depart.

After he'd gone, she read the newspapers over breakfast and her heart sank to her toes. A recognisable picture of her on Leone's arm featured in two different gossip columns. 'Leone's latest squeeze,' she was called in one and 'Another Andracchi beauty' in the other, which she knew that Birdie read every day. So far she had not been identified but how long was that happy state of affairs likely to last? After that wretched kiss Leone had stolen at Brewsters, local gossip would have got a headstart even before she'd headed for London. She realised that she had been really stupid to believe that she could get away with telling Birdie that she was *working* for Leone. Appreciating that she had to explain herself, she caught the train back to Norfolk and a cab ferried her out to Fossetts from the station.

By then, it was mid-afternoon and Birdie was in the sitting room fixing flowers at a table by the window. She looked up with a tranquil smile, only the faintest hint of concern in her bright eyes. 'I suppose you left *him* in London.'

'Birdie...I—'

'You're in the throes of a big romance and you didn't tell me,' Birdie scolded. 'But why are you looking so worried? I'm happy that you've met someone that you can care about again.'

Misty worried at her full lower lip with her teeth, not knowing how best to respond.

'Obviously you've moved *in* with him, as they call it these days,' Birdie continued ruefully. 'I don't approve of that aspect, but I do understand why you couldn't bring yourself to tell me.'

'I'm sorry.'

'You're a dear girl,' the older woman murmured with quiet affection. 'And if Leone Andracchi hurts you, he'll have me to reckon with.'

The ridiculous image of tiny Birdie calling Leone to account made Misty smile and she murmured gently, 'Stop fretting about me.'

'I expect Flash will now tell you that his heart is broken and he'll write a song about it. You had better brace yourself. There's nothing that young man loves more than a challenge…except perhaps an audience.'

Misty stayed on at Fossetts for a couple of days and took the train back to London on the Thursday afternoon, feeling pleasantly rested. When Alfredo opened the apartment door to her that evening, he was wearing a rather hunted expression.

'I really must have a key of my own,' she said gently.

'So that you can come and go as you please?' A familiar dark drawl launched from the lounge doorway. 'Not in this lifetime!'

Misty came to a dead halt in the centre of the hall. Leone was poised only fifteen feet from her. A green cotton shirt pushed up his muscular brown forearms, fitting black jeans sheathing his lean hips and long, powerful thighs, his sheer exotic appeal was only outweighed by the scorching anger glittering in his hard golden eyes.

'What's the matter?' she asked hesitantly, totally thrown by that greeting.

Leone spread both arms in a very expansive gesture. 'You are asking *me* what's wrong? Within hours of my flight to Paris, you walked out of here and vanished into thin air!'

'I've been at home with Birdie.'

'Not according to her housekeeper. I phoned and asked for you.'

Misty winced. Having identified her as being the woman with Leone at the première, a local journalist had repeatedly phoned asking to be put in contact with her. Mercifully having fielded his first call for herself, Misty had asked Nancy just to pretend that she wasn't there if there were any further enquiries in that line, and there had been several from different sources.

'So where *have* you been? Because if you've been with Philip Redding, I'm going to rip him apart!'

Misty surveyed him in growing wonderment.

'I should have dealt with him in the car park that night,' Leone framed with unconcealed aggression.

'Do you think you own me...or something?'

The silence sizzled.

'For the next few weeks...*yes*.' Smouldering golden eyes challenged her. 'If I find out that you've been screwing some other guy...'

Misty folded her arms and surveyed him with furious resentment and chagrin. 'You really do think I sleep around, don't you?'

'No...comment.'

'I was at Fossetts with Birdie keeping a low profile—'

'So *low* nobody knew you were there,' Leone slotted in unimpressed. 'Do you think that I can't recognise an alibi when I hear one?'

'Women do this to you all the time, then...do they?' Misty widened big grey eyes in mock sympathy. 'Sneak off to have it away with other men—'

'*Per meraviglia!* No woman has *ever* done that to me!' Leone sent her a flashing look of outraged denial. 'And don't stray off the subject. Were you with your ex-fiancé?'

'No...but to be honest, I don't think I'd tell you if I had been,' Misty confided. 'You didn't ask me not to leave

London. You said you'd see me on Friday and it wasn't Friday last time I looked at the calendar. As far as I was concerned, I was off duty.'

Leone was still endeavouring to swallow her first statement and it appeared to be a major challenge. 'You wouldn't tell me if you *had* been with Redding?'

'As I wasn't, it's a moot point.' Misty yielded a little for the sake of peace.

'Were you *on* or *off* duty in my limo the other night?' Her face burned. 'What do you think?'

With a sudden frown of exasperation, Leone glanced at his watch. 'I'm running extremely late for a dinner date. I'll see you tomorrow afternoon. We're flying up to Aberdeen and driving the rest of the way.'

Like a woman turned to stone by that careless speech, Misty watched Leone depart. He had a date. He… had…a…*date*. And he wasn't returning to the apartment either, so no prizes for guessing how *he* planned to while away the night hours. But then what did his sex life have to do with her? She had no idea, but she still couldn't settle at anything for what remained of the evening and she was dismayed to find her thoughts continually turning to what Leone might be doing. Obviously his current lover was either a very understanding woman or in on the secret that he refused to trust his fake mistress with. It was a job, just a job, and when had she forgotten that? When she had been writhing on the back seat of his limo? Hating herself for that degrading memory, she went to bed and swore that from then on she would not forget for one second that she was simply his employee.

The following day, she was taken to the airport to meet Leone. A paparazzo was standing by with a camera to mark the occasion and Leone greeted her with an embrace. Convinced that the photographer's presence was no accident and resenting that reality, Misty twisted her head away to ensure that Leone's kiss landed on her cheek instead.

'Why did you do that?' Leone demanded.

'Kissing's very personal…a hug is just as convincing,' Misty told him stonily.

'Really? I just hugged a block of wood.'

Matters were not helped by the four-hour delay on their flight, which followed as the result of an air traffic controllers' strike. In the VIP lounge, Leone worked at his laptop while she leafed through various magazines. Every time she looked at him, he annoyed her. He looked so sophisticated and handsome in his designer country casuals and a svelte blonde on the other side of the room kept on throwing him flirtatious glances, evidently having decided that Misty was merely an adjunct. And she wasn't important, was she? In fact, she was just nobody in Leone Andracchi's life. But last night, he had been with a somebody who *was*…

'Are you planning to defrost before we arrive with our hosts?' Leone enquired on the walk out to his private jet.

'I haven't a clue what you're talking about. I'm here, I'm all dressed up and I'm smiling. What more do you want?'

'You didn't sugar my coffee…it was quite deliberate and unbelievably childish,' Leone derided.

'You can fetch your own coffee from now on. I'm not your little *slave*,' Misty hissed like a spitting cat.

Not a word was shared during the flight, not even while the jet endlessly circled above the airport awaiting a landing slot. By the time they climbed into the car awaiting their use, after she had watched Leone attempt without success to call their hosts to explain why they would be so late, it was almost seven and their weekend trip was showing all the promise of a developing nightmare in which everything that could go wrong did go wrong.

'*Dio mio!* Why is no one answering the phone?' Leone growled. 'It's a castle...the Garrisons must have a large staff.'

'You mean, you haven't visited these people before?' Misty was quick to take the opportunity to satisfy her curiosity without losing face. A castle? Now that sounded interesting to her.

'Never. I hardly know the Garrisons but I believe they're quite elderly.'

Leone said that he knew where he was going even though he had never been there before and refused the offer of the tiny map inside the tourist brochure that she had picked up to amuse herself with at the airport. She fell asleep and at some timeless stage later was quite briskly shaken awake.

'We're arrived,' Leone said darkly.

'Where?'

'The end of the bloody world,' Leone growled with a distinct lack of appreciation.

CHAPTER FIVE

MISTY clambered out of the car, shivered in the surprisingly cool air and rubbed her hands over her bare arms before reaching for her jacket. All she could see beyond the car was a towering building with not a single light in sight. 'What time is it?'

'Ten.'

As Leone thumped at the massive front door knocker, Misty resisted an urge to ask if he had taken the scenic route to the castle. 'Did you manage to phone the Garrisons while I was asleep?'

'No.' After waiting two minutes, Leone hammered the knocker with greater vigour.

Several more tense minutes passed and then finally a dim light glowed into life above them and they heard a heavy bolt being drawn back. Leone looked only marginally less grim.

An old man wearing a wool dressing gown peered out at them. 'Are you wanting to wake the whole castle up? Have you no idea what time it is? It's after *ten*…'

Misty hid a smile under her hair while Leone, impervious to that censorious complaint, introduced himself, banded an impatient arm round her back and urged her over the threshold. A dying fire was flickering in the giant grate of the big hall, casting long shadows on panelled walls the colour of dark honey and the worn flagged floor.

'Oh, this is lovely…' Misty sighed.

'I'll show you to your room, then,' the old man grumbled.

'And you are?' Leone prompted in quiet command.

77

'Murdo, sir…'

'We'd like to offer our apologies for our late arrival to your employers,' Leone continued.

'You'll not be doing that tonight. They're in their beds.' Murdo led the way to the winding stone staircase in the corner of the hall. 'We only keep late hours at Castle Eyrie on special occasions.'

After a lengthy hike down gloomy corridors lit with very low-wattage bulbs, the old man opened the door of a bedroom. 'If you're wanting anything to eat, you'll have to see to yourselves. The kitchen's off the long corridor at the back of the hall.'

Watching Leone's lean dark features radiate disbelief at the offering of that helpful information, Misty hurried to offer an admiring comment about the bedroom which earned her a grateful smile from the lugubrious Murdo.

Only after the older man had gone did Misty wrench her appreciative gaze from the charming curtained oak four-poster bed and the carved wooden chimney-piece to contemplate the reality that they had only been shown to *one* room. Why hadn't that likelihood occurred to her before? And there was nowhere to sleep apart from the bed.

'*Per meraviglia*…it's freezing in here! It's probably damp.' An incredulous look of hauteur on his lean strong face, Leone glanced into the adjoining bathroom and barely concealed a shudder at the sight of the ancient fixtures. 'There's not even a shower!'

'There's only one bed…'

The bathroom doorknob came off in Leone's hand and he thrust it back on again. 'The whole castle is in an advanced state of decay. No wonder the Garrisons have the place on the market! I expect some romantic fool and his money will soon be parted.'

'There's only one bed…'

'Yes…as there are only three pieces of furniture in the

entire room, I *had* noticed that,' Leone derided. 'But right now, I'm rather more interested in heat and food.'

'You could light a fire and I'll make us something to eat.'

'This is not quite what I expected from a weekend in the country—'

'Will you stop complaining?' Misty gave him a look of reproach. 'It's obvious that the Garrisons are struggling to survive and can't afford more home comforts or staff.'

'You couldn't be more wrong. They're rich and stingy and famous for underpaying their workers. Their fortune was made in garment manufacturing sweatshops abroad,' Leone informed her drily. 'Save your compassion for more deserving parties.'

In spite of the kitchen being a giant cellar-like space that did not appear to have been updated since the Middle Ages, the fridge was large and well-stocked and in no time at all, blithely ignoring Leone's comments about the amount of logs it took to fill the grate in their bedroom, she had Spanish omelettes and a bowl of Caesar salad sitting on the old pine table. They both ate with appetite and little need for conversation.

Back upstairs again with the flickering fire casting a wonderfully atmospheric and flattering glow over the worn furnishings, Misty stole an embarrassed glance at Leone. 'I really *wasn't* expecting to have to share a bed with you.'

'Do you think our hosts, the Garrisons, actually still exist?' Leone mused, gazing down reflectively into the fire before he turned his dark head, vibrant dark golden eyes assailing hers with heart-stopping amusement. 'Or do you think old Murdo has done away with them and we're the next on the list? Do you want me to sit up all night armed with a poker?'

No, I want *you*, Misty thought in shaken acknowledgement of the jealous feelings of possessiveness and hurt that had been tormenting her since the night before. *I want you in that bed with me.* So stark was the voice telling her that inside her head that for an awful moment she actually feared that she had spoken those words out loud. Dragging her self-conscious gaze from him, she turned away. 'I'm going for a bath. I'll be quick.'

Gathering up her things from the case she had yet to unpack, she backed over the threshold in haste and then she paused, suddenly deciding to throw caution to the four winds and just satisfy herself. 'Who were you with last night?'

'With friends I hadn't seen in some time.' Leone studied her with veiled eyes that now betrayed a glitter of infuriating awareness. 'So *that* is what wound you up overnight.'

Feverish pink flooding her cheekbones, Misty closed the door in haste. Although on one level she wished she had had the self-discipline not to ask that leading question, on another she was too relieved by the answer she had received to care beyond the cringing knowledge that she had embarrassed herself. She soon discovered that the water was barely lukewarm and there was no temptation to linger.

'There's no hot water,' she said, returning to the bedroom shivering in the fancy silk nightdress that was all she had bothered to pack and striving to pretend it was nothing out of the ordinary for her to be sharing a bedroom with a man.

Already halfway out of his shirt, Leone rested measuring dark golden eyes on her hectically flushed face in the light cast by the flickering fire. 'Do I need to drench myself in cold water again tonight?'

The silence simmered.

Misty had not expected a question that direct. Dredging her shaken scrutiny from his bronzed muscular chest and the tangle of dark curls sprinkling his pectorals, she scrambled into the bed at speed. 'Yes,' she said tightly.

There would be no giving way to temptation, she told herself urgently, and she refused to look at him while she mustered her defences. Their current intimacy was deceptive. It wasn't real and it meant nothing. She fancied him like mad, had never known that desire could bite so deep, but her sane mind warned her that at best she would only be a temporary distraction for Leone Andracchi. Their only true relationship was an unusual working agreement and if those boundaries were breached it would get messy, embarrassing and far too personal. Indeed, she would just be asking to get a kick in the teeth.

Finding that her teeth were chattering, she sat up and finally noticed that the window was wide open, letting in a brisk breeze. In exasperation she leapt out of bed and hurried over to close it. No sooner did the fire get going than he opened a window! Where was the sense in that? She soon found out as smoke began to billow out of the grate and she was forced to throw the offending window wide open again.

The bathroom door opened. She hunched up under the covers but lifted her lashes a half-inch to see Leone emerge wearing only a pair of boxer shorts. She shut her eyes again but he was etched in her memory in glorious Technicolor: black hair still damp above his lean, chiselled features, wide, smooth brown shoulders, superb torso, sleek hips, long, hair-roughened thighs. Stop it, stop it, *stop* it, she urged herself guiltily.

The mattress gave under Leone's weight and then there was a ripping sound and he loosed a curse and vaulted back up again. As the covers were flipped back from her, she was forced to sit up and contemplate the long tear in the threadbare bottom sheet. 'How the hell am I supposed to sleep on top of that?' Leone demanded.

'I can fix it.' Misty was eager to be doing something and she got up.

'We should go to a hotel—'

'We'll manage fine.' Yanking off the bedding, Misty removed the bottom sheet and turned it so that the rip would lie below the pillows. 'Come on…help me!'

'It's a disgrace to treat guests like this,' Leone ground out.

'But it's such a wonderful old building, full of history and atmosphere *and*—'

'Damp and discomfort?'

As Misty straightened from tucking in the bedding again, something caught at her hair and out of the corner of her eye she saw a large moth and she yelped. 'Is it still in my hair?'

'It won't do you any harm.' With infuriating cool, Leone shooed the moth out into the night again.

Misty rested back against the foot of the bed, pale and struggling to catch her breath again. Leone studied her with shimmering golden eyes. The very awareness she had been seeking to avoid with too much chatter and an attack of practical housekeeping ripped through her taut length in a fiery charge.

'Standing there in the firelight you might well as be naked,' Leone breathed thickly.

Glancing down at herself in dismay, noting the way the flames shone through the delicate silk, she groaned and made a sudden move to dive back into bed. But before she could get there Leone reached for her and hauled her into his powerful arms.

As his hungry mouth came crashing down on hers, a startled squawk was silenced in her throat. Excitement hurtled up inside her like a lightning strike. Suddenly, without any warning or any sense that her brain was prompting her, she was winding her arms round him and clinging.

His fingers splayed across her hips, urging her into connection with the straining thrust of his erection, sending a sharp arrow of primitive need arrowing up from her pelvis, an instinctive reaction that had nothing to do with thought but everything to do with the stormy passion he had ignited.

He lifted her up onto the bed and tumbled her across it, following her down, kneeing apart her thighs with a confident domination that not a skincell in her quivering body wanted to resist. He was kissing her with a hard, deep urgency that was setting her on fire. She could not get enough of his mouth. Every so often she drew back to draw in an agonised gasp of oxygen and then went back for more, her hands curved to his well-shaped head, fingers sliding and curling through the damp black strands as she held him to her.

Finally Leone lifted his head, his own breathing harsh and uneven, brilliant golden eyes bright below ink-dark lashes. 'Are you protected?'

A shard of unwelcome reality pierced her brain. Protected? Protected from pregnancy, her thoughts completed. Oh, yes, she was protected all right, she thought with sudden bitter pain, protected by her own virtual inability to conceive. 'Yes...'

The tension holding Leone's big, powerful body taut over hers ebbed and he gazed down at her with burning satisfaction. 'This was inevitable, *amore*.'

'Was it?' While her intelligence prompted her to think about what she was doing, her entire being was a seething, seductive mass of response. The scent and the touch of him, the very weight of him against her thigh were a potent aphrodisiac. She could not bring herself to break free of him.

'The minute I saw you, I wanted you.' Leone reclaimed her reddened lips in a probing and erotic assault that was pure intoxication. 'The sun was coming through the window and your hair was like a halo of fire…'

Her eyes fluttered wide on his lean, strong face, heart racing as she checked out that he had actually said that. He screened his gaze, hard jawline clenching, faint colour scoring his incredible cheekbones as if he wasn't any more used to saying that sort of thing than she was used to hearing it. 'Sexy…'

The strangest shard of tenderness tugged at her as he ended with that rather lame but much cooler conclusion. And then he kissed her again and the world spun as if she were on a roller coaster, heart thumping, body braced in the teeth of the wind.

'I can't get enough of you,' Misty muttered in a daze.

Leone gave her a slow-burning smile, relocated them against the pillows and buried his hot mouth against her aching breasts, palming the small mounds through the fine silk, making her spine arch and her breath catch in her throat. 'I can be addictive… I should have warned you, *amore*.'

She closed her eyes while he took off her nightdress.

'*Dio mio*…you're perfect,' Leone growled, catching a distended pink nipple between thumb and forefinger and sending a spasm of tormented reaction through her, strong enough to make her moan.

Her eyes opened on the leaping shadows of light and dark that marked his darkly handsome features and she discovered that he was staring down at her with a slight frown. 'What?'

'You're lying there as if you are *so* shy,' Leone confided with a sudden husky laugh.

'I am… Just a bit,' she qualified, half under her breath, her own attention wholly captured by the wonder of his smile.

'It's a turn-on, *amore*,' he murmured huskily. 'But then I guess you know that.'

Thinking about all that she didn't know froze Misty for an instant, filled her with doubt, but then he lashed the lush pink peak of her breast with his tongue and closed his mouth over the straining tip and doubt vanished because there was no room for it any more. Indeed there was no room for anything but the raw intensity of her own driven response.

'We have all night…' Leone muttered hungrily, curving back from her to discard his boxers.

'I suppose…' She kept her eyes on his muscular chest. It was really going to happen. Her body was all heat and liquid eagerness but she was nervous: afraid it might hurt, afraid she might in some way betray her ignorance, for she did not want him to guess that he was about to become the only lover she had ever had.

After all, all he wanted was a casual tumble between the sheets, but *he* might start thinking that *she* wanted something more if he realised that she was a virgin. And, of course, she didn't. She was just madly attracted to him and that was that, and it was her own private business if she had decided that he would be her first lover. It didn't have to mean anything, she reasoned frantically with herself, fighting Birdie's moral conditioning with all her might, and it certainly didn't mean that she had special feelings for him. Developing special feelings for a male with Leone's reputation would be like shooting herself in the foot and she was far too sensible.

But as Leone drew her back to him with purposeful hands she met molten golden eyes and she burned and sense was nowhere to be found. He tasted her mouth and she trembled, her very skin feeling as though it were tightening over her bones, every inch of her taut and super sensitive.

'It's the way you look at me,' Leone confided with all male satisfaction. 'The way you react around me…it makes me *ache*…'

'I hated you…' Misty whispered in a tone of surprise, her mind refusing to comprehend how she had travelled from that violent hostility to the point where she could lie in his arms naked and it feel like the most natural thing in the world.

Leone ran light fingers through the silky tumble of hair spread across the pillow and gazed down at her as he let his other hand travel with caressing expertise up over her straining breasts. He watched her push herself up against his hand in an involuntary motion she could no more have resisted than she might have resisted the tide. Smouldering golden eyes surveyed her. 'You don't *now*…'

'No…' And conceding that reality scared Misty. In the space of days, he had somehow vanquished what had once been a certainty and she could not explain how or why.

But that possessive light in his stunning eyes was like a controlling forcefield surrounding her, shutting out everything she didn't want to acknowledge. The rapid beat of her own heart was leaving her breathless. The most enormous sense of excitement was penned up inside her, ready to break loose. The silence eddied in her ears, broken only by the ragged sigh of her own breath.

'I've never wanted anyone like this before,' she heard herself confide.

His eyes darkening, his lean bronzed features tautened and then suddenly he sunk one hand into her hair to raise her to him and he was ravishing her parted lips with his own again, letting his tongue delve into the moist interior of her mouth with explicit passion.

Her hunger came back at even stronger force. Her hands dug into his corded shoulders, loving the strength of him and the smoothness of his skin there. Indeed, for several intoxicating minutes she explored every part of him she could reach, but baulked at the most obvious.

'Touch me…' he urged raggedly.

And she was torn in two by excitement and nerves. He was hard and smooth and she was convinced there was far too much of him, but the fact that almost imperceptible tremors were running through his sleek, powerful frame empowered her. He groaned out loud with pleasure. She liked that: it meant she was doing things right. But before she could begin experimenting on him with greater daring, he pushed her back against the pillows and claimed a hungry, driving kiss.

'In the mood I'm in…a little goes a long way, *amore*…'

He lay half over her, playing sensually with her mouth while he toyed with the cluster of copper curls below her tensing tummy, slid her quivering thighs apart and traced the moist cleft at the heart of her. And from that point on she was all heat and electrified craving, every sensation driven by the aching tenderness there. He found the most sensitive spot and what remained of control was wrested from her with a vengeance. Her hips writhed and she sobbed out loud.

'Oh, please…'

'Waiting makes it better, *amore*,' Leone intoned against her parted lips as she sucked in breath like a drowning swimmer.

By the time he rose over her, sliding his hands beneath her squirming hips and pulling her to him, she was on fire with her own craving. He drove into her and a sharp rending pain momentarily gripped her, almost shocking her back to the real world again.

'You're so tight…' he groaned, gazing down at her with questioning eyes, a frown drawing his brows together. 'Am I hurting you?'

'Oh, no…' Misty hastened to assert through gritted teeth.

Leone surveyed her with veiled intensity and then he shifted with lithe power and eased himself very slowly and very gently deeper into her. '*Dio*…you feel incredible.'

The discomfort began to evaporate at the point where she was just about to tell him that she could not return the compliment. By then, she had taken all of him and was warming to the activity and the sensation so that by the time he began to move, she arched up and the frenzy of yearning desire flooded back to fill her almost in the same moment.

'I like it…'

Molten golden eyes collided with hers, sudden amusement flaring.

'With you,' she added jerkily.

He bent his dark head, brilliant eyes almost tender, and stole a lingering kiss. 'Sometimes you don't tell the whole truth.'

The excitement was rocketing again and, although she wanted to ask him what he meant by that, she couldn't find her voice. She moved under him, hot and abandoned, revelling in his sensual rhythm, letting the new wildness build inside her and pitch her higher and higher. His pace quickened and her heart slammed even faster, whimpers of sound torn from her while he drove her mindless with pleasure. At the furthest edge, she reached a climax of mind-blowing intensity, her entire body convulsed with fiery sensation and passion. He shuddered over her and ground out something in Italian and poured himself into her.

She held him close, conscious of a sweet, drowning pleasure in that simple act of closeness, acknowledging that in all her life she had never felt that close to another human being. In the circle of her arms, he felt as if he was

hers and she loved that. He released her from his weight
and then hauled her close again, holding her every bit as
tight as she wanted to be held, and for a time neither of
them said anything. Then he pushed her tumbled hair back
from her pink face, gazed down into her softened grey eyes
and then veiled his own.

'I've been thinking…I could help you trace your twin
sister.'

At that suggestion coming out of nowhere at her at such
a moment, Misty tensed in astonishment. 'Sorry?'

'Everyone ought to have family. It would only be a
small favour…no big deal, *amore*.' Leone shifted a smooth
brown shoulder in a slight dismissive shrug.

'No…nice thought but no, thanks,' Misty fielded tightly.

'Why not? Surely you want to meet her?'

'It's what *she* wants that counts and she's had my address and my phone number for four years now and she's
done nothing with them,' Misty countered unsteadily. 'So
just leave it.'

'I think you're scared—'

Inflamed by that comment, Misty pulled back from him.
'What would you know about it? I suppose you've read a
few of those nice cosy stories where people went looking
for long lost relatives and had a rapturous reunion…well,
there's *nothing* nice and cosy in my background, just the
hurt and damaged children our mum abandoned. There's
three of us that I know of.'

Disconcerted by her fiery emotional reaction, Leone had
thrust himself up against the pillows. Momentarily she was
distracted. He looked gorgeous, she thought painfully,
more gorgeous than ever with his black hair tousled and
his stunning eyes reflecting the firelight, his olive skin dark
and sexy and vibrant against the bed linen. In punishment
for her own dismaying susceptibility, she turned her head
away from him.

'You said, "three of us",' Leone reminded her. 'Three what?'

'Three sisters…maybe more, maybe boys too, for all I know!'

'Your mother had three children?'

'She married an older man when she was nineteen and she had a little girl by him. Social services told me that. Mum left him for my father but that didn't last and so Mum left my twin and I in care,' Misty advanced curtly.

'And?' Leone prompted as the strained silence dragged.

Her fine facial bones were prominent with rigidly restrained emotion. 'I met Mum's ex-husband when I was going through my "tracing my roots" phase. You see, I thought he might really be my father…stupid of me. I mean, why would my twin and I have ended up in care if he had been?'

Leone said nothing. He reached out to close a hand over her taut, clenched fingers.

Disdaining his pity, Misty jerked her hand out of reach. 'Her ex-husband was still really bitter. He called Mum a slut and told me to get off his property. He said I was a fool to imagine that his daughter would want anything to do with the likes of me!'

'*Dio mio…*' Leone was pale beneath his bronzed skin, undoubtedly, she felt, wishing he had steered well clear of the subject of family.

'Birdie's my family,' Misty stated tightly. 'I was crazy to go searching and digging into Mum's past. All I got out of it was rejection and humiliation.'

Leone closed his hands over her arms and tipped her back to him, ignoring her stiff defensiveness to assert with emphasis, 'I'll *never* mention the idea again.'

But he had stirred up emotions that were not so easily set aside again. Feeling raw and needing to be alone, Misty rolled away from him and took refuge in the bathroom.

She turned on the bath taps because tears were trickling down her taut face and she was scared a sob might escape and carry back into the bedroom. Taken aback to see steam rising above the bath, she put the plug in and eventually clambered into the warm water. She sat hunched with her head bent over her knees, wishing the pain and the confusion that had by then stretched to encompass that wild bout of lovemaking with Leone would go away.

Why had she told him all those personal things? She was torn with regret and embarrassment. She had seen the shock and discomfiture flash through his gaze. And she didn't even blame him for that clumsy and naive offer of his to trace her twin. He had no concept of what it was like to come from her kind of background. He probably knew every member of his own family tree back a few generations at least. Weren't Italian families supposed to be really close?

Some time later, a knock sounded on the door. She ignored it. The door opened.

'I've used up all the hot water,' she told Leone fiercely without even looking up.

'I raided the drawing room downstairs for some brandy and Murdo caught me in the act,' Leone said in a grated undertone.

Involuntary amusement infiltrated her strained defences as she pictured what must have been an extraordinary scene. 'Oh, *dear*…'

'So the least you can do is drink it.'

'OK…I'll be out in a minute,' Misty promised, a reflective little smile chasing the tension away from her soft mouth. She might, she just *might* sugar his next coffee for him as a reward.

CHAPTER SIX

MISTY shifted and stretched sleepily. A whole series of unfamiliar little aches and pains assailed her, reminding her of the night that had passed. Leone…the warmth of memory uncoiled inside her and overpowered every other prompting. All she wanted to do was luxuriate in the cocoon of happiness that had begun building at some stage of the night hours.

But it was only a casual affair, Misty reminded herself hurriedly. She stifled the misgivings threatening to surface: the awareness that she didn't really know what she was doing, the worrying fact that she had allowed temptation to overrule her usual sense and caution. Wasn't she a grown woman and old enough to make her own decisions? Just for once in her life, she wanted to live for the moment and drink every second dry of its promise. And at that moment her world felt filled to overflowing with promise.

She opened her eyes. The curtains had been drawn back. Soft misty daylight was filtering in and Leone was by the window, his tall, powerful physique enhanced by a casual jacket worn with well-cut dark chinos. She studied him with helpless appreciation. He was terrific company and he was a total fantasy in bed…and in front of the fire…and other places too. How had she ever imagined that she hated him? Had she used that as a defence to hide behind? A way of denying the reality that she was hopelessly attracted to him? She was so grateful that he had brought down her barriers, so grateful that she hadn't missed out on feeling as good about herself as he had made her feel.

His cell phone buzzed and he dug it out and began to

talk in low-pitched urgent Italian. His tension pronounced, he paced a little. She finally saw his lean, strong face and, simultaneously, happiness began to seep out of her like water in a cracked jug. Leone looked grim. Grim as he had looked that day he had spelt out his proposition in the office at Brewsters without any shade of humour or indeed any hint of the male who had been behaving like a passionate lover with her only hours earlier.

The lovely warm sensations inside Misty started to shrivel. He had regrets, great big screaming regrets, she decided painfully. He had got out of bed, dressed and left her sleeping. With one notable exception, it was like all the books she had ever read, all the films she had ever seen that covered what a guy did after a one-night stand that he felt had been a mistake. And the exception? He was still in the same room, still in the same building. And why? In the circumstances, he was pretty much trapped.

Had he just looked at her in the light of day and wondered what on earth he had imagined he had seen in her? Or was he one of those hateful womanisers who lost interest the moment the chase was over? Not that the chase had lasted long, she conceded. Had he even chatted her up? She didn't think so. He had read her signals and just moved in for the kill. As one-night stands went, she had been a very easy lay. Even thinking about herself in that light hurt but there was a part of her all too eager to rub that pain and humiliation in hard. There she had been kidding herself on that she was in control of events, able to handle whatever happened, and the minute things went wrong she felt like death warmed over and sick with pain and rejection all over again.

'What time's breakfast?' she asked with studious casualness as he ended his call, fighting her own agonising sensitivity with all her might.

Leone jerked round, lean, strong face taut. For a split

second his raw tension was visible in the way he held himself and then his wide, sensual mouth curved into a faint smile. It was a forced smile and twelve hours earlier she could not have told the difference, but a lot had changed within that time frame.

'I'm afraid you've missed breakfast. It's almost one,' Leone informed her.

Misty was so disconcerted by that news that she sat up, but as the sheet fell below her breasts she snatched at it, suddenly very uncomfortable with her own bare skin in his presence. 'You should've woken me up!'

'What for? The obligatory fishing trip in the rain?'

'Sorry...?' Misty discovered that she could not quite bring herself to meet his gaze levelly and that her ability to concentrate was at an all-time low. Emotions were churning up inside her, raw, wounded feelings of shame and self-loathing exacerbated by growing anger. Why hadn't he left her alone? Had sleeping with her been his cruel way of bringing her down and punishing her for standing up to him? Was that the sort of guy he was? She didn't know any more, she didn't feel she knew *anything* any more, but her pride surged to the fore to conceal her mounting turmoil.

'The rest of the guests came up from the local hotel and most of them have gone down to the loch to fish. I gather it's tradition.'

She could hear the rain thumping against the window and barely suppressed a shudder.

'I said you were very tired after our extended journey yesterday—'

'You said...*what*?' Accidentally she looked at him.

'I don't like fishing,' Leone informed her with veiled eyes, no more keen, it seemed, than she to make head-on contact. In fact he sounded just a little desperate.

'I'd have thought you could've tolerated it for a few

hours…after all, you did come up here to stay with these people. Are the women fishing too?'

'Some of them.'

'I'm sure there's a pair of wellies I can borrow. A pity you didn't warn me about the fishing because I don't have anything suitable to wear.' Misty was struggling to keep her voice even. 'We must seem like the guests from hell. We arrive late, we nick the brandy and I'm still in bed the following afternoon.'

'Ted Garrison is a political power broker. His sole interest in our presence is how much cash I might contribute to his latest cause,' Leone informed her wryly. 'We could spend the entire weekend in bed and he wouldn't give a damn.'

'No offence intended, Leone,' Misty murmured with a bright smile pasted to her numb lips as she snatched up her nightdress and pulled it on. 'The sex was a great way of whiling away a boring evening, but let's not kid ourselves it would rise to the challenge of amusing us for a whole weekend!'

Leone was very still. As she escaped into the bathroom she contrived to steal a covert glance in his direction. His bold profile was rigid. He was surprised, of course he was. He hadn't expected her to get the punchline in first, but no way was she about to give him the ego boost of believing that the previous night had meant anything to her or that she had the smallest wish to repeat the experience. After washing her face, she saw tears in her eyes and she wrinkled her nose furiously. No matter if it killed her, she was going to pick herself up again and act as though nothing had happened.

When she emerged the bedroom was empty. She teamed a gossamer-fine lilac top ornamented with fine beading with the skirt that fell to mid-calf and a velvet-trimmed cardigan, brushed her hair until it fell into style and applied make-up. Time to get into role: she was the fake mistress, more interested in fashion and an ultra-feminine appearance than fishing and unlikely to dress for practicality even on a country weekend in a Scottish castle.

As she descended the winding stone staircase with care in her high heels, she caught the sound of chairs being scraped back followed by the murmur of voices receding from the hall below. Stepping down into the echoing front hall where a welcoming fire burned in the dimness but there appeared to be nobody else present, she hesitated for a moment and then a slight sound alerted her to the fact that she was not alone.

A distinguished-looking man with dark hair silvering at his temples stood just inside the entrance, an exasperated expression on his face as he removed a jacket dripping with raindrops. He glanced in her direction and then froze, a frownline lodged between his brows as he stared at her with narrowed eyes.

'Hi…' Misty coloured beneath the intensity of his appraisal, wondering if the outfit she had chosen looked that outlandish. 'Do you know where everyone has gone?'

'Into lunch, I would think. I was hoping I wasn't too late as the prospect of picnicking by the loch in this weather didn't appeal.' Treating her to a flirtatious smile, he strode forward to extend his hand. 'I'm Oliver Sargent.'

'Misty Carlton…' The instant she heard his name she recognised him, for he was Birdie's favourite politician, given to uttering the kind of homely sentiments that were most dear to her foster mother's heart.

His hand tightened on hers and then fell away as she spoke, but before she could wonder at his withdrawal a grey-haired older woman in country tweeds was advancing towards them.

'My goodness, Oliver, you look grey. Are you feeling all right? You had better change out of those wet clothes.'

Without skipping a beat, the woman turned to Misty. 'I'm Peg Garrison. You can only be Misty. So nice to have some younger people staying for a change. I gather Leone has abandoned you—'

Misty tensed. 'Sorry?'

'Leone and Ted have taken a boat out on the loch. Ted called me on his cell phone. I doubt if we'll see them much before the party this evening. Ted rarely meets anyone as mad keen on fishing as he is himself, so he's sure to make the most of the opportunity.'

Taken aback by the content of that speech after what Leone had said on the same subject earlier, Misty found herself swept by her hostess into a chilly dining room where around a dozen older people were seated. She sat down and contemplated the minute portion of salad awaiting her.

'We always try to eat before we come,' her neighbour whispered with a rueful laugh. 'I believe you're staying here at the castle.'

'Yes.' Misty turned to smile at the faded blonde woman beside her.

'A mistake you'll only make once, as we did. The hotel is much more comfortable. I'm Jenny Sargent.'

'I think I met your husband out in the hall.'

'Oh, is Oliver back already? He's not very fond of fishing but Ted does rather expect one to share his favourite pursuits.'

'I'm Misty Carlton.'

'Is Misty short for something?' her neighbour continued chattily.

'Melissa, but I don't remember ever being called it,' Misty confided, tucking into her salad slowly in the hope of persuading her hungry stomach that it was a banquet, rather than a snack. She was picturing Leone on a boat in the lashing rain and hoping he got seasick, soaked through and had a thoroughly horrible afternoon.

Jenny's husband, Oliver, appeared midway through the meal and sat down beside his hostess, who was giving forth on how unnecessary central heating was while her luncheon guests tried not to let their teeth chatter over their miserly salads. Was Leone interested in politics? Misty could not help wondering why on earth he had come to stay for an entire weekend with such people. The other guests were of a different generation and all the talk was of politics, rather than business. Perhaps Leone wished to engage political support in some matter which affected Andracchi Industries, she thought vaguely.

On several occasions, she found Oliver Sargent skimming a glance in his wife's direction. At least she assumed it was his wife he was looking at, for she could not imagine why he should have any interest in her. Nonetheless, he had the coldest grey eyes she had ever seen and she knew that she would have to fib when she described him to Birdie. He was such a smoothie and he flirted like mad with every woman around him right under the nose of his infinitely nicer wife. But she would tell her foster mother that he was an absolute charmer rather than disappoint her.

Lunch was followed by a tour of Castle Eyrie's every room. Misty was surprised to find much of Peg Garrison's running commentary on the history of the castle directed at herself, although she was certainly interested. It was a fortified tower house with three storeys that had been altered several times over the centuries so that various staircases ran off in odd directions and corridors had ninety-degree turns, but the panelled rooms and casement windows had enormous charm and she thought it was sad that the Garrisons had neglected their summer home to such an extent.

'Now that the children have flown the nest, it's too large

for us and we intend to buy a villa in the South of France,'
her hostess informed her.

'Is Leone interested in buying this place?' Jenny asked
in some surprise when Peg Garrison had moved away. 'I
shouldn't have thought that it was his cup of tea.
Oliver…?'

Her husband approached them with a stiff smile.

'I was just saying to Misty. Peg seems to think that
Leone's gasping to acquire a Scottish castle.'

'Perhaps he is…' As Oliver Sargent treated his artless
wife to a frowning glance that made the kindly older
woman redden Misty found herself warming even less to
the man and was glad when his attention was claimed by
someone else.

'We got to know Leone through his younger sister…a
tragic business that,' Jenny Sargent sighed in continuance.
'Battista was working for Oliver at the time. She was a
delightful girl. Young people and fast cars…such a dangerous combination. Leone was devastated when she died.'

'Yes.' Misty was recalling the ashen colour Leone had
turned just squeezing out the admission that that pretty girl
in the portrait was his late sister and she realised that
Battista must have been killed in a car accident.

'I'm afraid Leone's avoided us ever since and I don't
blame him for it,' Jenny asserted, her sympathy clear in
her homely face. 'I'm sure whenever he sees Oliver and I,
it brings back unfortunate memories of the last few weeks
of Battista's life.'

Misty was finding it harder and harder to smile and chat
and it was a relief when the gathering broke up. Her
wretched subconscious was betraying her by serving up
images of the night before: Leone laughing about being
caught helping himself to the brandy and his promise to
Murdo that he would replace the entire bottle first thing in
the morning. She had been surprised that Leone had real-

ised that Murdo was afraid of being accused of having a
secret tipple and losing his job, and touched that the
younger man had cared.

She had never dreamt that such an extraordinary passion
could exist or that she could feel anything with such intensity. Being with him had felt so special but the cold
light of day had been harsh and revealing. Or had it been?
Had her own fear of rejection led her into overreaction?
Wasn't it possible that Leone's forbidding aspect might
have related to something that had nothing to do with her?
Even that phone call which he had been in the midst of
making? Well, she had jumped and that was that and it
was for the best, wasn't it?

Warmth greeted her as she opened their bedroom door.
A log fire was roaring in the grate and Leone was standing
in front of it, shivering and drenched to the skin. As that
was exactly what she had hoped on his behalf some hours
earlier, she was infuriated by the instant charge of concern
that filled her. His black hair curling with damp, his lean,
bronzed features still wet, his shimmering golden eyes assailed hers.

'Did you mean what you said earlier?' Leone demanded
with stark clarity.

Disconcerted, Misty trembled and angled back against
the door to close it. As her gaze centred on him in a frantic
search for some lead on how to answer that question her
heart began to thump inside her like an overwound clock,
racing and then threatening to stop altogether. In the fierce
set of his darkly handsome features she could see how
much was riding on her response and that shook her.

'*Dio mio*...you *didn't* mean it!' Leone ground out with
a flash of his even white teeth, shooting her a look of raw
anger. 'So why did you say it?'

Her triangular face had drained of colour and her knees

had developed a slight wobble but her chin came up. 'I got the impression that if I didn't say it, you would.'

'I wouldn't be that crude,' Leone sliced back at her, strong jawline at an aggressive angle. 'You talked like you were a whore!'

Colour drenched her cheekbones. 'I—'

'I don't want to hear you speaking like that again,' Leone cut in.

Misty bridled.

'How would you feel if I had spoken to you in that manner?' Leone demanded.

Gutted, she thought inwardly, her mind a sea of confusion that such a dialogue was even taking place between them. He still wanted her…he *still* wanted her. Indeed he cared enough to challenge her rejection of him. A whoosh of warmth at that knowledge surged up through her, wiping away the cold, sick feeling of having been used that she had fought to suppress all afternoon.

'Let me get you a towel,' she said unevenly.

Leone gritted something in Italian that sounded very rude.

'Don't swear at me,' Misty told him defensively.

'I wasn't swearing. I was telling you…don't *ever* do that to me again.'

'OK.'

Leone spoke again just as she reached the bathroom door. 'I would have hurt you less if you'd warned me that you were a virgin.'

Entirely unprepared for that sally, Misty spun round, pink flooding her cheeks. 'I—'

'I would've mentioned it last night but you seemed keen to conceal the fact.'

Misty met level dark golden eyes of enquiry and muttered, 'I was embarrassed.'

'I was stunned but very pleased that you chose me,' Leone murmured huskily. 'Yet with what I believed that I knew about you—'

'Flash and I shared the same foster home for years. We were more like brother and sister.'

Leone smiled. 'But you were engaged to Redding—'

'Not for very long and, really, that's none of your business,' Misty told him in a chagrined rush.

'Did you honestly think that I was complaining?' As she tried to step past Leone he caught her to him and claimed a drowning kiss, his sensual mouth hungry and demanding on hers, and the world spun crazily around her, her tummy clenching on the surge of raw desire. Her fingers closed into his wet jacket and began to drag it off him as she pushed into the hard, muscular heat of him. With a roughened laugh, he released her and disposed of the jacket himself. He backed her up against the bed and closed her back into his arms to lift her and bring her down on the mattress.

'I've got to get ready for the party—'

His stunning golden eyes darkened and veiled. 'Do you really want to go?'

'Leone…' Heart hammering but thoughts bewildered, Misty looked up at him and let her shoes fall off her feet. 'Of course we have to go—'

'There's no, ''of course'' about anything, *amore*.'

'Except when it comes to how you behave in someone else's home,' Misty muttered, watching him peel off his damp shirt, eyes widening on the breathtaking expanse of his bronzed hair-roughened chest. Just looking at him made her own body clench tight. She felt out of control, out of control of both thought and response.

Leone ran slow, provocative hands up her long, slender legs, lifting her skirt out of his path, and then he came to

the lace-topped stockings held up with suspenders and expelled his breath in a sudden groan of appreciation. 'That
is *so* sexy…'

'And you're *so* predictable…'

To try and prove her wrong, he bent his arrogant dark
head over her and ran his tongue along the bare skin above
the stocking tops. She managed a muffled giggle but damp
heat flowered at the very heart of her and made her shiver.
He tugged her up, extracted her from her cardigan and top
and kissed her with deep, erotic thoroughness in the midst
of the exercise.

'*Santo Cielo*…I need to be inside you,' he growled with
ragged urgency, coming down on the bed still half clothed,
dealing with her lingerie in a most summary fashion.

An uninhibited moan was wrenched from her as he
found the slick wet heat between her thighs. His unhidden
urgency only made her more wild for him. Aching with
the same driving need, she angled up to him and at last he
was there, plunging into her heated core with a delicious
force that made her cry out. His driving thrusts sent electrifying excitement leaping through her and the fierce
storm of his possession sent her flying to an ecstatic peak
and wave after wave of shattering pleasure.

Sitting up, Leone began to peel her out of her remaining
clothes, pausing every now and then to caress her with
expert hands, shocking her with the speed with which he
could rouse her again. She ran her fingers through his black
hair, curved them to his blue-shadowed jawline, reached
up and found his mouth for herself with new confidence.
She couldn't stop touching him but that felt all right because he was doing the exact same thing, but deep down
inside she now knew what made him special and the
strength of her own emotions frightened her…

*   *   *

So what *did* you do this afternoon?' Leone enquired as they crossed the landing to go downstairs later that evening.

Misty smoothed down the glorious white halter-neck dress she wore and glanced up at his lean, strong face with a teasing smile. 'I lunched…in a very small way, got the official tour of the castle…it's *really* beautiful, Leone. Oh, yes, and I got to meet Oliver Sargent—'

The hand Leone had at her narrow spine tensed. 'You can't have done. Oliver was on the other boat and it stayed out on the loch all afternoon—'

'He must have sneaked off it because he came back just as I arrived downstairs.'

Leone had fallen still and he stared down at her with narrowed eyes as dark as a midnight sky, his beautiful bone structure taut. 'Friendly, was he?'

'At first…and then, no, not really,' Misty framed uncomfortably, wondering what was the matter with him. 'I much preferred his wife.'

'You met her as well?' Leone breathed in a harsh undertone.

'Aren't they friends of yours?'

'No.'

'Did you expect me to skulk in the bedroom for the rest of the day just because you weren't here?' Misty asked.

'No.' Hard jawline clenched, Leone shrugged a wide shoulder with something less than his usual fluidity of movement. 'It's not important. Forget it.'

Of course, hadn't Jenny Sargent remarked that she suspected that Leone avoided them because they roused painful memories of his sister, Battista? And true to that belief, Leone was pale beneath his olive skin. Compassion stirred in Misty and her defensive stance evaporated. She wondered how long it had been since his sister had died and decided it must have been a fairly recent event for him still to be that sensitive.

It was a very big party and their first stop was the buffet laid on by the caterers. A large room had been cleared for dancing and adorned with beautiful flower arrangements. Misty drifted round the floor in Leone's arms, trying not to wonder where their affair could be going, reminding herself that no relationship came with guarantees. But she knew that for the first time in three years she was falling in love again, and that terrified her for it seemed to her that they had started out all wrong and she wished that she could go back and have a second chance.

An hour into the party she caught her shoe in the hem of her dress and went upstairs to pin it up. When she came back down again, Oliver Sargent stepped into her path. 'I'd like to offer you a friendly word of warning.'

His voice was slightly slurred, as if he had been drinking too much, and lines of strain were grooved between his nose and mouth.

'What about?' Misty frowned at him.

'Get out of Leone Andracchi's life,' the older man told her in a grim undertone. 'You can't trust him. He's *only* using you!'

Stunned by those daunting assurances from a man she barely knew, Misty stared at Oliver Sargent, but he immediately turned away and moved back into the crush. Now what was she supposed to make of that? It was obvious that the enmity between Leone and the older man was mutual. But why should she have been dragged into the midst of it?

CHAPTER SEVEN

IN THE early hours of the following morning, Misty lay watching Leone sleep.

Dawn light fingered across the bed, playing across his stunning dark features, highlighting the ridiculous length of his black lashes, moving on to rest on the relaxed line of his wide, sensual mouth. In such a short space of time he had become so important to her, but what sort of closeness did they have when she did not feel she could share Oliver Sargent's warning and ask why the older man should have approached her with such chilling advice?

But then what level of closeness did she expect when she and Leone had only been together for so short a time? Wasn't she being unreasonable? After all, Oliver Sargent had been drinking heavily and, if he didn't like Leone, he might simply have been trying to cause trouble. All the same, there had been something surprisingly sincere about the older man's manner, some quality that had spooked her. But then the man was a politician and made his living by being convincing, she reminded herself in exasperation, and she went back to studying Leone with possessive pleasure.

'I need to know where we're going in this relationship,' Misty admitted in the limo that was ferrying her and Leone back to the London apartment that afternoon.

The silence stretched like a treacherous swamp.

Inky black lashes screening his gaze, Leone murmured, 'I can't answer that yet.'

Misty drew in a slow, steadying breath but she had lost

106

colour. 'I won't be your mistress. I assume that I am still working for you…?'

Leone tensed and took a moment to consider that angle, which suggested to her that that role of hers was no longer as cut and dried as it had once been. 'Yes.'

'And you still have no plans to tell me what this grand pretence is all about?'

Leone assessed her taut face. 'No, not at present.'

'Then we go back to strictly business terms,' Misty decreed without hesitation.

Leone settled smouldering golden eyes on her, his incredulity patent. '*Porca miseria!* That would be ridiculous!'

'I won't feel comfortable with any other arrangement. You can't have it both ways,' Misty warned him, a sick, sinking sensation infiltrating her stomach.

'Blackmail just makes me more stubborn,' Leone spelt out sardonically.

Misty reddened. 'I am *not* blackmailing you!'

'I'll be in New York for the next week. Think it over while I'm away.'

As that unexpected little speech sank in, she realised that she was dealing with a master of one-upmanship. The mere thought of him vanishing for an entire seven days while matters stood unresolved between them was a body-blow. How had he got her that dependent so fast? She slung him a suspicious look, grey eyes silvering with a volatile mix of anxiety and resentment. 'I shan't miss you.'

'You sound as if you're about seven years old, *amore.*' Leone closed his hand over her coiled fingers where they rested on the seat between them. 'Why are you so keen to screw up something that's working?'

'Maybe it's not working quite as well for me,' Misty breathed stiltedly, but she held on to his hand.

She spent the first half of the following week with Birdie

and Leone phoned her twice. She was accustomed to busy days and the long hours were empty when she returned to London. On the penultimate night when she found herself watching the phone like a clingy, desperate woman, she made herself go out to the cinema. It was only when she was on the brink of falling asleep that evening that she realised that her period was several days late. Assuming that her emotional ups and downs had upset her cycle, she put the matter back out of her mind without concern.

Leone called her at two in the morning and she came awake with a sleepy sigh, defences at their lowest ebb as she listened to his rich, dark drawl and her toes stretched and curled.

'My flight will get in at seven,' Leone murmured tautly.

'Tonight?'

'In a few hours.'

'Oh…' In the darkness she smiled and smiled.

'So go back to sleep,' Leone instructed huskily. 'When you wake up, I'll be there.'

It sounded wonderful but she woke up again after five. Excitement had got her adrenalin going and, after wrestling with a cautious wish to play everything very cool, she finally gave way to what she really wanted to do and decided to meet him at the airport. By that stage, time was of the essence and she dressed at speed in casual white flared jeans and a vibrant turquoise top.

The cab she called picked her up late and she had to run through the airport. She was about twenty feet away when she saw Leone emerging into the concourse. Falling to a breathless halt, she thrust her streaming copper hair back from her face and waited for him to see her. He looked preoccupied and forbidding but stunningly attractive. And then he glanced in her direction and froze, what could only be described as an aghast look flashing across his lean, strong face.

As Misty read that unwelcome response to her appearance, she spun away in an uncoordinated surge and began to head fast in the opposite direction. A split second later, the world round her exploded into sudden noise and activity. A camera flashed, momentarily blinding her into a stumbling halt. Loud voices were shouting at her. She backed away in shock and confusion, truly not understanding what was happening, her mind far more full of the appalled expression Leone had betrayed when he'd recognised her and frozen in anguish on that image.

'Did you know Oliver Sargent was—?' a man demanded urgently, only to be drowned out by another, who yelled, 'Miss Carlton…how do you feel about what you've just learned? Angry? Bitter?'

Yet another camera focused on her as she kept on backing and backing away from the band of shouting men surrounding her. And then suddenly Leone was breaking through the crush, snatching the camera from the man waving it in her face and throwing it aside in a violent gesture that took her even more aback.

'Get the hell away from her!' Leone launched, hauling her under one powerful arm and immediately curving her round to shelter her with his body and prevent the intrusive lenses from capturing a shot of her shell-shocked face.

'What's going on?' she demanded.

A couple of big musclebound men waded in to clear their path and Leone urged her away from the fracas at speed.

'One of those journalists mentioned Oliver Sargent!' she gasped.

But there was no time for explanations. The paparazzi gave chase and when Misty and Leone finally reached the security of the limousine, Misty had a stitch in her side and couldn't find the breath to speak.

'It didn't occur to me that you'd come to meet me this

early in the morning,' Leone admitted with fierce regret. 'The press were waiting to ask me for my comments. The minute I saw you I realised all hell was about to break loose. Are you all right?'

'Please just tell me what's happening.' Misty raised an unsteady hand to her damp brow where a headache was beginning to pound, but she was relieved to appreciate that his discomfiture at her appearance at the airport had not been the rejection that she had read it as being.

'A tabloid newspaper is breaking a big story today and it involves you.'

Misty stared at him with rounded eyes. 'How on earth could it involve me? You mean, it's some story to do with you and I somehow got dragged in?'

'No…' His strong bone structure taut beneath his olive skin, Leone was choosing his words with visible care. 'A friend tipped me off while I was still in New York. He emailed a copy of the lead article…'

Leone extended a folded newspaper to her. 'I'm sorry…I'm sorrier than I have ever been about anything.'

What did Leone have to be sorry about? Misty shook the paper open and just gaped at the front page. Above a picture of her taken the night of the film première ran the words, IS THIS OLIVER SARGENT'S LONG LOST DAUGHTER?

'Where did this rubbish come from?' Misty regarded the headline and the smaller inset picture of the politician she had met at Castle Eyrie with wide eyes of incredulity.

'Without DNA testing, no such claim can be proved,' Leone breathed. 'But on the basis of the information that I have, there is a very high degree of probability that Sargent *is* your natural father.'

Together those two statements of fact cut through the fog of Misty's disbelief and focused her mind again. She stared back at him in horror, for initially all she could recall was her almost instinctive recoil from the suave older man. 'You honestly believe that this crazy story *might* be true?'

Dark eyes without the merest shimmer of gold rested on her, his level of strain palpable. 'Yes.'

Yes? And with that one little word everything Misty had known about herself seemed to collapse and shatter. When she had been much younger, she had often wondered who her father was, but since her late mother had refused to name him even to the social services she had accepted that she had no hope of ever finding out. So what could be more devastating than the discovery that a newspaper knew more about her parentage than she did herself?

The paper still lay on her lap unopened. Leone had been forewarned and must already have read it. She felt horribly humiliated and she was deep in shock. Could there be truth in such a wild allegation? Could Oliver Sargent have had a relationship with her mother all those years ago?

Her hand trembling, she began to open the newspaper.

'Leave it until we get back to the house,' Leone advised.

'House?' Misty queried.

'By now your apartment will be beseiged by the press. I can protect you better in my own home.'

She studied Leone, noting his low-key delivery and the gravity etched into every line of his lean, powerful face. He was trying to help and support her and, while on one level she was grateful, on another she was cringing with embarrassment. 'You came back early from New York because of this,' she said tightly. 'I'm sorry.'

'You have nothing to be sorry about,' Leone stated with unexpected harshness. 'I caused this.'

How had he caused it? By putting her in the public eye? By making her a source of interest to the press? Perhaps it was more her own fault, she thought numbly: she had refused to talk to the journalists who had initially contacted her. Had she given a few facts about herself, possibly nobody would have bothered to check out who she was in any greater depth. But how had anyone managed to establish what she had been unable to find out even for herself? Her brain still refused to come to grips with that headline. How *could* she be Oliver Sargent's daughter? And what were the odds against her having actually met the man face to face only a week ago? That had surely been the most amazing coincidence.

'Don't read that rubbish.' As Misty bent her head to scrutinise the newspaper article, Leone stretched out a lean brown hand and flipped it off her lap again.

'What are you doing?' Misty asked in bewilderment.

'Tabloids always sensationalise stories. Don't waste your time.'

Involuntarily, she closed her eyes and swallowed hard. She knew she would read it all and chew over every sentence, but she felt it might be wiser to do that without Leone as an audience. It had to be a pretty awful article if he was so keen to prevent her from seeing it.

Leone curved a protective arm round her and swept her up the steps of a big tall house before she could even get a proper look at it. Her bemused gaze darted over the spacious, elegant hall and then returned inexorably to the newspaper that Leone had in his other hand. 'I've *got* to see it,' she told him.

With a reluctance she could feel he extended it again.

'Let's go upstairs.' Pausing to address the hovering manservant in Italian, Leone led her towards the imposing staircase. 'We'll have some breakfast. I don't know about you but I'm hungry.'

'Yeah…' Misty couldn't have eaten to save her life, but she followed his lead, striving to behave as though the world she knew had not exploded beneath her feet.

'Try to understand that the press are much more interested in roasting Oliver Sargent alive in print than in your angle on this...try not to take it personally,' Leone urged.

At that piece of well-meant advice, Misty had to swallow the hysterical giggle tickling at the back of her dry throat. Why was it that men always shied away from the emotional fall-out of any event and concentrated on the practicalities? Did he really believe that even at her age she could find out from a newspaper that her father might be a famous politician and *not* take it personally?

'Sargent has made a lot of enemies in the media,' Leone continued with determination, shepherding her into a charming reception room already bright with early morning sunlight. 'They're out to get him, not you.'

Misty recalled reading one of Oliver Sargent's stern homilies on the number of babies being born out of wedlock and the effect that that had on society and on the children themselves. The older man was often both attacked and applauded for his moral stance. She could see that the revelation that he had fathered illegitimate children of his own and abandoned both them and their mother to their fate would crown him as the ultimate hypocrite in the eyes of many.

'I don't want you to get upset over this.' Leone's Sicilian accent had thickened to charge every syllable he spoke with the strength of his feelings.

Absorbing the first few saccharine-sweet sentences and the spread of pictures within the newspaper, Misty realised with shrinking discomfiture that she was to figure as an object of pity to the reader. Oliver Sargent's opulent country home was depicted beside the small terraced house where Misty had been fostered before being sent to Fossett's.

'Your mother's first husband was a generation older than she was. He was a college professor,' Leone stated without any inflection at all before she could get any deeper into the article. 'He encouraged her to enroll in further education classes. Sargent was a law student at the same university.'

'I can't imagine my mother studying,' Misty mumbled, already cringing with hurt at seeing in print the statement that she had been a troubled child, who had often played truant from school. It was true but she had become a regular attender after going to live at Fossetts at the age of twelve.

'The affair only became public knowledge when her husband discovered through hospital tests that you and your twin couldn't be his children. Your mother ran to Sargent for support but he turned his back on her. He had been engaged to Jenny all along.'

Misty thought of the pleasant woman she had met at Castle Eyrie and her stomach gave a protesting somersault. Jenny Sargent was about to discover that her husband had fathered another woman's children during their engagement. She too would feel betrayed and bitter and terribly hurt.

In the article, Misty's unhappy and rootless childhood was compared to Oliver Sargent's life of affluence and privilege, and she was skimming through that character assassination with an innate sense of distaste when she came on a section that turned her skin clammy. Her broken engagement to Philip was mentioned. 'Philip ditched Misty after she found out that she couldn't have kids a supposed and anonymous friend of hers had revealed.

'No…' A stricken moan was wrenched from Misty as she absorbed that cruel public exposure of her own biggest secret. She felt sick to the stomach.

Dragging the newspaper from her, Leone closed his arms round her trembling length. In hurt and shame and the agonising thought of him having read those same lines, she pulled away from him and a tearing sob escaped her.

'Go *away*…' she told him chokily. 'Let me deal with this by myself.'

But Leone was persistent. With a fierce objection in his own language, he tugged her back to him and he was too strong for her to resist. She could no longer restrain the great swell of tumultous emotion attacking her and the tears fell thick and fast. She could have borne the storm of Oliver Sargent being her putative father, for that still seemed quite unreal to her, but the painful reality of her own inability to conceive being put into print was more than she could stand.

'*Per amor di Dio*…I couldn't protect you from this. It was too late.' His rich dark drawl roughened with raw regret, Leone crushed her into the hard, muscular heat of his big, powerful body. 'Don't let yourself be hurt by it.'

Misty lifted welling eyes to his charged gaze, recognising the ferocious tension written into his devastatingly handsome dark features. 'I don't want you involved in this mess,' she confessed. 'That only makes me feel worse!'

'I *am* involved. I'm involved a great deal more than you appreciate.' Leone stared down at her with haunted dark eyes, ashen pale below his bronzed skin.

Misty assumed that he was blaming himself for putting her in the public eye in the first place and she shook her copper head in vehement objection, silken strands of bright hair flying back from her taut cheekbones. 'That's not true.'

'Everything in that newspaper story only emphasises what a very special woman you are,' Leone asserted with conviction.

'It is *so* special to be infertile,' Misty launched back at him in bitter pain. 'Oh, yes, *so* special!'

Tearing herself free of him in shamed and chagrined regret at having let that revealing response escape her, Misty spun away, but long, lean fingers closed over hers and entwined, preventing her from putting any real distance between them.

'That doesn't matter to me,' Leone insisted with harsh emphasis.

As Misty snatched in a sobbing breath, she could have wept in receipt of that assurance. Why on earth *should* it matter to him? After all, he wasn't thinking of marrying her. But, regardless of that reality, she recognised that she had still not wanted Leone to know her secret. She had feared that, just like her former fiancé, he might start thinking of her as being something less than other women.

He eased her back to him and the last of her prickly, independent defences subsided. She loved him, she loved him even more for being there for her when so many men leapt for cover at the first sign of trouble or embarrassment. Closing her arms round him in acceptance, she looked up at him, grey eyes silver with emotion. 'Make love to me,' she whispered softly.

Betraying disconcertion, Leone tensed. 'Misty, I...'

Misty turned white and thrust him back from her in such sudden rebuttal she took him by surprise. 'Forget it,' she urged strickenly.

In the act of stalking to the door, she was lifted bodily off her feet and up into Leone's strong arms. '*Santo Cielo!* How could you think that I don't want you? I wanted you every hour of every day I was away from you!' he grated rawly.

Relief travelled through Misty in a winging, weakening surge. At that moment, she had never been more desperate to lose herself in his passion and know that, regardless of those cheap tabloid revelations, he still found her attractive.

'But we have to talk first,' Leone completed in a hoarse undertone.

'Later...nothing else matters right now.'

'Misty—'

'Shut up,' she told him, reaching up in a desperate movement to cover that wide sensual mouth with her own.

With a feeling groan, he took her invitation with fierce urgency. He crossed the landing and shouldered his path into a bedroom furnished in masculine shades of green. There he laid her down on the wide divan bed and stood over her, lean, strong face taut. 'Are you sure about this?' he asked thickly.

'Well, if you want to have breakfast first, I'll understand,' Misty quipped unevenly.

His cell phone was buzzing. He switched it off and tossed it aside with heartening indifference, his smouldering golden eyes reluctant to leave hers for a second. What he said about the possibility of breakfast was short and succinct.

Misty was working really hard at not thinking about that newspaper story and Oliver Sargent. But it was impossible for her not to recall how the man who might be her own father had attempted to come between her and Leone by warning her that she could not trust the younger man. Now that she saw the most likely motivation for that approach, she was appalled. From the instant she'd given her name, Oliver Sargent would have known who she was and he had seen her as a threat to his precious reputation. His own behaviour virtually confirmed that he believed her to be his daughter. Had he assumed that she knew who he was too?

A shiver ran through Misty. She was seeing wheels within wheels and it scared her. At that point, another stab of comprehension assailed her and she turned dazed eyes on Leone. 'You knew all along that I might be Oliver Sargent's daughter!' she exclaimed to the male poised by the bed watching her every change of expression. 'Somehow you discovered that when you were having me checked out…didn't you?'

Wearing something of the aspect of a male in the dock on a murder charge, Leone nodded in confirmation, his tension pronounced.

'That's okay,' Misty assured him gently, eyes soft beneath her lashes, for even as she had spoken she was remembering Leone's equally offbeat behaviour that same weekend. He could have had no idea that Oliver Sargent would be visiting Castle Eyrie too and he had attempted to keep her and her putative father apart. Leone had been shocked when he had learned that she had already met the older man and had endeavoured without success to persuade her that there had been no need for them to go downstairs and attend the party that evening.

'I don't want to talk about this any more,' she confided unsteadily. 'There's no point. Now that I know the truth, I can see that Oliver Sargent was scared just being in the same room as me that weekend. But I've done without a father all my life and I'm hardly gasping for one now. *His* loss, not mine.'

Grave as a stone statue, Leone stared at her, and then he came down on the bed beside her and gathered her close. 'But you've been hurt so much by this.'

Her eyes watered and she mock-punched a wide muscular shoulder, tempted to tell him that nothing really mattered as long as she had him, that she could stand *anything* as long as she had him, but too cautious to risk such a frank confession. 'Stop being so wet!' she told him instead and she pushed him backwards, taking him by surprise so that he fell across the bed.

Startled, Leone looked up at her, brilliant golden eyes shimmering over her smiling face. 'You're a hell of a woman, *bella mia*.'

'Yeah…' Leaning over him, Misty tugged loose his tie

and trailed it off. 'And since you're being so shy about getting your kit off, I'm about to do it for you!'

'I hate to keep on repeating myself…but we *do* need to talk,' Leone framed half under his breath.

'You've stopped fancying me, haven't you?' Misty whispered jaggedly, all the colour draining from her tightening features.

Leone reached up and meshed long fingers into her hair before she could retreat from him again, and with his other hand he dragged hers down to the iron-hard thrust of his arousal beneath the tailored cloth of his trousers. 'Sorry to be so graphic but I'm always in this condition around you.'

Misty trembled in receipt of that proof. 'Always?'

'If I'd known what your ex-fiancé had done to you three years ago, I'd have torn that little creep limb from limb when I met him!' Leone ground out.

Reassured, Misty embarked on his shirt buttons. 'It's been a long time since I had any regrets in that line.'

Leone sat up and wrenched himself free of his jacket. 'Move in with me.'

At that sudden invitation, Misty stared at him in astonishment.

'I've never asked a woman that before,' he admitted with equally staggering abruptness.

It seemed obvious to her that Leone was unsure of the offer he had just made. She was shaken that he could be that impulsive, hurt that he could not hide his uncertainty from her, and she forced a determined laugh. 'I'd have to know you a lot longer before I would even consider moving to London on your behalf.'

She watched the disconcertion flare in his gorgeous eyes. He was so proud, so arrogant that her apparent amusement had flicked his ego on the raw. 'I'm not letting you go back to Norfolk.'

'The whole world doesn't turn at your convenience,'

Misty told him teasingly, and then he lifted her off him and rolled her under him instead. As he pried her lips apart with the plunging, ravishing heat of his sensual mouth she learned that her body turned and burned at his first passionate touch.

'I've had nothing but cold showers all week,' he groaned against her reddened lips.

He slid off the bed with pronounced reluctance and began to undress with all the hot impatience of a very aroused male. Just watching him did crazy things to her heartbeat. She wriggled out of her jeans, raised her arms, arched her spine and peeled off her top.

'You get to take off the rest…you're so good at it.' Misty reclined back against the pillows, confident that she was wanted, self-esteem restored.

Brilliant golden eyes set beneath spiky black lashes sought out hers. 'I was just practising for you coming along.'

Involuntarily, Misty giggled. 'I've heard some excuses in my time but that one is priceless!'

'You're so resilient.' Leone studied her with flattering fascination. 'I thought you'd still be coming apart at the seams over that tabloid story.'

He came down on the bed, all bronzed vibrant flesh, rippling muscles and magnificent arousal, and her mouth ran dry and she melted from inside out in response. No, she was not about to come apart at the seams while she had Leone in a supportive role, she conceded to herself without hesitation. She shivered as he released the catch on her bra, moaned out loud as he shaped the pouting swell of her breasts. She felt so sensitive there that the smallest touch on her taut nipples burned like fire through the rest of her and she blushed like mad.

'I ought to get points for appreciating how beautiful you

were when you were trying to hide your glory in shapeless suits the colour of concrete,' Leone informed her thickly.

'I never felt beautiful in my life until you looked at me,' Misty confided with helpless honesty.

He spread her like a willing sacrifice on the bed and worked his sensual path down over her straining breasts to her quivering tummy and, disposing swiftly of her panties, to the very heart of her. Her body ached for him with such immediacy that anything less than instant fulfilment literally hurt. Within minutes, she was lost in a sensual daze of writhing, gasping abandonment. She clutched at his hair, his shoulders and then gave herself wholly up to the voluptuous pleasure of what he was doing to her. Her climax took her like a tidal wave sweeping her to an explosive peak of hot, shattering delight that seemed to last for ever.

'I hope you don't have to go away any time soon again,' Misty mumbled in the aftermath.

'I missed you too, *amore*…' Leone drove into her with tender force and she closed her eyes again and let the wicked wanton pleasure take her by storm.

He pushed her to the heights again and it was wild and wonderful. Arching up to him, she matched his fluid thrusts and sobbed out loud when the frenzy of hunger controlled her afresh. But when that sweet, drowning passion of both body and senses engulfed her again, she came out of the experience with tears stinging her eyes, feeling that they had been closer than they had ever been and full of dreaming happiness.

Leone expelled his breath in a ragged hiss and kissed her and held her rather too tight for comfort. 'Now we're going to go and have breakfast and talk…and you're going to promise me that you'll reserve judgement until I've finished speaking.'

What on earth did he wish to talk about? His invitation

for her to move in with him? What else could it be? Why
the heck had she assumed that that was an impulsive suggestion? After all, Leone was not the impulsive type.
Indeed, most of the time, Leone gave her the impression
of being the sort of male who planned everything right
down to the final full stop. Furthermore, as he had been
referring to their need to have a serious talk since they'd
arrived at his house, it was much more likely that the idea
of her moving in with him had been on his mind while
he'd been in New York…

CHAPTER EIGHT

In the imposing dining room on the ground floor, Misty made an exaggerated show of sugaring Leone's coffee.

'Do you think you could be serious for a few minutes?'

Misty focused on Leone with ruefully amused eyes. She reckoned he looked serious enough for both of them but she couldn't concentrate. Only a couple of hours earlier she had believed that her world had fallen apart, but now, even though she knew she had still to deal with what she had learned about Oliver Sargent, her most overriding sensation was one of bubbling contentment.

The manservant whisked the metal cover from the breakfast fry she had cheerfully ordered. But as the familiar aroma of the bacon hit her nostrils, something quite unfamiliar happened to her digestive system. Attacked by an instant wave of nausea, Misty lurched out of her seat and bolted for the cloakroom.

Leone hammered on the door she had bolted behind her. 'Are you all right?'

Clutching the vanity basin to stay upright, Misty surveyed her drawn face in the mirror and suppressed a groan. Her tummy was still rolling and she felt rather dizzy too. Grimacing, she freshened up, thinking that it was just typical that she should succumb to some nasty, embarrassing bug at the very moment when she wished to look and feel her best.

Emerging again to receive Leone's questioning scrutiny, Misty said with determined brightness, 'I'm really not that hungry.'

'Are you feeling ill?'

'Of course I'm not feeling ill.' Misty was grateful that she had put some blusher on her cheeks and renewed her lipstick.

Back at the dining table, she sipped her cup of tea. 'You were about to get serious,' she reminded him cheerfully.

Leone had not touched his own breakfast and his strong bone structure was clenched hard. 'First, I want to tell you about my sister, Battista...'

Instantly, Misty understood what was making him tense and she was touched and pleased that he had decided to confide in her.

'Battista accepted a placement on Oliver Sargent's research staff last summer,' Leone advanced tight-mouthed. 'She was nineteen and she developed quite a crush on him.'

'Did she?' Misty looked surprised.

'He slept with her.'

Shocked by that statement, Misty frowned. 'Are you *sure* of that?'

'Certain. Her best friend was so distressed by her death that she told me the whole story. Sargent conducts his extra-marital affairs with great discretion. He owns a country cottage that only his lovers know exists.'

Misty lowered her attention from Leone's embittered gaze. So, the father who was a virtual stranger to her was *still* a womaniser, given to dishonesty and betrayal. No longer did she need to wonder what had caused the hostility between the two men, a hostility that Jenny Sargent had explained to her own satisfaction, ignorant as she had to be of the true facts.

'The night Battista died, she was driving Sargent down to his cottage, but I was unable to prove that he was in the car with her,' Leone admitted heavily. 'The car went off the road. There were no witnesses. She was trapped in the wreckage. He left her there and fled...'

Misty surveyed him in horror. 'Surely not?'

'It was well over an hour before an anonymous call was made to the emergency services. I very much doubt that he even risked making that call personally and, in any case, by then it was too late for Battista. My only consolation is that the medics told me that she couldn't have regained consciousness after the crash...' Leone's accented drawl had dropped low and roughened.

Misty was appalled at what he was telling her. 'How do you *know* that Oliver Sargent was with your sister?'

'I knew it the first time I saw him afterwards. I saw his guilt, his fear of exposure. He's a slick operator but he was terrified that I might be able to prove that he *was* with her that night. Unfortunately he has loyal friends willing to protect him.' His patent loathing for the man he blamed for his sister's death made Misty pale. 'One of those good friends let it be known that Oliver had spent that Friday evening driving down to Cornwall with him.'

'Have you ever confronted him?' she whispered sickly.

'He could sue me for making such an allegation without proof. His whole political career was riding on that alibi. I soon realised that, if I wanted to avenge Battista's death, I had to be even more devious than he is,' Leone admitted, lean, powerful face set in hard lines. 'Almost every public figure has something they want to conceal in their background. I had him investigated in great depth and that's how I found out about you...'

How I found out about you? That admission sent an alarm bell ringing in Misty's brain. She could see connections forming, the vague, horrendous outline of another dimension to their relationship that she could never have dreamt might exist. She sat there staring at him, willing him to tell her that her wild suspicions had no basis in fact.

'Oliver Sargent leads a double life. He's a corrupt politician and I wanted to expose him, but I also wanted him to suffer first.' Leone settled dark-as-midnight eyes on her waxen face. 'I chose you as my weapon.'

Misty parted bloodless lips. 'No…'

Leone sprang out of his seat and spread emphatic hands. 'I refused to see you as a person. I saw you purely as an extension of the man I hated beyond any other,' he told her with raw clarity. 'I had only the most cursory enquiries made about you and I was content to accept the rumours that you were far from being an angel. All that mattered to me was that your very *existence* was a threat to Oliver's reputation as the guardian of other people's morals.'

'Please tell me that this isn't true,' Misty mumbled in stricken appeal. 'Tell me I've woken up in a bad dream…'

'Nobody wants that miracle more than I do, *amore*,' Leone swore, studying her with fierce intensity. 'Do you think I *wanted* to tell you the truth? But I had no choice. Today you're in shock but by tomorrow you would've worked it all out for yourself. I hired you to pretend to be my mistress solely to get your face into the gossip columns and rouse the curiosity of the paparazzi…'

Leone was ten feet from her but that still felt too close. Sending her chair back in a sudden movement, Misty got up and backed away. A kind of fearful fascination held her attention to him, but really at that moment all she wanted to do was run and protect herself from hearing any more.

'I laid a trail so that the press could discover the link between you and Sargent for themselves. I intended you to meet him at Castle Eyrie,' Leone revealed with bitter regret. 'I changed my mind that same weekend because I saw what my revenge was likely to do to you. But by then it was too late to stop it…'

'Too late?' Misty questioned, her mind a bewildered

surge of incomplete thoughts, each one of which made her feel more betrayed than ever.

'I tried to prevent you from meeting Oliver because I knew that the moment he heard your name, he would realise who you were. I only went fishing to keep an eye on him but he got on the other boat and I lost track of him,' Leone reminded her, his strong jawline clenching hard. 'That same morning, while you were still asleep, I gave instructions that the evidence that linked you to Oliver Sargent should be buried again. But I had opened Pandora's box and I discovered I couldn't control what I had unleashed.'

Her legs were shaking beneath her and she sank down into an armchair. He had thrown too much at her at once for her to absorb it all immediately. Far from being his last option as a fake mistress, she had been his *only* option and hand-picked for the role. Sicilian business? Sicilian revenge. Her blood chilled in her veins. What kind of mind did it take for someone to use another human being as though they were an inanimate object of neither importance nor feeling? A very cold, calculating mind, she acknowledged, and the plan had been clever and callous in its very simplicity.

'No wonder you had to keep me in ignorance,' Misty condemned.

'Once I began to get to know you, I realised that what I was doing was wrong.'

But he had still got as far as taking her to Castle Eyrie to trail her in front of her father like a dumb fish lure there to hook a shark, so his regrets had only surfaced at the eleventh hour and only *after* he had slept with her. Up until that point she had simply been a thing, a cypher, a weapon and the very fact that he had paid her to take on that role of pretence must have made him feel even less compunction in using her to his own ends.

'Did you really think that money was likely to compensate me for what you've done to me?'

Leone released his breath in an audible rush. 'I'm ashamed to admit it…but at the beginning, yes, I did think that.'

'At least be honest!' Misty launched at him at sudden greater volume, colour beginning to fire over her cheekbones again. 'You didn't *care*.'

'I didn't want to consider that angle,' Leone countered doggedly.

With every minute that passed, she was grasping new realities. 'Was the idea of looking for a caterer to supply lunches for Brewsters all yours?'

Leone tensed. 'Yes.'

'And I got the contract because I was really the *only* applicant you wanted. It all went like clockwork, didn't it? Tell me, did you also hire a bunch of thugs to trash my business premises, knowing that I couldn't carry that loss and that Carlton Catering was that much more likely to go under?'

'Are you out of your mind?' Leone raked at her in angry, startled disbelief. 'I have no idea what you're talking about!'

'Just after I began that contract with Brewsters my premises were vandalised and my insurers refused to cover the damage.' Misty was impressed by the strength of his shaken rebuttal but impressed by nothing else, indeed far too deeply shaken to feel anything but alienation.

There was no more sobering or agonising discovery than the reality of learning that the man she had fallen in love with had been set on destroying her long before they had even exchanged a first kiss. He had planned her downfall, casting out the lure of that temporary contract and then sitting back to watch her take the bait and borrow on her prospects.

'You can't blame me for that misfortune or for the fact that you ran into financial trouble.' His dark golden eyes were grim on hers. 'But you can blame me for everything else that's happened to you!'

'Oh, don't worry,' Misty advised him unevenly. 'I'm blaming you, all right. But if my business hadn't got into trouble, how were you planning to persuade me to pretend to be your mistress?'

'I expected money to provide a sufficient persuasion.'

'And now I'm in debt to you to the tune of thousands and thousands of pounds and you are never going to see a penny of it back,' Misty swore between gritted teeth, striving to still the tremors of shock stealing through her taut, slender frame.

'I want nothing back. I rather hoped that we had moved beyond that point—'

'I don't think so. Before you went to New York, I asked you if I was still working for you and you said I *was*—'

Leone groaned out loud and flashed her a look of reproof. 'If I'd told you that our agreement was history after our weekend in Scotland, you would have walked out on me out of pride,' he breathed rawly. 'I believed that I had dealt with the threat of the press exposing your relationship to Oliver Sargent. But I needed the time to establish a more normal relationship with you.'

'So you phoned me twice from New York…you're *so* attentive when you're keen, Leone.' Misty made that crack with her fingernails scoring welts into her palms.

His lean, strong face tensed. 'I was angry with you when I left.'

'After all that you have done, *you* were angry with *me*.'

'I care a lot about you. I didn't want to lose you.'

Misty dragged her pained gaze from the hard appeal in his and twisted her head away. 'You don't treat people you care about the way you've treated me. I could never forgive you for going to bed with me in the first place. Just because my supposed father had an affair with your sister…well, I'm sorry, but someone should have warned her not to mess around with a married man.'

There was a ghastly silence but she could not bring herself to look at him. She felt as if he had broken something precious inside her that she would never, ever be able to put together again. And maybe that something precious was faith, and she knew with a sinking heart that her own next step would be to blame herself for every wrong decision that she had made.

'Misty…'

'At that party at Castle Eyrie, Oliver Sargent came up to me. He told me not to trust you and to get out of your life because you were only using me,' Misty confided in a tight, flat little voice.

'You didn't tell me that…' Leone bit out in strong disconcertion.

'I thought he was drunk and that he just didn't like you.' A laugh empty of amusement fell from her lips. 'But now I'll always wonder if he felt sorry for me, if some tiny kernel of paternal concern motivated him. Yes, he no doubt wanted me to perform a vanishing act so that he could breathe easy again, but what *he* told me about you was the complete truth.'

As Misty completed that statement she watched Leone flinch as though she had struck him. A knock sounded on the door and, when it was ignored, sounded again. Opening the door, Leone spoke to the manservant and she turned her head away, feeling empty and despising herself for that last weak, wanton hour she had spent in his bedroom.

'Someone called Nancy has been trying to contact you at the apartment. She wants you to phone.'

In a split second, Misty had flown upright, galvanised by fear as she appreciated that Birdie might well have already received word of that dreadful newspaper article. 'Oh, *no…*'

Leone settled a phone into her hand and she punched out the numbers. But what Nancy had to tell her was entirely unexpected. Birdie had gone into hospital two days earlier, had the operation on her heart only the day before and had come through the surgery successfully.

Misty was stunned. 'But when was all that arranged?'

'We've had the date for a couple of weeks but Birdie wouldn't agree to tell you. She didn't want you to worry or come back from London on her behalf. She insisted I keep quiet about it until after the operation,' the older woman confided apologetically. 'I did *try* to reason with her but I was scared of upsetting her.'

Misty breathed in deep and slow, perspiration dampening her short upper lip. 'And she's *really* all right?'

Minutes later she set the phone down again, her mind grateful for the release of being able to concentrate on someone other than herself. In addition, while her thoughts had been stalled on what she was to do next out of sheer shock, her path was now simple and clear. She would go straight home and visit Birdie in hospital.

'What's happening?' Leone murmured tautly.

Misty refused to look at him. 'Birdie's had the heart surgery she was waiting on. I'm going home.'

The silence stretched.

'I'd very much like to meet your foster mother.'

'I can't think of one reason why she would want to meet you.'

Momentarily silenced by that reroute, Leone said flatly, 'A limo will take you back.'

A limo would get her there faster than the train, Misty reflected. She walked out into the hall as if he weren't there and, in many ways at that moment, Leone *was* no longer real to her. The guy she had fallen madly in love with had evaporated before her eyes and she did not want to take account of a replacement who was chilling, callous and cruel.

'Give me the chance to make this up to you,' Leone ground out a split second before she departed from his house again.

With a frown of disbelief, Misty looked up at him and encountered fierce dark golden eyes, recognising the extent of the tension holding him still. 'But you *couldn't*,' she whispered. 'You scare the living daylights out of me...'

All the way back to Fossetts the expression on his darkly handsome face stayed in her mind's eye. He had looked so shocked. But what had he expected? At the end of the day, she had been faced with the hard reality that she had allowed her heart and her body to overrule all intelligence and common sense. What had she been doing, getting involved with a ruthless Sicilian tycoon? Hadn't she been well aware of his reputation even before she'd tangled with him? At what stage had she begun convincing herself that he was a real pussycat beneath the tough front? Warm and affectionate and caring? My goodness, there was no end to the things a woman in love could make herself believe...

Three weeks later, Misty sat in the waiting room in the local doctor's surgery.

Birdie had been released from hospital the week before but her foster mother had opted to spend her convalescence in Oxford with her sister, who had recently lost her husband. While scolding herself for being so selfish, Misty had been really disappointed that Birdie hadn't been coming home to Fossetts immediately.

Right at that moment, she was wondering why the doctor had asked her to wait for the test results. She was only feeling a bit off colour and she had been frank with him.

She had told him that she had had a recent major emotional upset and that her nervous stomach dated from that same day, and she had advised him to check her notes when he had asked her if she could be pregnant. Everything was Leone's fault: her misery, her dippy digestion, her vanished menstrual cycle, her newfound ability to go off into tears over the stupidest things.

Leone had phoned her and she had put the phone down on him. When he had not called back, she'd told herself that she was grateful that he had taken the hint. However, a week after that, she had been furious to learn that Leone had visited Birdie in hospital. Birdie had pronounced him charming and had got on like a house on fire with him. But then Birdie had not the slightest idea of what had happened between Leone and her foster daughter.

Misty could not understand how being without Leone could feel as if someone had stolen the sun from her world. After all, she had lived a long time without him and had known him for only a matter of months. Yet no matter how often she reminded herself that he had used her with ruthless disregard of the damage he might be inflicting, her sense of loss, emptiness and dislocation merely deepened with every passing day.

'Miss Carlton...' The receptionist indicated that she could go back in to see the doctor.

'Three years ago, you were warned that you might only conceive with the help of fertility treatment, but doctors tend to be very cautious when the prognosis is uncertain,' Dr Fleming told her gravely. 'Evidently you recovered well from the surgery that you had then because you *have* conceived.'

Barely having had the chance to sit down, Misty blinked. 'Sorry?'

'You're going to have a baby.'

She kept on staring at the older man, unable to absorb

the immensity of that announcement. At first, it felt like a cruel joke and she couldn't credit it, and then this great surge of hope swept through her and left her head swimming.

'Now, as I gather that this is an unplanned event...' he continued ruefully.

'It's not an unplanned event...it's a miracle,' Misty contradicted simply.

Fifteen minutes later, having listened unconvinced to the doctor telling her that he did not think her pregnancy lay within the realms of a miracle, Misty floated out of the surgery and straight down the main street into the nearest baby shop. She looked at the tiny clothes with reverent eyes, roved over to admire the buggies, and went off into a wonderful daydream over the soft toys.

Leone had got her pregnant. He had broken her heart, but what was a heart with a crack set next to a baby? A little boy, a little girl. She had no preference whatsoever. She bought a book on pregnancy. Leone's baby. She pushed out that thought as soon as it popped up. This was *her* baby. It was nothing to do with Leone. At least he had made himself useful in one direction, she reflected with a distinct sense of one-upmanship.

She noticed the board outside a newsagent's advertising the morning papers' biggest headline: SARGENT RESIGNS... It was not a surprise. In recent weeks, Oliver Sargent had rarely been out of the newspapers. Within days of Misty's existence being revealed, more serious allegations had been lodged against the older man: that he had accepted bribes in the form of expensive gifts and favours from dubious businessmen in return for using his influence on their behalf. As the evidence of his wrongdoing had mounted, his keen defenders had fallen silent and the ruin of his political career had seemed inevitable.

Momentarily, Misty felt sorry for the father she had

never known, but it was hard to care that much about a man who had made no attempt to contact her. Yet, apart from her twin and herself, he had no other children. Did he blame her for precipitating his downfall? Or was he just as uninterested in her now as he had been in her at birth? And did she even *want* contact with the man whom Leone believed had left his kid sister lying injured in a car wreck just to protect himself from scandal?

On the drive back to Fossetts, Misty thought about Carlton Catering and grimaced. During her absence, two of her three staff had found other employment. Although Misty had initially been delighted to be hired for several private dinner parties, her belief that her business was back up and running had been shortlived. She had suffered the excruciating embarrassment of being made to feel like a freak show by clients, who it seemed had largely sought her services so that they could tell their guests that she was Oliver Sargent's illegitimate daughter and the cast-off mistress of a Sicilian tycoon.

Now that she knew that she was pregnant, selling her business and just finding a job seemed a better option. Furthermore, with the proceeds of the sale, she could start repaying the money she had accepted from Leone before she'd realised that he had hired her to destroy her own father. She knew she would not be able to live with herself until she had begun settling that debt.

In the sitting room at Fossetts, Misty sat down to deal with the morning post. She was disconcerted to open a letter from the company that held the mortgage that contained a cheque written out to the exact amount of her last payment. Getting on the phone to ask why that payment had been refunded, she was astonished to be told that the mortgage had been settled in full prior to the arrival of her cheque.

Silenced by that shock announcement, she replaced the

receiver, instantly aware that only Leone could have made such an extravagant gesture. Sheer rage hurtled through her taut frame. So Leone still believed that he could buy her, did he? Well, she would soon disabuse him of that notion. She wanted nothing to do with him and no more of his wretched money either. As it was, she was likely to be paying him off for the rest of her days! Determined to confront him on the issue, she changed into a red stretchy dress that always made her feel feisty and she tidied her hair. Just as she was telling Nancy that she was going down to London, the doorbell went.

'Where's my red carpet?' Flash demanded, standing back to strike an attitude, spiky blond hair catching the sunlight, green eyes enjoying the effect he was having on her. Behind his metallic gold customised sports car a carload of minders built like human tanks were climbing out of their vehicle.

It had been five months since Misty had seen him, two since she had spoken to him on the phone. For a split second she hesitated, and then she threw herself into his open arms, eyes stinging with tears. He held her back from him and his keen gaze hardened. 'Why do you always pick bastards?'

'S-sorry?' she stammered as he walked her into the sitting room with the familiarity of a male who had often stayed at Fossetts.

'I may have been touring the US but I still follow the English papers,' Flash said very drily. 'You never called me once. Yet it's been all thrills and spills here. One minute you're swanking round in diamonds with this Mafioso type, the next you're discovering you have the long-lost daddy from hell...a politician...how low can you sink? And then you get dumped.'

Misty's chin came up. 'Excuse me? I dumped him.'

Resting back against the table, his lanky, compact length

complemented by a black T-shirt and faded jeans, Flash gave her a huge approving smile. 'That makes me feel a lot better. Where's Birdie?'

While she was explaining, Flash, who was rarely still for longer than ten seconds, picked up the fat paperback still lying on the table and grimaced. 'Who's reading this?'

Misty turned scarlet. It was the pregnancy book she had bought.

'What are you reading stuff like that for? You're only upsetting yourself!' Flash groaned with a look of incomprehension. 'I thought you'd got over that.'

She almost let his assumption stand and then guilt kicked in and she told him the truth. In shock, he closed his eyes and swore long and low under his breath.

'Something good has come out of something bad,' Misty muttered fiercely.

'It's a bloody disaster!' Flash launched at her angrily.

An hour later, he knew everything, right down to the fact that when he'd arrived she had been on the brink of heading out to catch a train down to London.

'So I'll take you instead,' Flash stunned her by announcing, an air of grim pleasure lightening his eyes at the prospect. 'And after you've told the Mafioso what he can do with himself, we'll go out and celebrate!'

Ten minutes later, an overnight bag hastily filled, she was in the car and it was roaring down the drive.

CHAPTER NINE

FLASH had not the smallest difficulty talking his way into the underground car park at Andracchi Industries.

When Misty arrived on the top floor, the receptionist called Leone's secretary with her name. With her mane of copper hair and the red dress that enhanced her lithe, shapely figure, she was attracting an uncomfortable amount of attention by then and her nerves were eating her alive. When Leone strode into view in person, a breath-taking smile on his lean, dark features, her mouth ran dry and her heart started beating like a war drum. After three weeks of cold turkey withdrawal symptoms and the kind of dreams that made her despise herself in the morning light, his stunning dark good looks and lean, well-built physique had a powerfully embarrassing effect on her.

Angrily ashamed of the leap of response attacking her treacherous body, Misty parted her lips and without even pausing for breath snapped, 'How *dare* you pay off Birdie's mortgage?'

Brilliant golden eyes shimmered over her from head to toe and he took his time over that appraisal before resting his attention back on her furious face. 'We'll go into my office.'

'What I have to say can be said right here!'

'But if you expect me to *listen*, you don't begin by abusing me in a reception area,' Leone murmured with icy cool.

Recalled to an awareness of their surroundings and genuinely mortified by her own thoughtless behaviour, Misty reddened to the roots of her hair and accompanied him down a corridor into an impressive office.

She stole a covert glance at him as he closed the door, taking in his bold, bronzed profile, the sleek, sophisticated cut of his suit and the slice of pristine white shirt-cuff visible above a lean, long-fingered hand. As a tide of aching regret charged her she swallowed hard. His every movement was measured and fluid and oh, so cool and she was intimidated by his apparent detachment. He offered her a seat but she declined.

'Can I abuse you now?' Misty enquired.

'I wouldn't advise it, *amore*.' Leone held eye contact far longer than was comfortable for her strained nerves.

'Don't call me that.'

'As far as I'm concerned, you're still my lover until I take another,' Leone imparted smooth as silk.

Another? That one word threatened to slice Misty in two. The very idea of him with another woman devastated her, froze her brain in its tracks and sent her heart swooping to her toes. Her fingers curled in on themselves as she willed herself back under control, but it took every atom of pride that she possessed.

'I'll ask you again.' Misty lifted her chin. 'What were you playing at when you settled Birdie's mortgage?'

A wry smile curved Leone's wide sensual mouth. 'I'm afraid you're out of bounds.'

Her temper began to rise again. 'I beg your pardon?'

'You heard me.'

'But I know *exactly* why you did it!' Misty condemned.

'Do you?' Leone surveyed her with veiled golden eyes that gleamed like the purest metal.

'Of course I blasted well know!' Misty fired back at him in furious frustration, unable to fathom his attitude. 'You're trying to impress me with your generosity and get me back—'

'No, I'm not.'

But Misty had worked up too big a head of steam to pay proper heed to that quiet contradiction. 'You think you can persuade me that you're really a nice person…you think you can *bribe* me back into your bed with the power of your money—'

'No, I don't.'

'And it's disgusting and what's more…a total waste of your time…' As Misty finally took in Leone's denials her voice faded away instead of reaching a crescendo. Silenced, she stared at him in visible confusion.

'I don't owe you an explanation but, since you've misunderstood the gesture, I'll tell you what motivated me,' Leone murmured evenly. 'In the guise of an anonymous well-wisher, I settled your foster mother's mortgage because I liked her.'

'Because you liked her…' Misty echoed weakly.

'I give millions to charity every year. I have no hands-on involvement.' Leone informed her. 'But when I met Birdie, I found myself wondering how often deserving individuals like her are passed over as being not sufficiently deprived to require help. Yet she and her husband, at no little cost to themselves, devoted their lives to working with troubled children.'

'Yes, that's true *but*—'

'If Robin Pearce hadn't quit his career as an award-winning architect forty years ago, his widow would've been left comfortably off. At this stage of her life, Birdie should not have to pay a price for their generosity towards others.' His strong jawline clenched. 'In short, if I choose to play Santa Claus, it's my money and my choice.'

The silence sizzled with as much danger as bare electric wires.

Misty was pale as death, for she could see that he meant every word that he had just said. And she wanted to sink through the floor. She wanted to shrivel into invisibility, anything sooner than be forced to bear the awful humiliation she had brought down on her own head. She had screeched at him like a shrew. She had accused him of going to extraordinary lengths to get her back. She must have sounded so vain, so self-absorbed, so far removed from reality. Even after soundly rejecting him, she had somehow contrived to go on believing that he remained interested in her.

'As I suspect that you virtually beggared yourself to keep your foster mother in that house,' Leone continued, 'you should be relieved.'

To Misty's horror tears stung her eyes in a hot surge and she spun away in panic, only to stagger as a blinding wave of dizziness engulfed her. Strong arms steadied her as she swayed and he backed her down into a seat.

'What have you been doing to yourself?' Leone demanded with audible concern.

As she sucked in extra oxygen to clear her head, the trickle of tears threatened to become a gush capable of washing him right out of his office again. Determined to hold all that moisture in, she bent her head and the dreadful silence stretched.

'Why did you come all the way down here to see me?' Leone breathed huskily.

'Rage.' Misty lifted her lashes and almost had a heart attack. Having dropped down into an atheletic crouch, he was right in front of her and only inches away.

'Start shouting again. At this moment, all I want to do is drag you down onto the carpet and lose myself in you again,' Leone confided thickly.

Misty collided with smouldering golden eyes and her heart skipped a beat.

His arrogant head angled to one side, he devoured her

with his molten gaze and then murmured, 'That's fantasy... I'd be more than happy to settle for dinner.'

She was appalled to realise that the reference to the carpet and sexual activity combined with him still had extraordinary appeal. At the speed of light she had gone from sick dizziness to burning, wanton lust and the most agonised craving. Soft, full mouth taut, she stared at him as though he had her imprisoned behind steel bars. Her brain was telling her to stand up and walk out, but her body was glued to the seat and shamefully hot and liquid with longing. At violent war with her own instincts, she trembled.

'No...I can't.' Desperate to think of anything but his proximity and her own weak reaction to him, Misty made herself concentrate on his benevolence towards Birdie. Like it or not, she too would benefit from that altruistic gesture, but at least it meant that she could immediately return a good deal of the cash he had advanced to her after that contract had been signed. Removing her cheque-book from her bag, she balanced it on her knee and began to fill out a cheque.

Leone frowned. 'What are you doing?'

Misty handed the cheque to him.

He quirked an ebony brow and vaulted back upright. 'What's this for?'

Her triangular face set and her eyes veiled, she stood up. 'It's the first payment on what I owe you,' she said stiffly. 'Primarily, I took your money to keep up the payments on Birdie's mortgage but you've taken care of that problem for me.'

His strong jawline had clenched. 'I told you that I wanted nothing back.'

'I didn't want to be involved in my father's downfall...unfortunately you didn't give me a choice about that. However, I *can* refuse to profit from his misfortunes,' Misty declared, her bright head high, but her heart twisting inside her as she saw the flare of angry reproach in his gaze.

She could imagine only too well how agonising it must have been for Leone when his kid sister had died in such appalling circumstances, and how embittered he must have been when he'd realised that Oliver Sargent could not be called to account through the normal legal channels. But two wrongs did not make a right and his ferocious need for revenge had hurt her a great deal, as well as highlighting the awful truth that there was no way on earth Leone could *ever* have a normal relationship with the daughter of a man whom he hated.

In the simmering silence, Leone tore the cheque in two.

Her legs feeling like hollow wood, Misty kept moving towards the door and opened it. 'I'll donate the money to charity, then.'

'You can't afford to do that either!' Leone dismissed in exasperation.

'I'm selling my business. If it doesn't find a buyer as a going concern, I'll sell off the equipment and the vans.'

Leone surveyed her with savage incredulity. 'Are you out of your mind?'

A bitter smile curved Misty's soft mouth as she allowed herself a final word. 'Thanks to all that publicity, I've acquired a certain notoriety locally. Listening from the kitchen while my clients and their guests discuss me is not my idea of fun.'

A line of hard colour scored his superb cheekbones and she knew she need say nothing more, for his pride was as strong as her own.

She hurried on down the corridor, her back rigid and her throat convulsing. Before the lift doors could shut she surged in and hit the button for the basement floor. Secure in the belief that she was alone, she rested her hot, damp forehead against the cold steel wall, just as the doors jerked back again and someone else stepped in. Flushed and discomfited, she turned round to find herself facing Leone again.

His smouldering golden gaze held hers in the pulsing silence. Her shoulder blades met the wall behind her, but the throb of awareness surged through her in an electrical storm of sensation. When he reached for her, she was breathing fast and audibly and the frantic ache stirring within her had no conscience. All that mattered in that instant was the hot, potent explosion of his sensual mouth on hers, the hard, satisfying strength of his hands as he plastered her up against every muscular angle of his lean, powerful frame. She was welded to him when the loud ping of the lift's arrival penetrated the fog of her excitement and she jerked back from him in dismay.

Her dazed attention fell on the car parked only about thirty feet away. The driver's door was already opening, a blond head appearing.

'I've got to go...Flash is waiting,' she muttered in a rush.

But as she made it out of the lift Leone closed his hand over hers to halt her. 'What are you doing with *him*?' he demanded with savage abruptness.

Misty tried and failed to pull away. 'That's none of your business—'

'Let go of her!' Flash demanded, striding towards them, his anger unconcealed.

In the background, Misty saw Flash's minders leaping out of their vehicle, scenting trouble and, by the expression on their tough faces, looking forward to the prospect. Every alarm bell she possessed started clanging. Leone against three men. Spinning round to face him, she gasped, 'Get back in the lift, you idiot!'

In a slow, emphatic movement, Leone released her. 'Stay out of this—'

Misty simply stepped in front of him. 'If you touch him, I'll never forgive you!' she flung at Flash in a passion. 'I don't want trouble and I won't have *stupid* male hormones taking over here!'

'I'm not about to stand by watching him manhandle a pregnant woman!' Flash growled at her. 'And stop embarrassing us. He's a big guy. He can look after himself.'

The angry colour in Misty's cheeks drained away long before the younger man finished speaking. Appalled by his reference to the child she was carrying and hearing Leone vent his breath in a startled hiss behind her, Misty gave her foster brother a stricken look.

'You're pregnant?' Leone exclaimed in disbelief.

Misty closed her hand round Flash's wrist and tried to drag him in the direction of the car. 'Come on...' she urged.

'Is it mine?' Leone muttered hoarsely.

And Flash swung round and went for him. It happened so fast, she had no hope of preventing that outbreak of aggression. She was just in time to see Leone duck and plant a punch on Flash instead.

'Stop it...stop it, the two of you!' she shrieked, her voice breaking with the force of her distress.

Ironically, Leone stilled just long enough to allow Flash the opportunity to return that punch.

At that point, registering that Flash's minders were staying out of the fray and no longer caring if the two men killed each other, Misty threw herself into the passenger seat of the car. *Is it mine?* She felt savaged. How could Leone have asked such a question?

Minutes later, Flash settled with a groan in beside her. 'Honour's been satisfied,' he informed her.

Misty stared out through the windscreen. Still as a statue, Leone was poised by the lift watching them, lean, strong features grim and set.

'You're supposed to thank me for defending your honour,' Flash told her. 'How was I supposed to know you hadn't told him about the baby? I mean...I assumed that was one of the *main* reasons you wanted to see him—'

'I only found out that I was pregnant this morning. I hadn't even thought about telling Leone yet,' Misty admitted tightly. 'And after what he said, I'm glad I didn't bother.'

'I wouldn't make too much out of Andracchi asking whose baby it was.' Flash grimaced. 'You were with me and he didn't like it...and me knowing what he *didn't* know would have made any bloke suspicious.'

'My goodness, you're really quite in charity with Leone now that you've thumped each other!' Misty responded with waspish bite.

'What are you planning to tell Birdie?'

Misty jerked and paled, for that was a challenge she had avoided even thinking about.

'She'll be devastated—' Flash forecast ruefully.

'Yes, I do *know* that!' Misty interrupted on the back of a guilty sob, knowing that Birdie would be shocked, hurt and very disappointed in her. Indeed, the older woman would very likely blame herself for some perceived and quite imaginary flaw in her own parenting skills.

'So, taking everything into account, I'm just amazed that you were carrying on in that lift with Andracchi!'

Her cheeks burning, Misty looked at her foster brother.

Flash cast her a mocking glance. 'You left lipstick on him.'

He took her back to his city apartment, ordered in a take-away for his entire entourage and sat down with them to watch the football matches taped for him while he'd been out of the country. Exhausted by her eventful day, refusing to think about Leone's forbidding reaction to the news that she was carrying his child, Misty fell asleep on a sofa. Flash woke her up several hours later to tell her to get ready to go out. It was already late and Misty was not in the mood, but, feeling guilty about being such a wet blanket, she washed her hair and made a special effort to look her most festive in the emerald-green and cerise top and hipster skirt she had packed.

A bank of cameras greeted Flash's arrival at his favourite London nightclub and she kept a bright smile pinned to her peach tinted mouth. If a photo made it into print and Leone saw it, she wanted to look as though she hadn't a care in the world.

Seated by the management at a reserved table, Flash closed an appreciative arm around her. 'You never complained once about the football—'

Misty grinned. '*Only* because I slept through it.'

'I've missed you, but you could be bad for my image,' Flash said with amusement. 'You tower over me like a Vegas showgirl!'

People kept coming up to talk to him. It was the early hours of the morning when Misty saw Leone through the crush. He was watching their table, lean, powerful face hard as iron. Her heart thumped, butterflies breaking loose in her tummy. Keen not to draw Flash's attention to him and knowing that she had to talk to Leone, she slid out from behind the table. But no sooner did she reach him than he simply closed one imprisoning hand over hers and began to press her towards the exit.

'What are you doing?' she gasped, but the music was too loud for him to hear her.

In the foyer, Misty rounded on him. 'I can't just walk out of here!'

'It's almost dawn and you're out dancing and drinking with another guy!' Sizzling golden eyes flared over her in furious derision. 'You're coming home with me—'

'No, I'm not, and the only thing I've been drinking is

pineapple juice!' Misty hissed back at him, wholly disconcerted by that attack.

Ignoring that plea, Leone turned to speak to one of the security men, and beneath her shaken gaze money changed hands faster than the speed of light. Leone curved a hand round the base of her rigid spine. 'Your pet rock star will get a message…OK?'

'No. I came here with Flash and I'll leave with him.'

Leone resting blazing golden eyes on her. 'You have two options, *amore*. Either you accompany me of your own accord *or*…I carry you out of here.'

Misty looked at him aghast. Already conscious that speculative eyes were resting on them, she reddened with angry incredulity. 'You wouldn't dare…'

'Wouldn't I?' Leone countered lethally. 'I've been trying to track you down since yesterday. Almost twelve hours on, I wouldn't say that my patience is at an all time high.'

At his admission that he had been looking for her ever since she had left the scene of that stupid fight, Misty worried at the soft underside of her lip and then walked out of the nightclub without further protest. Of course he wanted to speak to her after what he had found out. Was she afraid of what she was about to hear? Trying to avoid the unpleasantness? Naturally he had been shocked and angry the day before. What had been a casual sexual fling on his terms had had far-reaching consequences. He had asked her if it had been safe to make love and she had told him it had been, but she was now carrying his baby. She would be a fool to hope that from his point of view that could be anything other than very bad news.

Leone unlocked the door of a low-slung red sports car. She climbed in. He drove off and still the silence was maintained, worrying at her nerves, keeping her tension high.

'I'd like to know how you feel about this baby,' Leone confessed at the first set of traffic lights.

Fearing that he was asking that because he was hoping that she might be willing to consider a termination, she realised that she had to be totally honest. 'I'm sure you don't want to hear it…but I was over the moon when I found out,' she admitted tautly. 'I thought I couldn't have a child and to me it just feels like a miracle. But I don't expect anyone else to feel the same way. I know the circumstances are hardly ideal.'

Leone was listening with such intensity that the lights changed without him noticing and only the angry revving of the car behind recalled him to that reality. His masculine profile a little less taut, he drove on. She looked at his lean brown fingers where they rested on the steering wheel and felt her skin heat as she remembered the way he made love. Her colour heightening at what seemed the ultimate of inappropriate memories, she turned her head away.

'I had a surprise visitor shortly after your departure yesterday,' Leone breathed tautly. 'Oliver Sargent—'

Misty emerged from her self-absorption with a start. 'He came to see you? But *why*?'

'He finally confessed that he *was* with Battista the night she died. According to him he threw himself out of the car as it went off the road and he was knocked out. He said that Battista was dead by the time he recovered consciousness and that he panicked.'

'Do you believe him?' Misty whispered.

'Yes,' Leone ceded in a roughened undertone. 'By admitting that he had lied to the police when he was initially approached about the crash, he put himself in my power.'

'And are you planning to inform the police?'

'What good would that serve now?'

A shaken little laugh escaped Misty. 'So, really, it was *all* for nothing.'

'No. I got the truth and I don't regret helping the press to expose his corrupt practices in government. I only regret the harm I caused you,' Leone completed without hesitation.

She was disconcerted by the extent of her own relief at learning that her father had not left Leone's sister lying injured and alone. She could well imagine the older man's panic and fear of exposure in the aftermath of that accident and, although she could not condone his lies, she was pleased that he had had the courage and the decency to finally tell Leone what had really happened that night.

It was a surprise when Leone took her to the apartment where she had lived so briefly. As she walked into the hall he murmured in evident explanation, 'You left clothes here.'

He meant the wardrobe that he had bought her, not one item of which had she taken home with her. 'Yes…'

Misty sat down on a sofa, stiff with unease and a sense of being under imminent attack. Left to herself, she reflected, she might never have told him about the baby, reasoning that at least that way she retained her dignity and her pride.

Leone studied her from beneath black spiky lashes, stunning eyes intent. 'I want us to get married.'

'S-sorry?' Misty stammered, her silvery eyes widening in shock and her lips parted.

'No, don't start arguing with me. Hear me out first,' Leone said levelly. 'This is my baby too. I'd like my child to have my name and the same love and security that my father gave me.'

Unable to stay still, Misty stood up on legs that felt wobbly and stared at him, reading the gravity in his lean, darkly handsome features. Initially she was so shaken by that proposal that she could think of nothing to say. It was the very last response that she had expected from him.

'Sicilians have a very strong sense of family,' Leone asserted, his strong jawline clenching. 'You know that to your cost already, but there is a brighter side to the equation.'

'Is there?' Walking over to the tall windows with barely a sense of where she was going or what she was doing, never mind what she was saying, Misty could not drag her eyes from him.

'Do you want to be a single parent like your own mother?'

Instantly, Misty bristled. 'Don't bring my background into this. I could manage on my own—'

'But you don't have to manage alone. Don't punish our child for *my* sins,' Leone cut in with hard emphasis.

That warning shook Misty. Had she been trying to punish him? She had assumed that he would have little interest in a baby that had been conceived without his wish or agreement, for that had been true of her own father and equally true for many of the other foster children with whom she had grown up. She had also believed that only mothers had feelings and loyalties towards an unborn child and he had just proven her wrong.

'I wasn't expecting this,' she confessed unevenly, her hands closing together and then parting again. 'I mean…do you honestly think you could stick with a marriage over the head of a baby you didn't plan for?'

Flags of pink ran up into Misty's cheeks as she realised how revealing her own question had been. She had just betrayed the fact that she was considering his offer and computing the chances of him staying the distance as a husband.

'I want you back in my bed too, *amore*.' Leone held her startled upward glance with a frank and earthy intensity that made her breath catch in her throat and shame-faced heat surge at the very heart of her body. 'Marriages have survived on a lot less.'

She could have drummed up a dozen sensible reasons for marrying Leone. She knew exactly how difficult it was to be a single parent with nobody else to fall back on for support. Furthermore, if she married Leone, she would not have to worry about making ends meet or educating her child in the future. And last and not least their baby would benefit in many ways from having a father who cared.

But Misty was ashamed to acknowledge that not one of those worthy arguments would have made much impression on her had she not been in love with Leone. That was the crux of the matter. By stressing the needs of their child, he had given her a face-saving excuse to bring him back into her life and, much as she despised her own weakness, she knew that she was about to snatch at that excuse.

'OK…' Misty could not bring herself to look at Leone as she voiced that casual agreement lest he recognise the sudden intense spasm of relief assailing her at the realisation that she would be able to stop fighting herself every hour of every day. For that was what getting by without Leone had meant: a constant inner battle against her own weak-willed impulses and needs.

The silence lay heavy and she was tempted into glancing across the room. Leone was surveying her with narrowed dark eyes as though she had surprised him.

'I'm thinking of what's best for the baby,' Misty heard herself say as if she were a sacrificial lamb.

'Why not?' Leone countered, smooth as silk. 'If it wasn't for the baby, we wouldn't be having this conversation.'

Her fingers curled into momentary talons and then bit into her palms. She would have liked to unleash a stinging retaliation but he had voiced a humiliating and unarguable truth.

'We'll apply for a licence, so that we can have the wedding as soon as possible,' Leone continued.

Misty nodded, the delicate lines of her face icily composed.

'Would you like another pineapple juice to celebrate?'

'No, thanks. I'd like to go to bed now, if that's all right with you.' Pride prevented Misty from making any move towards him because she was determined not to reveal how strong her own feelings were for him. Yet she knew that her own assurance that she was marrying him solely for the baby's benefit had been ungenerous and cold. But she still very much wanted the coolness that had opened up between them to be bridged and took her time about leaving the room in the hope that he would say or do something to prevent her.

But Leone did nothing. As she glanced back over her shoulder she saw him by the window, strain etched in his hard male profile, savage tension emanating from the set of his powerful shoulders, and her throat thickened with tears.

He had shown neither censure nor resentment in a situation that would have tried most men. He had accepted responsibility for their child and he had asked her to marry him. But that did not mean that *he* was any happier than *she* was, for he knew and she knew that she was still blaming him for the manner in which he had used her to gain revenge on her father.

Yet he had acknowledged his mistake and tried not only to prevent her from coming into contact with her father that weekend at Castle Eyrie, but had also attempted to put a lid on the ensuing press revelations. That he had failed might be his own fault too for ever embarking on such a ruthless scheme, but was she planning to hold that against him for ever?

She lay in bed examining her own flaws: she was not

very good at forgiving those who hurt her. She had been hurt too often as a child and she had learned then to withdraw into a harder shell and to fight back to protect herself. She knew that Leone felt guilty and that guilt was destructive. Did she really want their marriage to suffer from that added burden?

She loved him so much it terrified her and maybe refusing to forgive him was easier than dealing with the reality that he did *not* love her, she acknowledged painfully. But had she been a little braver and a lot less proud, she would not be lying alone and miserable in bed aching for him with every fibre of her being...

In sudden rebellion, Misty slid out of bed, padded down the corridor and walked into Leone's bedroom before she could lose her nerve. Just as she entered he emerged from the bathroom stark naked and towelling his hair dry, six feet four inches of lithe, powerful masculinity. His stunning golden eyes locked to her and he let the towel fall as he strode forward.

A feverish flush colouring her face, she read the smouldering invitation in his raking scrutiny. Her heart pounded as he reached for her, tugging her up against his hard, muscular length and murmuring with roughened satisfaction, '*Dio mio, amore*...you always have the power to surprise me.'

She had surprised herself almost as much, only now thought was being overwhelmed by her own response. Her breasts were full and straining below the fine satin nightgown, tender peaks taut with arousal, and a dulled throb pulsed low in her pelvis. Weak with anticipation, she shivered, shocked by her own hunger. He picked her up and laid her down on the bed and peeled her out of the nightdress.

Leone released his breath in a sexy sound of appreciation. 'I'm so hot for you, I hardly know where to begin...'

He bent his dark head to encircle a rosy peak with the tip of his tongue and a low sighing moan escaped her as reaction shot right to the fiery heart of her. She closed her hands over his wide, muscular shoulders, loving the smoothness of his skin there, the masculine heat and scent of him, spreading her restive fingers in sensual pleasure.

'Kiss me...' she urged, letting her hands close into his damp black hair.

That long, drugging collision of their mouths left her quivering and hotter than ever. His fingertips teased through the nest of downy curls crowning her femininity and she arched up her hips and parted her thighs, wild excitement charging her as he discovered the slick wet heat of her.

'You drive me crazy with desire, *amore*,' Leone growled, rising over her in one powerful movement and sinking slow and deep into her.

She sobbed out loud with the wild, fierce pleasure of his invasion. All the seething emotional turmoil of the past twenty-four hours was finding an outlet in passion. She moved against him, all writhing heat and abandonment, letting the great swell of excitement snatch her up and control her until it flung her higher than she had ever reached before in a white hot blinding surge of fulfilment.

In the aftermath, she still felt as though she were floating and as Leone shifted back from her she leant over him, silver-grey eyes bright with emotion, and whispered, 'I died and went to heaven the day I found you.'

A wolfish grin of appreciation slashed his wide, sensual mouth. 'Are you sure you're feeling all right? You don't sound at all like yourself.'

'Enjoy it while it lasts,' she advised, happiness flooding through her as he curved her close and pressed a slow, sweet kiss to her reddened mouth.

'I didn't realise I'd found heaven until I stumbled into hell,' Leone traded feelingly.

She caught sight of her watch and tensed with guilt as she recalled the way in which she had left that club a couple of hours earlier. 'Flash is going to be *very* annoyed with me—'

His big, powerful frame tensed beneath hers. 'You don't need him. You have me—'

Misty laughed. 'I plan to hang onto both of you.'

'No.' Hauling himself up against the pillows, a virile vision of bronzed skin and rippling muscles, Leone studied her with hard dark eyes. 'I want him out of your life.'

'Well, what you want isn't always what you get,' Misty informed him gently.

'You ran to him when Redding dumped you three years ago…and you ran to him this time too—'

'You didn't dump me…I dumped *you*!' Misty heard herself launch at him full volume, temper roused by that unnecessary reference to her former fiancé.

'I'll treat that comment with the contempt it deserves.' Stunningly handsome dark features taut with anger, Leone threw back the sheets and sprang out of bed. 'I've seen how you behave with Flash.'

Taking that as an incendiary reference to her most embarrassing moment, Misty went rigid. 'I doubt very much that I'll be tempted to get up on a stage at our wedding and dance!'

'*Santo Cielo*! I'm talking about what I saw only *two* hours ago! He had his arms round you—'

'Flash is a very touchy-feely person and so am I—

'Not with me,' Leone slotted in between gritted white teeth.

Misty thought about that and it was quite true, but then she was in love with Leone and always on her guard around him. It was a case of…when he got affectionate with her outside the bedroom door, she would get affectionate with him. 'I don't think that's relevant. I'm very fond of Flash but we *are* only friends—'

'He has a lousy reputation with women—'

'He's only twenty-four…and, really, where *you* get the nerve to criticise *him* for that, I honestly don't know!' Misty exclaimed.

'If you're going to be my wife, you need to learn to listen to my point of view.'

That measured intonation sent a chill running through Misty and she paled. She dropped her eyes, wondering how they could be at daggers drawn when only minutes ago they had been in each other's arms. It was ironic that the crises in her own life had allowed her and Flash to rediscover their friendship over the past twenty-four hours. But possibly she was being unreasonable to expect Leone to forgive and forget the reality that he and Flash had been exchanging punches the day before.

'You'll be so busy planning our wedding that you won't have time to worry about anything else,' Leone informed her in bracing addition.

As she listened to the shower running. Misty slid back into her nightdress. Did Leone think she was a silly little girl he could distract with platitudes? She had no intention of severing her ties with Flash. Very tempted to ask Leone if his definition of a wife dated back to the old dark days of female servitude, she decided it would be wiser to return to her own bedroom.

Indeed, only when she got back into her bed did comprehension sink in on her. Leone was jealous. Why hadn't she recognised that? He was jealous of her close friendship with Flash. Recalling the manner in which he had reacted to Philip right at the start of their relationship, she started to smile. Leone was complex but very straightforward in some ways. He wasn't at all sure of her either. The more she thought about that, the more she loved him, for she had finally found a chink in his rock-solid self-assurance.

CHAPTER TEN

A WEEK later, Misty was dreamily removing her wedding gown from its packaging when Birdie called up the stairs to her.

'You have a visitor, Misty!'

In less than twenty-four hours she would be Leone's wife, and she was viewing their impending marriage along the lines of a campaign in which she would make herself so irresistible that Leone would fall for her like a ton of bricks. By the time she had finished with him, he really wasn't going to know what had hit him. She could plot and plan too, couldn't she?

The wedding arrangements had been made at the speed of light. No sooner had she phoned Birdie in Oxford to inform her of what was afoot than Birdie had persuaded her widowed sister to return to Fossetts with her and help to organise things. It was wonderful to see her foster mother regaining her old strength and energy, but a challenge to prevent the older woman from taking on too much too soon, she reflected ruefully.

Birdie smiled at Misty as she came down into the hall, but her bright blue eyes had an anxious light. 'It's your father…he's waiting in the sitting room.'

Both dismay and surprise assailed Misty. 'Oliver Sargent…he's come here?'

'It's to his credit that he has come to see you,' the older woman pointed out gently. 'Try to be equally generous.'

Torn between curiosity and discomfiture, Misty was as stiff as a plank of wood when she entered the room. The older man had lost weight since their last meeting and the lines of strain on his features aged him. He bore little resemblance to the opinionated and self-important man she recalled from that weekend in Scotland and simply looked tired and ill-at-ease.

'But for Leone, I wouldn't have come,' Oliver Sargent confessed.

Her eyes widened in sharp disconcertion. 'Leone?'

'He encouraged me to visit. I wasn't sure that you'd be willing to see me.'

'Please sit down.' Belatedly, Misty recalled her manners.

In the strained silence, he took a seat and continued, 'I imagine that you would first like me to tell you about my relationship with your mother.'

'Yes.' Misty was relieved that he had taken the lead on that subject.

'When we met, Carrie was only twenty-one but already married and a parent,' Oliver said with a sigh. 'Once she started classes at the university she was mixing with her own age group and she soon regretted tying herself down to an older man.'

'Were you *ever* in love with her?' Misty asked tightly.

'I was fond of her, but even then I was engaged to Jenny. However, Jenny was at home several hundred miles away,' he told her with a speaking grimace. 'I won't lie…I saw my affair with Carrie as being a safe outlet for both of us. I didn't appreciate that nothing is ever that simple until it was too late.'

'And when was that?'

'Our relationship ended when your mother admitted that she was pregnant. She believed that she had conceived by her husband,' the older man said wryly. 'It was only when *he* discovered through a blood test after you and your twin had been born that you were not his kids that the truth came out.'

'That news must have come as quite a shock to you too,' Misty said rather drily.

'Yes, particularly as Carrie then fled the marital home and arrived on my doorstep with her suitcases. Even though our relationship had been over for months, she expected us to take up where we had left off. It was a ghastly mess for everyone concerned. I didn't love her. I felt trapped. I was twenty-two and I wasn't ready to be a father either. I refused to go to the hospital with her to see you. My biggest fear at the time was that my parents or Jenny might find out what I'd been up to,' Oliver admitted with grim regret. 'When your mother realised how I felt, she moved out. I gave her a considerable amount of money and I never saw or heard from her again.'

'So you didn't see either me or my sister as babies.' That and the knowledge that he had at least offered her mother financial help somewhat eased Misty's desire to sit in harsh judgement over him. She could understand how he must have felt. He might have been slick enough to embark on what he had seen as a convenient affair with a married woman, but he had been far too young to handle the fall-out from a destroyed marriage, a woman as needy as her mother had been and instant fatherhood.

'Your sister…I believe she was adopted?' He gave her an awkward look of enquiry.

Misty confessed that she had no idea where her twin was and he subsided again. Nancy bustling in with a tray of tea created a welcome diversion.

'I *do* appreciate your coming here,' Misty said when they were alone again. 'I also like the fact that you've been honest.'

'This past week telling the truth has become a new habit of mine…' The older man wore a weary air of self-mocking acceptance. 'I've been trying to sort out the mess I've made of my life and Jenny's, but right now she's not willing to listen and I can't blame her. Before this, she was always there for me...'

'And now she's not?' Misty recalled the press revelations concerning his secret country love-nest. She had been relieved for Leone's sake that her father's brief affair with Battista had not become public knowledge, but she was not surprised that his marriage was in serious trouble.

'No...but I hope that that will change.' The haunted look in his eyes stirred genuine compassion in Misty, for he had already lost so much. In the space of weeks, he had gone from being a powerful man, fêted and flattered wherever he went, to being the target of distaste, condemnation and cruel amusement. But she sensed that the loss of Jenny might break him as nothing else might have done.

'When all the fuss has died down, I'd like to get to know you...if you're willing,' her father said levelly. 'But if you think it's a little late in the day for us to become acquainted, I'll understand.'

It was over an hour before he departed, for once the more sensitive points had been broached and dealt with Misty felt free to ask him other questions. He admitted that he had felt appallingly guilty for years afterwards at having taken the easy way out rather than offering her mother the ongoing emotional support that she had needed. He was leaving when Misty took a deep breath and asked him if he would like to come to her wedding.

He froze in surprise. 'Are you willing to have me there? I would like to see the ceremony. I'd keep a very low profile,' he promised with an eagerness that surprised and touched her.

Her first proper meeting with her father left Misty with a great deal to think about, but she was kept busy by the numerous last-minute checks that she felt that she had to make on the wedding arrangements. Early evening, she watched the florist and her assistants decorate the church on the outskirts of town and she could not initially understand why her spirits were so low. She loved Leone, didn't she? Loved him like crazy, so why was she suddenly suffering from a feeling of immense guilt?

Her hands shook as she attempted to position a tall, graceful lily with the same precision as the other women. All right, Leone didn't love her, but he wanted to do the best he could for their child and he did find her very attractive. But was that enough…was that really fair to either him *or* her? The horrid parallels between her own situation and the sad little story her father had told her earlier in the day were working on her conscience and her pride. Wasn't she now doing what her own mother had done?

Carrie had run to Oliver Sargent hoping that he would be willing to take responsibility for her and her twin babies. He had not been willing because he had not cared enough for her mother. Did she despise the older man for that honest confession? Or did she concede that he had probably made the right decision in opting not to offer marriage to a woman with whom he had only had a casual affair? Yet, even knowing that Leone was not in love with her, *she* was planning to allow *him* to go ahead and make her his wife…

That was wrong, absolutely wrong, Misty concluded, perspiration dampening her skin as she reached that agonising decision. Leaving the church, she got back into Birdie's car to drive home, her imagination focused on a frightening and wounding image of what such a marriage might be like a couple of years down the road. What would they have to share but the baby? He would get bored. He would live to regret sacrificing his freedom for a principle. He might even come to *hate* her…

She could not bear that idea. She needed to be strong. She *had* to talk to him before they both made the biggest mistake of their lives. He had been abroad on business since the day after she had agreed to marry him. His absence had made it so much easier for her to refuse to face what she was doing to him. But Leone was staying the night at the Belstone House Hotel and she would go over there to see him once he had checked in.

However, she turned into the driveway at Fossetts and was taken aback to see both Leone's and Flash's sports cars parked at opposing ends of the gravel fronting the old house. Flash strode out to greet her with an accusing look. 'Why didn't you warn Leone that I was going to give you away at the altar tomorrow?'

'I wanted to surprise him.' Pale as death, Misty muttered, 'But I may have dragged you up here on a wild-goose chase because I think I'm going to call off the wedding—'

'You've got cold feet…that's all,' Flash told her, unimpressed. 'You're nuts about him—'

'Tell me something honestly…' Misty studied her foster brother. 'If you had a one-night stand and got the woman pregnant, would you want to marry her?'

'Hell, no!' Flash exclaimed with a revealing shudder.

'Then *why* should Leone?'

Flash looked aghast at the connection she had made. But with a tight, hurting look of acceptance on her face, Misty went indoors, struggling to muster the courage to do what she felt was right even while her foolish heart was hammering just at the prospect of seeing Leone a few hours earlier than she had expected.

She could hear Nancy and Birdie chattering in the kitchen. Leone was in the sitting room. As she entered he sprang upright, his breathtaking smile flashing across his lean, bronzed features, his usual aspect of forbidding cool entirely put to flight. Connecting with his clear dark golden eyes, she felt her knees turn to jelly and her mouth run dry. Striving to regain control of herself, she went rigid when he closed his arms round her.

'*Dio mio*…I thought this week would *never* end,' Leone groaned feelingly. 'I couldn't stay away from you one minute longer. If you hadn't come back, I was going to drive over to the church.'

'Look…er…could we go out into the garden?' Misty asked jerkily. 'I don't want us to be interrupted—'

'Neither do I, *amore*.' Leone strolled over to the French windows to unlock them.

Misty stared at him; hungry eyes roaming over his chiselled profile, the sleek, elegant flow of his lean, powerful body as he moved. Then she shut her eyes tight in anger at her own weakness, hating the idea that she might not be strong enough to give up her hold on the man that she loved even though it seemed to her that that was the only sensible and fair thing to do.

'I want to call off the wedding…' Misty stated with driven abruptness, her voice sounding thin and harsh.

In the act of reaching out to unlock the door, Leone glanced back at her with a stunned light in his eyes. 'What did you say?'

'I'm sorry…but I don't think I should marry you,' Misty told him tightly. 'It wouldn't be right for either of us.'

CHAPTER ELEVEN

THE ghastly silence dragged.

Leone had turned very pale, his bone structure set taut beneath his olive skin. He stared at her in visible disbelief, a frown lodged between his brows as if he was having difficulty in understanding what she had just said.

'Let's go outside before someone comes in,' Misty urged, cringing at the risk of Birdie joining them with some chirpy reference to the wedding while she herself was already questioning the plunge she had taken. Having spoken those words, there could be no going back, no thinking better of what she had believed she ought to do, she registered fearfully.

'*Sì…*' In agreement, Leone sent a blind seeking hand travelling over the multi-paned French door in apparent search for the key he had been about to turn a minute earlier.

'I know this must've come as a bit of a shock to you—'

'A bit of a shock?' Leone repeated, his Sicilian accent very thick, lean brown fingers still wandering over the door but nowhere near the keyhole. 'You jilting me?'

'I'm *not* jilting you!' Misty gasped with tears of pain stinging her eyes and her throat closing over. 'I'm *trying* to do what's right and fair—'

'*Accidenti*…don't feed me bull like that!' Leone fielded hoarsely. 'I'm not a little kid.'

'You're only marrying me because I'm pregnant and you're going to end up hating me for it,' Misty condemned chokily.

Leone did not seem to be listening to her. He continued

to stare at her in as much apparent shock as if she had pulled a knife on him. There was no gold in the fixed gaze of his stunning eyes, only darkness. 'It's Flash…isn't it?' His rich dark drawl had a slight tremor. 'At the eleventh hour you've realised that you've always loved him—'

Misty was in a state of bewilderment, for Leone was reacting with a much greater degree of shock than she could ever have expected from so self-assured a male. 'Flash has got nothing to do with this—'

'You can get over him,' Leone informed her grittily, his strong jawline clenching. 'No guy in love with you would agree to give you away when you married another man.'

As someone rattled the doorknob from the hall, Misty fled over to the French windows to unlock them. Throwing them wide, she hurried out into the fresh air and struggled to make sense of what Leone was saying to her. Negotiating a path round the ride-on mower sitting parked, she spun round to face him again.

His whole attention was nailed to her with relentless force. 'I'm willing to wait until you come to terms with that. I see no reason why we should cancel the wedding…'

'Leone…I'm not and I've never been in love with Flash,' Misty stated in frustration. 'Yes, he fancied me for a while a few years back and it strained our friendship, but he's got over that now…it was just a phase. He's like my brother.'

Leone stared at her in silence, hard cheekbones prominent, fierce dark eyes glued to her pale, anxious face. 'Then why?' he almost whispered, but every word was underscored by raw-edged emotion. '*Why* have you changed your mind about marrying me?'

'Do you honestly believe that a shotgun marriage is likely to make you happy?' Misty demanded painfully. 'It was my fault that I even *got* pregnant and I know you haven't said a word about that, but you're only human.

Sooner or later, you're going to be thinking that and resenting me for it—'

'No,' Leone slotted in fiercely. 'You're talking nonsense and this is *not* a shotgun marriage—'

'How can you say that?'

'Because...' Leone snatched in a ragged breath, dark colour scoring his high cheekbones as he focused on her with strained eyes of appeal. 'Because I would have asked you to marry me anyway. Because I was bloody *grateful* when I realised you were carrying my baby as it gave me a second chance I wouldn't have got from you any other way. Because I screwed up every way there was but I do love you!'

Paralysed by that emotional speech, which carried not a shade of his usual formidable cool, Misty stared back at him in total shock, her heart thumping so fast and hard she felt faint. 'You...you *love* me?'

'I came here to tell you that tonight. I didn't want to say it on the phone last week because that's not romantic...and I would've said it the night I proposed if I hadn't felt so threatened by seeing you wrapped round Flash. The trouble *is*...' Leone paused in that halting flood of charged explanation to say with a defensive air of masculine discomfiture '...I haven't done this before and, even though I knew saying it might help, I just couldn't bring myself to say it...'

'That you loved me?' Misty prompted helpfully.

'You might have laughed and said you didn't believe me after the way I'd treated you...and I just couldn't work out how to say it convincingly.' At that point, Leone made a sudden movement towards her and fell over the ride-on mower.

And that was the instant when Misty knew beyond a doubt that Leone really really meant every word he had just said, for if he could fail to notice a three foot tall mower in his path, he was a definite lost cause to love. As he picked himself up with a profound aspect of incredulity at the size of the object he had tripped over, a hysterical giggle almost made it out of her throat. But she hastily sealed her lip for she had never loved him more than she loved him at that moment for being clumsy and uncool but very, very human. Even thinking of him having feared a derisive response to his declaration of love squeezed her heartstrings tight. Any desire to giggle had vanished and she was just on fire with love and sympathy for him.

'I'm convinced,' Misty mumbled shakily.

'I really thought I was *never* going to get you back... The baby was a miracle to me too and for you to say that it was your fault that that life-saving development took place...' Leone loosed a shaken laugh at that concept, dark golden eyes pinned to her with disbelief. 'Do you know why I couldn't protect you that weekend?'

Misty shook her head, joy beginning to unfurl inside her and take wings.

'I'm the bright spark who deliberately chose to leave the condoms behind in London because I believed that that would prevent me from dragging you into the nearest bed,' Leone admitted with a rueful light of self-mockery in his beautiful eyes that released crazy butterflies in her tummy. 'I took the risk. I took the risk knowing what I was doing because I couldn't resist you and I no more regret that risk than I could *ever* regret the consequences.'

'I believe you...' Misty felt pure *femme fatale* at that moment and her slim shoulders went back with pride. There he was, all gorgeous and sophisticated, but she had been too much temptation for him: he had been scared enough to try and control his own libido by doing something utterly crazy. She had been afraid that he might have slept with her that weekend just because she'd been available. The discovery that he had been as caught up and controlled by the overwhelming attraction between them as she had been freed her for ever from that fear.

'I swear that if you marry me tomorrow, you'll never live to regret it, *amore*.' His anxious gaze rested on her and then his eyes veiled, a tiny muscle tugging at the corner of his strained mouth. 'You don't need to share a bed with me if you don't want to…OK?'

'OK…' Misty was falling victim to fascination, her nicer side telling her she ought to confess that she loved him too, but her darker side keen not to miss out on discovering what lengths Leone might go to in his determination to persuade her to marry him.

Her Sicilian bridegroom received that agreement without perceptible surprise or objection. 'I know that it's likely to be a long time before you feel that you can trust me again—'

'We made love last week,' Misty reminded him.

'But that was like a comfort thing for you, wasn't it?' Leone muttered darkly. 'You had had a very stressful day and you didn't really know what you wanted from me that night—'

'Is that what you thought?' Misty was wounded on his behalf.

'I was just thankful you came to me…' Leone shot her a wry look. 'I'll take whatever you're willing to give on any terms. Haven't you worked that out yet?'

Misty was stunned by that assurance. She closed the distance between them and wrapped her arms tight round him, melting into the lean, hard strength of him and drinking in his achingly familiar scent with a deep sense of coming home where she belonged. 'The terms will be very easy,' she swore shakily into his shoulder. 'We're definitely getting married tomorrow. There's no way you're getting your freedom now.'

'I don't want it, *amore mio*,' Leone breathed thickly, a

slight tremor shaking through his big powerful frame. 'I felt like the roof had fallen in on me when you said the wedding was off. I couldn't handle it…I just didn't know what to say, what to do—'

'I'm so sorry I said it now,' she confided guiltily. 'It was just listening to Oliver talk today about how it had been with him and my mother. He didn't love her and, when I thought about it, I felt he was right not to let himself feel forced into continuing the relationship out of guilt because what did they have in common? All they had was physical attraction—'

Leone claimed a fierce, devouring kiss and then just held her tight before walking her in her still shell-shocked emotional state round the corner of the house to his car and unlocking the passenger door for her. 'We've got a hell of a lot more going for us than that, *bella mia*.'

'Like what?' she said ungrammatically when he swung in beside her.

Leone fired the engine into a throaty purr and turned to look at her with candid golden eyes. 'I can't live without you in my life.'

'Oh…' Misty surrendered to feeling happy. 'Where are we going?'

'I don't know but right now I feel like I might be scared enough to sit on your doorstep all night in case you change your mind about the wedding again,' Leone admitted half under his breath.

'I won't…I promise!' she exclaimed.

He parked in a layby down the road and threw back his proud dark head to study her with intent interest. When she thought about it she realised that he always looked at her that way and when she smiled, he smiled as if he couldn't help himself. All along his love had been there for her to see if only she had had the faith and the confidence to recognise it.

'I think I fell in love with you long before you ever signed that crazy contract. I was obsessed by you,' Leone confided with a rueful laugh. 'I was up at Brewsters every other week when I had no reason to visit, watching you every second you were in the same room—'

'So that *wasn't* my imagination.'

'And all the time I was thinking you were greedy and calculating and sort of hating and lusting after you simultaneously,' Leone groaned, shooting her dismayed face a glance of guilty regret. 'I wanted to believe bad stuff about you then. It put a barrier between us and I needed that barrier, but once I began spending time with you all that went pear-shaped on me overnight.'

'Did it?'

'Right from the start there was this weird sense of connecting…and then that first kiss…no kiss was ever that explosive for me! I couldn't keep my hands off you after that—'

'I would probably have died of disappointment if you had.' Misty was hanging onto his every word, silvery grey eyes clinging to his darkly handsome features as though her life did indeed depend on him. 'That wild attraction was very mutual but I hated you too at the beginning.'

Leone tensed and paled. 'I was a total bastard, so I can't blame you for that,' he acknowledged hoarsely. 'But I tried so *hard* to stop what I had begun with the press to protect you, and when I failed I knew what hell felt like. There you were suffering and I'd brought it on you and wrecked what I might have had with you.'

She reached for his coiled fingers. 'I was very hurt but you were wonderful—'

'Some kind of wonderful,' Leone breathed with harsh self-derision. 'I was panicking. I knew I would lose you the instant I told you the truth—'

'Is that why you asked me to move in with you?'

'I thought a marriage proposal after one weekend would make you lift the phone to call a psychiatrist for me. *Dio mio*…didn't you feel my desperation?'

'No, there was no mower for you to trip over and I was in deep shock,' Misty pointed out. 'But if you'd dragged out the L word then…the love bit, I think I'd have stopped a little longer to listen.'

He linked his fingers with hers, beautiful golden eyes tender and warm and lodged with flattering intensity on her. 'You said you were scared of me and that really tore me up. I knew I had asked for that, but it would have seemed like a *very* bad joke if I'd tried to persuade you then that I loved you after what I'd done to you.'

'No, if the woman is *in* love she might consider a love plea in those circumstances a bad joke at first,' Misty told him with immense superiority. 'She would think things like, I bet he doesn't really mean it…but then later when she had calmed down she would think about it more and maybe start making excuses for him having behaved like a toerag. Within the space of a few days she would be feeling much more forgiving and understanding.'

A bewildered frownline had lodged between Leone's winged ebony brows. 'Is that a fact?'

Misty nodded, a helpless smile building on her lush pink mouth. 'So you missed your best chance not going for the L word that day—'

'Are you saying that you love me?' Leone muttered thickly.

'Oh, yes…loads and loads. I was only trying to call off our wedding earlier because I felt so guilty about marrying you when *you* didn't love *me*.'

'You love me…and you still dumped me?' Leone seemed to be in shock again. 'And you call *me* ruthless?'

Misty waited for him to come to terms with her revelation.

Suddenly he was trying to haul her into his arms but there really wasn't room in the low-slung sports car for that kind of caper, so he tugged her out of the car, braced her up against the passenger door with feverish impatience and kissed her until she drowned in his hungry passion.

'I love you so much. I don't deserve that you love me too...' he muttered raggedly.

As a car horn cheekily sounded from a passing vehicle, Leone jerked back from her with a groan and settled her back into the car again. From his pocket he withdrew a tiny box embellished with a famous jewellers' logo. 'I also came over tonight to give you this.'

Holding her breath, Misty opened the box on a breath-taking diamond and sapphire ring. He took her hand and slid the beautiful engagement ring onto her finger. She watched the jewels catch fire in the sunlight and gave him a huge appreciative smile. 'It's gorgeous.'

'And then there's this...your wedding present.' Leone set a very large and very old ornate iron key on her lap.

Dreamy eyes still shining from the gift of the ring, Misty gazed down at the key in bewilderment. She knew some people collected old keys and, as old keys went, she supposed it was a top-notch find and she tried to sound appropriately impressed. 'It looks so old...it's just... er...fascinating—'

'Castle Eyrie is yours,' Leone murmured silkily.

Misty dredged her attention from the key and focused on him, wide-eyed. 'You *bought* the castle?'

'Why not?'

'You *hated* it!' Misty gasped helplessly. 'You said it was falling apart and it would be a money pit for the fool that bought it—'

'I can afford a money pit, and by the time the restoration is complete it will be a prime piece of real estate.' Perceptible dark colour underscoring his fabulous cheekbones, Leone screened his gorgeous eyes. 'You fell in love with Castle Eyrie and I feel it has some special memories for us,' he confided half under his breath. 'I bought most of the contents as well and persuaded Murdo to stay on in a supervisory capacity—'

Misty launched herself at him and locked her arms round his neck as best she could in the confines of the car. Eyes bright with love and tenderness and glowing appreciation, she told him he was the most romantic man she had ever met and he groaned out loud, but she could see he was pleased that she was so delighted.

'Just don't expect me to take up fishing,' he warned her with a shudder.

He really had to take her home again then. It was the evening before their wedding and she was planning on an early night. When Leone walked back into Fossetts and greeted Flash with an easy smile and not the slightest hint of unease, the very last of her concerns vanished.

At eleven the following morning, Misty walked down the aisle on Flash's arm and a collective gasp of appreciation filled the church as she came into view with her bridesmaids, Clarice and an old schoolfriend, following in her wake. Her copper hair fell in a shining curtain of silk to her bare shoulders while her green brocade sleeveless top hugged her slender curves and the full ivory silk skirt flattered her still narrow waist and swept to the floor like a ballgown. The same wonderful diamonds she had worn to the movie première glittered at her throat and her ears, for Leone had brought them down from London for her.

Misty had eyes for no one but Leone, who was watching her approach the altar with a satisfyingly transfixed expression on his lean, strong face. He was drop-dead gorgeous in his well-cut dark suit, but it was the look of love in his level dark golden gaze that made her heart race the fastest. After the simple ceremony, having signed the register, they walked together back down the aisle and she took time out from her own bubbling happiness to smile at her father, who was seated in a rear pew.

'I never thanked you for encouraging Oliver to visit me,' she whispered to Leone on the steps while the photos were being taken.

His arm tightened round her. 'He didn't need much encouragement, *bella mia*.'

Flash grabbed her hand before she could climb into the limousine and hissed, 'Who's the bridesmaid with the black hair?'

Misty gave him an amused glance and followed his gaze to where her friend and former employee, Clarice, stood flirting like mad with Leone's best man, a handsome Italian businessman, who seemed equally taken with the bubbly brunette. 'Her name's Clarice. She likes country music...and guys over thirty.'

'You're kidding?'

Misty grinned. 'Sorry, I'm not.'

Leone reached for her hand in the limo and gave her a slashing, self-mocking smile that turned her susceptible heart inside out. 'Until last night, I was so jealous of Flash I wanted to kill him every time I saw him!'

'I know...and I'm glad you don't feel like that any more. Like Birdie, he's family.'

'You look ravishing, *amore*.' He feasted his attention on her and his brilliant eyes smouldered gold before his black lashes dropped low to conceal them, a hint of tension tautening his strong bone structure. 'I should mention that you're going to have a special surprise today.'

'What kind of surprise?'

'I'm not at liberty to tell you, but I had very little to do with arranging it.'

'You sound like a bloke baling out in advance of a

crash.' Misty studied him anxiously. 'What are you keeping from me?'

'Nothing you need to worry about,' Leone swore in vehement retreat. 'I just want this to be the very happiest day of your life.'

And he thought that the surprise might not be a happy one?

'Is it something to do with my twin?' she asked right out of the blue.

He tensed. 'No.'

'You've invited all your ex-girlfriends to the reception?'

'Do I look like a man with a death wish?'

Reassured, Misty nestled under his arm. 'By the way, when did you break up with that blonde television actress?'

'The night I called her, "Misty,"' Leone admitted grudgingly.

Misty was tickled pink by that admission. 'And when was that?'

'Is this an interrogation?'

'Yeah…and if you don't tell me, Leone…how is this going to be the happiest day of my life?' Misty teased in a die-away voice of reproach.

'It was a few weeks before the contract I made you sign.'

Wreathed in smiles at that ego-boosting confession, Misty pondered what the surprise in store for her might encompass. Far more people were attending the reception than had been at the church, which had not had the capacity for large numbers. By the time she had shaken hands with what felt like five hundred people, most of whom were strangers, she had quite forgotten the matter. Midway through their meal, she glanced across the room and saw a young blonde woman staring at her and she had one of those faces that seemed to strike a chord of familiarity with Misty. But as their eyes met the other woman looked away with an odd air of discomfiture.

'Who's that blonde sitting beside the hunky dark guy?'

'What *hunky* dark guy?' her bridegroom growled, rising easily to the bait.

Misty giggled. 'They're at that table just inside the door.'

Leone tensed. 'That's Freddy and Jaspar al-Husayn.'

'Friends?'

'Recent acquaintances.' Leone seemed to be picking his words with quite unnecessary care. 'He's the Crown Prince of Quamar—'

'They're like…*royalty*?' Misty gasped. 'I don't remember seeing them earlier—'

'They arrived late. She's English. We'll talk to them later—'

'Leave me out of it,' Misty told him with a slight grimace. 'I wouldn't know what to say to a princess!'

Leone shot her a startled look. 'Freddy struck me as being very friendly—'

'I'm sure.' Misty was unimpressed by that accolade, thinking that men were not the best judges of beautiful blondes. 'But I've never met anyone royal before and I'd be scared of putting my feet in it.'

As the afternoon advanced she drifted round the dance floor secure in Leone's arms and cocooned in a dreaming daze of contentment. When it was time for her to go and get changed to head for their honeymoon in Sicily, she went upstairs to the suite set aside for their use. Her bridesmaids, who had promised to follow her up, failed to show and she had just finished donning an elegant blue shift dress when someone knocked on the door.

She was taken aback to find herself facing, or rather looking down at, Freddy al-Husayn, who was not very tall.

'May I come in and talk to you?' the other woman asked with an uncertain air.

Perplexed, Misty stepped back.

'I'm the surprise that your husband wasn't too sure he wanted you to have,' Freddy explained in an apologetic rush. 'He said he didn't want you to be upset, and when he explained how my father once turned you away from my home and told you that I would want nothing to do with you, I was *so* ashamed and angry. But at the same time I was overjoyed that, four years ago, you wanted that contact and I'm hoping you'll feel the same way now.'

Silenced by that bewildering conversational opening, Misty simply stared, a frownline forming between her brows.

'We had the same mother…' Freddy said awkwardly. 'But I'm afraid I'm not your twin, I'm only a half-sister. Jaspar and Leone both thought I should wait until you came back from your honeymoon, but that's weeks away and I'm not good at being patient when I've been looking for you for so long!'

'You're my sister…' Stunned as she was by that real- isation, Misty immediately found herself staring just as Freddy had stared several hours earlier. 'Oh, what a *won- derful* surprise! What on earth was Leone thinking about when he asked you to wait until after our honeymoon?' she exclaimed.

From that point on, it was a challenge to see who could say the most the fastest before the other interrupted with some question or comment. Words and explanations flowed at the speed of light. Misty laughed at the reality that her big sister was smaller than she was, and listened with deep pleasure to the news that it was eighteen months since Freddy had begun searching for her.

'It's only forty-eight hours since we found out where you lived but Jaspar didn't think just before your wedding was a very good time to confront you with a sister you mightn't even *know* existed!' Freddy rattled on ruefully. 'So he approached Leone first in London and swore him to secrecy because I wanted to be the first to tell you *who* I was...I didn't want it coming from anyone else.'

No wonder Leone had been apprehensive, Misty reflected fondly as she recalled her own angry, defensive reaction to his offer to help her trace one of her sisters. It made her smile too to think of their husbands conspiring to protect both of them as far as possible from the risk of hurt or rejection.

'My sister's a princess...but you're so normal!' Laughing, but with tears of happiness in her eyes, Misty grasped Freddy's hand in hers and they hugged, each of them knowing in that intrinsically female fashion that they had found a friend as well as a sister.

They were getting on like a house on fire when Leone appeared with Jaspar only a step in his wake. Misty only had to see Jaspar smile in relief at his wife's happy face to lose all fear of his exalted status. Leone and Misty went downstairs to say goodbye to their guests, but Jaspar and Freddy accompanied them to the airport. Having been reunited for such a short time, the two sisters found it hard to part so soon afterwards.

It was evening when Leone and Misty arrived at his country villa in the lush fertile hills above the town of Enna. A grand arched entrance embellished by tall gates opened off the steep winding road, leading them through a grove of olive and citrus trees before the beautiful gardens came into the view. In the centre sat the Villa Fortuna, tall, shuttered windows cast open now that the heat of the day had passed, tawny, weathered walls gold in the light of the setting sun.

'It's idyllic,' Misty whispered, thrilled to be seeing the house where Leone had grown up.

An hour later a light refreshing breeze fluttered the curtains in the bedroom as he pulled her close and she trembled at the touch and the feel of him. 'It's been the best day of my life,' she muttered shakily.

'It can still get better, *bella mia*.' A very masculine smile of promise on his lean, darkly handsome features, he drew her down onto the bed, watched her hair stream across the pillow like rich copper silk, and he gazed down at her with unashamed possessive intensity. 'I used to picture you like this in this room...in my bed.'

Misty curved an equally possessive hand to his stubborn jawline and looked up into his stunning golden eyes. 'Just one little question...did you *really* settle Birdie's mortgage for purely altruistic reasons?'

He tensed and then flashed her a rueful smile of breathtaking charm. 'Maybe fifty-fifty. I couldn't bear to think of you struggling to keep up the payments. But if I'd admitted that it would have been the kiss of death to my hopes of winning you back. When I saw Flash waiting down in the car park for you...it was probably the very *worst* moment of my life—'

'Honestly?'

He splayed gentle fingers against her still-flat stomach and surveyed her with tender eyes of loving satisfaction. 'But finding out about our baby was the equivalent of being thrown a lifebelt when I was drowning. I adore you, Signora Andracchi—'

Misty leant up to him and claimed his wide, sensual mouth for herself and the sweet, drugging heat of her own flaring response took over. He tasted her with a ragged groan and stopped to tell her how happy he was, only to be dragged back down into her arms and told that there would be plenty of time to talk later...

* * *

Eleven months on, in the atmospheric nursery at Castle Eyrie, Misty checked on their son, Connor. He was fast asleep. He had soft black curls and big trusting blue eyes and, at three months old, he was fascinating his adoring parents more with every passing day. Indeed, Flash had warned them that they were at risk of getting a little boring on the subject of his godchild.

It had been an incredibly busy and eventful year for all of them. Jaspar and Freddy had come to stay with them several times during Misty's pregnancy and Leone and Misty had since spent a fabulous vacation in the desert kingdom of Quamar. It was fortunate that Leone and Jaspar got on so well because Misty and Freddy pretty much left the men to their own devices when they got together. In fact developing a close relationship with her newfound sister and getting to know her nephews, Ben and Kareem, had given Misty a great deal of pleasure.

Just one thing marred that pleasure for both women, and that was their complete failure to discover any further information about Misty's twin. As time went on, it seemed less and less likely to Misty that she would ever trace her younger sister.

The hospital records of Shannon's birth still existed but the agency record of her adoption was missing—a fact which Leone considered suspicious, as those records *had* been intact when Misty had first attempted to contact her sibling. He believed that someone had since chosen to remove those records. He even thought that that brief letter of wounding rejection that Misty had received four years earlier might not even have been written by her sister. It had taken Leone to look at that letter and point out that the average teenager would scarcely express herself in such a guarded and very formal manner.

Suppressing her regret that she had celebrated her twenty-third birthday without coming any closer to finding her twin, Misty kissed her son goodnight and left the nursery. There was nothing chilly about Castle Eyrie now, for underfloor heating had been installed. The linen cupboards rejoiced in serried ranks of top-quality bedlinen and the bathrooms were splendid affairs. Every piece of antique furniture gleamed with the evocative sheen and scent of beeswax and Murdo, who flatly refused to retire even though he was seventy-five, took a brandy nightcap to bed every evening.

Misty loved the castle and Leone had grown to love it too, for when they were in the Highlands they got to spend the maximum amount of time relaxing together. A month earlier, her father and Jenny had spent a weekend with them. Oliver had managed to mend his marriage, but had only recently come through the stressful humiliating enquiries that he had had to withstand over his conduct during his time as a politician. However, her father was now putting his skills as an organiser to good use by working for a mental health charity. Although it was very much a backroom kind of job and unpaid, he had been extremely grateful that someone was prepared to give him the chance to work again. He was a changed man, a much more likeable man and he was very taken with Connor. Birdie was another one of Connor's keen admirers and was a regular visitor when she could tear herself away from her beloved garden at Fossetts.

As Misty counted all the blessings of her life with a dreamy smile, she concentrated on the most important person in it next to Connor: Leone. She just adored him, but she kept him on his toes too. He spent far less time abroad on business than he had when they had first met, and for her birthday he had presented her with a beautiful diamond eternity ring engraved with her name and his.

She was wearing a sassy ice-blue nightdress and her copper hair was loose round her shoulders just the way

Leone liked her to wear it. Her face warmed at the wanton heat already bubbling through her at the thought of his passion. Leone was peeling off his shirt when she entered their bedroom. He was an arresting sight and her mouth ran dry.

'Connor was asleep, wasn't he?' Leone teased her huskily. 'I *told* you I'd already checked on him.'

'I just like to check for myself.' Misty was embarrassed to admit that sometimes she just liked to look into her baby son's cot and glory in the sheer wonder of his existence. But, having been reassured that she would have no trouble in conceiving a second time, she wanted to wait a couple of years before she had another child.

'Come here...' Leone urged with smouldering dark golden eyes.

Heartbeat quickening, Misty looked back at him with a deep feminine appreciation undimmed by eleven months of marriage. He had always been gorgeous but he was just *so* male and sexy as well. She still woke up beside him some mornings and marvelled that he was all hers. She glided into his arms like a homing pigeon.

He curved her slender body to his lean, muscular length with a roughened sound of satisfaction and held her close. 'We'll go back to Sicily for our anniversary trip next month, *amore mio*.'

'Bliss,' she sighed in delight, thinking that life with Leone just seemed to be one long series of magical treats and grateful that he wasn't the workaholic that she had once feared he might be.

'And as a special favour, you'll bake mouth-watering *nucatoli* and *pasta ciotti* for me,' Leone said silkily. 'Just the way you did that first day. I found that very sexy—'

'*Sexy?* Me baking cakes?' Misty gasped. 'When I write my best selling book on how to trap a Sicilian tycoon and keep him happy, I'll be sure to mention that the good old home-cooking angle really hits the weirdest spot with some guys!'

In mock fury, Leone tumbled her down onto the bed and she curled up in a giggling heap. 'Of course, there is the bedroom angle too!'

Her husband came down beside her and gazed down into her laughing face with vibrant amusement. 'You're a hussy, *bella mia*—'

'But you love me loads,' Misty whispered, arching up to meet the devouring heat of his sensual mouth with a sigh of pleasure.

They both heard the phone by the bed ring. They both ignored it. But it went on and on and on and eventually Leone pulled back from her with an anguished groan of frustration and swept up the receiver.

'No...no, of course it's not too late to call us,' Leone swore and then he stiffened, a look of surprise tightening is strong bone structure, causing his dark, expressive brows to rise above golden eyes that were now focused with keen concentration.

'What's wrong?' Misty hissed anxiously. 'Who is it?'

'Birdie...' Leone turned to look at her. 'She says that your twin sister has been at Fossetts asking for you...'

In shock, Misty stared at him, and then as the news sank in she was gripped by such a fierce surge of joy and excitement that she could neither think straight nor put her feelings into actual words...

THE HEIRESS BRIDE

by

Lynne Graham

CHAPTER ONE

'SOONER or later, you will surely choose to marry *some-one*,' Sander Christoulakis pointed out, his emphasis of that last word reluctant. 'Why not Ione Gakis?'

Alexio made no response. On one level, he could not believe that this peculiar conversation was actually taking place. Once he would have laughed in his father's face at the very idea of an arranged marriage. But, for almost two years, Alexio had been living in a hell of grief from which he only escaped when he buried himself in work. In a desperate attempt to obliterate the yawning emptiness inside him, he had flung himself into a series of wild affairs but no miracle recovery had followed. Indeed, if anything, those shallow sexual entanglements had left him with a sour taste in his mouth.

'It is an honour that Minos Gakis should have approached our family with the offer of his daughter,' Sander continued with quiet persistence, watching his volatile son with hopeful measuring eyes for his reaction. 'He has a very high regard for your business acumen and his health has been troubling him. He *needs* a son-in-law whom he can trust.'

Alexio was grimly amused by that clever speech, which suggested that a marriage arranged between families rather than by the young people concerned was as common an event as it had once been in Greece—for it was anything but. He was also marvelling at how the attention of one of the world's richest men appeared to have blinded his

5

astute father to less palatable truths. 'Minos Gakis is an evil bastard and a thug. You know it and I know it.'

'Nevertheless, his daughter, Ione, *is* a well brought-up and decent young woman,' Sander continued with determination, convinced that only such a marriage would have the power to remove his son from the partying, headline-grabbing lifestyle that was currently breaking his adoring mother's heart. 'I see no reason why—given time—you shouldn't find happiness with her.'

No reason? Bitterness hardened Alexio's lean, powerful face, his brilliant eyes darkening. He could no longer imagine being happy with any woman. But Crystal, the woman he had loved beyond any other, was undeniably *gone*. But then the issue of his late fiancée was not a subject his father would care to tackle, for the older man was no hypocrite.

Alexio's conservative Greek parents had hated Crystal and had refused to accept her as a bride for their only son. Her wild-child reputation and chequered past had offended their sensibilities. When he had put an engagement ring on her finger, his father had been outraged and his mother had wept, and for months afterwards Alexio had cut his parents out of his life. Only in the wake of Crystal's death had the divisions begun to heal and, even then, only because he had initially been in such a haze of despair that he had been incapable of rousing himself to the effort of rejecting his family.

Yet since then every business deal he had touched had turned to solid gold. He was now infinitely richer than his father had ever been for, while Sander had inherited his shipping fortune and merely conserved it, Alexio had gone into venture capital and software development, taking risks that his more cautious father would never have countenanced. It was ironic that only his own massive monetary gains in recent months could have put him in a position where the billionaire tycoon, Minos Gakis, would consider him as a potential son-in-law.

'I have never even met Gakis's daughter,' Alexio said drily.

'You *have*,' Sander contradicted immediately, his brows pleating. 'According to Minos, you met her when you spent the night on Lexos.'

In his turn, Alexio frowned, but even more darkly. A couple of months back, his yacht had run into difficulty in rough seas off the coast of the island of Lexos and he had radioed for permission to dock there, for Gakis was notorious for the brute henchmen he employed to guard his private island from unwelcome visitors. As it had transpired, Alexio had been made very welcome, indeed lavishly entertained by the reclusive tycoon, but it had been an evening almost surreal in its ghastliness.

Although he was well into his sixties, Minos had had a mini harem of beautiful bimbos staying in his palatial villa and Alexio had been invited to choose one of those women to complete his night's entertainment. He had been revolted by how very willing the fawning females involved had been to satisfy the older man's jaded tastes. Even so, Alexio had not made the dangerous mistake of discussing Minos's proclivities with anyone on his return home. Minos Gakis would make an implacable enemy and only a fool would risk awakening the ruthless older man's wrath to no good purpose by talking out of turn. And when it came to anything that might threaten his thriving business empire, Alexio Christoulakis was no fool...

Surely one of those bimbos could not have been Ione Gakis? Beneath his father's bewildered scrutiny, Alexio vented a humourless laugh at that unlikelihood for, though Gakis was far from being a likeable character, he was not unhinged. But, plunder his memory as Alexio did, he could not recall meeting any other woman that night. Apart from the housekeeper who had shown him to his suite while he'd still been seething with thwarted fury over her employer's offensive amusement at his guest's refusal to sleep with a whore.

'Let me refresh your memory,' Sander Christoulakis breathed in some discomfiture, evidently having hoped that his son would recall the young woman without the prompting of the photograph he now set down on the table.

Alexio focused on the photo with incredulity and instant recognition. He muttered a sudden curse and reached for it. Having been taken in profile, it was not a very good shot, but he remembered that submissive bent head, that pale hair pulled back in a severe style and those fragile facial features.

'I thought she was the housekeeper!' Alexio confessed with a sound of frank disbelief. 'She behaved like one, *not* like the daughter of the house! Gakis snapped his fingers and she appeared and he spoke to her as if she was a servant. That timid little thing was Ione Gakis?'

'Minos did say that she's quiet and shy.'

'Colourless and mousey,' Alexio countered with ruthless bite, but a faint dark line of colour now scored his sculpted cheekbones and he swung away for, even in the mood he had been in that evening, he had not been impervious to her natural appeal.

He remembered her all too well: the delicacy of her fine features, eyes as green as emeralds and as startling and unexpected in a Greek woman as her fair colouring. A beauty without artifice and the absolute antithesis of the voluptuous and artificial party girls paraded before him by his host. He had never made a pass at a servant in his life but only her silent formality and his own innate sense of fair play had haltered him.

'I understand that Ione has hardly ever been off that island. Her father believes in keeping his womenfolk at home,' Sander Christoulakis remarked with the wry fascination of a man who had a wife and two daughters, who thought nothing of flying all over Europe merely to visit friends or shop.

'At some time in the future, I may well consider a marriage of convenience,' Alexio conceded, his beautiful mouth hardening on the smouldering reflection that Ione Gakis should have immediately identified herself to him. 'But I have no interest in marrying Gakis's oddball daughter. At the very least I would like a wife with some personality.'

'A little personality can go a long way.' Unwilling to surrender what he saw as a fantastic opportunity for his son, Sander argued with greater vehemence. 'And before you criticise Ione Gakis for what she lacks, ask yourself what *you* have to offer a woman.'

'In what way?' Alexio intoned very drily.

'If you have no heart to give, only a fortune hunter will want to marry you,' the older man warned in frustration. 'Your current reputation as a womaniser is sufficient to make most of our friends extremely reluctant to let their daughters come into contact with you.'

'But then I'm not in the market for born-again virgins or ambitious social climbers. So they're very wise,' Alexio drawled with dismissive contempt.

Sander Christoulakis suppressed a heavy sigh. He had done his utmost to persuade his son to consider the benefits of such a business alliance, hoping that the challenge of becoming involved in the vast network of Gakis Holdings would tempt Alexio as nothing else might have done.

He had also believed that Alexio might be drawn by the sheer practicality of a marital arrangement that would demand so little from him on a personal basis. Spelling out the very obvious benefits of marrying a young woman who would one day inherit all that her father possessed would not have made the smallest impression.

'Minos will be insulted by a flat refusal,' Sander pointed out ruefully. 'He wants you to meet with him and discuss the proposal. What harm could that do?'

Alexio regarded his parent with the grim dark eyes that his business competitors had learned to respect but, whether he was prepared to show it or not, his interest had already been ignited by his recollection of that night on Lexos. 'I'll think it over.'

Fierce strain in her jade-green eyes, Ione checked her reflection with care in the mirror, for so formal a summons from her father was rare and intimidating.

Her pale blonde hair was scraped back from her equally pale face. Her dull dark blue dress barely hinted at the shape of the slim young body beneath and the hemline fell to below her knee. In a crowd nobody would have noticed her and that was exactly how her father believed his daughter ought to look: modest, unobtrusive, sexless. That his ideas were fifty years behind the times and out of place in a wealthy, educated family meant nothing to him for he boasted of his peasant roots and saw no reason why the outside world should intrude on his feudal island kingdom.

Indeed, Minos Gakis was a positive god in his own household. A domineering controlling man with an explosive temper that could turn to violence in the space of a moment and, to him, a woman would always be a lesser being and a possession. While she was still a very young child, Ione had learned the correct code of behaviour to observe in her father's radius and she knew well how to control her tongue and keep her head down in a storm. On more than one occasion, after all, she had seen her late mother being battered by the older man's fists, and as she'd grown up, no matter how hard Amanda Gakis had tried to protect her daughter from similar treatment, she too had suffered from his brutality.

Her bedroom door opened with jarring abruptness and without the polite warning of a prefatory knock. Flinching, Ione spun round just as her father's sister, Kalliope, appeared, her thin, sallow face sour.

'Why are you always looking at yourself in the mirror?' Kalliope snorted with derision. 'It's foolish when you're so plain. But then, had you been born a Gakis, you would have been a beauty.'

Accustomed to the older woman's gibes, Ione resisted the dangerous temptation to ask what had gone wrong in Kalliope's own case, for even the kindest person would have been challenged to find attraction in those sharp features. As for that crack about her *not* having been born into the Gakis family, Ione was too well accustomed to the knowledge that she had been adopted to rise to that bait and give the older woman reason to complain to her brother that her niece had been rude to her.

Kalliope observed her brother's every household rule with religious fervour and received considerable satisfaction from reporting those unwise enough to transgress those rules. Furthermore, she liked Ione far less than she had liked Ione's mother, for, while Kalliope had continued to rule the roost over the gentle English bride her brother had taken as a wife, she had found their adopted daughter, Ione, a tougher nut to crack. Ione might not answer back and might show her aunt superficial respect. But ever since the day four years earlier, when Ione had been dragged back kicking and screaming defiance from Athens airport, there had been a silent stoic determination in the younger woman's clear gaze that made Kalliope feel like an angry, frustrated mosquito trying to sting an indifferent victim.

'Your father has exciting news for you,' Kalliope informed her curtly.

As Ione crossed the reception room beyond her bedroom in step with her aunt her pace slowed as apprehension gripped her. 'I shall look forward to hearing it.'

'Yet you've been such an ungrateful daughter,' Kalliope told her with harsh disapproval. 'You don't deserve what is coming to you!'

What was coming to her? Her aunt's resentment was unconcealed and Ione's curiosity flared even higher, but the sick knot of anxiety in her tummy only tightened. She could never be in her father's presence without feeling fear and he was not a man given to doling out treats. Indeed, Ione had often wondered if her father reaped a mean pleasure from ensuring that she was invariably denied what she most wanted. But then he did not love her, he had never loved her, and, soon after her adoptive mother's death, he had enjoyed telling her *why* she had been adopted.

Amanda Gakis had given birth to a son, Cosmas, within a year of her marriage but, in the following seven years, she had not managed to conceive again. Desperate for a second son, Minos Gakis had learned that sometimes after a woman had adopted a child her unexplained infertility could subsequently end in her becoming pregnant. In those days, the popular view had been that, having satisfied her longing for a baby, a woman might stop fretting and relax and conception was then more likely to take place. Sadly, however, Ione's arrival in the family had neglected to deliver the required result for her mother had not become pregnant again. As her father had regarded his adopted daughter as no more than the means to that hopeful end, there had been little chance of her securing much of a hold on his paternal affections in that disappointing aftermath.

Her aunt left Ione standing in the echoing marble hall outside her father's office suite. Kalliope knew as well as Ione did that she would be kept waiting. Taut with strain, Ione gazed out the window, untouched by the gorgeous view of the bay that the villa overlooked. Golden sunlight and blue skies reflected on the shimmering seas of the Aegean far below. Lexos was a beautiful island and the huge, fabulous house in which she lived possessed every comfort that wealth could buy. Unfortunately, nothing could compensate Ione for the reality that she was as much a prisoner in her father's home as a criminal in an isolation cell.

The freedom she craved was as much out of her reach as it had ever been. In four endless years she had not been allowed off the island, for her father no longer trusted her. Her attempt to run away had been ill-judged and foolish, a *wasted* opportunity, she reflected with bitter hindsight, for she had not planned it well enough and had merely forewarned her father of her intentions.

At the time, she had been receiving regular orthodontic treatment in Athens, and it had been relatively easy to slip out of the dental clinic past her unsuspicious bodyguards and dive into a taxi to head to the airport. But she had not had the foresight to check the timetables in advance and had not had the wit to just buy a ticket for the first available seat on *any* international flight. No, her goal had been London and she had sat around like a fool awaiting that flight only to be cornered and forced from the airport by her bodyguards before the plane had even landed. She shuddered at the recollection of the welcome home she had received from her outraged and incredulous father, who had never dreamt until that day that she might dare to try and escape his bullying tyranny.

After all, her mother never had. But then any spirit Amanda Gakis had ever had had been crushed out of her by her husband's sneering verbal attacks and even more punishing fists.

'Where would I go?' her adoptive mother had once asked Ione with open disbelief when her teenage daughter had suggested that leaving her abusive marriage was the only solution to her unhappiness. 'How would I live? Wherever I went, your father would find me. He would never let me leave...he loves me too much!'

Love, Ione thought with a pained cynicism far beyond her years. Love had made a victim of the beautiful mother she had adored. Love had been one of Amanda's favourite excuses for the violence she had accepted as her lot in her life, along with the stress of her husband's workaholic ways on his temperament and her own inexcusable stupidity. She had blamed herself. Even while she had lain terminally ill, she had blamed herself for lingering long enough to distress and inconvenience her husband and her son.

Eyes stinging as she realised just how much she still missed the woman whose love had cocooned her from the worst of her father's abuse, Ione stiffened with dread as the older man's smooth executive assistant emerged with a surprisingly unctuous smile on his face.

'Miss Gakis...come this way.'

Minos Gakis stood below his own flattering portrait in the lofty-ceilinged room. He was a big thickset man with an imposing presence but he had yet to recover the weight he had shed while he was being treated for cancer. Indeed, although his illness had been a well-kept secret and had been successfully treated, his harsh features looked even more lined and gaunt to her than they had months earlier and his complexion was the colour of putty. For the very first time, it occurred to Ione that his recovery seemed much slower than might have been expected for a man of his former health and vigour.

'Are you well, Papa?' she heard herself ask in instinctive dismay, for it had been several weeks since she had seen him as he had been abroad on business.

'I can see that my caring, compassionate daughter will be sadly missed in this household,' Minos responded with cutting amusement.

Embarrassed colour washed over Ione's pallor and only a second later did she begin wondering where she could possibly be going that she might be missed. Hope sprang up in her in so fast and strong a surge that her knees trembled as she stood there. Had he finally forgiven her for trying to run away? Was he now willing to consider allowing her to lead a more normal life?

'After all these years, you are *finally* going to be of some use to me,' the burly older man informed her with satisfaction.

Ione stiffened, recognising the foolish aspect of her wild hopes of being permitted a life of her own. When had her father ever done anything that had pleased her? He had broken down at her mother's graveside, but her surprise and relief that he had shown that amount of humanity had been ruined by her painful memories of the mental and physical damage he had inflicted on a woman who had never hurt another living soul by word or by deed.

'I have found you a husband,' Minos announced and paused for effect.

The shock of that revelation rocked Ione on her feet and, though she struggled not to betray any reaction, a faint gasp was muffled low in her throat. Her heart was racing but her keen mind was racing even faster. A husband? Why on earth would he find her a husband? There had to be a reason. It would *have* to be of profit to him in some way. She knew better than to utter a single question or exclamation for he would react to either response as if she had been impertinent.

'Speak when you are spoken to,' had been a lesson etched into Ione's soul during childhood. 'A respectful daughter does not question a parent.'

The silence lay like concrete slowly setting her feet into greater rigidity while she waited for him to speak again. A husband, she thought with dazed incredulity. Why had she not foreseen such a possibility? Well, principally she had not anticipated the development because she was painfully aware that her father revelled in keeping his family at his beck and call and wholly dependent on him in every way.

'If Cosmas had not died,' the older man stated with harsh exactitude as he referred to her older brother, who had been killed when his private plane had crashed the year before, 'I would have scorned any thought of making such a marriage for you. But you are all that I have now and some day you will inherit Gakis Holdings.'

If his first announcement had shaken her, that second made her lips part in shock and she whispered, '*I'm*...to be your heir?'

He vented a sardonic laugh. 'Who else is left? In the eyes of the law, you are my daughter even though you do not possess a single drop of my blood.'

Yet she was proud that she was not a Gakis, relieved that she need never fear the taint of his genes, and she stood there lost in her own increasingly frantic thoughts. She did not *want* to inherit Gakis Holdings. His huge international business empire was the monster that had created his unfettered power. Enormous wealth had made him untouchable. Without hesitation, he destroyed those who antagonised him and his sphere of influence stretched terrifyingly far and wide. Time and time again the greed of others had protected him for he bribed those who might have exposed his corrupt business methods...or even what went on in his own home.

Perspiration beaded her short upper lip as she registered the peculiar direction of her thoughts at that particular moment. Her father had just told her that he had found her a husband. Why wasn't she thinking about the shattering statement? As the silence buzzed around her she felt faint and sick and the sound of her own heartbeat seemed to be thundering in her own ears.

Suddenly she understood *why* she could not dwell on the news that she was to be married off like some medieval bride without any right to have a say in her own future. What was the point of agonising over what she could not prevent? For if she defied him, he would hurt her and harm what mattered most to her. He was remorseless and the process of intimidation would begin the instant she voiced a word of objection. He had turned her into a coward, a lousy, grovelling thing without the guts to take on a fight she knew she could not win.

'I'm impressed,' Minos Gakis informed her with a quietness of tone that sent a cold shiver down her rigid spine. 'You know your place in life now. That's good, for I won't take any nonsense over this matter. As your father, I know what is best for you.'

'Yes, Papa,' she muttered sickly.

'Don't you even want to know who your husband will be?' he mocked, revelling in her submission to his dictates.

'If you want to tell me,' she intoned half under her breath.

'Alexio Christoulakis.'

Her knees almost gave beneath her in shock. She glanced up and encountered her father's cold look of amusement. 'Alexio…Christoulakis?'

Slowly, painfully slowly, her triangular face drenched with colour for she recalled the night she had met Alexio Christoulakis with too great a clarity for comfort. Her long, naturally dark lashes dropped again to conceal her transfixed gaze. Alexio Christoulakis…the *numero uno* womaniser, who seemed addicted to making headlines in both the business section and the society pages. The guy who didn't like to sleep on satin sheets and who had insisted she changed them even though it had been the early hours of the morning. The guy whose bride-to-be had drowned in a drunken moonlit swim. The guy who had treated her like a maid and barely registered that she was human. The guy who was so achingly beautiful to look at she had stared and stared in spite of herself every chance she had got…

'I'm not surprised that you can hardly credit your good fortune,' Minos Gakis murmured unpleasantly. 'But I'm sure I don't need to add that you need not look for fidelity from him. This is a business arrangement. He will take the place that your brother once occupied and as your husband he will become part of this family.'

With his every successive word the blood in her veins chilled more. He was spelling out the brutal facts. She would only be the means by which Alexio Christoulakis could be put in a position of trust as a son-in-law.

'He's brilliant, single-minded, strong. It took a lot to persuade him to agree to this alliance. But I *need* him. When he arrives tomorrow, you will do whatever it takes to keep him content. Is that understood?' her father pressed coldly.

Pinning bloodless lips together, she nodded jerkily. 'Yes, Papa.'

'Even when you become his wife, your first loyalty will remain with me. You will not tell him that you are adopted. The Christoulakis family take great pride in their family tree. You will not embarrass or offend them with the news that you were born illegitimate *or* reveal that you have a twin sister, who is nothing more than a common prostitute. Nor will you again seek contact with her. Is that also understood?'

A faint shudder rippled through Ione's slight frame until she pulled herself taut again. Bitter revulsion and anger currented through her but it was backed by despair. She saw how her future was being mapped out: a future that would be as confined and empty as the present. He expected her to marry a stranger and spy on him for his benefit. He was demanding that she go on living a lie for he did not want it to be known that macho Minos Gakis had adopted his daughter, rather than sired her himself. And to drive the knife in harder, he abused the twin she had never met, scorning her sister for her lifestyle. Hatred made her very lungs burn and she turned her head away.

'Answer me, Ione,' he growled.

'Yes, Papa. I understand,' she said with all the expression of a robot.

The instant the interview was at an end, she headed straight for the gymnasium. There she changed into an exercise outfit and embarked on a rigorous training session to empty her taut, shivering body of stress. She overdid it and exhausted herself, finally slumping down on a mat, damp and shaking, to stare at the floor. And it was only then, at the last expected moment, that she finally grasped *why* she should be greeting the announcement of her approaching nuptials with joy and relief...

The minute that she left the island with her bridegroom would simply be the countdown to her eventual escape from the whole darned lot of them! Ione flung back her pale blonde head and her laughter suddenly echoed across the big empty gym. Alexio Christoulakis would be her passport to *freedom*, not her future keeper, not yet another lord and master in her life.

Having had experience of one bullying, aggressive male, she had no intention of accepting a second. But it was essential that Alexio marry her just to get her off Lexos. Not even her father was likely to suspect that she might choose to walk out on her bridegroom *after* her wedding. Especially not when it came to a male as eligible and good-looking as Alexio Christoulakis, who was rumoured to be the top pin-up in girls' schools across the globe.

Ione began to smile, soft mouth curving as she flung herself back on the padded mat and started to plan. When she reached England she would find her sister, Misty, for although it had been more than four years since that letter had arrived from her twin she still remembered every line of the address on it. Fossetts, her sibling's foster home had been called, and surely from that point it would be a simple matter to trace Misty even if she no longer lived there. Yet her own sister knew nothing about her, not even her present name, Ione acknowledged ruefully. At birth Ione had been given the name Shannon, but Amanda Gakis had chosen a new name for her adopted daughter. However, when she did finally get to meet her long-lost twin she really would have to work out some very tactful, very, very kind way of persuading her elder sister that she did not need to be the victim of rich, using, abusing men.

*   *   *

As the helicopter came in to land over Lexos, Alexio was thinking about the disconcerting meeting he had had with Minos Gakis forty-eight hours earlier and the commitment he had made in agreeing to marry Ione.

After having advanced an extremely advantageous business partnership that had taken Alexio by surprise, Gakis had laid *all* his cards on the table. In telling Alexio the truth about his health, the older man had to a very great extent put himself in Alexio's power, for the news that the billionaire tycoon might only have a few months left to live would send shock waves crashing through the business world and cause a steep fall in the value of the shares in Gakis Holdings, making it vulnerable to a takeover bid.

The Gakis empire ran only with Minos Gakis at the helm. His senior executives had been picked not for their ability to think on their feet but for the efficiency in following orders without question. Minos did indeed need a second-in-command, a son-in-law bound by family ties to hold the fort while he went into hospital for further treatment. For if he did *not* emerge again, what would happen to a daughter raised like a convent novice on an island and without the smallest grasp of what the real world was like? A young woman who would inherit billions and become the target of every smooth-talking greedy fortune hunter across the globe?

But without a doubt, Gakis was sick in more than body, a father jealous of his precious little girl's affections, for why else should he have raised his daughter in such unnatural isolation? Almost twenty-three and never had a boyfriend? Was Minos Gakis crazy? Didn't he realise that his daughter would fall madly in love with the first man who gave her some attention?

That's likely to be *you*, Alexio's intelligence told him

and, even though women who clung and looked at him with adoration turned him off big time, the shadow of a faint smile touched the corners of his strong mouth. Ione would be his wife, after all, and she had not looked like the demanding type. Different horses for different courses, he reflected with cool confidence. If she loved him their marriage of convenience might well run a great more smoothly. But what kind of a woman allowed herself to be bartered off like a commodity?

The 'commodity' in question was engaged in equally careful thought at that moment. Ione was working out how she could best put Alexio at ease and lull him into a false sense of security. After all, she did not want him succumbing to an attack of cold feet and spoiling her plans, and she had not forgotten her father's admission that it had taken a great deal to persuade Alexio into marrying her. She would have liked to show him that she could be a lot more presentable in appearance than her current circumstances allowed. Unfortunately that option was barred for her father might well lose his temper if she appeared wearing the cosmetics and the more flattering outfits that she sometimes put on to cheer herself up in the privacy of her bedroom.

Unfortunately, the only thought in Alexio Christoulakis's head when he first looked at her would be…sex. Her nose wrinkled. He would wonder what she would be like in bed; he wouldn't be able to help himself. He was Greek, he was *very* oversexed. And he had made an outsize fool of himself two years ago over a greedy little tart of a show-off with nothing else going for her but her ability to show her boobs and bare bottom off in public on a monotonously regular basis. Face it, she would be dealing with a very basic, testosterone-driven male, who left his supposedly brilliant brain outside the bedroom door. And here she was looking as plain and sexless as it was possible to look and he might well take fright. So she had to draw him in...*somehow*, ensure he got the impression that, no matter how devoid of instant appeal she might seem, the wedding night at least was likely to be a wow.

Of course, she didn't plan on sticking around for the wedding night, but he could have no suspicion of that reality. But then, he deserved *all* that he had coming to him, didn't he? What kind of a man agreed to marry a woman as part of a cold-blooded, callous business deal? A sexist, domineering, ruthless, power-hungry, insensitive pig!

As Alexio Christoulakis emerged from the helicopter he was gilded by bright sunlight. The selfish, spoilt pig who had demanded that she change his wretched bed sheets at two o'clock in the morning, Ione reminded herself as she stood like a small, rigid statue by her burly father's side.

But she had chosen to forget the sheer raw impact of Alexio in the flesh and the closer he got, the less she breathed and her chest tightened, for he *was* so incredibly good-looking. The golden light shimmered over the luxuriant blue-black hair cropped to his arrogant head, accentuated his superb bone structure, the stunning dark, deepset eyes, the bold brows, aggressive jawline and wide, charismatic mouth. His pearl-grey business suit was cut to fit wide shoulders, lean hips and long, powerful thighs that required no helpful enhancement from his tailor. He strolled towards them not one whit put out by a reception committee and a situation that would have filled ninety-nine out of a hundred men with a sizeable degree of discomfiture.

Her own heart was hammering with nervous tension and, had she not been holding herself taut with the self-discipline of years of training, she would have trembled. His vibrant self-assurance infuriated her, but on another level she could only be impressed by that show of strength, that cool, contained tough front. One wrong move, one word out of place and her father would ruin him. Didn't he realise that he was walking into the lion's den? Didn't he appreciate that if he married into the Gakis family he would be selling his soul to the devil?

'Ione...' Alexio looked down into eyes the same shade as precious jade, the most unreadable female eyes he had ever met, utterly empty of any impression, and the smooth and polished greeting ready on his tongue somehow died there. She had the pale, still face of a madonna, possessed of pure, perfect symmetry and...untouchable. At a distance she had looked like a doll, now she bore a very close resemblance to an ice statue: frigid from head to toe. The wedding night promised to be a *real* challenge.

'Alexio...' Ione squeezed out his name in acknowledgement, straining with all her might to get enough oxygen back to manage that feat.

Alexio watched the flow of warm pink colour burnish her cheeks, the uncertain flutter of her silky brown lashes and the brief relaxation of her taut lipline into soft, sexy fullness as she spoke. As he noted the tiny pulse beating out her tension below her delicate collar-bone, he recognised that she was neither indifferent nor cold, but raw with nerves and struggling to hide the fact. A primal sense of satisfaction lancing through him, his slow, dangerous smile curved his handsome mouth...

CHAPTER TWO

'BRING us coffee…' Minos Gakis rapped out to Ione the instant the three of them entered the air-conditioned cool of the villa.

Conscious of Alexio's veiled surprise at that harsh demand, Ione reddened. It was an effort at that instant to recall what mattered most, for somehow being treated like an object of derision in Alexio's presence hit her even harder than usual. However, suppressing her embarrassment, Ione pushed her head up high and lifted her slight shoulders back. Praying that her father was too busy talking to notice, she walked down the long marble hall with small, slow, measured steps that made her slim hips sway in what she hoped was a subtle but enticing manner.

She knew how experienced women practised such small visual wiles on the male sex. Goodness knew, she had had ample opportunity to observe the behaviour of the voluptuous giggling blondes her father brought over to Lexos when he entertained. Of course, on such occasions she was supposed to behave as though she were quite unaware of what went on in her own home and keep to her own wing of the villa, but as the years had passed Minos Gakis had become less discreet. She had often seen those women basking round the pool and had watched them switch on the seductive charm to attract lustful male visitors. Her soft mouth tightened with helpless distaste.

Engaged in listening to his host, Alexio watched Ione progress down the hall, a faint hint of a frownline marking his winged black brows as he questioned his own reluc-

25

tance to take his attention from her. The fluid slowness of her walk attracted his gaze first to the intrinsically feminine curve of her *derrière* and then to the soft rise of her hemline above her slender, shapely legs. She moved with the grace of a dancer but it was another, far more disturbing quality that caused the sudden startling ache of fullness in Alexio's groin.

Seconds later, Ione moved out of view and slumped back against the cold corridor wall, all of a quiver from the stress of a masquerade she found demeaning. But she *had* to try to engage Alexio's interest and convince him that she was content to marry him, for if he suspected otherwise he might change his mind and, if he did so, even her father couldn't force him to marry her and all hope of her getting off the island would be lost. She shivered at that awareness. Yet to attempt for the first time ever to attract a man and to do so in her father's vicinity demanded a degree of courageous subtlety she feared she did not possess.

She had worked so hard at forgetting just how unnerving a personality Alexio Christoulakis was, Ione acknowledged uneasily as she collected the already prepared coffee tray. His arrival had shaken her up a lot more than she had expected. With reluctance, she recalled their first brief encounter.

That night a couple of months earlier she had been relieved to be mistaken for an employee, for it was humiliating to be treated like a servant by her father in front of his discomfited guests. Alexio had been in too much of a rage to be more discerning, she recalled abstractedly. Dark eyes blazing gold with fierce pride, aggressive jawline hard as iron. And she had had a very fair idea of what hoops her father had put him through for his own amusement.

But she had still been struck as dumb as a tongue-tied schoolgirl when she'd first laid eyes on Alexio Christoulakis. Even though she had seen those same lean, dark, handsome features in the magazines she read, he had always looked so impossibly cool and reserved. She had not been prepared for a male so vibrant and so volatile in the flesh that raw energy literally sizzled from him.

And when he had called her back to change those satin sheets that her aunt believed to be the last word in sophistication, she had had no need to make that her own personal task for the villa had staff on duty twenty-four hours a day. Yet inexplicably she had hurried off to fetch fresh linen. When she had returned to his bedroom, he had been standing by the open doors onto the balcony, exuding a ferocious tension that had sent her own sensory processes into overload.

Guilty as a sneak thief but unable to resist her own fascination, she had kept on stealing covert glances at him. It had taken her for ever to make up the bed again, for her hands had been all fingers and thumbs. But he had seemed indifferent to her lingering presence and her lack of dexterity. Only once had their eyes met head-on and her mouth had run dry as she'd fallen victim to those spectacular golden eyes. A split second later he had swung away as though he were alone and had strode out onto the balcony where he had remained until she had departed again.

As she emerged from that unsettling recollection, perspiration beaded Ione's short upper lip. As she entered the main salon with the laden tray, she could see the shaded, vine-encrusted loggia outside where her father was seated in regal splendour and her heart sank at his choice of location. Evidently impervious to any fear of heights, Alexio was lounging back against the low retaining wall that was built into the very edge of the cliff, the relaxed angle of his lean, powerful frame pronounced.

Ione's hands clenched bone-white round the tray handles as she attempted to blank out the panoramic view and forestall the sick sense of dizzy terror that always threatened her in the loggia.

His keen gaze narrowing with questioning force on her drawn face, Alexio straightened and strode forward. 'Let me take that for you.'

Dismayed that he had broken off the conversation to offer her assistance, Ione froze. She collided with gleaming dark golden eyes fringed with dense black lashes and her heart seemed to crash inside her. He detached her death grip from the tray and strolled back to set it on the stone table. Screening her bemused gaze, she edged as close to the house wall as she dared to reach the table and serve the coffee.

'You're afraid of heights,' Alexio murmured.

Minos Gakis said drily, 'She must overcome it.'

Conscious of her father's annoyance that she should have interrupted their dialogue, Ione breathed jerkily, 'It's foolish, irrational. I mustn't give way to it.'

Alexio studied her. She was making a valiant effort to control her fear but she was as white as a sheet and the coffee-pot was shaking in her hand. And her father? He was smiling. Alexio had a sudden primal desire to tip his host out of his seat and suspend him upside down over that fearsome drop to kill that smile. It was an urge that shook him.

Ione sank down into the closest chair and struggled to get a grip on herself again. Accustomed as she was to being ignored in her father's company, she focused on Alexio while the two men talked business, and she reflected on what a poor impression she must have made in betraying her terror of heights. Hardly the right way to connect with a male once fabled for his taste in dangerous sports. He had the most amazing eyelashes, she thought, losing her concentration to momentarily dwell on the lush black sweep visible in his hard, angular profile.

As Alexio sent her a winging glance, brilliant dark golden eyes flaring into connection with hers, a surge of inflaming heat tremored through Ione in a shock wave of response. Her teeth set together as her breath caught in her throat and she tore her attention from him again. Highspots of colour formed over her cheekbones as she fought her own instinctive reaction to his raw masculinity with shamed and angry resentment.

She had no intention of following in her unfortunate mother's footsteps and letting her body rule over her brain. So he was gorgeous, but what was that worth? She had recognised her own foolish susceptibility three months earlier and had despised herself for her weakness. A womanising louse like Alexio Christoulakis figured nowhere in the future she craved. No man was going to break her heart. No man was going to control her. Once she had her freedom, if anybody broke hearts, it was going to be her. That ambition in mind, Ione curled back into her chair, arched her back a little and shifted her slim legs to let her hemline ride up ever so slightly.

Conscious of her every move, Alexio was entertained by her attempt to portray herself as a sensually exciting woman by exposing an inch of flesh above her knee, and he was equally conscious that her every provocative move was studied. Was she trying to turn him off the idea of marrying her? Or turn him onto it? Whichever, he was already appreciating that that smooth madonna face was deceptive.

Angling her blonde head back, Ione lowered her lashes

and let the tip of her tongue slide out to dampen her lower lip. His gaze zeroed in on her, black lashes screening his shimmering eyes to linger on the darting pink tip moistening her full, inviting mouth. Amusement ebbing, his lean, hard body clenched on a surge of sexual hunger strong enough to infuriate him. Why was she playing games with him?

Minos Gakis rose upright, his heavy movements betraying his weariness. 'I must attend to business, Alexio… Ione will entertain you. We'll discuss the wedding arrangements over dinner.

Ione was startled by that speech. If wedding arrangements were to be discussed, then their marriage was *already* a foregone conclusion. As it seemed that Alexio must have agreed to marry her even before he'd arrived on Lexos, her attempts to make herself seem more attractive had been a ludicrous waste of time and energy. On Alexio's terms, her true worth lay in her Gakis surname and her future dowry, not in her looks or her individuality. Her cheeks blossomed with chagrined colour. Once again she had been made to feel the sting of her own essential unimportance, but she realised that it would be unwise to suddenly abandon the act she had been putting on for his benefit.

'Shall we go inside?' Alexio drawled, taking charge with all-male decisiveness.

But for the reality that sitting out in the loggia was a punishment to her, Ione might have disagreed. Looking up at him to note how very, very tall he was from that angle, and filled with almost childish resentment by the intimidating nature of that fact, she got up with a nod.

Sudden angry suspicion gripped Alexio as he stood back to let Ione precede him indoors, his glinting appraisal resting on her undeniably sensual gliding walk across the terracotta tiles. How did he know that Ione Gakis wasn't a raving nymphomaniac with a father desperate to marry her off before she engulfed the family in scandal? If that were the case, the Gakis billions would be equal to preventing the spread of damaging rumours, but not the most optimistic of men could hope to hide such a shame for ever. The constant references to Ione's shyness and her protected upbringing added to her dowdy appearance might just be ploys to convince him that she was what her father said she was. But how could he know for sure? How did he *know* he wasn't being suckered into marriage with a woman who might try to make the Christoulakis name a laughing stock?

'Your father was a little premature in his reference to wedding arrangements,' Alexio imparted, smooth as velvet. 'I did tell him that you and I would have to talk before anything could be finalised.'

Ione stiffened, her nervous tension reawakening in a dismayed surge as she registered that she still had to win him over. Flustered, she muttered unwarily, 'I should've guessed. Papa…Papa can be impatient. He makes assumptions.'

'Which of us doesn't?' Alexio rested a light hand to her spine to guide her out of the bright sunlight into the vast salon and she was so ridiculously aware of his touch, his very proximity, that she imagined she felt his fingers burn through the dress fabric into the taut skin of her back. 'But you intrigue me. I'm not sure what to make of you.'

Something akin to panic shrilled through Ione. What was that supposed to mean? Intrigue? Didn't that suggest something covert? Did he suspect that her efforts to attract him were just one big empty pretence? How could he not? How could she possibly have believed that she could fool a guy who had slept with dozens of women into crediting that she would ever be a wow in bed?

'You don't know me,' Ione pointed out tightly, an unsteady hand sliding down over her dress to smooth it as she braced herself to try and redress the damage by reassuring him. 'But I can be *anything* you want me to be.'

The fall of silence that greeted that impulsive announcement was instant and it worked on her nerves like a chainsaw.

Taken aback by that startling assurance, Alexio frowned, dark golden eyes narrowing below winged ebony brows as he stared at her.

'I just don't know what you want from me yet,' Ione stated, gathering steam from the sheer level of fear holding her rigid, for if she had blown any hope of him wanting to marry her with her silly play-acting, she had *nothing* left to lose. Not only would her father lose his head with her, but she would also be buried alive on Lexos for years to come.

'What I want from you?' Alexio prompted in fascination, having recognised the spark of panic in her wide green eyes before she'd veiled them and the extent of the tension keeping her so still.

'I need to know what you want,' Ione told him again. 'Maybe you don't want me interfering in your life if we get married. That's fine. I *won't*. You don't need to worry about that. I'm a very practical person. Very quiet too. You'll hardly know I'm there. Once I know what you like, everything will be as you expect it to be.'

A shaken surge of angry compassion stirred in Alexio. Anger at her father for giving her the impression that such assurances would be necessary and compassion that she should feel driven to humble herself in such a way for his benefit. 'I have only one question that needs an answer. Do *you* want to be my wife?'

Eyes lowering, Ione trembled, compressed her lips, parted them again. An obvious question, one she should have foreseen but harder to answer than she could ever have dreamt, for by nature she was not a liar. And when she lifted her lashes and collided with the dark golden intensity of his questioning gaze, her breath feathered in her throat and her breasts seemed to swell inside her cotton bra. Embarrassment scythed through her as her nipples tightened into straining buds and an arrow of heat speared low in her pelvis. Yet *still* she could not take her eyes from his lean, dark, devastating features.

'Ione...I'm aware that your father has a forceful personality. If you feel in any way pressured into this—'

'Oh, no!' Ione broke in hurriedly, keen to make that denial for she could now see the direction in which the dialogue was going. 'How could you think that?'

'I don't know what to think,' Alexio said with the frankness that as a rule he only employed within his own family circle, his brilliant gaze pinned to her with penetrating force. 'I'm getting mixed signals from you.'

Sentenced to stillness by the sheer mesmeric effect of those beautiful eyes, Ione murmured half under her breath and without really knowing where the words had come from. 'I want to marry you more than anything else in the world.'

Darker colour accentuated Alexio's fabulous cheekbones for he had not expected that emotive a declaration. 'Why?' he heard himself say as if what she had just said was still not enough, though it was.

'I had a picture of you in my locker at boarding-school.' Her fair skin drenched with pink as she forced out that statement. 'Everybody had a pin-up. You were mine.'

Initially disconcerted at the news that he had been the focus of a schoolgirl crush, Alexio suddenly found himself smiling, and it was a smile full of so much natural charisma that it turned Ione's knees to cotton wool beneath her.

Gotcha, Ione thought with intense satisfaction in spite of that smile. He had fallen for it. And why not? The target of admiring and awestruck women all his adult life, he was accustomed to flattery. Actually, it had been one of her classmates who had languished over him at fifteen. Ione had thought love from afar was childish and a waste of energy and had kept cute photos of her dog inside her locker.

'I suppose we have to start somewhere,' Alexio conceded with a husky laugh of amusement.

Losing every suspicion of her motives, he castigated himself for the wildness of his own suspicions about her morals in the loggia. Her honesty was refreshing but naive. But then, after the sheltered life she had led, her naivety was understandable. In times to come, though, she might look back and hate him for having listened to that gauche little declaration, for what did he have to offer her in return? In the material line, nothing, and he didn't like that. Indeed, he had already decided how best to deal with that potential problem.

'I believe that our marriage will work best if you settle your future inheritance on any children we might have and we live on my income,' Alexio spelt out without hesitation.

Suddenly, Ione was grateful she had no plans to become a kept woman. He was *so* Greek: he wanted a dependant wife. How dared he suggest that she consent to that kind of an agreement merely to conserve his precious male pride? In her place, what man would agree to such an arrangement? It did not seem to occur to him that she might already be wealthy in her own right, yet Ione had inherited considerable funds from both her mother and her brother. As for having children with him, since the possibility was not going to arise, she didn't even think about it.

'Ione...I appreciate that that will be a very difficult decision for you to make, but I would like you to give serious consideration to the idea,' Alexio continued with level cool.

'I'll think about it,' Ione responded with castdown eyes. Love in a cottage Christoulakis-style? Had she been born of Gakis blood and truly intending to be his wife, at that point, all negotiations would have broken down. But money had no power over her, for immense wealth had brought her adoptive family nothing but misery.

His strong jawline clenched, dark golden eyes challenging. 'Your father will disapprove but I won't allow him to interfere in our marriage. You must accept that too.'

'Yes, of course.' But at that aggressive announcement of intent, Ione almost released a shuddering sigh of relief over the escape she was planning on. What Alexio had just said was grounds for a battle royal. Minos Gakis was no fond parent, but he set great store on his own pride and he would be outraged if his daughter was seen to live in anything less than a palace. But then the situation would never develop, she reminded herself impatiently, for her relationship with Alexio would not last beyond their wedding day. Furthermore, Alexio was only dictating terms for what was essentially a business deal rather than a marriage.

'I need you to voice your own opinions.' Exasperation currented through Alexio as she stood there like a slender statue revealing nothing of her thoughts.

No, he didn't. Since when had impervious demands required opinions? Ione regarded him from below curling brown lashes, green eyes cloaked, for every time she looked at him she was struck anew by his lethal dark attraction. 'But I agree with everything you've said.'

'You *must* have requests to make of me,' Alexio informed her.

'I would love to spend our honeymoon in Paris,' Ione dared, her low-pitched voice a tad uneven for so much was riding on his response. 'I believe you have a house there.'

'I also have a very beautiful villa in the Caribbean.'

Even that one little thing, he had to argue about, Ione thought fiercely. He couldn't help himself. An inability to give way gracefully to any will other than their own was the essential flaw in all ruthless, successful men. Well, whether he liked it or not, he was going to Paris. He *had* to take her to a city so that she could leave him. Staging a nifty vanishing act from a potentially remote Caribbean villa might well prove to be too great a challenge for her.

In some surprise, Alexio picked up on the antagonistic sparks in her silence. 'We could go sailing.'

'I get seasick,' Ione lied in a wooden little voice that concealed her panic at what was an even worse suggestion.

Paris. Paris where he had spent so much time with Crystal, Alexio reflected in instinctive recoil, but then he looked at Ione and, seeing the anxious light in her upward glance, he felt like a selfish bastard for denying her what appeared to be her heart's desire. 'Paris it is, then...'

Her smile, the smile she had not let him see until that moment, lit up her whole face to a startling degree. While he gazed into her shining green eyes and experienced a tightening sensation in his groin that was becoming all too familiar in her vicinity, he decided that it would be healthier to make new memories of one of his favourite cities.

'Let me show you round the picture gallery,' Ione suggested, daring to take the lead now that her battle was won and her worst fears vanquished.

Instead and without warning, Alexio reached for her and drew her close, his lean hands linking with hers and then releasing them to glide with smooth expertise up to her slim shoulders. 'First...'

No, no, no, *no*! Screamed through Ione's brain. Touching was absolutely not allowed. She stiffened, froze from head to toe, putting out defensive signals that a blind man could have sensed.

'You don't need to be nervous,' Alexio soothed in his dark velvet drawl, that roughened timbre setting up a chain-reaction echo down her rigid spine. But he knew he was lying. Every time she froze around him, he wanted to smash down her barriers, storm an attack through her defences and watch those beautiful eyes drown in him, cling to him, *hunger* for him.

She collided with smouldering golden eyes that made her head spin and her heart skip a beat in shock. She meant to step back out of reach but instead she found herself concentrating on just catching her breath. It shook her even more to feel her body wanting to push forward into the hard, all-male muscularity of his, for the rigorous control that had always been her saviour was nowhere to be found.

'Alexio...' Her own voice sounded strange to her, almost placatory.

He brought his wide, sensual mouth drifting down onto hers and then, with rueful amusement sounding deep in his throat, he pried her sealed lips apart with the tip of his tongue and explored the moist interior of her tender mouth. As the explosion of sensual sensation hit her she shuddered in its grip, her slim body alternately tensing and dissolving in the storm of physical feelings firing through her skincells. Crushed against the unyielding wall of his chest, her breasts pinched tight into throbbing peaks and the ache that stirred at the very heart of her almost hurt.

Alexio lifted his arrogant dark head to gaze down into her dreamy, bemused eyes with a sense of achievement entirely new to him. 'Am I the first?'

Having yet to regain mastery over herself in that moment and stunned by her own galloping heartbeat and excitement, Ione mumbled. 'The first to kiss me? No...'

In an abrupt movement, Alexio freed her. Who was she trying to kid? She hadn't even known *how* to kiss until he had shown her! But the dreaminess in her eyes had dissipated and she had lost colour. Indeed, she spun away from him as if he no longer existed for her and, registering that withdrawal, he immediately suspected the most likely cause.

'Who was he?' Alexio demanded, seized by a sudden dark anger that inflamed him into an instantaneous reaction.

Pale as death in the aftermath of that unwise admission, Ione could have bitten her own tongue out. Wounding memories were attacking her from all sides, but fear had risen uppermost again. If her father found out that she had mentioned Yannis, he would be furious. She did not consider Alexio's anger abnormal. Her father was a hypocrite too, preaching female purity one moment and taking solace with tarts the next.

'He was a fisherman's son. It was over two years ago. He k-kissed me. That's all,' she lied shakily.

Alexio's lean, powerful hands closed back into fists and slowly uncoiled again. Why shouldn't she have kissed someone else? And it was such a pathetic little confession that he was momentarily ashamed of himself for forcing it out of her. He could not explain the strength of his own irrational anger, and then he looked at her afresh and noted that she had turned a sort of sickly shade, her eyes refusing to meet his. That seething anger came out of nowhere at him again. He recognised that he wasn't hearing the whole story and was torn by a primitive desire to drag all the rest of it out of her as well, for her pallor told him that that fisherman's son had been a major event in her life.

CHAPTER THREE

'LET'S go and see those pictures,' Alexio breathed in a raw undertone. So he was unaccustomed to the experience of a woman reeling out of his arms to think about another man. But, in the circumstances, he knew his anger was unreasonable.

Ione was trembling. 'Please don't mention what I said to my father.'

Alexio flung her an astonished glance from his brilliant eyes and his jawline hardened. 'Of course not.'

Ione led the way to the ultra-modern picture gallery but her tummy was still churning. Yannis had been her first and only love and it had been sweet and innocent and harmless until the day that she'd been followed and her father's henchmen had forced her to watch as Yannis had been beaten to a pulp. Soon afterwards his family had left the island. She would never forget what *her* foolishness had cost *him*.

And what even greater foolishness it had been to admit to her bridegroom that she was not quite untouched by human hand! He was now thinking that she might not be a virgin. As she watched him view the magnificent paintings, which she believed ought to hang in a museum where at least they would be appreciated as something other than an investment, she recognised the lingering tautness in his strong, bronzed profile. Like her father, he was the contemporary equivalent of a caveman, who wanted a bride no other man had ever dared to touch. And wouldn't he just love it if she questioned him about his all-too-

numerous affairs? Even so, she was puzzled that he had
once intended to marry a woman like Crystal Denby,
whose reputation had been far from spotless.

But then Crystal had been totally, fantastically gorgeous, Ione conceded with wry acceptance. A woman
blessed with such undeniable attributes got away with a
great deal more than a plainer one. It must feel really good,
she thought with rueful longing, to have that kind of power
over a man.

'I'm sorry about the way I questioned you downstairs,'
Alexio remarked in a driven undertone, swinging round
without warning to level dark-as-night eyes on her triangular face. 'I have no right to question your past.'

His apology surprised her but she immediately sensed
that he wanted to know more about Yannis, was indeed
expecting and inviting her to respond with further details.
Angry defiance stirred in her and only with the greatest
difficulty did she resist the temptation to ask if he wanted
to tell her about *his* lost love. Instead she simply nodded
agreement in silence.

Even though she had thwarted him, grudging admiration
assailed Alexio. His wide, sensual mouth slashed into a
wolfish smile of acknowledgement that exuded such innate
masculine power over her that she found herself smiling
dizzily back at him without even thinking about it.

'I brought you this…' He drew a ring from the pocket
of his beautifully tailored jacket. 'It's the Christoulakis
betrothal ring, but if you don't like it it's not a problem.
You can choose your own ring if you prefer to do so. I
will admit upfront that my own mother considered it too
old-fashioned for her taste.'

Attacked by sudden discomfiture, Ione studied the diamonds that glittered below the gallery lights. A family
betrothal ring, an heirloom. A stab of guilt pierced her for,

whatever she might think of his motives, he *was* on the level about their marriage and she was not. 'It's beautiful...' she muttered and she made herself extend her hand in acceptance lest she betray herself.

Alexio reached for her hand and threaded the ring onto her wedding finger. 'I may not love you but I will do everything in my power to be a good husband,' he asserted.

In receipt of that little speech, Ione gritted her teeth together. Well, it was just as well that she had no intention of hanging around to test him out on that unlikely promise! Like any other woman, she deserved to be loved and she intended to be loved by someone one day. In the meantime, she would be playing the field with loads of different boyfriends. Well, if she could get one to start with, she conceded, climbing down from her mental soapbox to allow that until she had tested herself out on the dating scene she had no idea how much man appeal she might possess.

Although a boyfriend who kissed as Alexio did would be a very good start, she acknowledged. Without a doubt, his sexual expertise had roused her own much too enthusiastic response. However, seeking to deny him that small intimacy would have been a major mistake on all fronts. And it *had* only been her hormones that had got carried away, she told herself in consolation. Since she had been deprived of almost all the natural learning experiences that she should have had with men, she might even qualify as being sex-starved. So, why should she be ashamed of the wild excitement she had felt beneath that hard, hungry mouth of his? There had really been nothing at all personal in her response to him.

'Ione...' Alexio began, studying the smooth perfection of her shuttered face and yet far-away gaze and endeavouring to fathom what had stolen her attention from him yet again.

'Alexio…how *are* you? Ione should have brought you to me immediately,' a coy female voice shrilled from the entrance to the gallery.

Sprung from her introspection by the sight of Kalliope heading for Alexio with a delighted smile on her thin face, Ione breathed in deep. She need have no further concern as to how to occupy Alexio, for her aunt, who adored young, handsome men, was more than equal to the task. And over the following hour, while he endured Kalliope's voluble enquiries about every single member of his family near and far, Alexio demonstrated the most perfect manners, patience and courtesy.

'You don't deserve a husband from a good family.' Kalliope shot her niece a look of angry resentment as the two women walked back to their own wing of the villa to change for dinner. 'If Alexio Christoulakis knew the truth about your background, *nothing* would persuade him to marry a girl from the gutter!'

For once, in receipt of her aunt's venom, Ione felt only a weary compassion. Her mother had once told her that, twenty years earlier, Kalliope had fallen in love with one of her brother's executives, but Minos Gakis had reacted in fury and had refused his permission for them to marry. Kalliope had dutifully accepted his decision and now she was in her fifties, still unmarried and bitter over the lot life had dealt her.

But at least her aunt still *had* her life, Ione reasoned with a superstitious shiver as she selected another dull dark dress from her wardrobe. Cosmas had not been so fortunate. The night that her brother had crashed his plane, he had been under enormous stress and his resulting lack of concentration had killed him. If anything, Cosmas had been even more afraid of their father than she was.

Cosmas had had the Gakis head for business laced with their mother's sensitivity. Her eyes stinging as she thought about the big brother she still missed a great deal, Ione promised herself that, no matter what it took and regardless of what deception might be involved, she would do what Cosmas had been too scared to do: she would break free, she would escape before her self-will was crushed as his had been.

The first course of the lavish dinner had been served when Minos Gakis announced that the wedding would have to take place within two weeks as business commitments would keep him out of the country during the following month. Ione's startled gaze shot to Alexio, who seemed to be absorbing the news with a lot less surprise than she was. His lean, strong face was not even tense. Indeed, he shot her a long, lingering glance from heavily lidded dark golden eyes that burned hot colour into her cheeks and made her hurriedly look away.

'The ceremony will, of course, take place here on the island,' Minos decreed and he turned to study Alexio with a half-smile. 'I see no reason why you and Ione should not then take up residence here.'

Shock powered through Ione and her fork fell from her nerveless fingers with a clatter.

'In her own home, my daughter would have the company of her aunt while you are abroad and she would also enjoy the continued security of a full protection team.'

'No...*no*!' Ione gasped in horror, driven into defiance by the stricken conviction that such an arrangement could only have been planned from the outset.

Even as her dismayed aunt dug warning nails into her thigh below the table, Ione's red-faced father was flying out of his chair like a jet-propelled steamroller and raising a punishing fist as he roared down at his daughter in a rage, '*What* did you say to me?'

Mutely awaiting the blow about to descend and white as milk, Ione jerked as the crash of a chair falling backward sounded from the other side of the table.

'If you lay one finger on her, I swear I'll kill you!' Alexio thundered with a raw aggression more than equal to his host's.

A silence beyond any silence that had ever fallen in the Gakis household fell at that point. Nobody had ever challenged Minos Gakis like that. Sheer disbelief had paralysed the older man's heavy features as he slowly turned his big greying head to focus on his challenger. Ione wanted to throw herself across the table and stuff the tablecloth in Alexio's big, stupid macho mouth before he got himself beaten up. What madness had come over him? Where were his much-vaunted brains when he most needed them? Her father had said that he needed Alexio but her father would *still* throw him off the island and destroy him sooner than swallow such an insult.

Minos surveyed the younger man with outraged dark eyes and hissed. 'So you think she's *your* property now…eh?'

'*Yes.*' His lean, powerful face rigid, the surge of pure black rage that had powered Alexio was still in the ascendant.

With an abruptness that made his female relatives flinch, Minos Gakis threw back his head and laughed with a derisive appreciation that curdled Ione's quivering tummy. She would call the police. No matter what it cost her, if he let his henchmen hurt Alexio, she knew that *this* time she would call the police and inform on her own father.

But a split second later, she could only watch with a

dropped jaw as her father dealt Alexio a considering look of ironic approval. 'You're a man not unlike me. Possessive, protective of what's yours. Well, then, *you* keep your mouth shut from now on!'

Ione just closed her eyes, still sick from the threat of the violence that had so nearly exploded upon them all and equally sick with humiliation. The men resumed their seats. Alexio skimmed a probing glance at Ione and asked himself if he had been guilty of a crazy overreaction, for she did not seem grateful for his intervention. He had believed that her father had been about to hit her, but it was more probable that the older man had only been waving an angry fist in the air. After all, Ione had just sat there and would surely not have done so had she feared a blow. What grounds did he have to suspect Minos of abusive behaviour? And much might be forgiven of a man fighting terminal illness and looking death in the face, Alexio reminded himself with all the discomfiture of a young and healthy male.

'I feel unwell. Please excuse me,' Ione muttered chokily.

'Yes, go,' her father growled in a tone of disgust. 'You have already done your utmost to spoil our meal!'

Ione rose on knees that felt like jelly and left the room. Her head was pounding fit to burst and all courage was failing her. Alexio would agree to them living at the villa after their wedding. Why shouldn't he? Such an arrangement would be very convenient for him. After all, it would give him complete freedom and he wouldn't need to feel guilty about leaving her for long periods with her own family. Would there even *be* a honeymoon trip now? Alexio hadn't wanted to go to Paris in the first place and her father would soon persuade him that a honeymoon was a waste of business time and energy. Tears running down her convulsed face, Ione stumbled into her bathroom and stared at herself in the vanity mirror.

What an idiot she had been to believe that she could escape her father's control of every aspect of her life! He had been way ahead of her in the planning stakes and she had been stupid not to foresee that likelihood.

Ever since that letter from her twin sister had arrived within months of her eighteenth birthday, Ione's mail had been vetted and scrutinised. Her sibling, Misty, had wanted contact with her and Ione's father had been furious that the social services had unsealed the adoption records to aid such an approach to his adopted daughter without his consent. Ione had not been allowed to answer that letter and she only knew that her sister was or had been a Sicilian tycoon's mistress because that had evidently featured in a more recent newspaper story that had come to her father's notice. She had not seen that article herself. Her father had simply informed her that the sister she longed to be reunited with was a whore.

And ever since, Ione, far from recoiling in the disgust her father had hoped to evoke in her, had been just desperate to find her twin and help her. It had been no easy task for Ione to visualise a different life from that which she had always lived, but Misty had become her focus, her sole objective. Now she could see that goal receding further and further from her and she had no idea where to turn. Weary after the long stressful day and the effects of her own overtaxed emotions, Ione showered and slid into bed.

But her sleep was restless and peppered with confused dreams. Shards of old memories mingled with the disturbing events of the day and she tossed and turned.

* * *

As soon as his host retired, Alexio set off immediately to find Ione.

No longer did he marvel at his bride-to-be's startling offer to be whatever *he* wanted her to be. Over twenty years in the radius of her bullying father would wear down the strongest spirit, he conceded. Understandably the very idea of having to embark on their marriage on Lexos had filled her with horror. It was natural that Ione should want her own home, even more natural that she should want to see one of the most romantic cities in the world and enjoy the freedom that had until now been denied to her. But Ione *did* need to learn one fact. His expressive mouth quirked. He was not one of her father's employees, nor was he intimidated by him.

Ought he to warn her that Minos was still a very sick man and that, far from being on the road to recovery, there was only a small chance that further surgery would extend his life? Minos wanted neither his sister nor his daughter to know the truth. What right did he himself have to interfere? Yet how could he remain silent?

A maid led him to the door of Ione's suite. He rapped on the door, waited a moment and then strode into the spacious sitting room. For a bemused moment, he thought he had walked into a toyshop for there were soft toys everywhere he looked. On shelves, on seats, grouped round tables. Teddy bears. Giant bears, medium-sized bears and small bears, some fluffy and hairy but most of them pitiful specimens, whose garments could not conceal the awful truth that they were as ancient and as bald as coots. Pinned to the spot for an instant by the onslaught of all those watching beady eyes, Alexio suppressed a groan. He was hoping the bears didn't want to travel too.

The bedroom door was open and the lamps were lit, but it was a low-pitched gasp that recaptured his attention. He strode over to the threshold. Even though it was barely eleven, Ione was in bed fast asleep. Bloody typical, was his first thought, for when did a woman ever do what you expected her to do? He had assumed that he would find her distraught and in floods of tears, but she had simply gone to bed as though the sight of her father and her bride-groom almost coming to blows over her hadn't caused her an ounce of concern!

As she shifted position a shining loop of silk pale blonde hair uncoiled and fanned across the pillows and Alexio's ruminations found a more intimate focus. She had really beautiful hair and it was much longer than he had realised. And, although her appalling dress sense by day appeared to have stopped dead somewhere around thirty years before she had even been born, by night she wore the barest minimum of peach silk that clung to every lis-som curve. His attention lingering on the pouting swell of her small breasts as she arched her back in turning over, he decided he could live with maybe *one* bear.

Only as her sleep-flushed face turned towards him did he see the tracks of tears marking her fair skin, the tension still etched in her fine features. She shifted her head back and forth on the pillow while her fingers plucked at the linen sheet beneath her restive hand and her soft lips parted on a long, sighing moan of fear.

In her dream, Ione was back at the beach, her arms gripped in an imprisoning hold so that she was forced to watch every blow that Yannis withstood. She was trapped and so was he, but the responsibility was *hers* alone. Only her father could have ordered such a brutal punishment. Only her father could have instructed that his henchmen make her witness the devastation that her rebellion had unleashed.

Powerless to intervene, willing Yannis to stay down instead of stumbling upright again to invite another sickening punch from the two men set on inflicting the maximum possible damage on their victim, she flung her head and she started to scream. Over and over again, she screamed knowing that someone from the village would eventually come running, knowing that it was her only hope of bringing the brutal beating to an end.

As she came bolt upright in the bed on the back of that shrill scream her eyes flew wide and settled full of fear on the very tall, dark male shadowing her bed.

Alexio unfroze and came down on the edge of the bed in one forceful, fluid movement to close a strong arm around her. 'It was only a nightmare.'

Tremors of distress still trammelling through her slight frame, Ione jerked back from him and gasped in stricken disagreement, 'It *happened*... Yannis was beaten to a pulp!'

Unused to rejection, Alexio had stiffened, and at the mention of another man's name his lean, strong face set in formidable lines. 'What happened?' he prompted nonetheless, the need to know overruling all else.

But Ione had surfaced from her sleep-induced bewilderment and even as she bit back a sob she was wondering what Alexio was doing in her bedroom and endeavouring to pull herself together. It had been a long time since she had dreamt of that afternoon. Ione had learned in childhood to put distressing events behind her. What she could not influence, she had to tolerate.

As she flung herself back down on the tumbled pillows and flipped onto her side pale golden hair shiny as a child's obscured her drawn profile.

'What happened?' Alexio repeated as a shuddering sob tensed her again and he curved a soothing hand to her slender spine.

'I met up with Yannis secretly and Papa had him beaten up while I watched,' she whispered shakily. 'They laughed while they did it.'

Taken aback, Alexio snatched in a stark breath.

Ione shifted her head so that the glossy blonde hair tumbled back from her flushed triangular face, and unexpectedly stormy green eyes collided with his. 'He loved me and they nearly killed him for it.'

Alexio did not like what he was hearing, but other more primal responses were dulling the edge of that awareness. She was a study of unalloyed sensuality with her bright eyes and her full pink mouth and rumpled hair. Shoestring straps dissected her slim white shoulders and a fine wisp of silk defined her narrow ribcage and the provocative swell of her breasts. He hardened in urgent male response, sexual hunger flaming through him like an almost painful shot of adrenalin.

'Aren't you going to tell me that all Greek fathers have a duty to protect their daughter's virtue?' Ione pressed.

'No and not in such a way. But what future could a Gakis have with a fisherman's son?' Alexio enquired with lethal cool.

'Yannis was in his last year of med school and I had known him all my life,' Ione told him defensively.

While Alexio's intelligence warned him that the bad news about the fisherman's son was building to intolerable heights, he was simultaneously battling with a powerful urge to haul her into his arms caveman-style and imprint himself so powerfully on her that there would not be a thought in her head that did not centre solely on him.

The silence lay thick and heavy.

Ione meshed with molten-gold eyes enhanced by inky black lashes and the sudden burn of his gaze tautened her every sinew. Mouth running dry, she felt her heart thump

like a trapped bird inside her as her body betrayed her.
Her breasts were heavy with swollen and sensitive peaks.
Heat pulsed through her in a heady tide and settled with
a disturbing burn of awareness between her tensed thighs.

He bent over her, lifted a lean hand and let long brown
fingers slide through her tumbled hair and curve to her
cheek. Heart thundering and out of breath, she stared up
at him, scanning his darkly handsome features: the proud
jut of his nose, the slumbrous light in his gaze, the dark
shadow of roughness accentuating his aggressive jawline
and the lure of that wide, sexy mouth. Deep down in secret
places she could feel herself melting like ice cream on a
hot pavement and the pulse of excitement growing ever
more powerful.

'You haven't even asked me what I'm doing in here,'
Alexio chided huskily. 'I came to talk to you. I didn't
expect you to be in bed at this hour.'

Ione swept up her hand and let her fingertips glance in
an uncertain foray over the luxuriant black hair above his
brow. Her own hunger electrified and terrified her, but she
wanted to dig her fingers in and drag him down to her and
taste his sensual mouth again for herself. He caught her
trembling hand in his and flashed her a shimmering smile
of anticipation. 'If I touch you, I'll stay, but I believe that
we should wait for our wedding night.'

Hot, chagrined colour flooded Ione's slanted cheekbones. He spoke as though *she* had invited him to share
her bed and her pride was as stung as her thoughts were
in confusion. 'I—'

'Shush.' Brilliant golden eyes gleaming with very male
satisfaction, he studied her as if she already belonged to
him heart and soul and, smiling that heart-stopping smile,
he rested a silencing fingertip against her parted lips. 'I'm

flattered that you should be as eager as I am, but waiting always enhances the pleasure.'

As Alexio strode out of her bedroom Ione experienced a spasm of rage strong enough to deprive her of all breath and reason for several painful seconds. How *dared* he think that she would offer herself to him like some love-lorn, brainless wanton? How *dared* he assume that a momentary and slight desire to be kissed was the equivalent of an invitation to share her bed?

Alexio strolled back to his own suite at his leisure and smiled, thinking that marriage wasn't going to be so bad. Ione had been so deprived of freedom by her father that life with a tolerant and generous husband could only shine in comparison. He would not have to turn handstands to keep her content. And unless he was very much mistaken he had been blessed with a bride as hot-blooded as he was himself. Although he ached from the bite of a sexual restraint he was rarely forced to exercise, he was wholly confident that their wedding night would more than make up for that suffering...

CHAPTER FOUR

On Ione's wedding day eleven days later, a mysterious box wrapped in elegant gold paper was brought to her.

'Alexio's wedding gift.' Kalliope dealt her niece an impatient look. 'Well, open it up!'

Ione regarded the box with superstitious dread. She did not *want* to receive a present from the bridegroom whom she was planning to abandon within hours of their wedding! She had got nothing for him, had not even thought of an exchange of presents. Their marriage was only a cold-blooded business deal to be finalised in the church. Why was Alexio trying to personalise their relationship?

In exasperation, her aunt opened the box herself and lifted out an oval leather jewel case. Ione reached out in haste to take charge of the case. She flipped up the lid to expose a delicate emerald necklace adorned with fine diamond drops. It was exquisite but it meant nothing, she told herself. Alexio was simply going through the motions of what he believed was expected of him.

Kalliope frowned. 'Why that big box for that small case?'

Ione saw the edges of the tissue paper protruding from the carton and spread the paper back. Her heart missed a beat in shock when she saw the second gift. With reluctant hands, she lifted out the teddy bear that still bore the label of a world-famous auction house. He was a rare bear almost a hundred years old and he had a wonderfully expressive face. Her strained eyes misted with tears. Cosmas would have loved him.

'As if you needed another one of those things!' Kalliope exclaimed in astonished disappointment. 'Does your bridegroom think that you are still a little girl?'

Ione's brother had bought her teddy bears on his every trip abroad. After his death, she could not have made herself part with a single member of her collection for each and every one held a special memory of the big brother she had adored.

'Alexio would be well served if you took the toy to bed with you tonight instead of him!' Kalliope pronounced with earthy amusement. 'But he's clever and what a charmer he is. He knows how to touch a woman's heart. Who would credit that this marriage is only a business alliance arranged by your father?'

Face burning, Ione set the bear aside, struggling to regain her composure after that crack about sharing a bed with Alexio. That acid final comment from her aunt helped to speed up the process. Still tense as a bowstring, Ione looked in the mirror and twitched her short lace veil back into place. She had intended to allow Kalliope to choose her wedding dress. But when her aunt had demonstrated a desire to send her down the aisle weighted down with frills, bows and petticoats, she had changed her mind. After all, why *should* she appear before hundreds of people looking like a complete fright?

Her gown was a slender elegant sheath with a boat neckline and short sleeves and the very simplicity of cut flattered her diminutive height. Her wedding was a sham though, she reminded herself, and the gift of the bear merely proof that Alexio was worthy of his very bad reputation. Her chin came up. What womaniser had ever been successful without charm?

An hour later as the limo drew up outside the substantial church built by her father to celebrate her brother's birth almost thirty years earlier, Ione was no longer so sanguine. Her three bridesmaids were youthful distant cousins and virtual strangers to her. When the teenagers had expressed their surprise at the lack of the usual observances in advance of Ione's wedding, Kalliope had silenced them with an angry reproof. But the week before a Greek wedding *was* normally a social whirl of custom and fun experiences for the bride and her attendants. However, Minos Gakis had refused to allow his sister to fill the villa with female guests. Ione had been relieved, but she knew that her aunt had been very disappointed.

Sunlight gleaming over his proud dark head, Alexio was waiting on the church steps with a bouquet of flowers for her. Her heart hammered and her mouth ran dry. It was not a tradition she had expected him to observe and, immaculate in his well-cut dark suit, he looked spectacularly handsome. As she climbed out of the car his dark golden eyes raked over her with frank appreciation.

'Five minutes and counting,' Alexio teased under the voluble cover of the crowd of islanders calling out good wishes to them both. His keen gaze absorbing her taut pallor, he wondered if it was the prospect of the crammed church and the novelty of being the centre of attention that was making her so nervous.

It was a beautiful church and some of Ione's earliest memories were of her worship there as a child. Alexio's *koumbaros* or best man was his friend, Petros, and the other man carried out his duties with appropriate gravity. The service began with the elderly robed cleric blessing the exchange of rings and recognising their betrothal. Both bride and groom held a lit candle and Alexio linked his right hand with hers. Ione was trembling. With solemnity, they were crowned with orange blossom and then blessed by the priest. The timeless words of the ceremony roused her deepest and guiltiest misgivings.

As they sipped in turn from the wine that symbolised the sharing of all that life would bring, Alexio covered her hand with his, to steady her precarious hold on the cup. Ione was ghost-pale and she and her bridegroom circled the low table on which the bible rested and the guests showered them with rose petals and rice. The crowns removed, they were proclaimed man and wife.

'I thought you were about to faint,' Alexio breathed with visible concern as he urged her with all-male purpose through the crowds outside and straight into the limousine awaiting them. 'Are you all right?'

'I'm f-fine,' Ione stammered, fighting to suppress the uneasy feelings that had almost overpowered her during the service. What was done was done and there was no going back, she reasoned. Her hands knotted on her lap as she willed the driver to ferry them back to the villa at speed. The less time she spent alone with Alexio the happier she would be.

'You look very lovely,' Alexio commented.

'Thank you,' Ione muttered in a stifled voice.

'It's unfortunate that you couldn't meet my family before our wedding,' Alexio remarked. 'Is your father always so reluctant to entertain?'

'I'm afraid so.' Her father had no time for polite social courtesies and, as his sole interest in the Christoulakis family was Alexio, he wouldn't care if he had offended all of his son-in-law's relatives. She almost apologised on her parent's behalf until it occurred to her that, before very long, the Christoulakis family would have rather more embarrassing news with which to deal: her *desertion* of their son. Her heart sank and her tummy clenched.

When Alexio's parents and his sisters were the first to

approach her with warm smiles at the villa, Ione could not meet their eyes and did not know what she said in response to their friendly overtures. Her father signalled her from several feet away and, with a muttered apology, she hurried to his side.

Minos Gakis settled cold eyes on his daughter. 'You didn't smile once in the church. Make a better showing here before I lose patience with you.'

Just thinking that soon she would never have to cringe from such veiled threats again strengthened Ione. But an arm curved round her rigid spine and a rich, dark drawl sounded in her ear as Alexio murmured smooth as glass, 'But I have a lot of patience.'

Her father loosed a derisive bark of laughter. 'You'll need it, Ione may yet surprise you.'

At that crack, which Ione interpreted as a warning stab at the need to keep her illegitimate birth a secret, she coloured. As her father strode off Alexio's hold on her slight frame tightened and he looked down at her with pleated dark brows. 'Why is your father always so angry with you? What happened to create such a division between you?'

'We've just never been that close,' Ione muttered awkwardly, pained and embarrassed that he should question her on such a subject, for the strong bonds of affection between Alexio and his own family had been obvious even in the brief interaction she had witnessed.

Absorbing her downbent blonde head and her evasive manner, Alexio's brilliant eyes hardened. Why had Minos forecast that Ione might yet surprise him? Why was his bride acting as guilty as sin itself? It could only be something to do with the fisherman's son. That covert relationship was the most likely cause of the gulf between father and daughter. So why was she still dreaming about another man more than two years after the event?

Whatever, Alexio was already questioning his own protective and forgiving tolerance. She was a Gakis, he reminded himself. Any woman with the guts to defy Minos was no shrinking wallflower. Yet Ione had behaved throughout their wedding ceremony as though she were an early Christian martyr watching the bonfire being built.

During the luncheon that followed many speeches were made. Then came a lengthy performance from a famous singer and there was little opportunity for conversation between bride and groom. But by then even Ione had noticed the distinct chill that Alexio was exuding. Intelligence informed her that that was good, indeed even convenient in the circumstances, for it kept their interaction to the absolute minimum. Yet for some reason she could not content herself with that belief, could not prevent herself from sneaking anxious glances at him every chance she got and could not resist an inexplicable urgent need to rectify the situation.

'I never thanked you for the necklace…or the teddy bear,' Ione said uneasily half under her breath.

'Gratitude not required,' Alexio drawled.

'I didn't get anything for you…I didn't think,' Ione admitted, striving to understand why she had got into such a pointless dialogue and failing.

'I got you, didn't I?' Alexio countered with pronounced dryness.

As Ione glanced warily up at him, green eyes widening, the sheer strain stamped in her fragile features shook him. With a sharp pang of discomfiture, he remembered her telling him that she could be anything he wanted her to be. Only she wasn't accustomed to crowds and, thanks to her father's policy of keeping her at home, she knew hardly anybody. Yet, there was hardly a guest in the room who had not stared and stared at her simply because she was who she was: the Gakis heiress, whom precious few had seen before and even fewer knew anything about. Small wonder that she had been sick with nerves at the church and she needed reassurance, *not* censure.

Alexio closed his hand over her tense fingers and cradled them in his. 'This is a special day. Let's enjoy it,' he urged huskily.

His beautiful dark golden eyes connected with hers and her mind went blank as her breath caught in her throat. What he had said barely registered. She was conscious only of the warmth of his much larger hand engulfing hers and her own surge of relief that he had ditched his forbidding cool. Indeed, for a moment, she felt quite dizzy with the strength of that relief.

Alexio watched her pupils dilate, her cheeks blossom with colour and her lush pink mouth form into a tremulous smile, and felt like a very powerful magician. *Finally*, she was looking at him as a bride ought to look at her new husband. Almost imperceptibly she leant closer, her soft lips parting, and he released her hand to give a gentle teasing tug to the straying strand of pale blond hair brushing her cheekbone and waken her back to a sense of their surroundings.

'Later, *yineka mou*,' he promised huskily.

A split second after that, his best man, Petros, intervened. Grasping Ione's hand, the younger man urged her out of her seat and led her out onto the dance floor. There she hovered, staring back at Alexio while Petros marshalled guests into forming two circles around her. As the efficient Petros started off the dancing by signalling the band, traditional music filled the room and those in the circle got down on one knee to begin clapping. Still mesmerised by Alexio's eyes, Ione was more aware of the rapid thunder of her own heartbeat and a bubbling, unfamiliar sense of lightheartedness.

Alexio rose in one lithe motion, clapping in time with the music. He really *was* so beautiful he made her ache, she conceded helplessly, her bright gaze welded to his lean, strong features. In fact every time she looked at Alexio, he seemed to get more gorgeous, and he had been more generous in response to her awkward behaviour. But then how could he know *why* she had been so silent and strained? As her conscience again threatened her composure she locked it out and found it simplest just to watch Alexio.

When the last of the guests had completed the obligatory circling of the bride, Alexio folded Ione into his arms to dance. Kalliope smashed a plate on the floor, encouraging those at the top table to follow suit. Alexio winced at the racket, caught an amusing glimpse of his refined mother forcing herself to follow Kalliope's lead and laughed. '*Very* traditional.'

Ione turned her blushing face into a wide shoulder, for the smashing of crockery signified good luck, happiness and the permanence of marriage.

'While everybody is otherwise engaged...' Alexio curved a purposeful hand to the nape of her neck to tip back her head.

'Yes?' Ione met his smouldering golden scrutiny. Her mouth ran dry and she tensed. Suddenly the exuberant raised voices and the noise of breaking crockery receded from her awareness, leaving only the racing thump of her own heartbeat thrumming in her ears.

'I want to kiss my bride...' Alexio imparted, whirling her in one dexterous move behind one of the pillars in the grand ballroom and pressing her back against it.

Excitement claimed Ione even before he touched her. A wild leap of longing thrilled through her as he spread her back against the unyielding stone surface. He was all masculine mastery and cool but for the flare of hunger in his brilliant eyes. Arching her spine, tilting her head back was instinctive.

'...and my bride wants to kiss me,' Alexio savoured with lancing satisfaction, claiming her parted lips with a hot, urgent immediacy that took her breath away and sent her senses spinning.

The plunge of his tongue inside the sensitive interior of her mouth made her cling to him, dig her fingers into his broad shoulders and tremble. Her whole body felt hot and tight and charged. His sexual intensity electrified her. A flame fired low in her pelvis and the resulting rise of need provoked a stifled moan from her. She pushed forward into him, automatically seeking closer connection with his big, powerful frame. In a sudden movement, he was there, one hard hand curving to her hips to urge her into contact with his potent arousal while the forceful demand of his mouth sent her head back against the wall. Her senses sang, exhilarated by the raw, masculine strength and feel of him, the explosive hunger that answered her own.

When Alexio jerked back from her with a muttered curse word, dark colour scored his hard cheekbones and his molten gaze flared into hers only for a split second. She was pale, visibly shaken, wide eyes evading his and veiling. Alexio was so furious with himself that he almost punched the wall in frustration. Pinning his tiny virginal bride to a pillar and coming on to her as if he wanted to take her on the spot was downright crude. But when her lush, soft mouth had opened under his with such shy invitation, the force of his own hunger had almost overwhelmed him.

'I'm sorry,' he said flatly. 'Did I hurt you?'

Ione was so ashamed of herself, she couldn't even look him in the face. She shook her head in answer and she wanted to sink through the floor. *He* had pulled back from *her*, probably in surprise at the wanton way she had urged him on in a public place. It wasn't his fault. Men were useless at resisting temptation, which was why women were supposed to stay in control, Ione thought, cringing over her own behaviour. Pure lust had grabbed her and swept her away.

'Excuse me…' she framed in a mortified whisper and fled.

Assailed by all the stark annoyance of a male who prided himself on his every move around her sex, Alexio gave vent to his feelings and punched the wall. Flexing his bruised knuckles in the aftermath, he glanced up to see his father poised only feet away.

Sander Christoulakis spread rueful, expressive hands and grimaced. 'I know I shouldn't interfere…'

Then don't. Alexio ground his teeth together in outraged silence.

'But Ione's a shy little thing, *not* the kind of woman you're used to,' Sander pronounced in a tone of reproach. 'Treat her with respect.'

Ione headed for the library, which was one of her favourite retreats, but she hesitated outside the ajar door when she heard voices within.

'Ione's so drab…poor Alexio!' a youthful female voice was lamenting. 'This marriage is a tragedy. I bet my brother thinks he's never going to fall in love again after Crystal but he'll be bored and miserable with Ione and he'll end up taking a mistress.'

'Knowing your brother, probably *more* than one!' her

companion giggled. 'Do you realise that I've seen at least four women here that are exes of his?'

Alexio's kid sister, Delphia, was the first speaker and the other girl probably one of her pals. Ione remembered her aunt enquiring after Alexio's youngest sister. His fifteen-year-old sibling had been a late-born surprise when he and his other sister had been in their teens. He had smiled and confessed that Delphia was spoilt rotten by all of them. Ione had wondered then what it felt like to be spoilt rotten.

Drab? Well, she thought wryly, on a day when she was so much on show there had been good reason for her to maintain her usual unadventurous appearance. But that evening for the first time she would be stepping out wearing fashionable clothes and she was pretty sure that even a best friend, had she been allowed to retain one, wouldn't recognise her as Ione Gakis.

As for what Delphia had forecast? Out of the mouths of babes, Ione reflected with pained cynicism. Were she to stay married to Alexio, he would inevitably stray in search of more exciting conquests and she would be expected to turn a blind eye to his infidelity and be grateful for what small share she had of his attention. As long as he was discreet, as long as he did not divorce her and break up their family, few would think the worse of him for betraying her. She knew the rules of their society and it was still very much a man's world. Hadn't she grown up watching her mother pretend ignorance of her father's extra-marital forays?

What on earth had come over her during the past hour? With hindsight, she was aghast at her own weak-minded foolishness. All Alexio had had to do was reach for her hand and there she had been hanging on his every word and gazing at him as though he had just stepped down from heaven to grace her with his presence! She had even been dumb enough to get a sexual thrill out of being flattened against a pillar like some willing tart in a dark doorway. She lashed herself with that image. She had acted like an idiot.

Yet what might their marriage have been like had he *loved* her? That thought crept in, rebelling against her need to stifle it. But then what did a male like Alexio Christoulakis really *know* about love? Women had always fallen at his feet in large numbers.

Crystal Denby had been a sexy, provocative challenge, a tease and a flirt, who had played him at his own game until he'd finally given her an engagement ring. But had Crystal survived, would he ever actually have got around to *marrying* her? For Alexio was so essentially Greek. In his heart he really wanted to marry a virgin. And in a few hours' time, he would also expect his bride to spread herself happily across the marital bed even though she barely knew him. A sensitive guy? Throw her a teddy bear and jump her. About as sensitive as concrete laced with steel.

Although the reception would go on into the early hours of the morning, Ione went off to get changed. Her maid had laid out a green dress and jacket, the essential suit chosen by Kalliope, and Ione removed her wedding gown and put in on. Her heartbeat speeded up as she went into the dressing room to lift out the small attaché case stowed at the back of one of the wardrobes.

In the act of leaving her bedroom, she paused and glanced back at the forlorn teddy bear abandoned on the bed. The bear Alexio had given her. His name was Edward. It had said so on his label and he was an English bear, so didn't he deserve to go home to England with her? Biting her lip in indecision, she studied the rest of her bear collection and then hurried over to the bed, unlocked the attaché case and squashed Edward in.

Alexio watched his bride come down the main staircase. The suit was out of the ark in design but the shade enhanced her delicate colouring and nothing could conceal the grace of her slender figure. His whole body tensed on the hard, heavy rise of desire and raw exasperation flashed through him. What was it about her? Or was it the perverse knowledge that she was *his* now, his in a way that no other woman had ever been? He only knew that she excited him more than any woman had in a long time.

And he couldn't wait to take her shopping in Paris. A faint smile played over his wide, sensual mouth. He was already picturing the innocent pleasure she would find in a whole host of things that he and all the women he had ever known took for granted. He strode forward to greet her, but her aunt and her father and a vociferous clutch of guests demanded her attention.

Within twenty minutes they were boarding the helicopter that would drop them off at the airport. In a sudden movement, Ione turned back to Alexio, her profile taut. 'Will you ask the pilot to fly over the island first?'

'If that's what you want.' Alexio was surprised. Having witnessed enough throughout the day to confirm his suspicion that Ione appeared to rate little higher than the domestic staff in the eyes of her father and her aunt, he had somehow assumed that she would leave the island without a backward glance. He was too much of a cynic, he told himself. Naturally she was attached to her family.

As the pilot flew over Lexos, Ione gazed down at her home. Now that it would no longer be her prison, she could think of it as her home again and recall the good memories that in more recent years she had almost forgotten. She was leaving everything she possessed behind and she knew she would never see any of it again. Her father would never forgive her. He would have no need to do so with Alexio as his son-in-law.

'I hope you like my house in Paris,' Alexio remarked as they walked towards his private jet at the airport. 'It's…unusual.'

'I saw a magazine article on it once.' Had Ione's nerves not been jumping like electrified beans by that stage, she might have smiled at his selection of that particular word. In that magazine spread, Crystal Denby had been arranged on a sofa shaped like a giant pair of scarlet lips. There had been jazzy purple wallpaper in the background, an animal skin fur at her feet and enormous gilded blackamoor torcheres burning to either side of her. A quite unforgettable image of the sex kitten at home, Ione conceded. He had allowed his former fiancée to turn a gracious seventeenth century townhouse into the tasteless and showy equivalent of a bordello.

'Are you always this quiet?' Alexio enquired when the jet was airborne.

Ione pretended to stifle a yawn and sighed. 'I'm sorry…I'm so sleepy.'

When she appeared to drift off to sleep within minutes, Alexio resisted an ungenerous urge to shake her awake again. It *had* been a long day for her. Things could only get better; well, they could hardly get worse. He had almost forgotten what her voice sounded like. She shied away from his smallest touch and her beautiful eyes would not meet his. Possibly he deserved that, but it seemed to him that the young woman who had touched him with her confession that she wanted to marry him more than anything else in the world had suffered a distinct change of heart. And Alexio, who had never in his thirty years of existence had to make an effort to hold the attention of a woman, really didn't know how to handle that.

As Ione climbed out of the limo outside the Paris townhouse, she was so pale and tense that Alexio was afraid that a sudden movement might shatter her to pieces like glass.

'Are you feeling OK?' Alexio was amazed at how keen he was to hear that she was feeling dreadful. Illness he could cope with. Illness would explain everything.

'G-great...' Ione stammered like a schoolgirl, gripping her little case with tense fingers.

Alexio took a deep breath and lifted her off her feet into his arms. She loosed a startled cry as if she were under attack and strained green eyes finally met his in a head-on collision as he looked down at her. 'What are you doing?'

'Carrying you over the threshold.'

'Why...why are you doing that?' Ione gasped, clutching her case from beneath the lid of which Alexio could now see an edge of tartan ribbon protruding. Edward's ribbon. Out of all the rest of those bears, she had brought *his* gift with her. At a moment when he was in need of encouragement, it was a welcome revelation.

'It's an English custom. Your mother was English,' Alexio murmured gently.

The mere mention of England was sufficient to paralyse Ione. Both her natural mother and her adoptive mother might have been English, but all Ione could think about was the reality that she was planning to run off to London that same evening. As her colour fluctuated and her eyes veiled Alexio surveyed her with a questioning look.

He set her down in a spacious hall. A magnificent art

deco table sat in the centre, embellished with a glorious arrangement of white lilies.

'I believe the staff are ready to serve dinner.' Alexio cast open the door of a dining room furnished in similar style.

At even the mention of food, Ione's tummy churned. She had little more than two and a half hours left in which to get back to the airport.

'I'd like to freshen up,' she said tightly, unable to bring herself to look at him.

Alexio took her upstairs and showed her into the master bedroom suite. With a decor of dull gold and green and traditional furniture, it stood out like a major statement from what she had so far seen of the rest of the house. Ione understood. Since Crystal's death, he had had it re-decorated.

'I'll leave you…' But Alexio hovered and reached without warning for her clenched hands, forcing her to let go of the small case. '*Look* at me…'

'That's better,' he said.

Her mouth running dry, she connected with brilliant dark golden eyes and trembled. Her surging emotions threatened her superficial hold on her composure. He released one hand to brush a fine strand of blonde hair back from her brow. His long brown fingers surprisingly gentle. At the touch of him, a frisson of piercing awareness gripped Ione and her legs wobbled. Her nostrils flared on the already familiar male scent of him: husky and warm overlaid with a faint hint of some aromatic lotion.

She wanted more. Standing there quivering at that moment, she knew she wanted him as she had not known she could want any man. For she wanted Alexio against all reason, caution and self-preservation. Her nipples were swollen, sensitive buds pushing against the cups of her bra, and at the heart of her she was liquid with longing. Shame swept over her, shame that he could already have that much power over her.

He kissed her long and slow and deep and it was an entire banquet of sweet, sensual sensation. The stroke of his tongue within her mouth was unbearably exciting. The reality that no other part of their bodies touched only heightened her craving for the hard muscularity of him against her softer curves. Low in her throat, she heard herself moan, for the hunger tearing at her grew more powerful with every subtle movement of his sensual mouth on hers.

'I'll see you downstairs.' Freeing her, Alexio stepped back, hard cheekbones taut, smouldering golden eyes burning over the feverish flush on her triangular face with blatant male appreciation.

She moved back with unsteady abruptness and her shoulder blades met the solid wall and took support from it. She didn't want him to go. She wanted him to stay. Shock and fear of the unknown person that had surfaced inside her held her rigid. She stared at him, mesmerised by his lean, hard features; the play of light and shadow over his stunning eyes and chiseled cheekbones, the hard strength and command stamped into every angular line of his bronzed face.

Dragging her attention from him almost physically hurt and it took every ounce of her will-power. She deserved *better* than such a marriage, she reasoned in a frantic, feverish argument with herself. She deserved to be more than part of a callous business deal. And if she stayed, if she surrendered to the weak and dangerous promptings of her own heart, she would fall in love with Alexio Christoulakis and any hope of living her own life and any real prospect of finding happiness would be at an end.

She was a naive pushover for a male as sophisticated and sexually intense as Alexio. But that was only because she had no true experience of other men. Her sad little flirtation with Yannis scarcely counted. In fact, what she was suffering from now was probably no more than an intoxicating rush of physical curiosity and too many hormones in her bloodstream.

What she could not afford to forget was the *kind* of male Alexio was. A powerful Greek tycoon, who by their marriage would become all the more powerful. He had already acquired a name for ruthlessness that had been sufficient to impress her father. He would be no less ruthless when it came to his private life. For only a little while would she be a novelty, for she did not have what it would take to hold such a man. Neither the traffic-stopping beauty, nor the adventurous personality, not even the sexual expertise that would grip his attention for longer. If she stayed with Alexio, he would destroy her as surely as her father had destroyed her mother.

Her strength of purpose recaptured, Ione slipped out of the room to search for the most promising exit from the townhouse. After a nerve-racking exploration of the upper two floors she came back to the master suite in despair and only then discovered that a fire escape ran from the bathroom window down to an alleyway far below. Locking the door, she stripped and changed into the outfit in her attaché case. She left the note she had prepared. The transformation she achieved was done at speed, for she knew that she had little time left before either Alexio or one of the staff came to remind her about dinner.

Her heart was literally in her mouth as she opened the window, turned her back on the drop that terrified her out of her wits and climbed out. Her legs dangled before her feet finally connected with the small wrought-iron platform below the sill. She felt with damp palms for the balustrade. Rigid with fear, she descended the metal steps, edging round each landing to the next level while struggling to see where she was going without looking down. On solid ground again, she staggered and then, even though her legs were still shaking and she felt sick as a dog with nerves and fright, she forced herself to run.

Alexio was on the brink of going upstairs when Tipo, the burly head of Ione's protection team, appeared in the hall and rushed past him to head up there himself.

Minos had insisted that Ione would be at risk without round-the-clock protection. Alexio had considered four security men a quite excessive number for such a task until his father-in-law had admitted that he had had recent serious threats made against him. Well aware of how many enemies the older man had, Alexio had realised that his bride might indeed be in danger. On their honeymoon, she would be much more accessible than her parent on his private island.

'Where are you going?' Alexio was annoyed that his decree that the bodyguards must remain unobtrusive was already being disregarded. After all, what possible harm could come to Ione in his home while he was present?

'A window alarm went off up here!' the thickset older man called back and he was already talking into his handset to the rest of his team.

His lean, powerful face set in thunderous lines, Alexio reached the top landing in a couple of strides and went straight into the master bedroom where he expected to find that Ione had fallen asleep on the bed. Seeing the bathroom door closed instead, he knocked on it, outraged at the hue and cry being roused and the invasion of their privacy.

That fool of a man might have burst into the room while Ione was undressing!

'I'll break the door down,' Tipo offered.

'Ione?' Ignoring the bodyguard, Alexio rapped on the door a second time and then, motivated by genuine concern that his wife might have gone to sleep in the bath, he put a big shoulder to the solid wood and forced the lock.

'She's done a runner.' Drawing level with Alexio, Tipo scowled at the open window and the discarded garments lying on the floor.

'I beg your pardon?' Alexio breathed.

'She'll be at the airport. We'll bring her back,' his companion informed him and walked away.

For the space of a minute, Alexio was in total disbelieving shock, but during that minute he was anything but inactive. He strode through every bedroom and shouted Ione's name over the bannister in case she was downstairs in one of the other reception rooms. He could not credit the concept that she had vanished. Momentarily, his mind refused to accept what struck him as an impossibility. But his next thought was that someone could have come up that fire escape and kidnapped her! Sick at the tide of threatening images bombarding him, Alexio raced back to the *en suite* bathroom to study it again.

This time he noticed the sheet of paper wedged by one corner beneath the mirror. Even from the doorway he was able to read it.

'I'm sorry but I couldn't stay. Ione.'

Not a ransom note? A note from Ione herself. Alexio stared at it with fixed attention, striving to dig something out of that single sentence that might make the remotest sense to him. He reached the hall again in five seconds flat. Tipo was already barrelling out the front door.

'What the hell is going on?' Alexio demanded.

'You can trust us to handle this. Mr Gakis would like you to call him.'

At that suggestion, Alexio might have said something very short and succinct had he not been too preoccupied to waste the time. His bride had walked out on him...*why*? An image of her white, scared face flashed into his mind. Throughout the day, Ione had been a bag of nerves and evidently she had been a lot more distressed than he had appreciated.

Tipo cleared his throat. 'Mr Gakis wants us to fly his daughter home to the island where he can look after her.'

Raw outrage flashed through Alexio's lean, taut length with energising force. 'My wife is a Christoulakis and *I* will look after her!'

Three minutes later, Alexio climbed into his sports car. Determined to reach the airport in advance of Tipo and his bully boys, he used every short cut he knew. He was on automatic pilot because on one level he still could not accept that Ione could have done something so outrageous as leave him before the ink was even dry on their marriage licence. She had been scared. What of? *Him?* An incredulous laugh of dismissal started in his throat and then died there as he recalled the manner in which she had run from him earlier in the day.

He had had the dim idea that terrified virgins died out along with long skirts and clothed piano legs but Ione had had a rather strange upbringing, he acknowledged, striving to understand the incomprehensible. And then it dawned on him that Ione might have fled because she was *not* the wholly inexperienced bride he had been led to expect and that she might be afraid that her bridegroom would create hell over that discovery. As he mulled over what he had already learned about the fisherman's son Alexio's hard profile took on a forbidding cast. He reckoned a *lack* of virginity was the more likely possibility.

His brilliant dark eyes were grim. So he was disappointed, but he was also appalled that the matter could have assumed such proportions in Ione's mind that the only solution she could see was walking out on their marriage. An unpleasant recollection of Ione quailing beneath the threat of her angry father's fist assailed him at that point. Fear of her bridegroom's reaction might well have had sufficient power to make his bride bolt. How was she to *know* that he wasn't like her father?

In spite of her success in making it to the airport and purchasing her ticket, an increasing sense of bewildering misery and uncertainty was weighing on Ione.

The flight to London was delayed but, although she could have gone through the gates to wait in greater security and privacy, she had not yet been able to make herself take that final step. Having assumed that airports were very anonymous places, she was intimidated by the manner in which people seemed to be staring at her. Maybe she just looked odd. Maybe people could see how nervous and unhappy she was and were wondering what was the matter with her. It wasn't important, she told herself. Soon she would be in England and that much closer to finding her sister, Misty. Unfortunately that reflection did not bring the comfort she had believed it would.

What must Alexio think of her? That was all Ione could *really* think about: how Alexio must be feeling. He had to have found out by now that she had gone. He would not understand why she had disappeared. How could he? He would simply think that she was crazy. Would he feel hurt? His pride would certainly be hurt. He would curse the day he had first met her, for in no way did he deserve the shame and embarrassment her vanishing act would bring down on the Christoulakis family.

Alexio strode through the airport like a man on a mission. He checked the flight schedule. There was a flight to Greece in two hours. But *would* Ione go home to her irate parent? If not, where else would she go? She had had no close friends at their wedding. And then he recalled her discomfited reaction to his teasing reminder that her mother had been English. Of course, England. Surely she had to have some relatives there? The London flight had been due to take off in an hour but it was running late. He breathed a little easier.

Alexio saw Edward the bear before he recognized his wife. Her back turned to him, a young girl who looked like a teenager was gazing into a shop with a bear who might have been Edward's double tucked beneath her arm. Alexio stilled, his gaze welding to the glorious fall of platinum fair hair falling to the girl's waist. Ione? Could it be? In a chequer-board print skirt so tiny she should have been arrested for wearing it? Not to mention a pink crop top that exposed her bare midriff and absurd shoes with heels studded with stones that glittered?

Ione? Alexio was stunned, incredulous and awake to the reality that there was not a man within fifty yards failing to pay heed to her. He watched her stroll on to a magazine display and the slow, gliding walk was pure sex and Ione to the hilt. He saw her full face and snatched in a startled breath. The madonna perfection had been enhanced with cosmetics. She looked bloody spectacular, Alexio thought with a sudden stab of fury. He watched his wife produce an entire handful of high denomination currency to buy one little magazine. The guy on the stand was so entranced by the fairy-tale princess before him that he started to explain what the notes were.

A shy little thing, Sander had called her…

Having stuffed all the notes back into her miniature handbag as she moved away from the stand, Ione glanced up. When she saw Alexio, devastated disbelief stopped her in her tracks, for she could not imagine how he could have found her. He was only twenty feet away: very tall and dark and powerful, lean, strong face hard. Even before she clashed with his glittering golden gaze, her chest tightened and breathing became a severe challenge.

'What…w-what are you doing here?' she heard herself stammer foolishly.

'You are my wife,' Alexio breathed in a roughened undertone that was not quite steady.

And with those four words, he faced Ione with a reality that she had done virtually everything to avoid acknowledging. In the space of an instant, she was cast back to the outset of the day and the sombre and beautiful church service. For the first time an honest appreciation of what she had done crept up out of Ione's subconscious and overwhelmed her: she *had* married him.

In fact she had done even worse than that, her conscience told her. She had gone to great lengths to persuade Alexio that she could hardly wait to become his wife. In short, she had met his sincerity with deception and his honesty with evasion and lies. Ione, who had always prided herself on her moral values, was shattered by that belated reappraisal of her own behaviour.

'I don't know that to say…'

Alexio had plenty to say but sufficient self-control to know that a busy airport was not the place in which to give vent to his feelings. As to what those feelings were, he had not the slightest idea, for blistering anger had superseded all else. He closed a powerful hand to her wrist.

'You will explain yourself to me and then I will decide what *I* want to do.'

'Alexio…I—'

'Not a word until we have privacy,' Alexio grated with an explosive edge of his dark, deep voice.

Intercepting a poleaxed glance from a passing business-man lusting over his bride's scantily clad body, Alexio glowered at the offender in a righteous rage. Only nar-rowly overcoming an urge to remove his suit jacket and wrap Ione in it, he herded her into the nearest fashion shop instead.

Ione stood like a wooden image while Alexio swept a coat from the display and tossed it on the counter with a credit card. She was in shock. What on earth was he do-ing? And why was she letting him take control? He was her husband and as such deserving of a great deal more consideration than she had so far shown him. The guilt she was experiencing was now being followed by the strangest sensation of relief and acceptance.

The security tag removed, Alexio retrieved the coat and extended it to her. Embarrassed by the wide-eyed curiosity of the sales assistant, Ione dug reluctant arms into the sleeves. The raincoat was far too long for her and almost reached her ankles. But Alexio bent down and buttoned the coat right down to the last button in case it fell open.

'Why…?' Ione finally voiced her complete bewilder-ment.

'While you carry my name, you will not parade around in public dressed like a baby hooker!' Alexio informed her in a raw undertone in Greek, the vague suspicion that he might be overreacting stifled entirely by the fierce satis-faction he gained from covering every visible inch of her slender curves from the attention of other men.

Hot, mortified colour drenched Ione's pallor. A baby

hooker? How dare he? She was dressed in the height of fashion. He was just being cruel. But he was also betraying the exact same incredulous fury that her father would have exhibited had he seen her got up in such an outfit. She discovered at that moment that she could not keep a single thought in her head for longer than ten seconds. The sheer shock value of finally admitting to herself that Alexio Christoulakis was her husband seemed to have paralysed her brain cells.

He would take her to an airport hotel to talk, Alexio decided. Whatever happened, whatever she confessed, he would *not* lose his temper. But his intelligence was already drawing up scenarios that made him feel angrier than ever. Had he been a complete dupe? Was she *still* in love with the fisherman's son? What else was he to think when he found her at the airport dressed to kill and in no way resembling the shy and modest bride he had married? Had she run away to meet up with that bastard, Yannis, somewhere? On her terms had their marriage merely been an escape route from a domineering father determined to prevent her from being with a man of whom he disapproved?

CHAPTER FIVE

ONLY fifteen minutes later, Ione found herself standing in the centre of a large and luxurious hotel suite still clutching Edward, her bag and her attaché case.

'I want only the truth,' Alexio delivered with as near an approximation of level diction as he could manage, his lean, powerful frame rigid with tension as he awaited her explanation.

Ione gazed at him with a fast-beating heart, her attention roaming over his lean, dark, devastating face and the marks of strain there before going into guilty retreat. Her conscience almost slaughtered her. How could she tell him such a terrible truth? If he knew how utterly selfish and dishonest she had been he would never, ever forgive her. He would despise her for rewarding his integrity and trust with a tissue of unscrupulous lies and pretences. And it was only then, when she looked up and collided afresh with his scorching golden eyes, that she realised that she could not *bear* the idea of Alexio turning away from her in complete disgust. That second shattering piece of self-revelation shook her to her very depths.

In the humming silence, Alexio drew in a stark sustaining breath. 'Why don't you take your coat off?'

'I—'

'I'm your husband,' Alexio purred as he strode forward. Removing the bear and the bags from her, he tossed them aside. 'If a sudden attack of modesty didn't get to you in public, why should you shrink from displaying yourself to me?'

Ione was paralysed to the spot as lean, deft fingers dealt summarily with the buttons of her coat. Her frantic thoughts had gone into free fall when she'd registered that her biggest fear now was that Alexio would walk away. But her brain and her tongue would not unite, for registering that Alexio had mystifyingly become more important to her than her quest for her own sister and freedom filled her with stricken and genuine bewilderment. 'You said I looked like a baby hooker—'

'I was too kind.' Alexio flung the coat aside and stepped back to let his shimmering scrutiny wander at a leisurely pace over her.

Ione tensed even more beneath the surprising discovery that, when Alexio looked at her in that certain indefinable way, she felt half naked and horribly self-conscious. As his insolent appraisal rested on the upswell of her breasts, her nipples pinched tight and butterflies broke loose in her quivering tummy. He raked his scrutiny down to her sleek bare midriff and the tight little skirt that merely accentuated her slender shapely length of leg. He forced his attention back up again to her exquisite face, his big, powerful body taut and throbbing with sudden fierce but furious sexual hunger.

Inflamed with squirming discomfiture by that intimate reconnaissance of her figure, Ione felt like a slave on the block. She could hardly breathe and her heart was banging up against her breastbone in panic. Yet she could not dredge her dilated eyes from him or control the frisson of disturbing heat curling up from low in her pelvis.

'Silence doesn't become you in that outfit,' Alexio drawled with cutting candour. 'So, assuming that you weren't cruising in search of an illicit sexual thrill from a complete stranger on our wedding night…where *were* you going and why?'

Ione had no idea what to say, for she had already recognised that the truth was beyond the bounds of all forgiveness. 'I don't know...'

'You don't know,' Alexio repeated as he prowled round
the room like a lion ready to spring and then he flung back
his proud dark head, fixed her with eyes as hard as granite
and roared. 'What sort of an answer is that? This morning
we got married...this evening you sneaked down a fire
escape, got tarted up like a streetwalker and raced for the
airport! Now either you are in severe need of therapy or
you had a good reason for doing that!'

'I was going to fly to London.'

Alexio froze at that confirmation and marvelled at his
own incredible reluctance to accept the obvious. His strong
jawline clenched. Had he thought she had fled to the airport simply to watch big aeroplanes land?

'How did Tipo know that you would be at the airport?'
he demanded.

Ione gave him a shaken look. 'Tipo is *here*...in Paris?'

Alexio watched her pallor grow. Clear as day, he saw
her fear at the mere mention of the older man's name, but
his anger only hardened when he recognised his own instinctive stab of concern that that should be the case.

'I thought we were on our own here...' A weak little
laugh fell from Ione's dry mouth as her tummy somer-
saulted on a mental image of the treatment she would have
received had her father's henchmen found her first.

'I called you my wife but a woman who walks out
within hours of taking her wedding vows is *no* wife of
mine,' Alexio framed with biting clarity. 'However, I have
a right to know *who* you were planning to meet!'

'Meet?' Ione gave him a blank look, her mind still endeavouring to cope with that first grim statement. Of
course, he did not want such a wife. No man would want

such a wife. A wife without loyalty, decency or honesty. She cringed. What else could she expect? She had burnt her boats. A hollow shell-shocked feeling began to engulf her in the wake of that acceptance. She was still free, she tried to tell herself. Not being as naive as she had been at eighteen, she knew that her bodyguards could not force her to go anywhere against her will if she was ready to fight back with the threat of a public scene that might reach the newspapers. But somehow that reality was of little consolation.

'The truth!' Alexio thundered back at her in explosive frustration. 'I want the truth. Who is waiting to meet you in London?'

'No one…no one even knows I was going there,' Ione muttered, failing to catch his drift.

'Not even Yannis…?' Alexio prompted in a dark-timbred drawl that fairly bristled with incipient threat.

'Yannis?' Ione parroted in confusion. 'Why would I be meeting with Yannis after all this time? I don't even know where he lives.'

The silence hung there like a sheet of glass waiting to crash.

Still seething with brooding suspicion, Alexio studied her. All trust was gone. He had not thought her capable of what she had already done. Every time he took in another appraisal of her startlingly provocative appearance, he became more incensed. 'Ione may yet surprise you,' Minos had quipped. And Ione had. But Alexio would allow no woman to make a fool of him.

'If there's not another man involved, why were you heading for London?' Like a perfect living doll, he reflected, rating the fabulous hair, the stunning face, the delicate but shapely curves and perfect legs. Every guy's fantasy right down to the innocent look of anxious appeal in her huge green eyes. Only a bride who did a runner on their wedding night was not *his* fantasy.

'Of course there's not another man involved!' Ione was shocked that he could suspect her of such a thing and then flung into deeper shock by the recollection that she *had* been planning on finding a boyfriend, who kissed as he did. As if men were interchangeable objects and one was as good as another. As if their marriage and her vows of fidelity had meant nothing to her. And too late, Ione was discovering that she was not as fearlessly unconventional nor as single-minded as she had believed she could be. At least not when it came to the prospect of for ever saying goodbye to Alexio Christoulakis.

'There is nothing more to say.' Lean, powerful face set in rigid forbidding lines, Alexio surveyed her with stormy golden eyes, for, even though he was willing to accept that no third party had precipitated her departure, he could not overlook what she had done or avoid interpreting it. 'It's clear to me that you had second thoughts about our marriage even before you got to the church. You would have saved us both a great deal of embarrassment had you had the courage to admit that then.'

Tears of bitter regret stung Ione's shaken eyes and she gulped back the painful ache in her throat. She had been so stubborn, so set on protecting herself and thinking the very worst of him that she had deceived herself right up until the last possible moment. She hadn't gone through the gates to await her flight, for getting out of there again without creating a huge fuss would have been a challenge. She had hung around restive and indecisive, fighting her own turmoil, refusing to admit even to herself that she didn't actually *want* to leave Alexio. She had behaved like a stupid child and what she was getting now was her just deserts because *he* wasn't a child, he was an adult.

'I thought I wanted to be free…' Ione explained half under her breath. 'I've never been free. Until tonight when I left this house, I have never been anywhere alone in my whole life.'

Alexio was taut, still, silent, but his gaze was lodged to her lovely green eyes and incredible eyelashes. When she blinked those long, dark lashes almost hit her cheekbones.

'I thought the worst of you…I panicked,' Ione confided in a breathless appeal. 'But I didn't think through what I was doing.'

At that moment, thinking was not uppermost in Alexio's mind either, but a word like 'panic' did dovetail beautifully with his earlier suspicion that his bride had bolted because she was a more delicate flower than he in his crude masculine insensitivity had appreciated. While his ferocious anger drained away at remarkable speed, his attention extended to take in the lush, moist pink of her mouth and he tensed in exquisite physical discomfort while at the same time assuring himself that no woman had ever got round him with eyes the colour of emeralds and soft, persuasive words.

'Do you think…do you think you could give me another chance?' Ione whispered, cringing for herself even as she voiced that plea, but knowing in her heart that she had no choice. He was Greek and she had injured his pride. Compromise wasn't his style. If he walked out, he was never, ever coming back.

Rationally, Alexio thought that might be possible with perhaps ten new security men on constant alert. She was a little wired. There was no escaping that conclusion. Any woman who had to go down a fire escape and get as far as the airport before she could recognise that she wanted to stay married to him was…? Sensitive, fragile and needed careful handling. And a word about not lugging

Edward the bear about in public might not go amiss. Not to mention the danger of wearing extraordinary shoes encrusted with what he suspected were genuine diamonds and flourishing enormous sums of money at news stands.

'Alexio…?'

'I'll think about it,' Alexio drawled with husky superiority.

Flames of discomfited colour lit Ione's face at that ungenerous response.

'It's more than you deserve, *yineka mou*,' Alexio informed her, brilliant dark golden eyes striking hers in unashamed challenge. 'You still have a lot of growing up to do. So persuade me to reconsider my options.'

Her soft mouth compressed, her eyes flaring before she hastily veiled them, outraged by that comeback but biting her tongue. She could not understand her own desire to fight with him. She never fought with anyone. Her battles had always been by necessity more subtle. His mobile phone shrilled. He switched it off. The silence came back humming with seething tension and the nape of her neck tingled until she lifted her head again.

'I don't like silence…I don't like sulks.' Alexio surveyed her steadily and stretched out his hands. 'Come here…'

And Ione didn't like that either. In fact, being ordered around was exactly what she hated most, but when Alexio fixed those expectant dark golden eyes on her it was as if her backbone and her pride went into retreat. She was just so shaken up by what had happened and still in so much turmoil, for she had yet to work out when and how he had contrived to steal her brain from her body and leave her feeling that no other man could replace him. That was nonsense, total nonsense and she loathed herself, but her feet moved even though she tried to will them into paral-

ysis and that terrible, helpless craving for him streaked
through her like a banner of shame.

'Naturally, I want to make love to you,' Alexio confessed in a roughened undertone. 'If you don't want that,
go now because I can't live with a wife who shrinks from
me.'

Ione reddened. 'I'm not going to shrink!'

Alexio dealt her a wolfish smile that sent her pulses
crazy. 'I don't need a virgin bride either. I might have
liked the experience just once. What Greek male could say
otherwise? But I can live without it and think no less of
you than I do of myself. Marriage lasts a lot longer than
the wedding night, *yineka mou.*'

He lost Ione there, for she could not credit that he could
be seriously suggesting that she had had other lovers. But
she was too wary to question him lest she fall into some
trap of the manipulative verbal variety at which her own
father excelled. In any case, she was far too taken up with
the quivering inner heat of her own body because, barely
twelve inches from Alexio's big, powerful frame, anything
more mentally strenuous demanded too much of her. He
just smiled and deep down inside her somewhere it was
as though her very bones were melting.

'The first time I saw you...*really* saw you, you came
into my room with the linen to change the bed.' Alexio
drew her up against him, molten golden eyes roving over
her with heated appreciation. 'I burned for you then. You
looked so wholesome that you were a walking temptation.
I imagined peeling you out of that shapeless dark dress
that I mistook for a uniform and laying you down on that
bed—'

Ione was listening to him with hot cheeks and wide,
doubting eyes. 'No...you hardly looked at me—'

'You were too busy trying to achieve hospital corners

on the bed to notice. So what was a Gakis doing changing beds?' Alexio bent and swept her up into his arms for the second time that day.

'I don't know.' Leaping nervous tension suddenly made Ione start talking a mile a minute and her heart was racing like an express train. 'I should've called the maids but I didn't. I knew you didn't realise who I was—'

Alexio lowered his arrogant dark head. She clashed with the midnight glitter of his beautiful eyes and her breath caught in her throat as he outlined the ripe curve of her lower lip with the teasing tip of his tongue. 'I realised when I saw your photograph and I was furious with you but very intrigued.'

He lowered her down onto the big bed in the bedroom next door. He reached out to remove one of her shoes, only to find himself clutching a shoe empty of a foot as Ione snaked at speed off the other side and backed awkwardly towards the bathroom.

'I'm sure you'll understand if I ask you not to lock the door, open any windows or seek a fire escape,' Alexio enumerated and he wasn't entirely joking. He watched the stones studding the entire heel of the shoe glitter with rainbow fire in the lamp light. 'Who gave you these?'

'Cosmas.' Her lovely face shadowed on that reference to her brother.

'Are they diamonds?' Alexio enquired.

His bride shrugged with all the innate unconcern of a Gakis born to wealth beyond avarice. 'Probably.'

'It's dangerous to flaunt that kind of wealth in public. It's also rather tacky,' Alexio delivered in exasperation.

Ione stiffened, kicked off the other shoe and went into the bathroom. 'You're a snob just like Papa said you were!' she slung.

As she vanished from view Alexio felt rather like a man

trying to imprison quicksilver between spread fingers. He dropped the offending shoe. 'Ione—?'

'Looking down on us because my grandparents weren't rich, important people. If I want to wear tacky shoes, I'll wear them!'

Ione may yet surprise you, Alexio reminded himself on the back of a suppressed groan.

With tears welling up in her eyes, Ione stared at her own reflection in the vanity mirror. If he regarded her adoptive family as vulgar people with tacky taste, how much more would he reel in horror from her true ancestry? A natural mother who had become pregnant with Ione and her twin during an extra-marital affair? A natural father who was a former politician brought down by his own corruption? A sister who carried on with rock stars and Sicilian tycoons? So was she now making a choice between finding that long-lost sister and staying married to Alexio?

'Ione…?'

Ione appeared back in the doorway. 'I shouldn't have shouted at you.'

Even bearing a close resemblance to a miniature ice queen, Alexio conceded with driven appreciation, his bride was incredibly beautiful.

'Do you want me to take my clothes off now?' Ione asked stonily, striving to act cool about the offer she was making.

Alexio parted his lips and then swallowed an appalling urge to laugh out loud. 'No, definitely not. I think it would be safer if we just go to bed and act like we've been married at least forty years and very rarely indulge in that sort of thing.'

Ione stared back at him in visible confusion and then reddened, uttered a strangled gasp and slammed back into the bathroom. Alexio heard the bolt ram across the door without surprise. He wished he had checked the window first. She was as skittish as a cat on hot bricks. Why was everything so complicated with her? Was it him? Or was it her? And how was he planning to lure her back out of the bathroom?

Torn apart by a sense of humiliated rejection and hurt, Ione ran a bath for want of anything better to do. Tears were running down her cheeks. Why had she listened to all that stupid soft soap about him having been attracted to her from the very first time he had seen her? Why hadn't she just asked him why he hadn't done something about that supposed attraction at the time? Men said stuff like that but didn't mean it. He had to think that she was as thick as a brick to swallow a story like that. Burning for her? The chilliest and most reserved burn she had ever seen! Why, he hadn't even spoken to her that night three months ago except to tell her that he would not sleep on satin sheets!

Self-evidently, it had been a massive mistake to try and assert herself sooner than be suspected of shrinking. Though whose fault was it that she was nervous? Her fault for plunging herself into a wedding night that she had never expected to play a part in? Or his for keeping on lifting her off her feet with that awesome strength as though she were some kind of little toy doll? And what right had he to assume that she wasn't a virgin? How dared he insult her like that? For make no mistake, that was a grave insult to the honour of her family! He might sleep around…she did not.

Somehow that last unfortunate reflection only increased Ione's turmoil. He was her husband and she just didn't know what to do with him, didn't know what was going on inside her own head either. Surely she couldn't be falling in love with a guy who had tried not to laugh when she'd offered to take her clothes off?

Wrapped in a giant bath towel, Ione slid the bolt back and slowly opened the door. The bedroom was empty. Instant panic filled her. Had Alexio got fed up and abandoned her in the hotel? Had he done to her what *she* had done to him? An awful chill gripped Ione and she fled across the room to look into the sitting room.

Having made several necessary calls, Alexio tossed the phone aside, straightened from his elegant lounging stance against the dining table and smiled at her. The relief that washed over Ione made her knees knock together. Steadying herself with one hand on the door handle, she went pink. 'I'll…I'll just go to bed, then,' she announced breathlessly.

'Good idea,' Alexio commented deadpan, suppressing his irreverent grin with all his might. For once, her lovely face had revealed her every thought. No, there was nothing dense about his bride and she might not look Greek but she thought like a Greek, all right. The very instant she'd found him absent, she had suspected revenge. She didn't trust him, not one inch. In fact he very much doubted that she had ever trusted any man and he frowned as he made that deduction.

Dropping the towel, Ione scrambled into the bed and lay between the cold sheets trying not to shiver. If practice made perfect, he was sure to be really good at it, she told herself. He was a great kisser. But there was a huge amount of other stuff that came between the kissing and the rest of it. She supposed she would have to pretend she liked it even if she didn't. She wondered what pretending would demand of her and whether or not he would be able to tell the difference. He was certainly taking his time about joining her.

Ione checked her watch. Ten minutes had passed. Not exactly enthusiastic, was he? Her soft mouth compressed. He just had no consideration. He might be gorgeous but he was an insensitive pig. She should have said no up front. Wedding night or not, she should have told him that it was absolutely medieval for him to expect her to sleep with him so soon! But then how many women had slept with him on the first date? She wished they had had the chance to date. He would still have been *waiting* at the end of six months!

Alexio strolled into the bedroom. He was feeling good about the decision he had just made. It had finally dawned on him that possibly a little restraint in the bedroom might pay dividends in the field of bridal trust and appreciation. His father had been quite right on one count. Alexio was not used to women who ran in the opposite direction. In fact the shock of that experience was still sinking in on him. That with her fear of heights she had also negotiated a two-storey fire escape stung.

As Ione's gaze settled on Alexio's lean, dark, devastating face a helpless little shiver of apprehensive heat travelled through her taut length. She met brilliant dark golden eyes and her heart hammered.

'I just came in to say goodnight,' Alexio imparted.

'S-sorry?' she stammered.

'I'll sleep in the other room. It's very late and you must be exhausted,' Alexio murmured smooth as glass.

Clutching the sheet to her chest, Ione stared at him with widening green eyes of total disconcertion. 'But…but this is our wedding night—'

Alexio shifted a fluid, expressive brown hand. 'We have the rest of our lives to spend together. Sharing a bed is only one small part of marriage…'

Only one *small* part? It was their wedding night and he

couldn't be bothered making love to her! The shock of such casual indifference from a male of his reputation hit Ione hard. Humiliated beyond belief, she fell back against the pillows and shut her eyes tight as she sucked in a tremulous breath. He didn't want her. He didn't even intend to occupy the same room.

'I'm prepared to wait,' Alexio completed huskily.

Even the vaguest notion of herself as being appealing now for ever buried, Ione sat up again in one driven motion. 'You can wait *for ever* as far as I'm concerned!' she gasped strickenly. 'I've never been so insulted in all my life!'

'Insulted? *How* have I insulted you?' Alexio demanded, the volume of his voice rising.

Ione was blinded by tears and her throat was closing over, but rage and hurt were eating her alive. 'First, you accuse me of dressing like a hooker. Then you accuse me of not being a virgin and finally...'

'Maybe you should have stayed off the fire escape,' Alexio slotted in lethally as she paused to gather in a sustaining breath.

'And *finally*,' Ione relaunched in sobbing condemnation, 'you tell me you don't even *want* me!''

'What sort of nonsense is that? Is this the reward I get for trying to be considerate and unselfish?' Alexio raked back at her, his volatile temper flaring on the strength of his annoyance at having what he had deemed to be a major compromise and sacrifice thrown back in his teeth. 'If I'd followed my own inclinations, I'd have busted down that bathroom door, hauled you out of that bath and flattened you to that bed an hour ago!'

Ione focused on him in sharp disconcertion.

Belatedly conscious that that had not been the most confidence-inducing confession he could have made, Alexio raked long brown fingers through his luxuriant black hair and breathed between gritted teeth. 'But that was only a fleeting fantasy born of frustration, naturally *not* an urge I would have acted on.'

Stilling, Ione processed that new information and her soft mouth fell open. Considerate? Unselfish? Those were not words or indeed abilities she had ever associated with men. Men always put themselves first. Even the brother she had adored, the brother who had been so kind to her, would never have made himself uncomfortable on her behalf. But when it dawned on her that Alexio was actually offering to sleep elsewhere because he had assumed that that was what *she* wanted even though it wasn't what *he* wanted, she was utterly transfixed by the concept. In that instant, he rose in her estimation one hundred per cent. In fact he soared so very high in her blitzed imagination that a pair of wings and a halo would not have been out of his reach.

Ione gave him a dizzy smile of appreciation that just grew and grew until her whole face glowed. 'Of course, I want you to stay…you're my husband,' she reminded him unevenly.

Entrapped by that glorious smile, Alexio stared back at her with shimmering golden eyes and then, without any perceptible thought preceding the action, he came down on his knees on the bed and reached for her in the same motion.

Each of them heading in the same direction, their mouths crashed up together and locked in a passionate onslaught. He framed her face with his hands, beautiful eyes hot with desire, snatched in a ragged breath and went back to her lush mouth for more. He captured her lips again and again, sensual, searching and so intense that her whole body trembled in the circle of his arms. Her hands curved to his well-shaped head and then her fingertips laced into his springy black hair to hold him to her.

It was as if there were a hungry fire inside her, licking up through every skincell. The plundering quest of his tongue only sent the flames shooting higher. A low moan was dredged from her as he tipped her back against the pillows with easy strength and crushed her beneath his superior weight. She arched her back helplessly, conscious only of the throbbing ache of her nipples and the shockingly strong need to push her sensitised breasts into abrasive contact with the fabric of his jacket.

'I'm wearing too many clothes,' Alexio husked, angling back from her to shrug free of his suit jacket, but losing concentration at the sight of her small, beautifully formed breasts crowned by delicate buds the colour of tea roses.

Only then realising that the sheet between them had slipped, Ione felt hot colour flood her cheekbones and she wrenched at the sheet instinctively, but it was pinned in place beneath a powerful male thigh.

'Don't…you're perfect,' Alexio breathed hoarsely, his sizzling gaze pinned to her breasts with flatteringly intense interest as he lowered his proud dark head to taste a straining pink peak.

As a tiny whimper parted her lips, the shimmering dart of almost painful arousal jackknifed through her and centred at the honeyed heart of her. Heartbeat hammering and breathless, she looked up at him, met his extraordinary eyes set beneath curling black lashes and felt the surge of wildfire reaction roar through her. Her whole body felt haywire, restive, hot with wanton craving. She did not have the will-power to shift so much as an inch from him, and the strength of her own response to him terrified her.

* * *

'I'll take my time, *agape mou*,' he swore in dark-timbred sensual promise, brushing his fingertips along the fragile curve of her jawbone. 'I'll make it good.'

In a lithe movement, Alexio sprang off the bed and began to undress. Dry-mouthed, Ione watched him unbutton his shirt, disclosing a muscular wedge of bronzed chest sprinkled with a riot of dark curls. Peeling off his well-cut trousers to strip down to a pair of dark boxer shorts, he discarded everything in a careless heap. Her fascination struggled with the return of her tension. From his wide shoulders to his long, powerful, hair-roughened thighs, he was all hard angles and lean muscle, potently male, breathtakingly spectacular. The boxer shorts travelled south. He angled a wicked grin over the dismayed eyes she shut just a second too late, surveyed the pink blossoming in her cheeks.

'Now you know for sure that I want you,' Alexio teased, the mattress giving beneath his weight as he shifted closer and let his breath fan her burning face before delving the tip of his tongue in a provocative slide between her parted lips.

'Yes.' Ione collided with his vibrant eyes and her head fell back on a long gasping sigh as he ran the palm of his hand over her straining nipples.

'You're so sensitive there, *yineka mou*.' With an appreciative groan, he cupped her swollen breasts, stroking the distended peaks with his fingers and extending the sweet torment with the hot, hungry provocation of his mouth.

Ione trembled and moaned out loud, twisting closer, pushing up to him and finally digging her hands into his hair to drag his lips back up to hers. Her head was swimming with the force of her own explosive response, every part of her slender, straining body on red alert. With every probe of his tongue, the taunting pulse of need between her thighs became more unbearable.

'Let me pleasure you,' Alexio said throatily, plotting a leisurely path down a quivering slender thigh through the pale soft curls to the moist, damp centre of her.

'Oh…' Without warning, even the smallest trace of control was wrenched from Ione by sensation. Her hips executed a feverish shift against the sheet, her hands clenching as the beat of her own hunger grew and she was powerless to prevent it. The wild excitement was building higher, tiny cries breaking on her lips as she squirmed, feverishly struggling to somehow satisfy the ache of her own tortured longing.

He shifted over her, hard, handsome features intent, golden eyes molten on her passion-glazed face. As he tipped up her thighs, he pressed a tender kiss on her swollen mouth and muttered hoarsely, 'I'll be gentle…I don't want to hurt you.'

The hot probe of him against her tender entrance was a sensual shock that made her still and then he entered her inch by incredible inch, all heat and pressure and alien maleness. She tensed in apprehension, astonished by the pleasurable feel of his invasion. At the momentary stab of pain she loosed a stifled moan and then he sank deep into her and she rose against him in startled response. The frantic excitement pounded through her again, electrifying, utterly controlling and she surrendered to the dark, deep, pulsing pleasure until he dragged her resistless to some crazy height where nothing but sensation ruled. Sharp, sweet ecstasy raked through her and expanded into an explosive cascade of delight and blew her into a thousand glittering pieces.

He shuddered over her in his own completion and a fierce burst of tenderness filled Ione and she closed her arms round him even more tightly, tears of wonderment sparkling in her softened eyes.

'That was extraordinary…' Alexio lifted his tousled dark head and looked down at her with dark-as-midnight eyes, noting the faint purple shadows that betrayed her exhaustion. His heart-stopping smile curving his wide sensual mouth as he rearranged them into a more relaxed huddle. Holding her slight body close, he dropped a kiss on her brow. 'Go to sleep now, *agape mou*. It's almost dawn.'

But he was the one who fell asleep and she lay watching him, in thrall to her own fascination and the quite unfamiliar sense of buoyant happiness consuming her. He slept in a careless sprawl with the sheet tangled round his hips and took up more than his fair share of the bed. She knew she was falling in love, knew there was not the slightest thing she could do about it. The freedom she had craved had been superseded by an infinitely more powerful craving to be with him.

All that was demanded from her was a leap of faith and the willingness to believe that Alexio would never treat her with the same callous lack of feeling that her father had demonstrated towards her mother…

CHAPTER SIX

ALEXIO watched Ione emerge from the changing room.

Radiant in an emerald-green shift dress that was a stunning foil for her bright eyes and wealth of platinum fair hair, Ione did a twirl. 'Well?'

Alexio was in search of a flaw but the dress wasn't too tight, wasn't too short and only her slim arms were bare. Even so, he still thought she looked too eye-catching. Paris was a very cosmopolitan city but heads turned wherever they went. Ione had the stylish cool and confidence that all true Parisians admired, but more than anything else she had that most basic and blatant of currencies: classic and sensational beauty of a calibre rarely seen.

'You've got to like this one,' Ione insisted with an impish smile. 'What's the matter with you?'

Alexio really didn't know. He had no idea why he always wanted to cover her up. He was not a possessive man. Crystal had worn outrageous clothes and, aside of his irritation over her constant hunger for attention, what his late fiancée had worn had never bothered him. But Ione only had to allow his chauffeur a glimpse of thigh as she alighted from the limo and he could feel his tension rising. She just didn't have a clue how beautiful she was. But sooner or later the supreme power that was hers would dawn on her and Alexio definitely didn't want that to happen when he was not around.

Ione's lush mouth pouted and she glided up to him. 'Are you bored?'

'No, I love a floorshow...I just prefer it in private,'

Alexio confided, his dark, deep drawl lowering to an intimate purr that sent a responsive shiver down her slender spine.

Drawn by the flare of gold in his smouldering gaze, Ione leant closer, starry eyes welded to his lean, dark, devastating features. Bare inches from him as she was, her senses delighted in his achingly familiar male scent. Three weeks of round-the-clock exposure to Alexio had barely touched the surface of her joy in him and certainly brought her no closer to satiation. She had been delighted when he'd sent her team of bodyguards back to Greece and replaced them with men who treated her with respect. In fact, the more time she spent with Alexio, the more she marvelled at the sheer rightness of their being together.

But throughout those same days and nights Ione's conscience had weighed ever more heavily on her. If Alexio ever found out the truth of *why* she had married him, how would he feel? If he learned that she had planned from the outset to walk out on their marriage, any trust he had in her and any respect or affection would be destroyed. No man deserved to be used by a woman merely as an escape from an unhappy home life. A chill of fear ran through her at the very thought of Alexio ever discovering how low she had once been prepared to sink.

Suppressing that anxiety, she made herself think instead about the wonderful honeymoon they had shared. Alexio had gone to public school in England but he had spent his university years at the Sorbonne. He spoke fluent French and he had shown her an insider's view of the city he loved. He had let her drag him round the Musee Marmottan to see Monet paintings and then had delighted her a week later with a surprise trip to Monet's house at Giverny. She had been enchanted by the pink villa with its green shutters and the glorious gardens and ponds cre-

ated by the famous artist to serve as inspiration for his
own paintings.

But the images that would remain longest with her were
more intimate: getting soaked by the unpredictable water
jets in the Parc Citroen and then thoroughly kissed even
though she looked like a drowned rat; walking hand in
hand along the Seine while Alexio explained that he had
never been romantic and, in the midst of that macho proc-
lamation, told her that when the breeze caught her hair she
resembled a maiden from Arthurian legend; watching excited children sail toy boats in the Luxembourg gardens
until Alexio pulled her into the circle of his arms and
groaned, 'I don't know what you're doing to me but for
the first time in my life I can honestly see myself wanting
to have a baby with a woman.'

That particular recollection still filled Ione with a deep
and happy sense of acceptance. And last but not least was
the fabulous birthday cake which he had ordered for dinner
the night before in honour of her twenty-third birthday.
She fingered the Victorian ring that he had given her. It
was a 'regard' ring, the first letter of each jewel spelling
out that message, and she had been touched and pleased
that he had taken the time to choose something so special
as a gift.

Leaving the boutique on the Champs-Elysées, they went
back to the townhouse to dine. Later they were attending
the opera. As they went upstairs to dress after their meal
Ione said ruefully, 'I'll be sad when we leave Paris—'

'We don't have to yet. Allow me thirty-six hours in
London and I'll come back and base myself here for one
more weekend—'

'You have business in London?' Ione looked up at him
in surprise. 'Could I come with you?'

'You'd be bored out of your mind, *agape mou*.' Alexio

sighed. 'I'll be tied up in meetings all day and the company apartment I use over there isn't up to much.'

Brimming on her lips was the assurance that she wouldn't mind in the slightest, would indeed even consider camping out on a park bench if it meant she could stay near him. But common sense and pride mercifully intervened. After an entire three weeks of his attention, it was greedy of her to begrudge him a single night away from her. Nor was being possessive and demanding the way to impress him with her newfound maturity. Indeed, that sort of behaviour would only alienate him.

She loved Alexio with an intense passion that she had never dreamt she could feel and she was happier than she had known it possible to be. He might not love her, but he certainly did seem to care about her and he treated her better than she had ever been treated in her entire life. He was affectionate, humorous, charming and incredibly sexy at any hour of the day and sometimes she just couldn't believe that he was hers.

'Think of how rampant I'll be when I fly back,' Alexio growled in sensual threat, tugging her backwards into his arms on the threshold of their bedroom.

Ione grinned, snaking back into contact with his big, powerful frame. 'You're always rampant,' she teased, and she loved that reality for his passion made her feel like the most irresistible woman in the world.

'Stop doing that,' Alexio groaned as she arched her slim hips in sinuous, shameless encouragement into the hard, virile maleness of him.

Ione reddened, momentarily taken aback by her own behaviour, but the knowledge that they had only one more night before their idyllic honeymoon came to an effective end was a more potent inducement and she whispered unevenly, '*Make* me...'

'Not too long ago your idea of an invitation was looking longingly at me across a dining table. It was rather sweet but this is more exciting,' Alexio confided with hoarse appreciation as he spun her round and without hesitation captured her lush mouth with the hard, drugging force of his own.

The sheer hunger he made no attempt to hide exploded through her slender length like a depth charge that sent ripples of sensual shock through her every fibre. With a helpless little moan, she leant into him for support and he gathered her up, sent the door crashing shut with a powerful shoulder and tumbled her down on the bed.

'Day or night, I can't get enough of you…' Lean, strong face taut with all the passion of his volatile temperament, Alexio gazed down at her and, for the merest instant, his stunning golden eyes betrayed a mixture of surprise and faint discomfiture as he made that acknowledgement.

Gotcha, Ione reflected in an entirely different spirit of one-upmanship from that which she had once embraced in his vicinity. Her face stilled as she instinctively concealed the first revealing rush of her own happy satisfaction with that state of affairs. Any time of the day or night, he was welcome. Desire was only a beginning: she knew that, but without that desire any hope of his returning her love some day would have been doomed. For a male as passionate as Alexio, it would take more than a meeting of minds and goals to build a strong marriage.

'What are you thinking about?' Alexio demanded huskily as he stood over her, wrenching off his clothes with a flattering degree of impatience. 'You're wearing that little sneaky look you get when you're plotting something.'

'Sneaky?' Startled, Ione looked up at him in dismay. 'Plotting?'

His irrepressible wolfish grin slashed his bronzed features and made her heart clench on a fierce flood of love. 'I'm onto you *agape mou*. That tranquil lack of expression invariably means you're deep in intriguing thoughts.'

He was right and that shook her.

'I guess concealing your emotions comes naturally to you. That's how you operate around your father.'

Conscious of the more serious note in his dark drawl and the penetrating light in his keen scrutiny, Ione paled and turned her head away.

'Minos is an intimidating man. Strong men shake when he loses his temper,' Alexio remarked with a studied lightness of tone. 'But you don't need to practice that kind of caution in my vicinity. I may lose my temper occasionally but I don't ever lose control of my fists.'

'That's good to know...but I really don't know why you're taking the trouble to tell me that.' With a slight tremor in her strained voice, Ione refused to be drawn, for it was not the first time in recent days that Alexio had raised a similar subject and she knew that she could not afford to trust him with any confidences of what her life had been like on Lexos. For to do so would put him at risk.

Didn't he know that curiosity had killed the cat? The habit of silence on the subject of her father's abuse was as engrained in her as it had been in her mother and her brother. But her father's violent outburst that night over dinner just over a month ago had left Alexio uneasy and, as time went on, she was aware that he had become more suspicious of exactly what he had witnessed and interrupted. She had the uncomfortable feeling that something in her own behaviour must have served to rouse those suspicions.

Frustration currented through Alexio as he saw her exquisite face shutter. The past was a closed book to Ione.

It was as if she had been born on the day of their wedding for she never mentioned her childhood or indeed any of her relatives, living or dead. And now her withdrawal was pronounced.

'Now, where were we?' Alexio teased, switching mental gears with ease and coming down on the bed beside her to angle her up against his bare, hair-roughened chest and run down the zip on her dress.

With sure hands he removed the garment and pushed her hair out of his path to let his expert mouth trace a provocative path across the exposed nape of her neck. She quivered, suddenly wild with hunger for him, and in an awkward movement she twisted round and pushed her mouth in a seeking, blind gesture into his. She felt safe, so safe with him, but she also knew that if she told him too much he would *not* be safe from her father's fury.

Alexio held her back from him for a moment. His eyes were the colour of rich honey as they sought her evasive gaze. 'What's wrong?'

'Nothing…' Even as he looked at her with those glorious eyes, the heat and the promise of his hard male arousal was already gaining mastery over her. Her breasts ached, their tender peaks swollen and stiff.

Spreading her slender thighs to either side of his, he undid her bra. Suddenly breathless, her heart pounding in her own eardrums, she let her head fall back and arched her spine so that her pouting, sensitive flesh grazed the dark thicket of black curls hazing his pectoral muscles.

'We're going to be late for the opera…' Alexio breathed with thickened purpose and, knotting one hand into her bright hair, he tilted her back with care until her taut spine met the mattress and then brought his urgent mouth down to tease at her straining nipples.

Fire leapt straight to the moist triangle between her

thighs. She jerked and gasped and then fell into the plundering kiss that followed like a drowning swimmer. Her fingers woven into his luxuriant hair, she surrendered to the dark pleasure of pure sensation as his expert hands roved over her quivering, sensitised body.

'You're an enchantress...' Alexio growled, staring down at her with smouldering intensity, his appreciative gaze absorbing her rapt expression. 'When you lose yourself in my arms, I have a hell of a job staying in control.'

'That's a complaint?' Ione whispered before he pressed his warm, carnal mouth to a pulse-point beneath her collarbone and his lean, sun-darkened hands proceeded to plot an erotic path down over her squirming, responsive length.

Within a very little while, she was even more inflamed with longing and whimpering beneath his electrifying caresses, her entire being in thrall to his. No longer could she resist the urge to touch him in turn, and her exploring fingers followed the narrow furrow of dark hair that bisected his taut, lean stomach and almost reached the hot, hard tautness of his throbbing shaft before he clamped a restraining hand over hers with a rueful groan.

'I can't wait.' In a purposeful movement, Alexio rearranged her. Anchoring himself between her parted thighs, he entered her with a slow, delicious strength that made her moan out loud with pleasure.

And then there was nothing but him and the way he could make her feel driven, possessed and yet weak with love. She felt him tremble with the force of his own fierce need and she curved round him in abandonment, scanning the raw tension of passion etched in his darkly handsome face. He urged her to explosive fulfilment with powerful thrusts and the stormy excitement overwhelmed her in a breathtaking surge of ecstasy that wrung her out in the aftermath.

'We'll be very, very late, *agape mou*,' Alexio husked, dropping a kiss on her slight shoulder and licking the salt from her skin with an earthy enjoyment that made her melt. 'Do you mind?'

'Mind?' She minded nothing that he did while he held her close and looked down at her with those wonderful dark eyes that made her heart leap. 'No.'

'It's amazing how well we match,' Alexio informed her with indolent male satisfaction and she almost smiled at his innocence.

For even in the space of three weeks, Ione had been careful to pick up on his preferences and adjust herself accordingly. She had been mortified when it had finally dawned on her that she had rather juvenile tastes in fashion. She supposed that in some ways that was understandable, for she had never got to go through the natural phase of defining her own identity by what she'd worn in adolescence.

Somehow, without ever actually saying so, Alexio had managed to let her know that the type of outfit she had worn to the airport was most popular with teenage girls. And, at almost twenty-three, she ought to have been beyond that stage. Quite how his attitude meshed with the often spectacular fashion statements flaunted by his late fiancée, Crystal, Ione had no very clear idea. But one reality she did accept: Alexio had loved Crystal and love could be blind. As she had no such bank of reassuring love to depend on, it had seemed to her that she had no choice but to put his approval above her own inclinations.

So, her beloved shoes with their diamond heels that seemed to strike Alexio as the ultimate in vulgarity had remained in her wardrobe. Then there was the fact he liked to get up very early in the morning, not to mention his decided preference for Greek food when she would have happily sampled international cuisine at every meal. It was all a case of been there, done that for him, she reflected with loving forgiveness.

'I'm not fond of opera,' Alexio confided lazily.

Ione suppressed a sigh.

Alexio leant over her, brilliant eyes mocking. 'But I know you've been looking forward to it all week, so we will go.'

'Then we'd better hurry!' Galvanised into action, Ione peeled off her watch to toss it on the cabinet by the bed and snaked free of him to flee into the bathroom to have the fastest shower on record.

Thirty minutes later, her hair swept up to hold the magnificent amethyst and diamond tiara that matched her necklace and earrings, and clad in a figure-hugging lilac sheath that split just above the knee to reveal a glimpse of slender leg, Ione looked in vain for the watch she had carelessly discarded. It was in neither the tumbled bedding nor on the carpet, and then she recalled that the top drawer of the cabinet had been lying open before she'd gone for her shower and she tugged it wide again. Smiling as she reclaimed her watch from the drawer, she saw a photograph.

Sliding the watch back on her wrist, she nudged aside the condom packet, for it was Alexio's cabinet, and reached for the photo of the smiling bikini-clad brunette. Her heart hammering chokily in what felt like her throat, she slowly sank down on the side of the bed to study Crystal Denby. Alexio's socialite fiancée had been extremely attractive and even Ione's critical eye recognised the appeal of her voluptuous figure and long, perfect legs, not to mention the provocative sparkle of her dark eyes and sexy smile. Alexio had taken that photograph. She knew it in her bones. Crystal had been posing for her lover, confident of his admiration.

Her tummy queasy and her skin chilling over, Ione replaced the photo where she had found it and shut the drawer again. But she was trembling and she felt as if Alexio had stuck a knife into her without warning. Why did he keep a picture of Crystal within easy reach of their marital bed? How often did he look at it? Well, obviously it was there to be looked at, *grieved* over…

She felt hollow inside and simultaneously sick with rage and pain. Throughout their honeymoon, she had been determined not to think of Crystal. She had been equally careful not to ruin her own contentment with the reflection that Alexio had probably shared many of the same outings and much of the same passion with the lovely brunette. Such wounding thoughts would have been pointless, but the discovery of that photograph had blown her liberal and sensible approach to their marriage right out of the water.

Alexio emerged from the dressing room. She stole a single glance at his lean, dark, devastating features, imprinting him on her mind's eye with agonised hurt and resentment foaming up inside her. She had ditched her pride for him, even taken a rain check on her longing to be reunited with her twin sister for him, and she had exerted herself in every way to be the wife that *he* wanted. And wasn't that where she had gone wrong in the weakness of loving him to distraction? What about what *she* wanted?

'Turn round,' Alexio murmured in his dark, deep, throaty drawl. 'You look amazing in that dress.'

Slender spine taut, Ione spun round from the window, eyes glittering bright as emeralds in her triangular face. 'I saw the photo of Crystal Denby you have in the drawer by the bed!'

A very slight frownline drew his winged ebony brows together and his stunning golden eyes narrowed in a questioning look. 'And?' Alexio prompted, refusing to react having always been his first line of defence in potential scenes with her sex.

That single word sent Ione rocketing from hurt to blinding, ungovernable rage. *And?* As if it should mean nothing to her that her husband cherished another woman's picture, as if she had no right whatsoever to comment on the fact, as if only a very unreasonable woman would dare to object. Ione read meanings into that single word that he could never have dreamt.

'If you don't get rid of that photo, I'm leaving you!' Ione heard herself fling back, and her own shock at the melodramatic threat that emerged of its own seeming accord from her lips was greater than his.

Alexio regarded her with sardonic disbelief writ large in his lean, strong face. His wide shoulders were squared, long, powerful legs braced slightly apart. 'If we don't leave now for the opera, it won't be worth our while going.'

Momentarily silenced by that complete sidestepping of the entire issue, Ione stared at him in a tempestuous fury. 'You think I want to go and watch a stupid opera when you've got a picture of another woman in our bedroom?'

'Don't shout at me,' Alexio countered very soft and low, stormy golden eyes resting on her with a silent intimidation she could feel.

Ione's stomach flipped over, the same sick sensation of fear that came over her in her father's presence attacking her for the very first time in Alexio's. But the same defiance that had brought her into regular conflict with Minos Gakis while her mother had still been alive leapt up even

stronger. 'You have insulted me,' she framed with fierce
conviction.

Alexio was cursing the inefficiency of the domestic
staff, who had been instructed to make a clean sweep of
all such memorabilia, for he had made little use of the
townhouse over the past two years. But then, only a wife
would rifle through his personal effects, Alexio reflected
with all the annoyance of a male who hated complications.

'In what way have I insulted you?' he murmured, and
that precise tone of boredom had in the past proved more
than sufficient to deflate most women.

That laconic intonation had the same effect on Ione as
hot coals shovelled onto a dying fire.

'I'm your wife. She was a tramp!'

The instant that inflammatory word left her lips, Ione
was ashamed of herself. So disrespectful and cruel a reference to a woman who had been dear to him was decidedly beyond the bounds of what was forgivable.

Alexio froze in receipt of that allegation. Outrage flashing into his stormy golden gaze, he surveyed her with a
distaste that was more than sufficient punishment for her
reckless tongue. 'I respect her memory and so must you
for I will not tolerate your jealousy,' he said harshly.

'I'm not jealous of her...' Ione whispered hoarsely, her
aching throat closing over on that anguished denial.

But Alexio said nothing. He simply strode out of the
room. Disconcerted, Ione closed her eyes in despair over
her own foolishness. A minute later, she hurried after him,
but by the time she reached the top of the stairs the front
door below was thudding shut on his departure.

Jealous, *yes*, Ione then conceded painfully. She *was* bitterly jealous of the woman who had once held Alexio's
heart. It didn't matter that Crystal was dead: her memory
lived on. He never mentioned her, but then she had not

asked any questions for, the more important Alexio became to her, the less she had been able to bear any thought of his late fiancée. But why shouldn't he keep a photograph of Crystal? It had not even been on open display. Now because she had not had the wit or the self-discipline to mind her own business, she had ruined the last night of their honeymoon.

Hopeful that he would return and determined to make a sincere apology, Ione went down to the drawing room to wait. She was all shaken up and really scared of the damage she had done to their relationship. Why was it, though, that she was always doomed to be second-best in the eyes of those she cared about?

The same hurting thread seemed to stretch through her whole life. Cosmas had been the child most dear to his parents' hearts, Ione merely the baby in need of a home who had roused Amanda's loving and generous compassion. And here she was, second-best to her husband as well, for Alexio would never have married her had Crystal still been alive. Yet in spite of that knowledge she had still contrived to fall head over heels in love with him and hold back from what had once been her most driving ambition: her desperate longing to be reunited with her twin sister.

Of course, she did eventually intend to defy her father and tell Alexio the truth about her background in the hope that he would understand how much finding her sister, Misty, meant to her. So why hadn't she done it yet? Why hadn't she told him? And the answer came back loud and clear and made her ashamed of her own cowardice. She had stalled on telling Alexio that she was adopted because she was afraid that if he knew he would think less of her for not being a true Gakis. After all even Cosmas, who had loved her, had heartily pitied her for not being *born* into the family.

But now she had to live with the knowledge that Alexio had walked out on her in total disgust at her unpleasantness, which was much, much worse, Ione reflected wretchedly.

When Alexio entered the drawing room some hours later, his lean, strong, face taut, he found Ione clad in very fetching silk nightwear and curled up on a sofa fast asleep.

Ione woke up only when Alexio scooped her up into his arms. Looking up at his bronzed, dark features and the faint smile curving his wide, sensual mouth, she blinked in confusion and her heart crashed against her ribcage, but she still spoke the last thought that had occurred to her before she'd drifted off into slumber. 'How would you like it if I kept a photo of Yannis in our bedroom?'

Alexio stopped dead in his tracks, complete disconcertion powering through him in receipt of that sudden question. 'I wouldn't have it,' he growled without a second of hesitation, and silence stretched before comprehension stepped in and dark colour scored his hard cheekbones.

Mollified by that admission, Ione screened her gaze and muttered ruefully, 'I shouldn't have said what I did.'

Infuriated by that crack about Yannis and recognising that he had been stitched up, Alexio shrugged and began to undress. Nothing short of thumbscrews would have persuaded him to mention the fresh opera booking he had made for the weekend.

Aware that she had ducked the genuine apology she had intended to make, Ione breathed guiltily, 'Alexio, I—'

'I have a six o'clock flight to make in a few hours' time,' he incised in cool interruption. 'Let's shelve any serious conversations until I get back.'

Realising in dismay that the topic of Crystal now appeared to be a total no-go area, Ione slid out of her wrap, got into bed and breathed in deep. 'But I have something I want to tell you and if I wait, I might lose my nerve.'

A frown pleating his ebony brows, Alexio focused on her with smouldering dark golden eyes.

'It's a family secret and Papa warned me not to tell you because he doesn't like it to be known,' Ione rattled off in a rush. 'But I wasn't born into the Gakis family…I was *adopted* into it.'

Alexio regarded her with unconcealed disbelief. 'Have you been drinking?'

Ione scrambled back out of bed, disappeared into the dressing room and emerged again in a breathless surge. 'That's my sister, my twin…' Ione extended the tiny baby snap she had dug out of her attaché case. 'Her name's Misty.'

Alexio took the little black and white baby photo between thumb and forefinger and stared back at Ione with a stunned light in his gaze. 'You are serious about this?'

He both looked and sounded so shocked that Ione paled and dived back into bed. 'A nurse took a picture of her before we were parted.'

'Adopted…' Alexio sank down on the edge of the divan, frowning golden eyes lodged to her. '*When* were you adopted?'

'I was only a few weeks old.' Ione went on to explain that she had not been as healthy as her twin at birth and her natural mother had decided that she could not cope with a second baby who would require extra care and further medical treatment.

'What was the matter with you?' Alexio demanded.

'I was underweight and I had feeding problems…and the birth also left me with dislocated hips,' Ione said with a grimace. 'Papa wanted Mama to adopt a boy but she wanted me. He hoped that adopting me would somehow miraculously help Mama to conceive another son.'

'I have heard of that happen.' Alexio's keen gaze was intent on her strained profile, his intelligence warning him that he had strayed into a verbal minefield in which he had not the smallest experience. 'When did you find out that you were adopted?'

'I was so young, I can't even remember.'

'Where were you born?'

'London.'

Alexio could not conceal his astonishment. 'You were adopted from England?'

'I don't have a drop of Greek blood in my veins,' Ione admitted, sudden piercing regret assailing her when it was far too late to think better of what she had confided. He was appalled. It was written all over him. And she had not even got as far as admitting to her less than presentable birth ancestry, not to mention the unfortunate plight of a sister who was the mistress of some tycoon.

'To be Greek by adoption is the next best thing,' Alexio asserted in haste, his lean, sun-darkened hand closing over her clenched fingers in sincere sympathy. To comment that missing out on the Gakis gene pool might well be no great cause for sorrow would not be tactful. He was still in shock.

Ione didn't want his pity and an all-too-familiar sense of wounding rejection was gripping her. She cared, she cared far too much about what Alexio now thought of her. But why? What difference did it really make? She was *still* the Gakis heiress, *still* his wife and he *still* kept a picture of Crystal Denby in their bedroom. Yanking her hand free of his, she turned her back on him and closed her stinging eyes tight.

'I just thought you had the right to know,' she said flatly. 'But I don't want to talk about it any more. Goodnight.'

When Ione wakened the following morning, she was miserable when she realised that she had slept through Alexio's departure. But an enormous basket of beautiful flowers was brought to her an hour later. She opened the accompanying card.

'You are a Christoulakis now,' Alexio had written in the evident belief that it would be a comfort for her to know that no higher honour could be conferred upon a woman, and her eyes swam with tears even as she laughed.

Had she misunderstood him the night before? Foisted her own insecurities onto him? He had been very taken aback by the news that she had been adopted, but surely he could not have written that message had he been seriously concerned by what she had told him? She longed to be with him again and was furious with herself for giving way to her own emotional turmoil and freezing him out in the aftermath of their first row. Now she had thirty-six hours to wait until he flew home again. Why did she never have any sense when it came to Alexio?

She could always fly over to London and surprise him! The instant that idea occurred to Ione, it possessed her. The staff would know the address of his city apartment and when he finished his working day, she would be there waiting…

CHAPTER SEVEN

IONE was in an exuberant mood by the time the limousine her bodyguards had acquired for her pulled up in front of the apartment block late afternoon.

She was in London for the first time since her birth. Thanks to her adoptive mother, she was bilingual, but she had feared that the English that Amanda Gakis had always used with her children when she'd been alone with them might have grown a little rusty since her brother's death. However, she had tested herself out on the businessman seated next to her on the flight from Paris. He had been extremely chatty and had boosted her confidence by telling her that she spoke his language with only a slight and very charming accent.

Ione emerged from the lift and walked to the door of the apartment. Thinking better of using the spare key she had been delighted to find available in the townhouse, she rang the bell first just in case there were staff or indeed someone else staying there. She was on the brink of employing the key when the door swung wide.

A tall brunette with a mane of hair the colour of glossy chestnuts, her shapely figure enhanced by a smart black suit, looked out with a brimming smile that fell away in slow motion when she saw Ione.

Surprised, but assuming that the woman worked for Alexio in some capacity, Ione walked on into the hall. 'I'm Ione Christoulakis.'

'Pascale Fortier.' The svelte Frenchwoman let the door snap shut again on its own.

'Do you work for my husband?' Ione asked, strolling ahead into the main reception room and surveying it with some disappointment for it was so bland it might have been a hotel room. But then he had said it was a company flat and the presence of a third party made the possibility of a romantic dinner for two unlikely, Ione conceded in seething disappointment. Registering that that unexpected guest was taking a long time to respond to her question, Ione turned her head in enquiry.

'No...I don't work for Alexio.' Pascale was staring at her, coins of colour marking her exotic cheekbones, her attractive face hard. 'Was Alexio expecting you?'

'No.' Wondering why the brunette was emanating angry defensiveness, Ione tensed up as well. 'I gather you're staying here?'

The other woman shrugged a designer-clad shoulder and then gave her a malicious little smile. '*Tiens.* I suppose a wife must take precedence over a lover and I shall have to pack.'

Ione heard nothing beyond the first part of that declaration. Her skin turned clammy, shock reeling through her in an explosive wave. A *lover*? There was a rushing sound in her eardrums and the other woman's voice seemed to be coming from very far away. Then, in the space of a sickening instant that made her tummy lurch, everything fell into place: Alexio's smooth assurance that the London apartment wouldn't suit her and that he would be too busy to spend time with her. How foolish and blind she had been to the obvious!

Alexio had not wanted her to accompany him to London. He had had other plans for this thirty-six-hour break away from her. Ione felt as if the walls were closing in around her and the floor were breaking up beneath her feet. Heart clenching, she made herself look at Pascale with much keener attention. Another tall, beautiful and confident brunette in the style of Crystal Denby and very much the kind of woman that seemed to define Alexio's taste in her sex. So, how had she ever believed for one moment that a wife who was a small, slight blonde could have any enduring appeal for such a male?

Without another word, for pride alone was holding her together, Ione walked back out of the apartment. A tiny bead of perspiration trickled down between her breasts. Shattered by that encounter with Alexio's mistress, she was shaking. Yet it was also as if her brain had been cut in two. While on one level she was possessed with a blind, helpless craving to find some *other* explanation for the Frenchwoman's presence in Alexio's apartment, on another level she was already accepting that Alexio had planned to spend the night there betraying her in the arms of another woman. After all, hadn't even her own father warned her that Alexio would be unfaithful?

Her bodyguards awaited her in the ground floor reception and escorted her back to the underground car park. She knew exactly what her family would expect her to do in such circumstances: fly back to Paris, behave as though she had never come to London and indeed act as though nothing had happened. She had been raised to the tune of such double standards, taught that, while a woman must always maintain a decent reputation, a man might do as he liked as long as he was discreet. Her own mother had ignored her husband's infidelity to the best of her ability. But no such martyred soul eager to break out existed inside Ione.

Devastated as she was, she was already getting angry. When had she chosen to forget that their marriage was more of a business alliance than a personal relationship? When had she stopped thinking about Alexio's bad reputation for loving and leaving women? Love had blinded her. Love had filled her with unrealistic expectations and left her sick with humiliation and anguish. It was time to acknowledge her mistakes, call a halt to her own weakness and let Alexio know in no uncertain terms that she had no intention of tolerating his infidelity. Snatching up the phone, she ordered the chauffeur to take her to Alexio's office.

'No, don't announce me,' Ione told the wide-eyed receptionist who rose to greet her on the executive floor of the elegant building that housed Christoulakis Enterprises. 'I want to surprise my husband. Where is his office?'

Impervious to the obsequious secretary, who fell into step by her side and talked in anxious apology about some *terribly* important meeting due to begin in five minutes' time, Ione thrust open the door. Walking in rigid-backed, she leant back against the door to close it again.

Alexio was talking on the phone. Sunlight cascaded through the tall window behind him to pick up the sheen of his luxuriant black hair, the stunning angles and hollows of his superb bone structure, and then fire his extraordinary eyes to mesmeric pure gold as he looked up with a frown to see who had entered his office without permission.

Springing upright in one lithe, powerful motion, he exclaimed in surprise, *'Ione?'*

At first sight of Alexio, the cautious vein of protective detachment that Ione had thrown up between her brain and her emotions evaporated. Her heartbeat lodged in the foot of her tight throat and hammered there, making it difficult for her to breathe. His breathtaking smile flashed across his sensual mouth, lighting his lean, bronzed features with the mesmeric charisma that was so much a part of his raw, masculine appeal. That smile disconcerted her, for any onlooker might easily have been convinced that Alexio was delighted by the sudden arrival of his wife in London. But then didn't his ability to conceal his true reactions simply emphasise how truly low and sneaky and cunning he was?

Deep, dark anger stirred higher in Ione. Her already taut spine notched up another inch in rigidity and her chin lifted. Yet even while she hated him, she knew that she still loved and wanted him. 'I have only come here to tell you that our marriage is over.'

Smile ditching fast, Alexio lodged level dark golden eyes on her in apparent bewilderment. 'I beg your pardon?'

'Our lawyers will deal with the legalities of our separation,' Ione stated and snatched in a stark breath. 'I do not want to see you again, nor will I discuss my decision.'

'Believe me, *agape mou*...you are going to discuss this until dawn breaks tomorrow,' Alexio countered soft and low, brilliant eyes shimmering with a blaze of incredulous anger. 'I don't care what notion you have got into your head, you are *not* walking out on our marriage!'

Ione's facial muscles were so tight, she felt as though she were talking through a mask and the lips she parted were bloodless. 'I met your mistress at your apartment.'

Computing that new fact into the situation, Alexio's big, powerful frame tautened and his eyes darkened, his strong bone structure setting hard. 'I don't have a mistress. Pascale is an ex of mine, nothing more. She still has a key to the apartment and she contacted me when she arrived in London this morning. I told her that she could stay the night there but I said no to the dinner invite.'

A jagged laugh was wrenched from Ione as she remembered Pascale's face falling when she'd realised that it was Ione and not Alexio on the doorstep. 'What sort of a fool to you think I am?' she prompted tightly, fighting the high note of stress she could hear in her own voice.

'You're my wife and I expect you to *trust* me,' Alexio grated on a sudden fierce note of fury. 'I told my secretary to book me into a hotel for the night.'

'Of course, you wouldn't admit the truth unless I actually caught you in the *act* of betraying me,' Ione countered in bitter reproach, infuriated by what she deemed to be smooth and clever lies intended to make her doubt her own judgement. 'But I've seen enough to convince me that you're still the womaniser you always were. I won't live with an unfaithful husband—'

'Have you listened to one thing I've said?' Alexio launched back at her with savage bite, his golden gaze shimmering, his strong jawline set at an aggressive slant. 'No, you haven't. You judged me guilty before you even entered my office. You're not even giving me the chance to defend myself!'

'I know your reputation with women.' Ione flung her pounding head so high, her neck ached, her hard-won composure beginning to unravel at the seams. 'I won't accept such a marriage. I won't live with lies and pretences—'

'*Theos mou*…you're not going anywhere until this is sorted out!' Alexio thundered as he strode towards her, his outrage unconcealed.

'Thumping me or threatening me won't work either!' Ione gasped, backing away a step in spite of her attempt to make herself stand her ground.

'Thumping you?' Alexio froze as though she had exploded that same ground from beneath his feet. Pale beneath his bronzed skin, he surveyed her with shattered intensity, his brilliant eyes locking to the taut white triangle of her half-fearful, half-defiant face. 'You think that I would hit you?'

A shiver ran through Ione as she realised what she had betrayed in her distress.

'Your father *did* hit you…' Alexio framed a split second later, shock roaring through him in spite of the suspicions he had had. 'Do you think all men are like that? I've never struck a woman in my life, nor would I! How could you think I would harm you?'

Ione was trembling, her teeth chattering together. He had backed off from her as though she had attacked him. He was appalled by what he had learnt but there was a look of blunt masculine reproach in his level gaze that she could have believed him capable of meting out similar abuse. In shamed perplexity, she spun away for she had always felt safe with Alexio, had somehow known right from the beginning that in that way he was not at all like her father.

'For your own protection,' she breathed unevenly, 'you mustn't ever let Papa know that you know. He has ruined men for less.'

Alexio said nothing. Instead, he simply closed his arms round her from behind, magnifying the enormous confusion she was struggling to overcome. It was a warm, reassuring embrace, calculated not to either threaten or invade her space too much. What shook her was her own rampant desire to lean back into him, flip round and feel the hard strength and heat of his lean, muscular body against her just one more time. Just *one* more time before she walked away.

'He will never get to lay a finger on you again, *agape mou*,' Alexio swore hoarsely. 'I swear that. You will never return to Lexos. You will never be alone with him again. As long as he lives, you will be safe.'

Her eyes filled with anguished tears for she knew he meant every word of those assurances. And every skincell in her body was jumping, every pulse on red alert to make proper physical contact with the man she still loved. Making herself step away from Alexio in that instant was the hardest challenge she had ever faced. But he was bad for her, she reminded herself painfully. He might not be *all* bad but she could not live with a faithless man she could not trust. He had already hurt her and it was her duty to protect herself. If she stayed in their marriage, he would destroy her as surely as Minos Gakis had destroyed her adoptive mother.

'I need more,' Ione breathed shakily and, straining every sinew to overcome her own weakness, she moved out of the protective circle of his arms and turned round to face him again. 'More than you can give me.'

Alexio rested raw dark golden eyes on her. 'I haven't been unfaithful to you…and I will not be in the future either.'

Possibly he fully believed that, Ione thought wretchedly. Perhaps because she had caught him out before he could even succumb to the provocative Pascale's charms, guilt was making him credit that he could change. But it was too late. The writing was on the wall and she was painfully aware that there would be countless occasions when temptation came Alexio's way. He was an extraordinarily good-looking man and that reality combined with ruthless power and enormous wealth would encourage all too many women to see him as a challenge.

'It was a nice honeymoon,' Ione whispered with ragged sincerity. 'But I mean it as no offence when I say that I can do better than stay married to a man like you. A man who buried his supposed heart in another woman's grave—'

'Ione—' Alexio ground out in raw interruption.

'I want a man who loves me for myself and I would

sooner be alone than accept anything less. All my life, I've accepted less, but I won't do it any longer,' she swore in an agonised undertone. 'I deserve a life of my own and I intend to find my sister, Misty, and get to know her.'

'I will help you to find your sister but I won't help you to make a life *away* from me!' Lean, powerful face taut with strain, Alexio reached for her clenched hands and engulfed them in his. 'This is crazy. I don't think you've absorbed a single word I've said and you're very upset.'

Ione swallowed back the awful thickness in her throat. Leaving Alexio felt like trying to sacrifice one of her own limbs. As she dragged her hands from his the door opened without warning and Alexio expelled his breath in a driven hiss of frustration. Then silence fell. A bulky older man wearing an Arab headdress with his suit stood on the threshold with an expectant air of impatience.

'Your Excellency...' Switching into business mode, Alexio strode forward to greet him.

After exchanging several phrases in what Ione assumed to be Arabic, Alexio swung back to draw her forward and introduce her as his wife. The older man was an emir, whose lengthy foreign name went right over Ione's buzzing head. She forced a polite smile to her stiff lips, conscious that he had to be the VIP whose arrival Alexio's secretary had tried to warn her was imminent.

As the emir's party entered in his wake, Alexio tugged open the door into an adjoining office and, recognising that neither of them had any choice but to accept the interruption with good grace, Ione walked on through. 'Twenty minutes...please wait,' Alexio urged in a charged undertone, searching her evasive green eyes for agreement.

As he hesitated, visibly unwilling to leave her without that assurance, Ione nodded. The tension easing in his darkly handsome features, he closed the door again, leaving her alone. Ione drew in a sustaining breath and walked straight out through the other door into the corridor outside Alexio's office. It was easier this way, she told herself as she entered the lift, closely followed by her protection team. No more unpleasant arguments, no dragged-out, emotionally draining scenes at which she might risk losing impetus and conviction. She was weak where Alexio was concerned but she had meant every word she'd said to him. He could have all the Pascales he wanted now and continue to cherish his photos of Crystal, but she would have a life of her own too.

She told one of her bodyguards to call her a taxi and remove her suitcase from the limousine. When the taxi arrived, she informed the men whom Alexio had hired to dog her every footstep that she did not wish to be accompanied or followed. She asked the driver to take her to the station from which she could most easily catch a train to Norfolk.

She was taking the first necessary step towards finding her sister and it was a journey that she had dreamt of making many times in the past. Yet now, when she had finally claimed the right and the freedom to make that journey, she was choked by tears and literally torn apart by the knowledge that it was unlikely that she would ever see Alexio again. The actual prospect of living without him hit her then like a giant rock dropped from a height…and telling herself that she had been strong and had made the right decision was not of the smallest comfort.

It was after nine that evening when Ione got off the train and wearily waited for yet another taxi to pick her up from the rural station.

But she was finally within only a few miles of the house

where her sister had been living when she had written to Ione almost five years earlier. The taxi driver told her that Fossetts was a local landmark: a tall, narrow building with a steep roof and attic windows that from a distance lent it the quaint charm of a doll's house. As she thought about that letter, which her father had not allowed her to reply to or retain, Ione's throat ached. Would her sister be able to forgive her for that lack of response? And what were the chances of there *still* being someone living at Fossetts who either knew or remembered Misty?

Asking the driver to wait as she planned to spend the night at a local hotel, Ione approached the front door. She was very nervous. A well-built middle-aged woman answered the bell.

'I'm sorry to disturb you at this hour but I'm trying to trace a woman called Misty Carlton,' Ione explained tautly. 'She lived here about five years ago.'

The woman looked bemused. 'But not now, I'm afraid. Misty got married last year.'

'Married?' Ione echoed in considerable surprise.

'Why, yes…to Leone Andracchi. He's a very successful businessman and they have a little boy called Connor now. Misty's foster mother, Birdie Peace, still lives here but unfortunately she's out this evening.'

Shock and excitement made Ione's heart beat very fast. 'Could you give me Misty's address?'

Her momentarily chatty informant seemed discomfited by that more bold request. 'Well, I'm not sure I'm at liberty to do that. May I ask why you're trying to get in touch with Misty?'

Ione drew in a charged breath. 'I think…I mean, I *know* that she's my twin sister. I was adopted but she went into foster care. I've wanted to find my sister for a long time.'

For several tense seconds silence stretched while the

woman stared at Ione in frank disconcertion. 'My goodness, will you come inside and wait for Birdie to come
home?'

'Thank you, but I've been travelling all day and I'm
very tired.' Ione was reluctant to have to deal with the
brimming curiosity now visible in the older woman's face.
'Perhaps you could give me Misty's phone number…'

Minutes later, Ione got back into the taxi on knees that
felt as weak as cotton wool. She had it, she *had* the phone
number! She had also learnt that her sister was a couple
of hundred miles away in Scotland where she and her husband had a second home, but nothing could dim her joy
at finally having a concrete link to the twin from whom
she had been parted soon after birth. At that moment, believing that she might actually lift a phone and hear her
long-lost sister's voice on the line was almost too much
for Ione to credit.

Furthermore, it seemed that her father had lied about
her sibling's lifestyle, for the adventurous sister whom
Ione had naively believed would need her support and advice was already both happily married and a mother. She
was embarrassed by her own clear misconceptions about
her twin and grateful that she had had no opportunity to
reveal them and cause offence. Yet that discovery was also
another humbling moment of truth for Ione, who could not
help comparing her sister's apparent security with the humiliating reality that her own marriage had barely lasted
the length of the honeymoon.

Checking into the Belstone House hotel, Ione requested
a suite. In the seclusion of the gracious sitting room, her
first act was to order a meal for she was feeling dizzy from
lack of food. Then she studied the phone again and the
piece of paper bearing that all-important number. Common
sense told her that late at night was hardly a sociable hour

at which to call in the hope of speaking to her sister for
the first time.

Baulked from the one act that might hopefully have
banished Alexio to the back of her mind, Ione strove not
to think instead about what her estranged husband might
be doing at that exact moment. Hadn't she given him his
freedom back? So why should he not take advantage of
it? Alexio might well have enjoyed the romantic evening
with Pascale that, at the outset of the day, Ione herself had
hoped to share with him. After all, what would he have
left to lose?

And that had been *her* choice. She trembled, tummy
churning at the awful turmoil threatening to eat her alive.
In a determined movement, she stripped all the rings he
had given her from her hand and set them on the coffee-
table. Walking through to the bedroom, she decided to
have a quick shower and change into something more
comfortable before her meal arrived.

But just suppose, another little voice piped up while she
was in the shower, just suppose the explanation Alexio
had given her about Pascale had been the truth? A pushy
ex-girlfriend showing up without warning and making herself at home in the apartment with a view to persuading
him into continuing their relationship in spite of his recent
marriage? Ione groaned in shame at her own revealing
train of thought. To even think in such a manner was to
risk becoming the kind of wife who buried her head in the
sand and swallowed any excuse, no matter how improb-
able it was.

Surely she would fall out of love again with Alexio?
Surely her awareness of his true character would kill that
love stone dead? But why was life so cruel? Why, when
Yannis had been so fine a man, had she only been able to
admire and respect him? And yet when Alexio had come

along, she had seen all his flaws yet *still* she had let him steal her heart!

As she tied the sash on her light silk robe the noisy clackety-clack approach of a low-flying helicopter made Ione wince. She moved over to the window. Her heart skipped a beat in sheer shock when she saw a craft emblazoned in the unmistakable colours of Christoulakis Enterprises skimming in low over the hotel's illuminated topiary gardens and coming in to land out of view…

CHAPTER EIGHT

As ALEXIO sprang from the helicopter he was still light-headed with the rage that had roared through him unabated all evening.

When he had walked into that office next to his own and found it empty, he had been shattered by what felt like the ultimate stab in the back. That Ione should have agreed to wait and had then broken her word had been, on his terms, an unconscionable act of betrayal. Prior to that, he had been ready to make allowances for the fact that she was the daughter of a man who had had more affairs while married than most men managed while single. He had even acknowledged the unwelcome spectre of his own womanising reputation with gritted teeth and conceded that as some excuse for Ione's refusal to immediately believe his side of the story on Pascale.

However, events had then taken a much more disturbing turn. Calling her security team to discover where she was, he had been appalled to realise that she had dismissed her bodyguards. Ione with that ridiculous attaché case packed full of cash and diamond jewellery was out *alone* and *unprotected*? Ione, who had no more idea of how to look after herself in the real world than a cartoon character?

He had been furious that he had not raised the subject of the contents of that case while they'd been in Paris! But he had been reluctant to hurt or embarrass her. After all, who did not have their little quirks? And if she could not bear to be parted from her late mother's hoard of jewellery and only felt secure with a vast amount of cash in her possession, where was the harm when she was guarded every place she went?

He had been on the brink of heading straight to the police when one of her bodyguards had admitted that she was actually being tailed by two of her team, but that, unsure whether he would have wished them to disobey her direct orders, their plea of initial ignorance had seemed wiser. His almost sick sense of relief had combined then with the first stirrings of an anger stronger and deeper than anything Alexio had ever felt in his life.

Awaiting a knock on the door of her suite, Ione stood taut, her head high, her chin at a defiant angle. It *had* to have been Alexio in that helicopter! She could not credit that coincidence could have brought one of his executives to the same country hotel. But beyond that level, her mind was in a loop. Even as she reminded herself that she was not afraid of anything that Alexio might say, panic and the most lowering sense of excitement were tearing her in two opposing directions.

No knock sounded. Instead there was a click as the card-entry mechanism was utilised and the door swung wide. Alexio powered in with his long, purposeful stride and the door thudded shut again in his wake. Golden eyes ablaze, his lean, strong face was rigid with forbidding constraint. Her heart banged up and down inside her like a ball being bounced on a very hard surface.

'How *dare* you register here as a Gakis?' Alexio launched at her without even pausing to gather his breath. 'How dare you deny my name?'

As an opening salvo, that was an unexpected one and Ione parted her lips, failed to think of anything cutting enough to say in response and closed her mouth again, keenest of all to retain her dignity.

'But then you have a remarkable degree of arrogance!'

Alexio shot at her in wrathful continuance. 'In that you are a Gakis right down to your little pearly fingertips!'

Green eyes widening, she stared back at him in genuine shock. 'That's not true—'

'Isn't it? What right did you have to tell me that our marriage was over? Are you the only person in this relationship? Are you always right and never wrong? Do you make a habit of judging others on the slightest of proof? Well, it's good to know that when our marriage hit its first minor storm, you baled out so fast you left a smoke trail!' Alexio completed with savage sarcasm.

Ione set her teeth together and refused to react.

'But then you're a Gakis...how could you possibly be wrong about anything?' Alexio punctuated that sardonic aside by setting a small disc recorder down on the dining table by the window. 'Only this time, as you're about to find out, you've made nothing but a bloody fool of yourself!'

'Really?' High spots of outraged pink had formed over Ione's cheekbones. 'What's that machine about to do? Paralyse me into stupidity?'

'*All* my office phone calls are recorded.' Alexio depressed the button with one stab of a long, punitive forefinger.

Ione stiffened as the disc began to play. She heard Alexio accepting the call from Pascale and the other woman's husky voice struck an immediate chord of recognition with her. She was surprised though to hear Pascale address Alexio in fluent Greek. Pascale announced that she was in London overnight and that, knowing that Alexio was in town as well, she was hoping that they could be together. As still as a marble image, her angry colour slowly draining away, Ione listened to the brief exchange that followed. The coolness edging Alexio's dark drawl was patent once he realised that Pascale had already made herself at home in the apartment, but the persistent brunette still tried to keep him chatting before suggesting a second time that he join her for dinner.

'Give me a break,' she heard Alexio say drily. 'Use the apartment tonight if you must but leave the key on your way out. I won't be visiting.'

'But you'll still know where to find me if you change your mind,' Pascale pointed out in a provocative purr before she rang off.

A deathly silence stretched then. Ione's hands continued to thread the loose ends of her sash back and forth between her restive fingers. Inside herself, she was coming apart at the seams with the craziest urge to shout and scream with joy and relief. She had been wrong, oh, yes, she had been very, very wrong and she was happy, indeed downright *ecstatic* to learn that she had misjudged her husband. The weight of sheer misery that she had been fighting off for endless hours fell from her in the space of an instant.

'Alexio…' Ione fixed shining eyes on him, her low-pitched voice hoarse with the fierceness of her emotions. 'I'm—'

'No.' Alexio lifted a lean, emphatic hand, shimmering golden eyes raking over her with contempt. 'Don't you dare to think for one moment that sorry is going to cut any ice with me *this* time around!'

Studying him with startled eyes, Ione breathed, 'But I *am* sorry—'

'You said you'd wait in that office but you *lied* to me. I've never stayed with a woman I can't trust. I also expect my wife to have the highest standards of loyalty and honesty. And you don't appear to have either quality!'

'But, I…' A thickness was blooming in Ione's throat

and clogging her vocal cords and she was so tense her muscles ached. She was devastated by that condemnation.

'No buts.' Lean, dark handsome face set hard, Alexio treated her to a raking head-to-toe appraisal that judged and found *her* wanting. 'You walked out on me when the very least you owed me was a hearing. At the first sign of trouble, you trashed everything we had and took off!'

'What was I supposed to believe when I found Pascale in your apartment?' Ione demanded emotively, her delicate bone structure drawn tight beneath her skin as she tried to defend herself.

'You were *supposed* to believe in me. You were *supposed* to value our marriage enough to stay and discuss the situation like an adult. But all you could think about was putting the boot in first and saving face,' Alexio derided. 'Nothing else mattered to you. You listened to nothing I said—'

'Pascale told me that you were lovers—'

'*Were* being the operative word. It's over two months since I last saw her and our casual arrangement ended well in advance of our wedding.'

'All right, I overreacted.' Desperation was beginning to get a strong grip on Ione. 'I should have given you more of a chance to explain...'

Alexio rested grim dark golden eyes on her. 'But that's not enough, is it? If Pascale had called me on my mobile phone, I wouldn't have been able to prove that I hadn't set up a meeting with her. But she didn't have my most recent number so she had to call me at the office. Where would we be now if I hadn't had a recording of that phone call?'

Ione turned bone-white as he floated that scenario before her.

'I think that without that recording I'd have been up

that four-letter word of a creek,' Alexio framed, his declaration raw-edged with bitter anger. 'If you can't have faith in me, we can't have a marriage.'

That tone of savage finality made Ione's heart sink to her toes. She had gone from ennervated defensiveness to soaring shame laced with joy, only to be cast down again. She had accused him of something he hadn't done and refused to trust his word. Indeed, she had been all too ready to believe him guilty. *Why?* she now asked herself in an agony of self-reproach. Why had she been so quick to judge him? She thought back to the glorious weeks they had shared in Paris and the high of happiness she had been on when she had arrived in London earlier that day. Dimly, she grasped what had gone wrong.

'You see...' Ione's voice emerged riven with strain...I'd never been so happy before and, perhaps, I couldn't quite believe in it. When Pascale said what she did, it was like I'd been expecting you to betray me all along. I just accepted it. It seemed much more realistic and familiar than all that happiness.'

Alexio was giving her an arrested look from beneath frowning black brows, his intense golden eyes locked to her, his big, powerful frame whip-taut with his growing tension as he listened.

'I think I'm very cynical. I don't think I'm arrogant. I think I try to protect myself because I've been hurt a lot,' Ione admitted in a tight undertone. 'I grew up in a home where my only strength was my pride, but I still had to sacrifice it to keep myself safe. I'm not accustomed to being able to depend on or trust anyone else but...but I can *learn*.'

Alexio endeavoured to conceal his shattered response to what she was telling him, but it was as though she had landed him a sudden hard punch in the stomach. He realised just how much his own contented and uncomplicated childhood had influenced his expectations of life and other people. He saw that what he had always taken for granted Ione had never had. Not the security, not the safety, not the trust that all needs would be met and definitely not the love. And that realisation just gutted him.

Closing the distance between them in a long stride, he hauled Ione into his arms. She stiffened in surprise but her heartbeat picked up speed like an express train. 'I don't want your pity—'

'Is lust OK?' Alexio broke in faster than the speed of light.

A ragged laugh escaped Ione. Suddenly pliant as a rag doll, she let him crush her close to his broad, muscular chest and squash her damp face into his shoulder. He smoothed her platinum-fair hair with a hand that wasn't quite steady and she registered that he was as shaken up as she was. 'I'm so sorry I put you through this,' she mumbled painfully.

'Forget it. I just realised that I was coming from a place you haven't got to yet,' Alexio delivered an assurance that she found incomprehensible in a wry undertone. 'But I didn't marry you to play around with other women. I've had years and years of total freedom to do whatever I liked and I *did* and I'm ready for something different now. You have to accept that too.'

'Yes…'

Someone knocked on the door and Alexio groaned. 'Who the hell is that?'

'It's probably the meal I ordered.'

Releasing her, Alexio opened the door. A waiter wheeled in a trolley, laid out the dishes and departed again with a very fat tip in his hand. Ione gazed at Alexio, every sense drinking him in: the brilliant, beautiful eyes that tied her in mental knots, the long, lithe strength and vitality of his lean, athletic frame, the supreme self-command that was as at home with blunt, open anger as affection and tenderness. He was a hell of a guy and she didn't feel she deserved him, didn't even know if he was willing to forgive her and didn't have the courage to ask.

Alexio lodged his intent gaze on her and the atmosphere sizzled. 'How hungry are you?' he enquired thickly.

'Not…' The instant that Ione recognised the smouldering flare of sexual hunger lighten his stunning eyes to pure mesmeric gold, her voice cried up on her and she couldn't find the rest of the words she needed.

But it seemed that Alexio understood for his slashing smile lightened the tension in his bronzed, masculine features. 'I want you too, *yineka mou*' he admitted, backing her step by step in the direction of the bedroom. 'You have no idea just how much.'

Relief cascaded through her and the breath caught in her throat. 'Still?'

'It's a round-the-clock obsession,' Alexio husked in hoarsened syllables as he reached for her and brought his mouth crashing down with raw passion on hers.

His sheer energy and unashamed need pulsed through Ione like an adrenalin charge. The explicit plunge and withdrawal of his tongue inside the tender interior of her mouth was so incredibly erotic that she whimpered helpless encouragement and clung to his shoulders, standing on tiptoes to aid him. With a rueful sound of frustration, Alexio lifted her off her feet and settled her down on the wide divan in the bedroom.

'I should still be mad with you,' he groaned. 'I don't chase all over the countryside after women. I don't *do* that kind of stuff—'

'You won't have to do it ever again,' Ione swore.

'You want to write that down and sign it in triplicate?' Alexio teased, capturing her lips in a long, drugging kiss that fired every fibre of her being while he extracted her from her robe with deft hands.

Wrenching himself back from her to undress, he rested molten eyes of appreciation on her. Ione lay there naked, face burning at the awareness that her nipples were visibly taut and swollen and that she ached for him.

'You're so beautiful,' Alexio breathed, coming back to her, all hard contours of powerful masculinity and overwhelmingly sexy.

He took her lush mouth again. He was all passion and plunder, ravishing her lips apart with his own, and she couldn't get enough of him, couldn't still the wild, trembling eagerness that had seized hold of her. She had thought they might never be together again and she ran her hands over his muscular arms, arched her spine up so that her tender breasts rubbed the hair-roughened wall of his chest, parted her thighs in instinctive invitation.

'Don't wait,' she muttered fiercely, letting her teeth graze a smooth, hard shoulder.

Alexio lifted his dark, tousled head, shimmering golden eyes ablaze with need and raw satisfaction. 'You want me that much?'

'*Always…*' she moaned as he discovered the slick, wet heat at the heart of her.

Slow and sure, he eased himself into her and the sensation was so intense that tears stung her eyes and her back arched in ecstasy. She strained up to him and sobbed out loud with frustration and excitement until his pagan rhythm matched her frantic fervour. The blinding instant of release convulsed her in a glorious overload of pleasure that sent shock waves splintering through her every skincell.

'I suppose I should let you eat now,' Alexio sighed with pronounced reluctance as he stole a last lingering kiss. He lifted her on top of him and closed his arms round her in a possessive hold that pinned her to every damp inch of his big, powerful frame. 'After all, I know that you haven't eaten since you stepped off the plane from Paris, *agape mou*.'

Brows pleating, Ione emerged from her somnolent daze of contentment to lift her tousled head. 'How do you know that?'

'You were tailed from my office. How do you think I found you so fast?' The teasing light in his gaze ebbed to be replaced by a more serious expression. 'Don't dismiss your bodyguards like that again.'

Ione coloured. 'If I was followed, they didn't listen to me.'

Alexio laced his hands into the wild tumble of her bright hair, level eyes censorious. 'I was very grateful they didn't listen. In Paris, you left that vanity case you take everywhere lying open one night in the dressing room and I *saw* the contents.'

Ione froze and lost every scrap of natural colour. He had actually seen the money that had once figured as her escape fund from their marriage? She had had no idea how to dispose of that money without running the risk of alerting Alexio to the reality that her flight on their wedding day had been a pre-planned event.

'That cash ought to be in the bank and the diamonds should be in a safe,' Alexio murmured gently.

Dry-mouthed, Ione nodded in instant agreement and fearfully waited for him to ask the obvious question of why she had found it necessary to carry round a case stuffed with money and her late mother's jewellery. But Alexio just smiled, that heart-stopping smile that always left her weak with love. Almost as weak with relief that he had not enquired further into the matter, Ione buried her discomfited face in his shoulder, her guilty conscience weighing heavy. She would never be able to confess the truth. If he ever found out how selfish and foolish she had been before their wedding, he would not forgive her.

'So…' Alexio drawled with studied casualness. 'You called at a house before you checked in here. What was that about?'

Ione grinned, her attack of conscience falling to the back of her mind as she thought about her twin. 'That house belonged to my twin's foster mother. I said who I was and *now*…I've got Misty's phone number!'

Alexio sat up in a sudden movement that took her by surprise. 'What did your sister say when you called?'

'I haven't called yet…I thought it was too late at night—'

Alexio unleashed a groan and made her tell him exactly what she had said and to whom at Fossetts. 'Don't you realise that your twin's probably sitting by the phone right now *waiting* for that call? People don't keep information like that to themselves. I'm sure she's already been told that you went to her foster mum's home and got her number.'

Ione reddened. 'I'll call first thing in the morning.'

Vaulting out of bed, Alexio strode into the sitting room to retrieve the piece of paper he had noted earlier lying on the coffee-table. He was amused at himself. Why on earth had he got the crazy idea that that might be Yannis's number? The fisherman's son was old history.

Minutes later, Ione found herself seated with a phone planted into her hand while her husband stood by, his magnificent body interrupted only by a pair of grey jersey boxer shorts. 'It's after midnight,' she protested tautly. 'It's just not right to call this late.'

'You're scared and she's probably scared too. Get on with it,' Alexio instructed.

The phone was answered by a breathless female voice even before Ione heard it ring at her end of the line. 'I'm Ione Christoulakis,' she said unsteadily. Is that Misty?'

'Yes. Are you my twin?' the voice asked anxiously.

'Yes. I don't know what to say to you…now I've found you—'

'My head's in a spin too. In fact, I'm thrilled to death. I was terrified you weren't going to call and I couldn't *believe* that Birdie's cousin had let you go without even getting your name or your address!' Misty's voice had gathered steam and pace to become bright and excited. 'If we arrange a special flight for you, will you fly up here tonight?'

Ione's eyes rounded in astonishment and she turned to speak to Alexio in Greek.

'No,' he pronounced at decisive speed. 'You're already on the edge of exhaustion. Tell her, we'll fly up early tomorrow morning.'

'Who are you with?' Misty asked with intense curiosity. 'And what is that language you're speaking?'

And from that point on, all awareness vanished. While Alexio ordered fresh meals for them both on the hotel's internal phone, Ione curled up on the sofa and rushed to answer her twin's surge of eager questions before finally gaining the confidence to press her own. Alexio went for a shower. Supper arrived and Ione ate it with one hand in tiny morsels because she couldn't stop talking. Only when it got to the point where she was smothering yawns through every sentence did she reach the stage where she could face saying goodbye to her twin for a few hours.

Then she just slumped with a dazed and happy smile on her weary mouth. 'My sister lives in a castle,' she informed Alexio.

Alexio lifted his wife off the sofa, carried her through to the bedroom and slotted her between the sheets. Even in the time it took him to reappear with the rings he had scooped off the coffee-table, and which he had steadfastly desisted from commenting on, she had gone out like a light into a deep sleep. He threaded her wedding ring back onto her limp hand and then wondered why it had seemed so important to do that.

By the time the helicopter landed the following day at the private airstrip at Castle Eyrie, Ione was bubbling over with a heady mixture of excitement and nerves.

'Misty's going to love you,' Alexio forecast, enclosing Ione's taut fingers in a reassuring hold as he helped her climb out. 'You got on like a house on fire on the phone last night.'

All Ione's attention centred on the woman hurrying towards them and the big smile of welcoming warmth on her twin's vibrant face.

'Let me look at you…' Copper hair streaming back from her brow in the breeze, Misty bounded up with the lithe grace of her very long legs, bright silver-grey eyes engaged in a fascinated appraisal of her smaller, tenser twin. 'Oh, my goodness, you're tiny…and really, *really* beautiful,' she gasped, slowly shaking her head. 'Our gene pool was a real lucky bag. But you're the living image of our paternal grandmother. Our father has a portrait of her. She was a legendary beauty in the thirties.'

And as Ione met her sister's emotive gaze and saw the tears there that mirrored her own and heard those words, which for the very first time connected her to another family, her heart felt as if it were ballooning inside her. She didn't know who made the move first but they engulfed each other in a clumsy hug, laughing and crying at the same time. Then Misty's arm wrapped round her, Ione was urged over to a sports car, tucked into the passenger seat and wafted back to the castle with her chattering sister at the wheel.

Meanwhile, Leone and Alexio had been introducing themselves, standing back at a distance, striving not to spoil that special moment when their respective wives saw each other for the first time in over twenty years.

'Bloody hell…' Leone breathed in disbelief as the car sped past about thirty feet away. 'Misty's stranded us!'

Silence reigned for several seconds while both men waited for the car to slacken speed and turn. Alexio and Leone exchanged a brief glance of mutual male incredulity, but neither felt it necessary to remark on the fact that they had been overlooked like left luggage in the general excitement.

They strolled back to the castle and Leone broke the news that there was yet another sister called Freddy. A half-sister, born of Ione's natural mother's first marriage and married to the Crown Prince of Quamar. 'She talks a lot too,' Leone commented. 'And Misty was on the phone to her at dawn today, so I suspect you're going to be meeting Freddy soon as well.'

'The more the merrier,' Alexio quipped with easy amusement. 'Ione doesn't have much in the way of family.'

'Minos Gakis?' Acknowledging that he was already aware of exactly *who* Ione was, Leone absorbed Alexio's momentarily grim expression and relaxed a little more. 'I suggest we go for lunch—'

'Leave them to their reunion, stay out late.' An appreciative smile formed on Alexio's wide, shapely mouth. 'Just how long do you think it'll take our wives to miss us?'

Curled up at either end of the same sofa in the lofty drawing room and sharing a pot of coffee, Misty and Ione only remembered the husbands they had abandoned when Murdo, the elderly butler, came in to announce lunch and asked if his employer and Mr Christoulakis would be back in time for the meal. Aghast expressions crossed Ione's and Misty's faces at the exact same moment. They met each other's eyes and then went off into a guilty fit of giggles at what they had done.

'Have you ever forgotten about Leone before?' Ione whispered chokily.

'No, and I bet he's furious,' Misty groaned. 'What about Alexio?'

'I wouldn't think it would have made his day,' Ione confided, but, learning from Murdo that their husbands had returned to the castle and departed from there in Leone's four-wheel drive, the sisters relaxed again. The first part of the day had passed with Ione keen to hear her sister describe their late mother and learn about Carrie Carlton's ill-starred affair with their natural father, Oliver Sargent. She'd been truly thrilled at the news that she still had another older sister, Freddy, to meet. But the afternoon passed with the simple pleasure of cradling her adorable little nephew, Connor, on her lap and just talking and getting to know her twin.

That evening, Ione stood at their Gothic bedroom window in the castle watching the sun go down over the shimmering loch and released a wondering sigh of contentment. Alexio, who had reappeared with Leone just in time for what had proved to be a very entertaining dinner, tugged her into his arms and turned her round to face him. 'Good day?'

She looked up into his spectacular eyes and, acknowledging how very special he was, she just melted from outside him. 'Heavenly.'

'We should buy a house over here.'

Ione tensed and then, appreciating that it was past time that she practised greater openness with Alexio, she took a deep breath. 'We don't need to. I inherited Cosmas's London townhouse and my adoptive mother left me Caradore Park, her family's country home. I haven't visited either property but my father makes use of both when he's in England.'

Lean, strong face clenching hard, Alexio was very still. 'And you didn't consider those facts worth mentioning before now?'

Ione evaded his incredulous gaze and contrived a shrug. 'It just didn't seem important. You know...I think I'll go for a bath,' she muttered in the sizzling silence, heading for the *en suite* at supersonic speed.

Alexio drew in a slow, deep sustaining breath. He caught the bathroom door before it could snap shut. 'There's more, *isn't* there?'

Taut as a bowstring, Ione gulped. 'Mama and Cosmas left me everything.'

One glance at Alexio's rigidity was sufficient to assure Ione that her husband had a very good idea of what everything encompassed and an awful silence stretched while he absorbed that revelation.

'So...' Alexio drawled with noticeably flat diction. 'You place it all in trust for our children.'

The silence fell thick and quiet again.

'No...' Ione almost whispered.

Glittering golden eyes backed by all the force of

Alexio's powerful personality locked to her. 'I've already given you my views on this subject.'

Paling at that fair and true reminder, Ione bent her head.

'Every Greek husband regards it as his right to provide for his wife,' Alexio declared with stubborn conviction.

His ferocious pride was getting in the way of his intelligence, Ione reflected with gritted teeth. She could not credit that his partnership with her father would last the course and she was trying to protect them both. Sooner or later, Minos Gakis would do something underhanded in business that would alienate Alexio. When Alexio attempted to dissolve that partnership, her father would try to destroy him. A time might come when even Alexio might appreciate that advantage of not having a dependent wife whose wealth was tied up for posterity in trust funds.

'I won't compromise on this score,' Alexio warned her with a lethal quiet assurance that sent a shiver down her slender spine. 'It is a matter of what is *right*.'

As he shut the door on her again with a definitive snap, she jerked and accidentally up-ended an entire dish of fragrant bath bombs into the tub. They fizzed like noisy fireworks sending out a rainbow of streaking colours that blurred beneath her fraught gaze. So much for honesty!

By the time she emerged Alexio was in bed, lying back against the banked-up pillows, one long, powerful thigh exposed by the covers he had disarranged. Shimmering golden eyes locked to her and her mouth ran dry, heart jumping, pulses speeding up. The sheer, gorgeous impact of him continually knocked her flat and left her breathless.

'As I see it, *agape mou*,' Alexio murmured levelly, 'this too is a matter of trust. Do you or do you not have faith in my ability to look after you?'

Instantly, Ione saw the drawbacks of having allowed that keen, cutting intellect of his the space to come up with the most devastating argument available to him. 'How can you be so low as to ask me that? What can I say to such a question?'

'Yes...or...*no*?' Alexio traded, refusing to back down an inch.

Aware that even a hint of a negative on that score would outrage his pride and undermine their marriage, Ione did something she had never done before: she slid with the most seductive wriggle she had ever contrived out of her nightdress. She felt the sudden sexual burn of Alexio's intent gaze on her pouting breasts and slim hips, the sudden instant shift in atmosphere that resulted as his all-too-potent virility focused him on earthier pleasures. Barely breathing and her face hot, she sauntered over to the bed and got in beside him, arching her back as she shook her silvery mane of hair back off her narrow shoulders.

'Yes...of course, yes,' she whispered sweetly.

'You're a witch,' Alexio growled, scorching golden eyes flaring over her exquisite face as he locked one hand into her glorious hair. Hauling her caveman-style down on top of him, he locked his hungry mouth to hers and claimed a fiery kiss that currented through her quivering length with the efficiency of a heat-seeking missile.

Over the weekend that followed at the castle, Ione talked to her half-sister, Freddy, at length on the phone and agreed to meet up with her natural father, Oliver, for lunch on her next visit to London. It was time for her and Alexio to return to Greece and, although she knew it would be a wrench to leave her twin behind, she could bear that better than she could have borne being parted from Alexio. Their marriage was too new and she was far too much in love to accept Misty's invitation to stay on at the castle without Alexio for another few days.

Minutes before Alexio and Ione embarked on their flight

to Athens, Alexio received an urgent call that he took in private. Only after the jet had taken off did Ione notice the lines of tension holding his lean, darkly handsome features taut and the sombre look in his gaze.

'What's wrong?' she asked.

Alexio released his breath in a slow, pent-up hiss. Shock was still coursing through him. He had just received the news that his father-in-law's condition had, with very little warning, worsened. His doctors had decided that the planned surgery was now out of the question and that there was little more they could do for him. Assailed by the total innocence of Ione's enquiring gaze, he cursed his own reluctance to break his word to Minos.

'Ione…your father is seriously ill,' he imparted.

Before his eyes, Ione's face went white. 'Since…since when?'

Alexio closed his hands round hers and told her exactly what her father had told him over six weeks earlier.

CHAPTER NINE

HER shattered expression a clear indication of the level of her shock, Ione dragged her fingers from Alexio's in a driven jerky movement. 'Papa is dying...and you *knew* and you kept that from me?'

"It was your father's wish that neither you nor your aunt were told. He was to have surgery in a few weeks. Now that's not an option,' Alexio conceded tautly while Ione continued to stare at him with accusing and stricken eyes. 'But I believed, as Minos believed, that the crisis point was still some time away.'

'The crisis point...' Ione trembled, spun away from him like an uncoordinated doll. She remembered that her father had looked ill when he had come home from his last trip abroad, but she had put that down to overwork for he had always driven himself too hard. How could she *not* have realised? How could Alexio *not* have warned her?

'I believed that I still had plenty of time in which to prepare you,' Alexio admitted with audible regret.

'And you are the man who *dared* to tell me that I did not meet your standards of honesty?' Ione slung at him with quivering force, lashing out wildly at him because she was being eaten alive by guilt. Guilt that she had been so absorbed in her own problems months earlier that she had neglected to note her father's declining health. Guilt that she had so recently planned to leave the Gakis family for ever in a manner that would have caused her father immense public embarrassment and annoyance.

'I did not like to break my word to him.' Making that

150

admission in a driven undertone, Alexio spread speaking, fluid hands in an expressive movement that was wholly Greek.

'So even Papa has more rights in this marriage than I do!' Ione hurled at him, taking off on another tangent without skipping a beat. 'You put your word to him above your loyalty to me, but this is a *family* issue…and you are *not* a Gakis!'

Shaking like a leaf, Ione collapsed down into her seat. She could not look at him because she knew that what she was saying was unfair. He knew too well what her home life had been like. But, for the first time in many years, Ione was registering that, in spite of everything, she cared for her father, could not *help* caring for her father, could not think of herself as anything other than Greek and a Gakis because that was where her earliest remembered roots were and always would be. Finding her twin, Misty, had filled her with joy, but she had felt oddly detached from their discussions about their natural parents and only now did she appreciate why that had been so: twenty-three years of living another life could not be set aside or overlooked.

'You'll be on Lexos by this evening,' Alexio assured her.

With difficulty, Ione swallowed the ballooning thickness in her throat. 'Papa hates to be fussed over. I understand why he chose not to tell me or Kalliope about his condition. It's not your fault.'

In the early hours of the following morning, Ione left her father's room where only medical personnel now held sway. Her father had been so ill that throughout the hours she had sat by his bedside he had not once seemed aware of her presence. Seeing the parent who had always dominated the household in such a weak state had been a considerable shock for Ione. No, there would be no improvement, the doctor had informed her: the older man had suffered a major heart attack.

Conscious that it was too late to go and talk to her aunt, who was so distraught over her brother's condition that she had yet to emerge from her rooms to speak to either Alexio or her niece, Ione went back to her own suite. It had been several hours since she had seen Alexio for her father's lawyers, in company with his top executives, had been anxiously awaiting her husband's arrival at the villa. Alexio was now in official charge of the Gakis empire and Ione was painfully aware that the demands on both his time and his attention would be immense.

As she entered her sitting room she was surprised to see the doors spread back on the balcony, and then her heart quickened when she saw Alexio there, his jacket and tie discarded and his formal shirt open at his strong brown throat.

'I thought you'd still be working…'

'Not when I have to start work again in a few hours' time, *agape mou*.' Alexio held out his arms in an expansive motion that made her strained eyes sting with tears. She hurtled into that embrace like a homing pigeon.

'And then how could I go to bed without first pausing to admire your teddy-bear collection in the moonlight?' Alexio remarked deadpan, casting meaningful eyes at the room a few feet away where the bears sat around on display.

A chokey little laugh escaped Ione at that sally. She loved him so much that sometimes it almost hurt to be that close to him. Weak at the knees, she curved into his big, powerful frame, taking strength from the warmth and strength of his hard, muscular body, drowning in the husky, familiar scent of his skin. 'Cosmas was planning to have cabinets built for them—'

'A most indulgent brother.'

Ione looked up at him with rueful green eyes. 'I like bears but it was Cosmas who was totally crazy about them.'

A pleat formed between Alexio's winged ebony brows. *'Cosmas?'*

With a sigh, Ione murmured, 'He was gay…'

Taken aback, Alexio stared down at her with astonished dark golden eyes.

'Another Gakis secret known to very few,' Ione conceded with wry acceptance.

'Did Minos know?'

'Of course not. Papa was always telling Cosmas to find a wife.' In the moonlight, the pale, perfect triangle of Ione's face shadowed at that memory. 'The last few months of his life, Cosmas was under enormous strain, but he couldn't face telling Papa the truth.'

'I can imagine what a challenge that would have been.'

'In different ways,' Ione breathed in a wobbly undertone, her full mouth tremulous, 'both I and Cosmas were great disappointments to Papa…and now when I *see* him so—'

'Shush.' Alexio's strong arms tightened round her. 'Losing someone else always brings guilty feelings to the surface but what is done is done. Had I accepted that sooner, I would've dealt better with Crystal's death. But instead I blamed myself for what happened to her.'

Ione tensed in surprise at that admission. 'But why?'

Alexio lounged in a fluid motion back against the wrought-iron balustrade. His lean features were taut, black lashes low over his reflective golden gaze. 'Crystal and I had a row the day she died.' His expressive mouth compressed. 'She wanted me to set a date for the wedding and I refused. We'd had the same argument on several occasions. But that particular night we were staying in a beachside villa on Corfu—'

Ione studied his lean, dark, devasting features with keen interest. 'Why wouldn't you set a date?'

'During one of our many periods apart, she slept with another guy.' Alexio pushed long brown fingers through his luxuriant black hair and shifted a wide shoulder, his jawline squaring as Ione failed to conceal her disconcertion at that blunt revelation. 'Although I still wanted to *be* with her, I couldn't forget that. Our guests on Corfu were her friends. They liked to drink and horse around pretty much round the clock and I was bored. I left them and went off to work in another room. I never saw her alive again.'

Ione swallowed hard and touched his arm in an awkward movement, needing to show her sympathy but unable to find adequate words.

'A crowd of them went for a midnight swim. By the time they realised that Crystal was missing, it was too late. I felt like I'd *killed* her,' Alexio admitted with a quiet, charged force that shook Ione.

'*No*...' Ione breathed fiercely, closing her arms round him in turn and finally understanding why it had taken so long for him to get over Crystal Denby. Guilt. He had blamed himself for that final argument and for not being there in the water when his fiancée had needed him. 'It was a horrible accident...it was the same as Cosmas crashing his plane. There was nothing anybody could have done to prevent it.'

'But I'd never have let her go swimming after she'd been drinking. That *is* a fact,' Alexio countered ruefully.

'However, I don't beat myself up about it any more. Crystal often took crazy risks and rarely heeded advice.'

Tensing, Ione worried at her full lower lip. 'I must seem very dull stuff after her...'

'Are you kidding?' Vibrant amusement flashed through Alexio's stunning eyes and, throwing his proud, dark head back, he laughed with rich appreciation. 'I never know what you're going to do next!'

Colour warmed her cheeks. 'I won't ever walk out on our marriage again.'

'I don't plan to give you cause, *agape mou*.' With a husky sound low in his throat, Alexio captured her lips with sweet, delicious expertise and the anguished insecurities that had tormented her throughout the previous day fell into abeyance for what remained of the night.

Ione was up by eight and by then Alexio's side of the bed was already empty. Having talked to the doctor watching over her father and learned that there was no change, she went for breakfast.

Kalliope was already seated at the table in the superb panelled dining room. As Ione greeted her the older woman dealt her a resentful look and two highspots of pink marked her thin cheeks. 'So *at last* you are gracing us with your attention.'

'Had I known that Papa was ill, I would have come home sooner,' Ione protested.

Kalliope pursed her lips. 'You're lying. Don't lie to me.'

One glance was sufficient to warn Ione that her aunt was in a more than usually difficult mood. A look of sincere bewilderment on her face, Ione tensed in receipt of that condemnation, but she said nothing for she had no wish to be drawn into a hostile exchange with the older woman.

On the threshold of the room and unobserved by either

woman, however, Alexio came to a halt when he heard that same accusation. A censorious light in his gaze, he frowned at Kalliope Gakis.

All Kalliope's attention was centred on her niece. 'I spoke to Tipo after your husband dispensed with his services in Paris. I found out that you walked out on your marriage only a few hours after the wedding—'

Belatedly understanding exactly what her aunt was getting at, Ione jerked and lost colour and began talking fast in her own defence. 'That was all sorted out. I made a very foolish mistake but Alexio and I are happy together now.'

'A mistake? Is that what you call it?' The Greek woman raised an unimpressed brow. 'I let Tipo complete his investigation. He discovered that you booked that flight to London a full nine days *before* you even married Alexio Christoulakis!'

In the act of striding forward to draw attention to his presence, Alexio switched his attention to Ione at supersonic speed. 'Is this true?' he demanded of his wife before he had even allowed himself to absorb the full meaning of what he had just overheard.

The glass in Ione's hand tipped between her suddenly nerveless fingers and spilt a puddle of orange juice onto the polished surface of the dining table. While a gasp of dismay erupted from her aunt at Alexio's sudden appearance, Ione felt like someone frozen in time and space. Paralysed with horror at the knowledge that her husband had heard Kalliope's accusation, she stared across the room entrapped by Alexio's stunned dark golden eyes.

'I believe I asked you a question,' Alexio breathed with lethal quietness.

Pushing her chair back, Kalliope stood up. Her aghast scrutiny flickering between her niece's shattered face and

Alexio's menacing stillness, she muttered a stifled apology and hurried out of the room.

Ione set down her glass with a trembling hand and rose unsteadily upright. 'Alexio—'

'Shut up,' Alexio incised, cutting and quiet as a rapier blade. 'You know what I am asking you. Is it true that you booked that London flight nine days *before* our wedding?'

The hideous silence clawed at Ione's nerves for she did not know how to respond. Yes, it was the truth, but it was an appalling truth that might destroy their relationship. If she gave that confirmation, she would be admitting that she had agreed to marry him solely to use him and their wedding as a means of escape from her father's domination. She would be confessing that she had *never* intended to be his real wife, *never* intended even to live with him. And to make such a confession now when they had found such happiness was more than Ione could bear.

Torn apart by fear of the consequences, she gazed back at him, her skin clammy, her heart sinking like a stone. His superb bone structure was prominent beneath his bronzed skin, ferocious tension etched into the hard line of his mouth and his strong jaw as he waited for the response that she would have given ten years of her life at that moment to avoid.

'I'll ask you one last time...' Alexio breathed with raw emphasis. 'Is it the truth?'

Ione's rigid shoulders slumped as she recognised the complete impossibility of sidestepping that leading question. Pale as milk and trembling, she parted bloodless lips and muttered heavily, 'Yes. I wish I could say it was a ghastly lie but unhappily for me...it *is* the truth...'

In the depths of his brilliant dark golden eyes she saw all that she had feared: shock, incredulous disgust but, worst of all, she saw his angry pain that she could have sunk that low, cared so little for his feelings, indeed considered nobody but her own self. That single lancing look was the very worst punishment he could have given her and it filled her with the most terrible guilt and remorse she had ever experienced.

'It was wrong...but at the time, I was desperate. Papa hadn't allowed me to leave the island for four years. I was like a prisoner here,' she reasoned sickly, her agonised gaze clinging to his lean, hard features and the pallor spreading round his taut mouth. 'I wasn't thinking straight. I wasn't capable of thinking about how my plans would affect you—'

'Or even caring?' Alexio slotted in lethally.

Pained colour flared in her cheekbones. 'It was selfish and stupid and I regret that I ever thought that way—'

'You went through our wedding *knowing* what you were planning to do...' Alexio loosed a ragged laugh of disbelief, viewing her with renewed recoil. 'How could you do that? How could you go into that church and lie as you took the same vows that I took in faith and sincerity? Is there no end to the deception you're capable of?'

'I changed my mind at the last minute—'

'You changed your mind because I confronted you,' Alexio countered with harsh clarity.

'No...even before you found me at the airport, I had already had second thoughts about what I was doing!' Ione argued feverishly. 'I felt terrible. I couldn't bring myself to leave you—'

'Maybe the thought of that big wide world of freedom was a little too threatening for you by that stage. I don't accept that belated loyalty or decency had *any* sway over your behaviour. And we'll never know whether or not you would have got on that flight, will we?' Alexio pointed out in the same fierce tone of condemnation, his lean, powerful face grim and hard.

'I already had feelings for you...and I was f-fighting them!' Ione stammered in increasing turmoil. She could see the way the dialogue was going. He had just given her a frightening glimpse of how complete was his loss of faith in her.

His beautiful eyes as dark as the midnight hour, he viewed her with fierce condemnation. 'You just used me like I was nothing on your terms. Well, you have now proved to my full satisfaction that you require no blood bond to be a Gakis through and through...for only a Gakis would act with such total disregard for others!'

Her gaze lowering from his in shame and turmoil, Ione flinched for she could not excuse herself. Her original intention to use their marriage to her own ends had been indefensible and she had abandoned her escape plan too late to impress him. Had she turned back before she'd returned to the airport in Paris on their wedding day, it might have made a difference to his outlook, but she had not.

'I deserve that but I *couldn't* tell you the truth afterwards—'

'Had you admitted the truth that day at the airport hotel, I would have let you go,' Alexio interrupted with cold, brutal conviction. 'Our marriage would've been annulled. Indeed nothing on this earth would have persuaded me to give you a second chance!'

Ione tried and failed to swallow and mumbled unevenly, 'I very much wanted that second chance, Alexio.'

He shook his proud dark head in slow motion. 'I can't credit what a fool I've been! Your behaviour at our wedding...the cash and the jewellery in your luggage...the weakness of your excuses. I actually told myself I was dealing with a nervous virgin. I was ready and willing to be suckered. Do you know why?'

In sick dread of what he might say next, Ione shook her own head.

'No woman had ever ditched me before and at least a dozen women had tried to get me to the altar,' Alexio confided with seething self-derision stamped into his devastatingly handsome features. 'I was prepared to believe any excuse sooner than credit the ego-zapping truth: the woman I had chosen to make my wife, the woman I expected to grow old beside, was happy to walk out on our marriage a few hours after the ceremony!'

Despair was building in Ione by the second. 'Don't judge me for what I did weeks ago when I hardly knew you,' she pleaded. 'I'm not the same person any more and our marriage is the most important thing in my life now. I *care* about you—'

'So much that a mere hint of infidelity made you abandon our relationship a second time,' Alexio incised with lethal timing.

That destructive and dangerous reminder sent a wave of desperation travelling through Ione. Nothing she had said seemed to have made the smallest impression on him. In addition, Kalliope's revelation was now encouraging Alexio to put an even more damaging slant on more recent events.

Alexio spread two lean hands in a curiously clumsy movement that lacked his usual fluid grace. 'Our relationship is a lie...' he murmured in a roughened undertone. 'All of it right from the beginning—'

'No...no, it wasn't!' Ione cut in frantically.

Alexio cast her a look of murderous reproach. 'Are you seriously asking me to believe now that you ever had a photo of me in your locker at school?'

And it was with that unsettling and least expected final comment that Alexio strode out of the room. Ione slumped down into her chair, buried her face in her hands and sobbed her heart out. She was trying not to think of how many times she had stolen a look at those pin-up pics of Alexio over her classmate's shoulder.

Some minutes later, she jerked when someone squeezed her shoulder in a brief, awkward gesture of sympathy. Lifting her head, she was disconcerted to see her aunt looking down at her with guilty concern.

'I didn't mean to cause trouble between you and your husband,' Kalliope declared tautly. 'I like Alexio. He is part of the family now. I was angry with you. But I *wouldn't* have spoken had I known he was there to hear.'

'I know,' Ione conceded heavily.

Kalliope nodded in her more usual brisk manner, her relief that her niece had not chosen to make more of an issue of the matter palpable. 'Then let us both go and sit with your father now.'

Minos Gakis passed away late that afternoon. Alexio came to Ione within minutes and said and did everything that might have been expected of him. Kalliope collapsed into his arms in tears. Ione was grateful for his support, but painfully conscious of the shuttered look in his brilliant gaze and the new distance she sensed in him. She hoped to talk to him that evening, but Kalliope's extreme distress, the arrangements for the private funeral and the demands of business all intervened. When Ione finally fell into bed exhausted that night, Alexio was still working, and when she woke up the next morning only the dent in the pillow beside hers was evidence that he had shared the same bed at some stage of the night.

Later that day, Alexio joined his wife and her aunt for lunch. There was no opportunity for private conversation

and Ione could not help wondering if that had been why
Alexio had chosen to put in an appearance at the table.
She could not approach him in the office suite where he
was surrounded by staff. Her troubled eyes fixed to his
lean dark face as she strove to fathom what was going on
inside his head and whether or not it was perhaps wiser
for her not to force another discussion at such a stressful
time. And what more could she say that she had not already said? Yet how could she remain silent when every
passing hour seemed to be deepening the distance between
them?

When Alexio had not returned to their room by midnight that same evening, Ione could stand being without
him no longer. Scrambling out of bed, she pulled on a
hand-painted floral silk robe and set off for the office wing.
She found Alexio so deep in work at her father's giant
desk that he did not even register her quiet approach.

For a moment, Ione just hovered, feasting her hungry
eyes on his hard, bronzed profile, the lush darkness of his
lashes as he scrolled down the page on the laptop computer he was using, the luxuriant black hair that gleamed
in the lamp light. Thinking of how he had once accused
her of baling out of their marriage at the first sign of trouble, she straightened her already taut shoulders. She did
not want to lose him. Indeed the mere thought of losing
Alexio terrified her.

'Are you coming to bed soon?' Ione enquired stiltedly,
sheer nervous tension working on her vocal cords and dry-
ing her mouth.

Alexio glanced up, dark golden eyes shielded by his
spiky lashes. Thrusting back his chair, he rose with innate
good manners to his full commanding height. 'I doubt it.
Your father's lawyers wish to read his will tomorrow and
they require these figures.'

'Couldn't someone else do it?'

'I'm afraid not. I mean no offence,' Alexio murmured levelly, 'but the most senior executives in the Gakis empire couldn't tie their own shoelaces without a direct order.'

Ione coloured. 'Papa liked to stay in control.'

'Yes, but it does leave me, in the short term, without a normal company infrastructure to rely on,' Alexio pointed out in the same even tone.

He was speaking to her in the same courteous, reasonable manner he had utilised since the previous day. Not as he had once spoken to her with warmth and intimacy. Her heart ached inside her and her eyes burned with unshed tears. 'Are you ever going to forgive me?'

His strong dark features set and unreadable golden eyes met hers in the briefest of collisions. 'What is there to forgive?' he enquired. 'I have a very good idea of what your life was once like. You were powerless and you chose the only means at your disposal to seize the chance of another life—'

'But at what cost now to *us*?' Ione broke in emotively, troubled rather than relieved by that logical concession. 'You're telling me that you understand *why* I did what I did but that's not what I asked—'

'I said there was nothing to forgive,' Alexio reminded her. 'You made a rational decision and, in your position then, I might have done the same myself. Ethics really don't enter the equation when it comes to survival.'

Ione was so tense that her legs had begun shaking. 'Right from the start, I was drawn to you but I fought it every step of the way. I wouldn't allow myself to trust you…I wouldn't let myself *think* about what I was doing to you—'

'I don't think we need to talk about this.'

She focused on his strong, stubborn jawline where a bluish shadow of stubble was already visible and she could have wept. She had hurt his pride, destroyed his trust in her and shattered their marriage and yet he was standing there evading the issue with a determination that shook her.

'But one matter I should mention…' Alexio continued in his cool, measured drawl. 'I was wrong to ask you to put your wealth into trust funds for our children. I had no right whatsoever to demand such a sacrifice and in retrospect it does seem rather ridiculous—'

'No, it wasn't ridiculous,' Ione interrupted chokily, ready to sign away all that she possessed at that instant if it would heal the giant, terrifying chasm that had opened up between them.

'Of course it was.' Alexio dealt her a weary, mocking smile that turned her inside out with anguished regret. 'Tomorrow, you will become one of the richest women in the world.'

'What is mine is yours,' Ione protested in despair.

'I signed up to take care of the Gakis empire and profit only through my partnership with your father. Now that he is gone, I will take nothing that is yours,' Alexio imparted with quiet dignity.

'If that's going to become another barrier between us, I'll *give* it all away!' Ione threatened wildly.

Alexio expelled his breath in a stark hiss of censure that shrivelled her where she stood. 'You have a duty of care and responsibility towards many thousands of employees. If the Gakis empire is broken up, the asset strippers will move in and there will be huge redundancies.'

As Ione gazed back at him in visible dismay, Alexio added, 'I think you should also take into account the reality that you might find being poor something of a challenge.'

Catching the slight quiver in his dark, deep drawl, Ione recognised the sudden amusement he was struggling to conceal, for of course what she had said had been foolish. As it was the first crack she had seen in his disturbing detachment, she took strength from it.

'I'll wait up for you.' Ione backed towards the door as she made that breathless promise. 'And, by the way, those pin-ups of you might not have been in *my* school locker but I often took a sneaky look at them!'

At that leading reference to his own bitter words the day before, Alexio went rigid. Shimmering golden eyes lit on her with all the angry turmoil he had worked so hard to conceal from her, but then lingered to make an almost involuntary appraisal of her tumbling silvery blonde hair and the lissom, feminine curves enhanced by fine silk. For a split second as she collided with his intent gaze the atmosphere was electric with an excitement that fired her every skincell and she trembled. Then the phone buzzed and the moment was lost as he swung away to answer it.

Heart beating very fast, Ione returned to bed. He still wanted her, didn't he? Well, she wasn't too proud to take advantage of that chink in his armour. Maybe she ought to have thrown herself across his desk there and then. Or maybe she ought just to have told him how much she loved and needed him.

But in the end all those frantic, feverish thoughts proved to be a waste of time and energy for when dawn broke the skies Ione was still alone and in an even more distraught frame of mind than she had been earlier. Alexio had ignored her unspoken invitation. Alexio, who had never, ever said no to her, had rejected her for the first time. In turmoil, Ione started wondering if he was planning to divorce her once he had dealt with all the vast complications of her father's estate. Might that explain why he had been so careful to state that he would not profit in any way from anything that was hers?

CHAPTER TEN

'WHAT would *I* have done in your position?' Misty mused reflectively on the phone to Ione a week later. 'I think I would've lied like a trooper.'

'Misty…' Ione groaned.

'There are some things that men are just not equipped to deal with,' her twin informed her with complete cool. 'Admitting that you planned to desert him within hours of taking your marriage vows *definitely* falls into that category! Alexio is a real romantic…don't you appreciate that? He greeted you with flowers on the church steps on your wedding day. He thought it was sweet that you fancied him as a schoolgirl. I think it's time you told him how you really feel about him.'

'I told him how *much* I cared—'

'I care about lots of people but I don't *love* them. Alexio's been spoiled by women most of his life and then he got hitched to you and, since then, *he's* been the one doing the spoiling!'

'Yes,' Ione acknowledge thickly, her throat closing over with the threat of tears. 'But he's been away so much on business, I've hardly seen him this week and I know that that is not his fault but it's not helping matters.'

Misty sighed. 'I just wish you'd let Freddy and I fly over for the funeral. We could've given you support and talked so much better face to face.'

'I was fine and I'm still fine,' Ione had observed the wishes that Minos Gakis had expressed in his will and only a tiny handful of his closest surviving relatives had

167

attended the event. Although she would have loved to have invited her sisters, she had also had to consider Kalliope's likely reaction to the presence of strangers at such a time.

When Ione had finally relinquished the comfort of talking her problems round in circles with the outspoken sister whom she was already beginning to think of as a best friend, she walked out onto the glorious flower-decked balcony beyond her new sitting room. In one brief week so many changes had already taken place, she reflected.

She had looked round her own rooms, which she had occupied since childhood, and had decided that she would make a special display in honour of the teddy bears and her brother's memory, but that it was definitely time to make a move to less girlish accommodation. She just wasn't the same person she had been a couple of months earlier.

Freed of fear, she had grown up all at once and, had the memory not now been so painful to her, she might have smiled when she recalled the absurdly juvenile outfit she had donned to run away on her wedding day. As it was, she had enjoyed installing herself and, of course, Edward the bear into a suite on the first floor of the villa. That had given her occupation and also the sense that she was making a fresh start within her own home.

Alexio had stayed on the island only until the will had been read. He had then flown to the Gakis headquarters in Athens to embark on the task of reorganising her father's holdings into a twenty-first-century business empire that would be open, accountable and efficient. Ione knew he was working eighteen-hour days and understood why he had made only a brief trip back for the funeral, but that did not ease her anxiety above the state of their marriage. It was now over a week since they had even kissed, never mind shared the same bed. Was this how it was all going to end? With Alexio just drifting further and further from her until finally she would have to face the fact that the man she loved no longer wished to be with her?

Yet never had Lexos looked more beautiful to her, Ione conceded ruefully. Against the backdrop of the glittering sunlit turquoise sea, the mountainous green slopes studded with the tall, arrow-shaped cypresses that seeded themselves naturally on the island looked breathtaking. She had not truly appreciated how much she loved Lexos until Kalliope had startled her with the news that she was leaving almost immediately to set up home in Athens.

'Your father liked me to live in his household and, of course, I was able to make myself useful here because your mother, Amanda, had no interest in domestic matters,' her aunt had pointed out with perfect truth. 'But I've always wanted to live in the city where I will be close to my friends. I know that my brother would not have approved but I am as excited as a girl about buying a first home of my own.'

For Ione, it had been an enlightening glimpse from another perspective of how restricted and empty Kalliope's life had been. Her aunt had never had the freedom that Ione herself had sought. The older woman had spent the greater part of her life running her brother's home and as that had been a role for which she had received little thanks, it was not surprising that the experience had soured her nature. Yet since Ione had abandoned her former rigid reserve with Kalliope, their relationship had improved and Ione had been embarrassed when her aunt had asked her permission to have friends visit her at the villa that afternoon.

Recognising that she ought to put in at least a brief appearance at that gathering, Ione suppressed a sigh and changed into a simple dark blue dress that nonetheless shrieked its Parisian origins and elegance. She had not even spoken to Alexio the day before and she felt rather too emotionally fragile for the challenge of making polite conversation. Indeed she was afraid the slightest thing would send her off into tears.

At about the same moment that Ione was treating her aunt's visitors to a welcoming smile, Alexio's helicopter was coming in to land on Lexos and a young man was coming up the steep drive to the villa after a long trudge up from the ferry docked at the harbour. An apprehensive expression on his thin, intelligent face, his jacket slung over one slim shoulder, the stranger paused to catch his breath.

Alexio was heading for the front entrance when he noticed him standing there and, with the natural courtesy that distinguished him in no matter what company he found himself, he approached him and introduced himself.

The young man said warily. 'My name is Yannis Kanavos. I…wondered if I could see Ione.'

Alexio froze in so much recoil from that declaration that he could not for an instant trust himself to speak. It was, he recognised, his worst nightmare come true at the very worst moment imaginable. The fisherman's son, Ione's one and only love, from whom she had been forcibly parted by her father. The rise of his own aggressive instincts was immediate.

'I see that you recognise my name.' Yannis stood his ground but he looked very young and apprehensive.

Kalliope had taken her visitors out to the loggia to admire the magnificent view but Ione had remained in the salon. As the door opened she glanced up. When she saw Yannis she could not believe her eyes and, without even realising it, she half rose from her seat. Her attention locked to the strained features of the young man whom

she had known since childhood, she did not see Alexio
enter in his wake. Indeed she was so much taken by surprise that only as Yannis spoke her name did she accept
that it was truly him. Hurrying forward, she stretched out
both hands for him to grasp.

'It *is* you—'

'Yes, it is I,' Yannis mumbled, as overcome with emotion as she was.

'Where have you been?' Ione whispered shakily, tears
blurring her vision even as her face shone with happiness.

'I've been training with a medical relief team in
Kosovo. I only heard of your marriage when I came home
on leave.'

Entering the salon from the loggia, Kalliope Gakis recognised the unexpected visitor and the reunion taking
place with an expression of unconcealed surprise and disapproval. She shot a startled look at Alexio and sped over
to him to whisper, 'What is the Kanavos boy doing here?'

'He asked to see Ione.'

'And you allowed this?' Kalliope surveyed her niece's
husband as though he had taken leave of his senses.

Alexio's sense of honour had triumphed over his more
primal instincts. He had a very good idea of the courage
it must have taken for Yannis to come to the Gakis home
and he respected that, even if he wished him in hell, but
what he was witnessing was no reward for his generosity:
it was sheer punishment and torture. He had never seen
Ione so relaxed and natural with anyone but himself, and
certainly not with a man, but she had gone from joyful
tears to laughter and was now engaged in deep conversation with her former boyfriend. Alexio stood there with
his big hands clenched into controlling fists, painfully
aware that Ione had not even noticed his arrival.

Only as Ione directed Yannis into a seat did she see

Alexio standing so straight and tall just inside the door. One glimpse of his lean, strong face was enough to make her heart leap, but the brooding darkness of his expression killed the delighted smile of relief that was ready to curve her lips.

'Alexio...' she said unevenly, wondering how long he had been there watching her making a fuss of Yannis, and feeling rather embarrassed and discomfited.

'I'm sure you and Dr Kanavos must have a lot to catch up on. I'll see you at dinner.' Alexio strode back out again, leaving her hovering in the centre of the room.

After Yannis had exchanged politer pleasantries with her uneasy aunt, Ione was keen to talk to him in private. 'Let's go for a walk,' she suggested and, responding to the older woman's scandalised appraisal with a soothing look, she left the room with Yannis.

They went straight down through the gardens, then towards the beach, for Yannis did not have long to spend on the island. With his usual independence, he had turned down her offer of a flight back to the mainland and he didn't want to miss the ferry, which only docked at Lexos for a couple of hours to offload supplies.

'Was it *your* decision to marry Alexio Christoulakis?' Yannis finally asked as they walked along the strand that would eventually wend round to the harbour. 'That's why I felt that I had to see you. I was afraid that your father had bullied you into the marriage.'

'I love Alexio,' Ione said simply.

Yannis smiled. 'I'm happy for you. I had already noticed that *he* loves *you* to bits!'

'Really?' Ione was dully amused by the confidence with which Yannis made that pronouncement.

'The minute Alexio realised who I was, he saw me as a threat. He didn't want to let me see you but he's a decent man. What have you been telling him about us to make him react that way? You were never in love with me,' Yannis reminded her with his sober smile. 'At most, we were loving friends. Isn't it strange how things can turn out for the best, only one doesn't see it that way at the time?'

Behind his father's back, Cosmas had helped the Kanavos family to make a fresh start on the mainland, but Yannis admitted that his parents would like to return to the island and Ione assured him that his family would be warmly welcomed home. Resolving to have their village home, which had been boarded up after their hurried departure, freshly decorated and aired in readiness, she watched Yannis depart on the ferry and then strolled back slowly and lost in her own thoughts to the villa.

Where Alexio was concerned, she *had* to stop hiding behind her pride, Ione acknowledged heavily. What true effort had she made to redress the damage that Kalliope's revelation had done to their marriage? How could she have believed that just telling Alexio that she would wait up for him a week ago was *any* kind of an olive branch? That had been an invitation to make love to her, to paper over the cracks with sex, she conceded in deep shame. It had been a shabby, superficial response to the situation and she could not blame him for reacting with contemptuous dismissal.

Wishing very much that God had allowed man to create a pair of binoculars that could see through hills to the harbour, Alexio was on his third stiff brandy by the time he saw Ione's tiny figure climbing the hill. His whole body leapt with relief. He had watched her walk away with Yannis and had not had a clue where she'd been going. He had gone through hell while he'd waited to find out. He had pictured her wandering hand in hand onto the ferry in some idyllic dream with Yannis. Letting her go had been the hardest thing he had ever done in his life, but he had done it only for *her* sake. But the instant Ione had been out of his sight, it had begun to seem like the craziest and stupidest thing he had ever done.

As Ione mounted the stairs Alexio was already striding across the vast galleried landing to greet her. 'You have come home…'

Wondering why he found it necessary to comment on the obvious, Ione collided with intense golden eyes and her ability to think straight vanished. She had to make a conscious effort not to just hurl herself at him as all the lonely, anxious insecurity of recent days welled up inside her.

'You're staying?' Alexio breathed hoarsely.

In silence, Ione nodded, beyond working out where he might imagine she could possibly have been going. He reached out a long-fingered hand and stroked his forefinger down her cheek in a curiously tender gesture before he let his lean fingers lace slowly into her hair. Her heart started thumping somewhere in the region of her throat, leaving her breathless. And then, in a sudden movement that shook her, Alexio hauled her up against him and brought his wide, sensual mouth down on hers with an explosive hunger that slivered through her like a flaming arrow hitting a target.

All the turmoil of the past week found release in the wild collision course of that fierce kiss. Lifting her off her feet, Alexio carried her across the sitting room where Edward the bear sat in innocent splendour and through to the bedroom beyond. She found herself on the bed sucking in oxygen even as Alexio came back down to her again, wrenching at his tie, throwing off his jacket, trying to do too many things at once but still a supreme success at continuing that kiss with the same fervour.

'Oh…' Ione gasped, excited to death and wholly delighted by his enthusiasm, but totally bemused.

'If you'd got on that ferry, I was going to follow you and tear the good doctor to pieces. I *couldn't* let you go…I just couldn't!' Alexio growled. 'Do you know what he said to me when I brought him indoors?'

'Er…no,' Ione mumbled, still striving to work that first reference to her getting on the ferry. He had believed she was about to run away with Yannis? Was he insane?

'Kanavos said that all that mattered to him was that you be happy and I could have happily killed the pious little jerk!' Alexio ground out with raw resentment. 'I want you to be happy too, but I want you to be happy only with *me*. I'm your husband. And if you're not happy with me, I want you to work at being happy. You don't belong with a guy like that. He wouldn't have any time for diamond-heeled shoes and teddy bears.'

'I know…Yannis is very serious and he would never run away with another man's wife. He also mentioned that he's on the brink of getting engaged to a nurse.'

Alexio gazed down at her with astonished dark golden eyes.

'I'm very fond of him. He was my brother's friend when we were children and I always liked talking to him, but even two years ago I knew I wasn't in *love* with Yannis,' Ione admitted ruefully. 'He's a special person and so good and kind but I was really just flirting with him—'

'Flirting…?' Alexio echoed thunderously.

'That's why I felt so dreadful when Papa assumed it was something more serious and had him thrown off the island. All that trouble because of me,' Ione sighed with deep regret.

With apparent difficulty, Alexio hinged his jaw shut again and breathed. 'And was he in love with you?'

'Infatuated, I think, at the start…but he felt we didn't have enough in common to even consider a future together.'

'I thought he'd come here to declare undying love in an effort to try and take you away from me!' Alexio launched down at her in condemnation.

'So you let me go all the way down to the ferry with him and thought I might not come back.' Comprehension had finally struck Ione and she surveyed him with shaken disbelief. 'What sort of a husband are you?'

A dark rise of blood accentuated Alexio's sculpted cheekbones.

Anger flared in Ione. 'I'm your wife. How could you think for one moment that I would take off with Yannis?'

'I wanted you to choose between us,' Alexio breathed tautly.

At that driven admission, Ione stilled in shock.

'You never made a free choice to be with me.' As her lush lips parted as though she intended to argue that point Alexio rested tormented golden eyes on her exquisite face. 'No, don't argue with me. Only answer one question. Did your father tell you you *had* to marry me?'

The silence thumped all around her while she attempted to find a way round that question but, if she was not prepared to lie, there was no way out. Her eyes stinging, Ione compressed her tremulous lips and she nodded in pained affirmation.

Alexio turned ashen pale beneath his olive skin. 'I should've known. So I was right. You had no choice and only after I tracked you down at the airport did you suddenly change your mind and decide to try and make a go of our marriage—'

'You're making things sound worse than they were—'

'No…there *is* nothing worse than finding out that you were *forced* into marrying me,' Alexio confided with a ragged edge to his dark, deep drawl.

Seeing the depth of his shock in his beautiful eyes and his instinctive recoil, Ione felt torn apart 'But—'

Alexio pressed his fingers against her lips to silence her. 'You were raised to be a dutiful Greek daughter. Yes, you originally planned to walk out on me. But when it started getting messy, when I confronted you…wasn't it easier for you just to make the best you could of our marriage?'

Ione was appalled when she finally grasped exactly what had been going through Alexio's mind over the previous nine days. He had worked it all out, put all the facts together to come up with a big picture that depicted her as a powerless victim throughout their entire relationship. 'No…it wasn't!' she argued with vehement conviction. 'In fact, it was one of the hardest things I ever did. As for being a dutiful daughter, at that point I didn't care. I'd spent *years* plotting, planning and dreaming about how I was going to trace my sister and build a new life. Then you got involved and all of a sudden I didn't know what I wanted any more. At the airport, all I could think about was *you* and how you would feel when you'd realised I'd gone. I wanted to be with you and that's the only reason I stayed…'

'Is that the truth?' Alexio's extraordinary eyes were pinned to hers with unashamed intensity.

'It doesn't matter how we started out…it only matters where we end up,' Ione whispered shakily. 'And I just want to end up with you. That's all. Nothing else. Just you.'

'I was so scared it would be Yannis,' Alexio conceded unsteadily, the strong bones of his face taut with tension.

'And I asked myself…how could I truly love you and yet stand in your way? How could I keep you with me when I already suspected that you had been forced into marrying me?'

How could I truly love you? A thousand butterflies were unleashed in Ione's tummy and she studied him with wondering fascination. 'I thought you buried your heart with Crystal…'

'My grief was real enough but it was based on guilt. I had to meet you before I understood that.' Alexio grimaced but candid golden eyes as rich as honey sought and held hers. 'By the time Crystal died, our engagement was on the skids, only I was too stubborn to accept that. I'd made a huge stand with my family over her and I didn't want to admit I'd made a mistake. That's not to say that I wasn't still very fond of her. We were together a long time—'

'You just didn't want to marry her any more,' Ione slotted in gently, her heart singing at his honesty. She knew what he wasn't saying: had his family not created such an outrageous fuss over his relationship with Crystal and challenged him, he might never have got engaged to her in the first place.

'I had to fall in love with you to understand that I'd never really been in love before, *agape mou*,' Alexio confided huskily. 'I cared more about you than I did about me. Pretty basic that, but that's the best definition.'

'And a very special one,' Ione whispered, tears catching at her throat.

'But I was devastated when I realised you'd booked a flight to leave me before we even got married because, while *you* were doing that, *I* was counting the days to our wedding! So finding out about that booking blew me away…I didn't know what to do…what to say. For the whole of the last week, I've been flailing around trying not to think about it and just burying myself in work—'

He loved her. He really, really loved her, but the more he bared his own emotions, the more she wanted to cry. 'You were so distant—'

'How do you act when you find out the woman you love was forced into marrying you? What do you say when you even understand why she did the things she did? I was very hurt...I felt like an idiot for not working it out for myself, but I didn't *want* to work it out,' Alexio admitted with an honesty that only made her tears flow faster and prompted him to tug her into his arms and hold her close while he smoothed her hair in an almost clumsy gesture because his hand wasn't steady. 'Once you told me the truth, I just felt like I had no right to *be* with you any more, no right even to think of you as my wife...because what choice had you had?'

'But I love you too,' Ione said in a wobbly voice. 'I love you so much. I was too scared to tell the truth in case I lost you—'

Alexio tilted her back from him and searched her swimming eyes with raw intensity. 'You love me too?'

Ione nodded.

'Then why are you crying?' Alexio demanded in bewilderment.

'I just felt *so* sad when I realised how miserable you'd been feeling all week—'

In a sudden manoeuvre, Alexio tipped her back against the pillows. 'Stuff the sad bit...are you just saying you love me because you feel sorry for me?'

'N-no,' Ione squeezed out with even greater difficulty. 'It's just that I spent all last week feeling more sorry for *me*—'

'You really love me?' Alexio still wasn't convinced.

'I'm crazy about you!' Ione gasped, irritation at his refusal to credit her declaration driving back the overemotional tears as nothing else could have done.

A slashing grin transformed Alexio's lean, strong features. 'How crazy?'

'Can't live without you crazy…head over heels.' Happiness bubbling up inside her, Ione melted in the adoring appraisal her husband was giving her.

'There will never be another woman in my life, *agape mou*,' Alexio swore. 'I love you so much it hurts…'

He kissed her and she savoured the flood of hunger and love that enveloped her. It was pure bliss to know she was loved, to look into Alexio's tender gaze and know how important she was to him. The passion that followed as they struggled out of clothes and fell back into each other's arms with an extreme lack of cool was wild and stormy, for both of them needed to express that love and lie wrapped round each other afterwards, just revelling in the warmth of renewed intimacy.

'So…' Ione murmured, feeling wondrously relaxed and decidedly smug as she rested her appreciative but thoughtful gaze on Alexio's darkly handsome face, 'what about the…''what's mine is yours'' angle?'

Alexio tensed and then regarded her with considerable discomfiture. 'I couldn't stand for you to think that I would take advantage of you in any way. It was my pride talking…what little I had left after hearing Kalliope speak. I'm no fortune hunter—'

Ione studied him with a world of tender understanding in her gaze. 'I found my fortune in *you*,' she stressed. 'I need you as much as I need air to breathe.'

His breathtaking, teasing smile tugged at her heartstrings. 'I adore you…but give me five or ten years and I swear that *I'll* be keeping *you*!'

'I don't want you working such long hours that you're never with me!' Ione protested in dismay.

Laughing huskily, Alexio tumbled her down on top of him. 'When you're out of my sight for an hour, I miss you...*trust* me.'

And she did, she discovered with an instant lightening of her heart—she trusted him with every fibre of her being.

Eighteen months later, Ione spread an appreciative maternal appraisal between the pair of canopied cots in the nursery of the London townhouse.

Even three months after the birth of their twin son and daughter, her sense of achievement was still immense. Apollo had big brown eyes and dark curls and he slept like a log between feeds. Indeed Alexio had joked that their son only woke up to eat. Diantha was smaller and slept less and demanded much more attention. But each was utterly adored by their proud parents for the very different little personalities they were already beginning to display.

A wicked smile curved Ione's lips. She and her sisters had decided that it would be really great if they *all* had their children within a few years of each other so that their kids would fall into a similar age group. They had not thought it necessary to mention that ambition to their husbands. Freddy, of course, had had a headstart with little Ben and Karim, and had just recently given birth to a daughter, Azima, who was a perfect doll. Misty was eight months pregnant with a second son, who would be just great company for his brother, Connor. Ione had been delighted when she'd realised that she'd been carrying twins and to have a boy and a girl together had been the icing on the cake for her.

Not that Alexio had had that attitude. He had been really

worried when he'd realised that she'd been pregnant with two babies and she had got very tired during the last weeks, but there had been no complications during the birth. For Ione, it had been secretly wonderful just to have known that Misty and Freddy had been waiting outside the delivery room because Alexio had been so nervous that day he hadn't been able to hide it from her.

Her close relationship with her sisters was one of the greatest joys of Ione's once lonely life. She had met her father, Oliver Sargent, and, while she had found him charming company, she had been rather disappointed to feel no stronger bond, yet she had got on with his wife, Jenny, who was no relation at all, like a house on fire. But where her sisters were concerned, there had been no such disappointment. Freddy was so kind, Misty so full of life and fun, but both were equally loving and supportive. Mind you, it took Misty to throw her and Freddy for a loop, Ione conceded with a rueful smile of recollection…

Six months earlier, Alexio had thrown a fabulous surprise party for the twenty-fourth birthday his wife shared with her twin. That evening, Misty had arrived early with her arms tightly wrapped round a shabby cardboard shoebox and a look of uneasy strain on her vibrant face.

'I have a confession to make,' Misty confided guiltily to her sisters. 'There is one piece of information about our background that I've always held back from both of you. Our mother, Carrie, remarried when I was still a little kid. I couldn't make myself tell you that because it was just about the most hurtful thing I ever found out about her. All the time she'd been talking about how she was going to make a home for her and I and take me out of foster care, she was married to this guy who hadn't a clue I even existed!'

Feeling increasingly uneasy about withholding those

facts from her sisters, Misty had tried to make amends for her silence by discovering more information about their natural mother. It had been Freddy who had first learned when and where Carrie had died, but there had been a gap of quite a few years in their knowledge of how Carrie had lived between walking away from her twin daughters and her death alone in a city boarding house. Misty had traced their mother's landlady in the hope that she might remember Carrie. She had been shaken when the elderly woman had asked her to wait and had then reappeared clutching an old shoebox.

'It just seemed cruel to throw her keepsakes away and there was nobody to give it to for she never had any visitors. I always wondered who the kiddies in the photos were,' the older woman had explained.

Inside the box had been mementoes that had touched all their hearts and softened their attitude towards the woman who had brought them into the world, yet abandoned all three of them in turn. In worn envelopes they had found baby photos and locks of hair belonging to each of them. But the biggest surprise had been the revelation that there were *four* envelopes, not just three. And in the fourth envelope had been a lock of auburn hair and a colour snap of a tiny toddler with a shy, endearing smile that wrenched at their hearts, for they had known that that little girl must have been deserted by their mother just as they had been…

'I think we have another sister somewhere.' Misty was as usual the first to say out loud what Freddy and Ione were thinking. 'She might have been born during Carrie's second marriage but, as we don't know what her husband was called or anything at all about those years, we don't have a single lead to find her and I doubt if she even knows *we* exist! She may well be years younger…I mean,

Carrie was only in her early twenties when she had us…what if our little sister is in foster care all alone and with nobody?'

It could not be said that Alexio was overjoyed to be mopping up Ione's tears in the aftermath of all the worst-case scenarios Misty had come up with. Their husbands, Leone, Alexio and Jaspar too, swore that every effort would be made to find that little girl who had to be their sister. But there had been no trail to follow without establishing Carrie's whereabouts during those missing years and, so far, there had been no lucky breaks.

A powerful arm curved round Ione's slim shoulders, springing her back out of her rueful thoughts into the present. 'You're gloating over the twins again,' Alexio sighed in mock reproof.

'Why not? Being a mum is still so new to me.'

'You're a wonderful mother,' Alexio assured her.

Ione watched him studying his baby son and daughter with a pride and satisfaction that he could not hide and smiled. It did not occur to her even to mention that her thoughts had been on that fourth forlorn little sister in the photograph, for it would only remind Alexio that his efforts to discover a single fact that might lead them to her had been no more successful than that of her sisters' husbands.

And Ione, more than many women, knew just how lucky she was to have found real, lasting love with the man of her dreams. Every time Alexio looked at her she knew her feelings were equally matched by his. They spent a lot of their time based in the London townhouse that had once belonged to her brother. The decor had been rather outrageous when they'd first moved in and Alexio had been stunned by the spectacular swimming pool in the basement. Indeed the pool complex with its light displays, waterfall and mini-island could have starred on any film set. They had redecorated the rest of the house, and London, with the country house that they used on weekends, was their true home now.

The villa on Lexos was for holidays, the occasional business conference or for loaning out to Freddy and Jaspar or Misty and Leone for a romantic break because, love the island as she did, Ione found it rather too isolated after a couple of weeks. On the other hand it was the best possible place for her and her sisters and their families to get together because the house was so enormous. They also often entertained Alexio's parents and his sisters there. Ione had grown to love his family as much as her own and had a wonderful, warm relationship with her mother-in-law.

Alexio closed his hand over hers and tugged her out onto the landing, where he brought his mouth swooping down hungrily on hers with a roughened groan of satisfaction. 'Missed you today,' he muttered thickly before drowning out any possibility of a response with a second kiss.

'Missed Apollo and Diantha too…' The third kiss extracted a responsive moan from Ione's throat and Alexio took that as an invitation to sweep her up in his arms and carry her into their bedroom.

Alexio had had an evening meeting to attend, which he always hated, and Ione revelled in the comforting knowledge that he had been so keen to get home to her. But as he gazed down at her with possessive love in his eyes there was something about his smile, that oh, so sexy, wolfish smile of satisfaction, that etched a slight pleat between her brows.

'What happened today?' Ione asked.

'I'll tell you later…' Alexio's smile had a distinct triumphal edge now, but as he followed it up by telling Ione how gorgeous she was and taking off his shirt, an exercise which always entranced her, she lost the plot at that stage.

'I adore you, Mrs Christoulakis,' Alexio murmured indolently about an hour later, arms still tightly wrapped around Ione. 'Don't ever think I don't appreciate you.'

In a dreamy-eyed state of blissful contentment, Ione felt totally appreciated, indeed blessed.

'But sometimes I'm very selfish. I came home tonight with news I couldn't wait to break and then I took one look at you and I knew you'd be on the phone to Misty and Freddy half the night...and I stalled,' Alexio completed with a grimace.

'Sorry?' As Alexio sat up Ione braced herself against the pillows and looked at his darkly handsome features in bewilderment, for she had not a clue what he was talking about.

Alexio settled the phone helpfully on her lap. 'I've got a lead that may hopefully help us to trace the *fourth* Carlton sister...'

'Oh, my goodness!' Ione exclaimed, thrilled to death. 'What did you find out?'

As Ione grasped that Alexio had found out the surname her natural mother must have used during her second marriage her green eyes brightened. Now that they had a name to work with, it would surely only be a matter of time until they traced their sister.

'I bet this annoys the hell out of Leone,' Alexio forecast.

'Why are men so competitive?' Ione reproved.

'And you're *not*?' Vibrant and amused golden eyes raked over her. 'Then tell me how I know that next year it'll be your turn to get pregnant again?'

Ione flushed. 'That's not being competitive.'

Alexio stretched like an indolent tiger and grinned.

'Don't worry about it, *agape mou*. Leone and Jaspar and I agreed that we quite enjoy the process.'

In the midst of dialling Misty's number, Ione gave him a mock punch in the ribs for that crack. He laughed and pulled her back into his arms. 'I love you,' he whispered huskily, sending a surge of happiness cascading through her, and on that particular night she didn't stay on the phone to either of her sisters quite as long as she might have done.

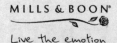

Modern
romance™

BEDDED FOR REVENGE by *Sharon Kendrick*

Cesare's pride had been wounded but he planned to bed Sorcha, and then dump her...all for revenge! And revenge was sweet. Sorcha Whittaker was still the sexiest woman he'd ever seen, and their passion was incredible. The hard part now was walking away...

THE SECRET BABY BARGAIN by *Melanie Milburne*

Jake Marriott was clear about the terms of his relationships – no marriage, no babies. So Ashleigh Forrester ran because she was pregnant with his child. But Jake is back, and the striking resemblance to her son is too obvious to ignore. Now Jake wants to buy her as his wife...

MISTRESS FOR A WEEKEND by *Susan Napier*

Nora Lang wants the most dangerous man she can find! Enter top tycoon Blake Macleod. When Nora acquires some business information that he can't risk being leaked, Blake has to keep her in sight – he'll make love to her for the whole weekend!

TAKEN BY THE TYCOON by *Kathryn Ross*

Nicole and her handsome boss Luke Santana work hard and play hard, with no strings attached. But Nicole finds herself wanting more than Luke can give, so she ends their liaison. What will Luke do when he uncovers the secret Nicole carries with her now...?

On sale 4th August 2006

Available at WHSmith, Tesco, ASDA, Borders, Eason, Sainsbury's and most bookshops

www.millsandboon.co.uk

MILLS & BOON®

Live the emotion

_Medical

romance™

BRIDE AT BAY HOSPITAL by *Meredith Webber*

Bad boy Sam Agostini left the bay thirteen years
ago, leaving Nurse Megan Anstey broken-hearted.
Now he is back, still devastatingly handsome, still
undeniably charming, and a highly respected doctor.
As Sam fights to make up to Megan for his past, new
secrets start to bubble to the surface…

THE FLIGHT DOCTOR'S ENGAGEMENT
by *Laura Iding*

Air Rescue:
High flying doctors – High altitude medical drama

Flight doctor Zach Taylor is intrigued by his partner
– fiery paramedic Jenna Reed. There is more to
Jenna than meets the eye – and he is intrigued by her
determination to rescue everyone and everything.
Zach can see that it's Jenna herself who needs saving
– his plan is to do exactly that and, hopefully, also
win her heart!

IN HIS SPECIAL CARE by *Lucy Clark*

Despite being Mt Black Hospital's only full-time GP,
Dr Claire Neilson always finds time for her patients.
But Claire doesn't let anyone care for her…until
the new specialist – incredibly handsome, enigmatic
Dr Declan Silvermark arrives in the small Australian
town and turns her carefully ordered world upside
down…

On sale 4th August 2006

0706/03b

The child she loves…is his child.

And now he knows…

THE SEVEN YEAR SECRET BY ROZ DENNY FOX

Mallory Forester's daughter needs a transplant. But there's only one person left to turn to – Liddy's father. Mallory hasn't seen Connor in seven years, and now she has to tell him he's a father…with a chance to save his daughter's life!

HIS DADDY'S EYES BY DEBRA SALONEN

Judge Lawrence Bishop spent a weekend in the arms of a sexy stranger two years ago and he's been looking for her ever since. He discovers she's dead, but *her baby son* is living with his aunt, Sara Carsten. Ren does the maths and realises he's got to see pretty Sara, talk to her and go from there…

Look for more *Little Secrets* coming in August!

On sale 7th July 2006

M&B

FROM *SUNDAY TIMES* BESTSELLING AUTHOR PENNY JORDAN

They had shattered her past.
Now she would destroy their futures.

Pepper Minesse exuded sexuality and power. She presented a challenge men wished they could master. But Pepper had paid dearly for her success. For ten years, her thirst for revenge had fuelled her ambition and made her rich.

Now it was time for the four men who had taken something infinitely precious from her to pay too – their futures for her shattered past.

On sale 7th July 2006

Sexy!

Three steamy, sultry reads to get the temperature rising this autumn

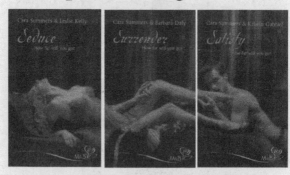

Seduce

The Proposition by Cara Summers &
Wickedly Hot by Leslie Kelly

Available 21st July 2006

Surrender

The Dare by Cara Summers &
Kiss & Run by Barbara Daly

Available 18th August 2006

Satisfy

The Favour by Cara Summers &
Good Night, Gracie by Kristin Gabriel

Available 15th September 2006

www.millsandboon.co.uk

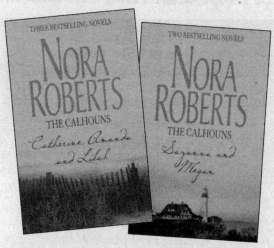